The Sin in the Steel

The
SIN
in the
STEEL

Ryan Van Loan

TOR

A Tom Doherty Associates Book
New York

THE SIN IN THE STEEL

Copyright © 2020 by Ryan Van Loan

All rights reserved.

Maps by Tim Paul

A Tor Book
Published by Tom Doherty Associates
120 Broadway
New York, NY 10271

www.tor-forge.com

Tor® is a registered trademark of Macmillan Publishing Group, LLC.

The Library of Congress Cataloging-in-Publication Data is available upon request.

ISBN 978-1-250-22258-9 (hardcover)
ISBN 978-1-250-22257-2 (ebook)

Our books may be purchased in bulk for promotional, educational, or business use. Please contact your local bookseller or the Macmillan Corporate and Premium Sales Department at 1-800-221-7945, extension 5442, or by email at MacmillanSpecial-Markets@macmillan.com.

First Edition: 2020

Printed in the United States of America

0 9 8 7 6 5 4 3 2 1

For Rachel, who never wavered.

Kanados

Port au' Sheen

The Southern Expanse

The Ring of Fire

THE
SHATTERED
COAST

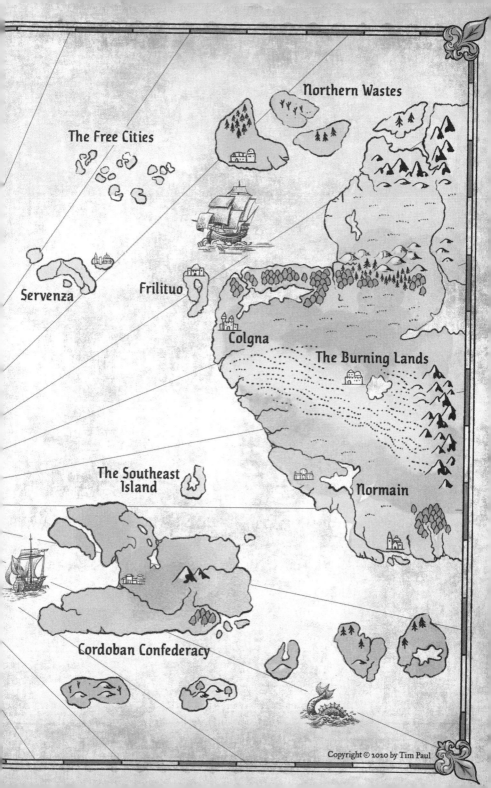

Northern Wastes

The Free Cities

Servenza

Frilituo

Colgna

The Burning Lands

The Southeast Island

Normain

Cordoban Confederacy

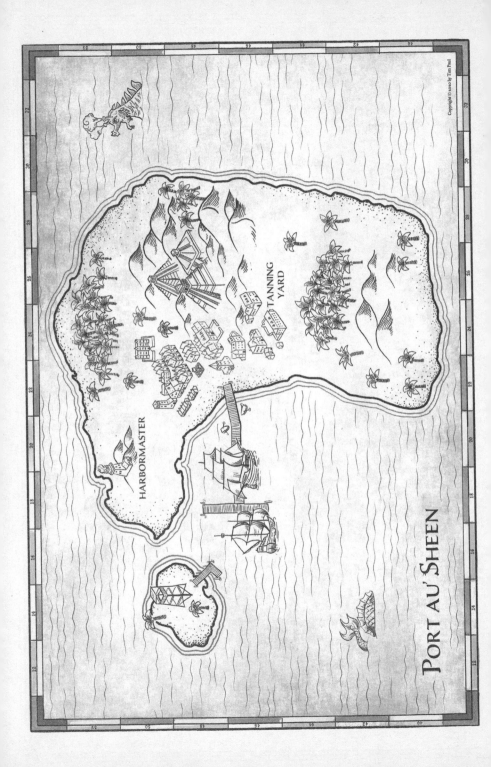

TANNING YARD

HARBORMASTER

PORT AU SHEEN

Copyright © 2020 by Tim Paul

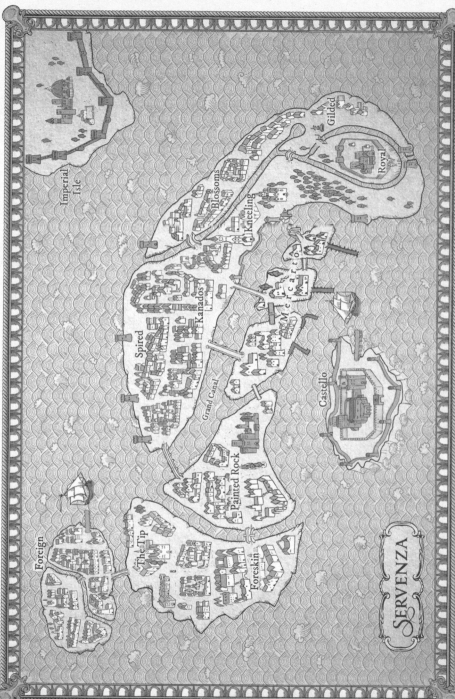

Imperial Isle

Gilded

Royal

Blossoms

Kneeling

Mercatto

Spired

Kanados

Castello

Grand Canal

Painted Rock

The Tip

Foreign

Foreskin

SERVENZA

Copyright © 2020 by Tim Paul

The Sin in the Steel

1

Before I learned how to read, I thought knowledge was finite, dead and decaying inside old men's skulls. Now I know the truth, that knowledge is living gold threaded through layers of dead parchment, just waiting to be mined. But while the world may be driven by knowledge, it runs on gold. The hard kind. And if my plans were to succeed, that was the kind of leverage I needed. I saw my chance, placed my wager, and took my seat at the table.

For that I was being shoved at bayonet point down a marbled hall lined with frescoes and landscapes of a hundred ports that shared a similar theme: palaces and outposts of the mighty Kanados Trading Company. The Imperial Guard pushed us forward at a breakneck pace; it was a wonder I didn't trip over my blood-soaked dress. I must confess, the bayonet at my back was wonderful motivation. Eld stumbled beside me, weak from the knife he'd taken in one shoulder.

A knife meant for me.

I'd tossed what I thought were loaded die, only to see them come up pips, and unless the odds changed fast, we were likely to swing for it. The Imperial Guard wouldn't look the other way like the Constabulary, and even the Constabulary wouldn't look away from a room full of dead guards and a mage whose God would be missing their magics soon enough. Not when I'd been caught holding the still-smoking pistole. *Maybe with enough lire?* Unfortunately, I'd need as much gold as it cost to buy the palace they'd brought us to and even then, the Imperial Guard doesn't bribe easily. I've tried.

No one gets off with just a bribe when you've murdered a mage. Not that we had. Murdered a mage, that is, but perception was reality and reality saw us swinging before the day's sun had fully risen.

A pair of heavy wooden doors that rose from floor to ceiling swung open of their own accord as we approached. I saw the hint of a muddy footprint and filed it away before the guard behind me hit me low in the back. I went down, caught up in my bloody skirts. Eld tried to catch me, then cried out when I hit his bad shoulder, and we both sprawled across the marble floor, sliding to a stop in front of a gilded table built over turnstile cabinets. I picked myself up, making it to my knees before the hard octagonal iron of a musket barrel pressed against the base of my skull and sent a chill running down my spine.

"Eyes down or your brains will decorate the floor," the guard growled.

"I've read blood leaves a bitch of a stain on marble," I said, before I could think. Eld groaned beside me. *Number eighty-eight, Alyce's* On Sculpting. The guard growled again. I heard a pair of heels click on the floor. Lavender skirts pinned back and sewn with thread o' gold swished around the table in front of us. I risked a glance up through a few errant strands that had pulled free from my loosely braided dark curls and saw a pale woman with blond locks piled down the left shoulder of her gown—

which had sleeves that covered her to the wrist, as was the latest fashion.

She met my gaze with a smile that made her appear younger than she was, thin lips or no. An older woman in dark Imperial armor, with crimson plumes of rank swaying atop her helm, walked past us to stand beside the blonde. She moved with the loose, stalking saunter that I associated with enforcers the street gangs employed. She held up—making sure we could see it—an all-too-familiar pistole, then set it down on the table, out of view. Once that was done, she crossed her gauntleted arms, staring at us from eyes darker than her sun-darkened face, as if sizing us up.

"You've a need for friends," the woman in the lavender gown said.

I looked up at that, expecting to see a dark room awash with lantern light glittering off the blades and saws and pincers meant to pry the truth from our lips whether we willed it or no.

"Do we now?" Whatever else I meant to say caught on my tongue as my eyes finally took in the room they'd brought us to. *Gods.* Guard forgotten, I looked past the woman and felt my mouth slacken. No torture table here, but something far more dangerous.

A library.

They'd brought us to a library—at least that is the only word our tongue has for it—but "a library" meted it poor justice. It was labyrinth-like in its shelves that rose from floor to ceiling and wall to wall, with the far wall a dim specter in the distance, barely illuminated by a score or more of chandeliers. It wasn't the size of the space but the sheer quantity of what it held that made my throat clench as if in want of water. Books . . . no, tomes, packed side by side on every shelf, sometimes stacked double in height. Everywhere my eyes turned there was another cover in mismatched bindings and sizes and colors staring back at me, another voice to be discovered, another bit of information to banish my ignorance, another morsel of magic to be consumed.

Three hundred and sixty-seven. Even Eld hasn't read as many books as I have, and he's old. I'd thought myself well-read, versed in the subjects of enlightenment, but here was a treasure to beggar my meager achievements. Here was a sun to my mere pinprick in the darkness. *I could spend a dozen years here and not finish.* I inhaled deeply, absorbing the dusty incense into my bones; a shiver covered me in gooseflesh. *A dozen years.*

The musket barrel pressed harder against my neck, bringing me back to the reality of my situation—on my knees with a gun to my head and enough evidence painting Eld and me as murderers to see us executed on the spot.

"You've a need for friends."

"I *have* friends," I said, trying and failing to keep my gaze from wandering across the shelves behind her. One. Anyway. "But I'm not sure I follow you."

"Oh, I think you do, Sambuciña," the woman said. Her light cheeks dimpled when she saw my astonishment, and she smiled again. I never know why people do that. Smile. Are they amused? Happy? Trying to disarm? Almost certainly the last, even if some of the other emotions play into it, but it's hard for me to discern.

The eyes, on the other hand, rarely lie. Hers were bright and hard, and searching. *For what?*

"You were on your way to the gallows, to be hung for disturbing the Empress's peace, for larceny, and for half a dozen counts of murder, but as a *friend,* I interceded on your behalf." She made a motion with her hand and the barrel against my neck disappeared.

"That's pleasant of you," I muttered. The guard growled yet again.

"Buc!" Eld hissed. He's polite like that. He looked pale in the lamplight. I hoped that was from the shock of the arrest and not blood loss. He was the muscle and I the brain, and weak muscle was no muscle at all. Besides, he was the only soul that would call me friend. I can't lay claim to many years, but I've learned it doesn't pay to toss that away.

Not with these stakes.

"Is there a name we should use, to thank you?" Eld asked.

I tried not to roll my eyes.

"Salina," the woman said after a moment. She arched an eyebrow. "I can save you from the noose, but only if you're useful."

"Very noble," I said.

"We're not noble, Sambuciña; we're a trading company. Omnia cum pretio."

"'Everything has its price,'" I repeated. It was the one phrase in the New Goddess's tongue that didn't twist in my mouth.

"Precisely," Salina said, favoring me with another of her false smiles.

"We've rights to a judge's ear before we swing," I reminded her. "And last I checked, self-defense wasn't a hanging offense."

"Self-defense?" Salina snorted. "You were caught surrounded by dead bodies, pistole in hand. That hardly seems like self-defense."

"Looks can be deceiving," I said.

"They can indeed," said a new voice. A man in a powdered wig marched out of the stacks behind Salina; his naturally tanned skin, somewhat pale from lack of direct sunlight, looked paler still beneath the bloodred robes he wore.

"That's why," he said as he settled himself into the gild-backed chair behind the cataloging table, "it requires the judiciary to sift through the evidence, to sort"—he gestured toward the stacks with a flick of his hand—"fact from fiction, as it were."

"You did say you wanted a judge's ear," Salina said, that small, insipid smile catching the edge of her lips. "Do you know why Servenza hangs criminals, Buc?"

"Because rotting bodies send a message," I said.

"That's part of it," the female Imperial officer beside Salina said. Given that she'd brought the murder weapon in, she was likely the one giving the orders when we were captured. *Damn her.* Her plumed helm turned her into some anonymous grim defender of justice, the executioner to the judge's judicial pronouncements.

"The other part is that it's cheaper to hang them than it is to shoot them," the judge added.

"But the Kanados Trading Company isn't so cheap," Salina said.

"You can't hold a trial in here," Eld protested.

"Oh, but we can," Salina said.

"Court is in session," the judge pronounced, his lips thinning in the vaguest suggestion of a smile. He produced a gavel from his robes and rapped the table thrice. "The honorable Judge Cokren presiding."

The sound of the guard cocking his musket was loud in the silence.

2

Eld began arguing with the judge, protesting the venue, the domain, and anything else under the sun he could think of, but his arguments were as weak as he was, given the massacre we'd come from. A massacre of—Gods damn it—*my* doing. But there were odds to be had, if I could see the angles in time, only my head was spinning still and I could taste iron in my mouth. *That blow didn't help things.* I'd been sloppy, to let the woman catch me with her fist, however glancing, but we'd been outnumbered three to one and us unarmed. *Enough time to analyze what went wrong later. If there is a later.* I waited a breath to let the men build themselves up, until Judge Cokren's face began to take on some color of its own.

"Your Honor!" My shout cut off the two men's voices. "W-would it please the court to hear our version of events? So that you may ascertain the truth?"

"It would," Judge Cokren said, smirking at my stammer.

Let a man think you weak, let him think you vulnerable, and he'll never see the blade until it's planted in his ribs. This time the blades were of the verbal kind. There'd been enough blood spilt, and most of it on my dress.

"It was self-defense, Your Honor . . ." I began.

"Oh?" Salina crossed her thin arms, drawing her gown tighter about herself. "Do tell."

I ignored her, shooting a questioning look at Cokren, who nodded fractionally in approval.

"Some philosophers think knowledge a burden, a millstone round their necks dragging them down with its power, but they're all fools," I said, speaking softly as I eyed the books surrounding us.

My vision was still a little unsteady, but I couldn't stop drinking in the thousands upon thousands of tomes waiting to be discovered. But first, I needed to discover why we had been brought here. Last I'd checked, the Kanados Trading Company didn't hang murderers inside their headquarters.

"Knowledge isn't power; knowledge is a loaded pistole waiting to be fired. Knowledge is opportunity."

I smelled the warm, welcoming scent of parchment, thick in the air, and for a moment the ringing in my head subsided. My mind raced ahead, leaving words behind for me to follow, but I had to take my time. Judge Cokren needed a clear picture if we were to walk free. For the first time since Eld had taken that knife in the shoulder, I could feel the odds shifting, albeit ever so slightly.

"We solved a dozen cases that other would-be investigators failed miserably at, just to get to this point," I continued. "To find a merchant who needed someone like me, someone who could look at a score of disparate clues and piece them together to complete the puzzle." *A merchant who could open doors that would give me what I've wanted ever since I left the streets, burning everything behind me.* "A merchant who—"

"Wasn't completely clean," Salina finished. "Grift and bribery, I shouldn't wonder," she added for Judge Cokren's benefit.

"No, Salazar wasn't spotless," I agreed. *Then again, neither am I.* No one leaves the streets without some grime on them, and I'd left with it smeared into my bones. Eld thinks me too young to have lived more than one life, but I grew up on the streets, where most lives never made it past a dozen years. I can lay claim to seventeen and if I have it my way, I'll claim scores more before I draw my last breath.

Watching my old life burn had left glowing embers within me. I'm young, but I'm no fool—change requires power and in the Empire, power comes from gold. The hard kind. The kind Salazar could provide.

"I didn't think Salazar was fool enough to cheat us after we'd solved his case for him," I said.

"Are you arguing that this fight was over a failure to pay for services rendered?" Judge Cokren asked, leaning forward over the table.

"That is what brought both parties together, aye." I nodded.

"And you went into his own warehouse to collect?" Salina shook her golden locks.

"Sounds more like revenge than anything else," the female officer put in. She'd seen the blood and bodies strewn about Salazar's office.

"I knew what I was doing," I growled. "We were there to talk . . . to discuss payment options." Both women arched their eyebrows and I swore. "You can't take money from the dead."

"Not if you're caught before your robbery is complete anyway," the officer said in a low voice.

Salina clicked her tongue. "Now, that was ill done, Colonel. Let Buc give us her version of events."

"It is Captain, signora."

"For today, yes, but tomorrow?"

"To return to the matter at hand," Judge Cokren said, his tone making both women look away from each other. He adjusted his crimson robes and his dark eyes pierced my own. "Girl, you came to talk to this merchant Salazar and ended up murdering half a dozen."

"Five," I corrected him. All three stared at me. Beads of sweat slid down my forehead. *Must be the lights.* "The mage murdered Salazar."

"The mage murdered his employer? That's your story?" Salina cut in.

"You know mages are loyal only to their God," Eld said with a shrug.

I winced. "And you know that the Kanados Trading Company employs scores of mages to keep tabs on their estates, right, Eld?"

"I—uh, had forgotten that detail," he admitted. His pale features burned, so at least he had enough blood left in him to blush. "But Buc speaks the truth, Your Honor. The mage blew Salazar's brains out."

"And left you holding the pistole?" Judge Cokren chuckled mirthlessly. He adjusted his powdered wig. "This may be the shortest deliberation I've ever had and I tried the man who nearly killed the Empress last summer."

"It was the fastest fuckup I've ever seen," I said.

"Certainly one of the fastest I can remember," Eld supplied. "If you weren't there, you wouldn't have believed it. One moment we're talking, Salazar is trying to bargain down his price, and then the mage ends the conversation."

"That's when the killing started," I said. I closed my eyes and was back in the darkened warehouse, in the room Salazar's lackeys had led us to after stripping us of our weapons. I could remember the smell of the dust, heavy in the air until blood flowed, its sharp iron scent cutting through everything else. "Salazar's man slung a blade at my face." One of the first lessons the streets taught me was that if you flinch, you miss the next move. Do that and you won't have to worry about another move because you'll be dead in the gutter. "I didn't flinch."

"Aye, and why would you when it took me in the shoulder?" Eld asked, shrugging his wounded side.

"You were wounded at the outset?" the captain asked. Her hand strayed to the sword at her side. "And still killed half a dozen?"

"Five," I reminded her.

"I've been wounded before," Eld murmured. He glanced at me. "And, uh, I had some help."

"Look, Salazar was trying to slip out of paying after we'd gone and found his missing merchandise. That was bad enough," I said. "But then he had one of his lackeys go and put a knife through Eld. Not paying's one thing—killing my friend's another." I snorted. "They were fools; by that point Eld had dropped three of them with fisticuffs. He'd have done for more if our weapons hadn't been taken away."

"She exaggerates," Eld protested, but Judge Cokren held up his hand and motioned for me to continue.

"But they'd already made their second mistake."

"Oh?" Salina asked.

"They gave me a knife," I said, unable to keep the hint of a smile from my lips.

"That hurt," Eld growled.

"Did it?" I asked, shaking my head.

Salina sniffed.

"In close quarters and outnumbered, you can either curl up in a ball and wait for their knives—or you can attack."

"Wait, wait," Judge Cokren said. "You were unarmed and outnumbered and you attacked?"

"Recall I had a knife by then," I said.

"From my shoulder," Eld said.

I shrugged. "Like I said, I hate failure, so I attacked. Put one of the shorter bastards up against the wall before he could blink. He tried to scream—"

"Tried?" The captain's brow furrowed.

"It's hard to scream with a blade buried in your throat," I told her. Salina made a choking sound and looked as if she were going to sick up. I could feel the dried blood on my face crack and my smile made her turn another shade of green. "I think that was number five."

"And then what?" the captain asked.

"Then Buc reminded Salazar what happened when the Montays tried to double-cross us," Eld said.

"The Montays?" Salina asked. "From the Foreign Quarto by way of Colgna? Didn't the younger brother go missing last winter?"

"I'm not sure," I lied. Eld grunted from my elbow in his ribs. "I'm not familiar with any of that name within Servenza's jurisdiction. To continue," I said in a louder tone, "it was about then that Salazar started running away at the mouth with excuses."

"Which was when his mage reached for something in his coat," Eld added.

"Ah, this is where the mage comes into the picture?" Judge Cokren asked.

"Sort of," Eld said. "He was the one who ordered the goons to rough us up—hence the three I'd put down before they started trying to kill us."

"You went face-to-face with a mage?" Salina asked, disbelief written boldly across her features.

"We were about to," I said. "I was still trying to work the knife loose from that skinny bastard's throat when the mage's eyes rolled to the back of his head."

"His eyes rolled?" the captain asked in her low voice. "Like he had a fit?"

"Was he using his magic?" Salina asked.

"No," I said. "Maybe?" I shook my dark curls. "All I know is, he froze suddenly, as if some puppeteer pulled his strings taut, as if every muscle had suddenly seized."

"He didn't stay frozen," Eld said. He shivered. "He pulled a pistole out from his coat before I could blink and I thought I was dead."

"Mages were ever poor shots," the captain said. The plumes in her helm shook with her head. "Comes of relying too much on their magic."

"Oh, he didn't miss," I said.

"We told you we didn't kill Salazar," Eld added.

"And we didn't. Salazar's lips were just starting to move when the mage blew his head off in a plume of smoke and blood and brains." I closed my eyes and could smell the gunpowder sharp in my nostrils.

"In the middle of this murderous maelstrom, the mage decides to blow his employer's brains out?" Judge Cokren asked.

"Never trust a mage," I said. Something I'd known as a child on the streets even before I'd learned to read. Something Salazar would have done well not to forget.

"Wise words," Judge Cokren said, avoiding Salina's sudden gaze as if just remembering she employed mages by the score. "And your story does contain elements of self-defense. . . ." He tapped his fingers on the table. "What happened to the mage after he murdered Salazar?"

"Salazar's body hit the floor . . . ," I began. *Eld caught up a sword off one of the lackeys and buried it in his neck.* I could still see the blood squirting like a fountain around the bright steel. "The mage reached into his coat with his other hand. I thought he was going for another pistole and I . . ." I took a breath and shook my head. "I screamed," I whispered.

"So there is some fragment of rational thought in you after all," Salina murmured.

I glared at the other woman, but Eld saved me from replying.

"I thought the mage had done something to Buc with his magic," he said. "She doesn't scream. Ever. So I stabbed him with a sword, I'd, um, borrowed. And he died."

"Mortal after all," Judge Cokren said.

"He died hard," I told him. "I looked for any clues about where he'd been before we met, but he was clean, save for powder marks." I shook my head. "Too clean, really, given the heat and the dust-filled streets outside. He'd bathed not long before our meeting.

"That's when I plucked up the pistole, hoping to find some clue there," I explained. "And that's about when the honorable captain"—I nodded toward the armored woman—"and her guards burst in." *With me holding the still-smoking pistole. Never trust a motherfucking mage.*

"It's an intriguing story," Salina said.

"It is," the Imperial officer admitted. Her lips twisted. "But the mage murdering Salazar makes no sense."

"'As easy to understand the sun as a mage's mind,'" Salina quoted.

This was the crucial moment, where Eld and I either walked free or went to our deaths. Looking at Judge Cokren's expression, I could practically read his thoughts. *What was the mage's motive?*

"The tiny chunk of rock we stand upon rotates around the

sun," I said, drawing every gaze to me. "The sun is large in our skies, but were you standing on the surface of the sun and not incinerated from the heat, our chunk of rock would be a pinprick of light, indistinguishable from all the other pinpricks. Read Felcher's *Discourse on Planetary Bodies*."

I shot Eld a look as I shifted my feet. I started to cross my arms, but the dark leather bands around my wrists prevented me. They were a shade darker than my skin, and padded, so they restrained without biting, unlike the cold iron I was used to. I'd nearly forgotten I was wearing them. "If I can understand somewhat the sun's purpose, then I think I can understand the mage's."

"What number book was that?" Eld asked beside me.

"Thirty-seven. I should have read Ducasse first though, as a primer. That was fifty-two."

"What's thirty-seven? Fifty-two?" Salina asked.

Eld smirked as he inclined his head. I wasn't sure if he'd picked up my signal or not, but I knew I could count on him for a distraction when I needed it. The less said about the mage's motives the better, because I knew fuck all why the mage had chosen that moment to betray Salazar, but given what followed—our arrest—it was damned convenient. *Even if the bastard died for it. Why?* Too many questions and not enough clues to sink my teeth into.

"So at the end of it all," Judge Cokren said, speaking slowly, his off-white teeth too even not to be fake, "you two are the only ones left drawing breath. There are none to gainsay your claims of self-defense. You also"—he touched the pistole lying on the desk before him—"possess the murder weapon."

"Only Salazar died by musketry," Eld reminded him.

"Did you think we'd dump that motley collection of cutlery we found at the scene atop such a fine desk?" the captain asked. She snorted and removed her helm to reveal shorn hair that barely covered her scalp and would need months before they could form proper curls again. "Your Honor, the girl tells a pretty story, but it's just that: a story. Pronounce your sentence and let me take them out back to the midden heap. It'll be but the work of a moment."

"The captain . . . colonel? Whatever"—Judge Cokren waved a hand—"does make a point." The officer shrugged as if it were of no consequence. And perhaps for her it wasn't; she was just following the law. The judge sighed and adjusted his crimson robes before turning toward Salina. "Well, signora? I could be *persuaded* either way."

"Why don't you go for a walk, Your Honor?" Salina said finally. "Have you seen our gear-work arboretum? I assure you it's worth a visit."

"Aye?" The old man pushed himself to his feet. "How much?"

Salina eyed the officer standing beside her, whose eyes looked like they were going to pop out of her head at the bribery going on in front of her, and grinned. "The same as last? I'll send for you when your services are needed in here."

"Perfect." He glanced at my dress and shook his powdered wig. "Bloody perfect," Judge Cokren said as he strode past us, his robes swishing softly against the marble floor. "Send for some wine while you're at it, won't you?" Then he was out the door, leaving only the faintest whiff of powder in his wake.

3

"Before we get off on the wrong step entirely, let's start again," Salina said.

"Before?" Eld choked. "You've threatened us with execution by firing squad!"

"Eld's a little put out," I explained. I took a deep breath, letting the last few minutes distill in my mind. An image was starting to form, but it was still hazy. "And I'm not too thrilled myself."

"Ah yes, an amends?" Salina asked. She gestured toward the stacks. "By all means, help yourself. As many as you like." I held my hands up to show my leather restraints, and Salina's smile was replaced with a hard line that made her lips disappear.

"Colonel, release our young friend. These aren't violent prisoners."

"No?" She raised an eyebrow and touched the pistole on the table. "Were you listening to the same story I was?"

"Colonel."

The older woman sighed, but she moved to my side, produced a stiletto, and cut the leather from my wrists. Her dark eyes never left mine as she moved. "It is done."

I twisted away before she could confirm the sheath tied to my left wrist beneath the tight silk of my riding dress. It was empty, but she didn't need to know either piece of information. I strode past her and stopped in front of the nearest shelf. *The newer system.* Numbers ran in gilded script across the bottom of the shelf, much more preferable than the older systems, which sorted books alphabetically, by titles or subject or some strange combination of the two.

Disciple of the Body. I plucked the book from the shelf without thinking and someone exhaled behind me, but my mind was in a time nearly two years ago. Book number twenty-four, a disheveled copy lacking a cover that kept me distracted from the pulling of the oar that ferried us from Servenza to Frilituo, toward a pair of murders carried out by a nobleman's distraught maid with eyes above her station. Verner had a way of writing that opened the mind the same way his book opened the body for all to see. I closed Verner and reached for another.

With my hands free, it was the work of but an instant to collect half a dozen books. When they filled my arms, I set them carefully down upon the marble floor and reached for another. I had never calculated the number of books needed to sink a barge, but if I kept going, I might have to.

"Buc?" Eld's voice was soft, but I heard the edge. There was that streak of politeness again. I didn't knock him for his fault, but imposing it on me was tiresome. And burdensome. And a whole host of other 'somes as well.

Salina laughed. "No, it's all right. Your friend is free to choose as many as she likes. Well," she said, her laugh deepening, "perhaps as many as the pair of you can carry. Now then." Salina's heels clicked loudly on the floor as she moved around the table behind me. "You're probably wondering why you were brought here."

"Either you've lost something or you're baffled by a mystery. Or you really had a soft spot for old Salazar," I said, pausing to add Robesier's *Soliloquies* to the pile. I've never had an ear for verse, but enough nobles had quoted him to me while deep in their cups to warrant a reading. "Forewarned is forearmed," as they say. "You didn't find us by accident, not with how fast we were arrested, which means you were following us. The Imperial Guard answers your commands, but they don't like it." I heard the officer snort.

"I'm told they can't be bought and if they could be, they wouldn't be used in so simple a manner, so clearly you've the backing of the Empire in this matter, whatever it is. And you brought along a judge who *can* be bought, so I don't think you're weeping over Salazar's losing his head. A mystery, then? And one that involves the most powerful trading company in the world and the Empire—which means it must involve commerce and commodities."

I turned around to gauge their reaction and saw Salina staring at me. "My only real question is, why now? I'd almost believe you paid Salazar to renege on our deal, but we were nearly killed and your soldiers too far away to prevent it." I frowned. "Unless that was the final test, to prove if we were worthy of your time?"

"You ascribe too much reason to fate," Salina said quickly, "thereby displaying your ignorance in the matter."

She would have been right, save I hadn't really believed the last, just wanted to make sure Eld and I didn't have an expiration date waiting for us at the end of whatever contract she was about to propose. Yet, her attitude rankled; for hiring someone to help her accomplish something she was unable or unwilling to do, she seemed to take a perverse amount of pleasure in seeing me fail. *You're not like the others. It's the white dog that's chased out of the pack. You're different and that will scare some and threaten others.*

One of the first things that Eld told me when I let him save me from the streets. Some of the tension loosened in my shoulders now that I had the read of her.

"Perhaps, but there is a mystery, no? And you need us to demystify it for you."

"You are as astoundingly apt as advertised," Salina said. She turned back to Eld. "I have a special case I'd like you to consider, sirrah."

"Then you'd best address the girl," I said. I willed my voice to be light, but I couldn't judge how successful I was over the sound of my teeth grinding together. *Gods, but I can't wait until I have grey hair. Or breasts.* "I hold the keys to 'aye' or 'nay.'"

She stared at me, then her gaze flitted back to Eld. He shrugged, wrists still bound. "I can't complain; it has worked out so far."

Salina eyed his shoulder, bloody from the knife, and his torn vest, but said nothing before taking a very deep breath and turning back to me. "I have a special case," she said again.

"So you said."

Her nostrils flared. "I can send for Judge Cokren at any moment and have him pronounce your sentence. She"—Salina gestured toward the officer—"wouldn't hesitate carrying it out."

"I wouldn't," the captain agreed. Her pink lips, bright against her skin, crept up, finally changing toward something approaching a satisfied smile. "Not when it comes to murderers."

"I wondered if it was going to be bribery or blackmail," I said. "You know, to sweeten the deal, for us? So you didn't pay off Salazar. The guard was waiting to arrest us on some trumped-up charge for aiding him off the books, but you got lucky and caught something that can be spun to seem much worse."

"So we understand each other."

"No, we don't." I touched my chest. "I understand you; you don't understand me. Blackmail won't work."

"I've found the firing squad to be a convincing argument," she countered.

"Generally, you'd be right," I agreed, "but I'm not like everyone else. How many times have you been threatened with death in your life? Perhaps once? Every breath I ever took, growing up, carried the threat of death with it."

"And you'd let her condemn you to this fate?" Salina asked, turning back to Eld.

"If it were up to me?" He snorted. "No, signora."

"That's why I call the shots," I snapped, pulling her attention back to me.

"Because you grew up with death? On the streets?" She glanced down at the table, at a sheaf of papers beside the pistole. "Sambuciña Alhurra. Aged seventeen or so years. Mother, Southeast Islander. Father unknown, likely of Imperial descent. First mention was seven years ago in the Painted Rock Quarto, detained by the Watch on suspicion of pickpocketing. Next appearance was with your sturdy friend here, preventing the attempted heist of the Gilderlocks' formerly impregnable vault." She looked up from the papers. "Formerly, as you emptied the safe yourselves. Without telling Gilderlock."

"'To catch a thief,'" I quoted. "Your information is most impressive, but only to the truly infantile." Eld's groan just reached my ears. "My skin is the color of your library's shelves, which means one of my parents was either Southeast Islander or from the Burning Lands. We know how many of the last find their way to our shores, so Southeast Islander it is. Skin color is passed on the mother's side. I was never detained by the Watch on suspicion of anything." I left unsaid that that was because my marks never knew their pockets were lighter until I was streets away. "That was my sister. And everyone who knows of us knows about Gilderlock."

I snorted and nodded back toward where I'd seen the muddy prints as we were dragged in. "Next time you have someone race to get you information before we arrive, you might want to go to the trouble of cleaning up their boot prints, so the ones you're try- ing to impress can't figure out how you know what you do. The judge was a nice touch, I'll grant you that." The woman's face had grown steadily darker and flits of color danced along her cheeks as she opened her mouth.

"Wait!" Her face managed to gain another shade. I dug in my coat pocket and pulled out a rolled paper that was almost too crumpled to be of use. Kan is a funny leaf. Quite literally. Smoke too much and you'll find yourself laughing at every pass- ing breeze. Smoke enough of it and your eyes will develop the haze, the world will turn strange colors, and you'll die because you've forgotten to eat. One paper takes the edge off, slows down most, but I've found what it does for me is slow my brain down enough so I can speak to the slower types . . . everyone else.

Right then my mind burned with the intensity of a thousand suns, connecting the guard to Salina to the judge and everything else in between—but none of that was useful if I couldn't push Salina to where I wanted—no, *needed* her to be. My first toss of the dice had failed, but I'd been handed the cup again. Double or nothing. I dug a match out and struck it with my thumb.

"With your permission?" I asked. Salina nodded, though her eyes flashed. The herb was bitter in my lungs, but with the first pull I could feel my thoughts slow from a sprint to a mere run. "Eld, will you explain to her? I'm making a mess of this."

"When did you develop self-awareness?" he asked.

"It's only temporary," I assured him.

"Uh-huh. Signora," he said, turning back to Salina, "what Buc is trying to say is that your information on us . . . it's not enough to blackmail us with. We only take on cases that interest us, cases that no one else can solve, cases that matter."

"How did Salazar's case of missed payment matter?" she asked.

Eld blushed and glanced at me. I exhaled my third and final pull. I was at a swift jog now; I didn't want to slow to a walk. I didn't want to know what it was like to be normal.

I glanced at the tiny bit left in my hand and sighed. It's one of the few expressions I can do well. So well, it almost felt real, even to me. "Everyone makes mistakes," I said. I wasn't going to tell her the truth, not with that judge wandering around waiting to order us shot. "Not me, usually, but you caught me on a bad day."

"Well, if the charge of murder and the threat of having your brains blown out isn't enough to encourage you, perhaps our circumstances will. All of our agents have failed . . . in one form or another." She gestured around her. "You've seen the merest hint of our resources. You know the Empire is involved as well. Let that sink in for a moment and let me know if my *case* meets your criteria."

I crushed the last bit of kan between my hands and watched the flakes fall to the floor so she wouldn't see the interest in my eyes. *The Empire failed.* I nodded after I'd schooled my face. "Point taken, continue."

"You're familiar with the sugar trade and its origins?"

"Vaguely," Eld said. "It's supplanted kan as your number one commodity; that is common knowledge."

"It grows mainly on the Shattered Coast," I added.

Salina looked at me. *There's that smile again.* "Yes, and while there are minor merchants and even another trading company in production there, we dominate the plantations. Six months ago ships started disappearing. Look." She produced a key from a hidden pocket in her dress and turned something within the table. There was a loud click, then the sound of gears spinning. The tabletop began to rise and slide to the side, revealing an intricately diagrammed map of . . . the world. Gilded lines of latitude and longitude ran across its length, intersecting with a gold star that marked Servenza. Squares within the table, out to sea, opened to reveal tiny wooden ships.

The map rose to the table's previous height, then the tabletop slid back beneath the map and disappeared from view as everything snapped into place with a final click. Salina's smile faded.

"It was a few at first, here and there, but it's still a wild sea dotted about with scores of islands, some that haven't even been charted yet." She turned the key again and dozens of ships began to move across the map, driven by the gears spinning beneath the table. Several sank down in their squares, replaced by open water. More began to disappear, and yet more, until the seas looked a lot less crowded than they had a moment before.

"Accidents happen," Eld supplied.

"Just so. Unfortunately, the numbers continued to grow, so three months ago we started looking into this seriously. Especially when we noticed that the only ships disappearing were those carrying sugar."

"What other cargoes do your ships carry?" I asked.

"A few exotic fruits, some special varieties of kan, things of that nature," Salina said. "None of those ships have disappeared. And from what our"—her eyes flicked to the captain and back again—"spies can tell, the other trading company's ships seem unaffected as well."

"The other trading company?"

Salina hesitated and the captain stiffened before inclining her head ever so slightly. "Normain."

Eld whistled.

"We are at peace, no?" I asked. Something didn't quite make sense. True, Normain was one of the few powers on the coastal mainland that had not only held out from Imperial rule, but had managed to grow its territories inland as well. No small feat, given the Burning Lands bordered them on two sides. But for all that, they weren't the naval power the Empire was. *So why risk their colonial holdings over sugar?*

"We are," the officer said. "If Normain is aware of their advantage, they haven't shown it yet."

"Yes," Salina said. "Plus, there have been no signs that they've been hoarding sugar. Quite the opposite, in fact. That's the only reason our own slackening of supply hasn't been remarked on until now. But the whispers have started. Our stockpiles are running low and we've only one ship we're sure will make landfall within the week. That only gives us a fortnight until we run out of sugar."

"And then?" Eld asked.

"And then the nobles have to drink their tea bitter, like the rest of us," I said. "And no sweets after dinner. Oh bother."

"Hardly," Salina said, drawing the word out in a high tone that erased any doubt she was herself a commoner. "Then our stock plummets and our shareholders are ruined."

"Isn't one of your largest shareholders the Empress?" I asked. Her face blanched. I grunted. "The fucking Empire itself? This?" I gestured at the shelves around us. "And that out there? All financed by sugar and backed by the Imperial lira?"

"So you see," Salina said, her voice drawing tight, "why we must find the reason why our ships have been disappearing, and put an end to it. Immediately."

"Well, within a fortnight, anyway, aye?" I asked.

"You really are the most perfect arsehole," she said.

4

"I can have you on a ship within the hour," the woman said, ignoring my too-wide smile.

"We'll need more information first," Eld said. "The disappearances could be due to pirates, a change in the weather patterns—maybe the hurricanes are returning to their former strength after the past century of peace—and there's still Normain," he said, ticking off the points one by one on his fingers.

I grunted agreement. "Even leaving aside our neighbors . . ." The Imperial officer cursed under her breath. "The Shattered Coast is a labyrinth of remnants of lost civilizations, waters that turn compasses upside down, artifacts of the Gods—"

"To say nothing of an attempt at a hostile corporate takeover," Eld added.

Hostile corporate takeover? That sounded interesting. With the kan in my lungs, my mind didn't ferret out all the possibilities as quickly as it might have, but it let me savor them more. I found everything much easier to savor now that the judge in blood robes wasn't staring at us from beneath that ridiculous wig. The lack of a gun pressed to my skull didn't hurt either.

"We've already considered all of those," Salina cut in sharply, ripping me out of my head and back to the present. *Bitch.* "In the end, it's all speculation; the Shattered Coast is half a thousand leagues distant, and the only way to know for sure is to have boots on the ground." She reached beneath the map table and pulled out a leaf of papers. "If it's information you require, then I'll make sure packets detailing our previous attempts are awaiting you. On board the ship."

"We'll also require payment," I said. "We aren't doing this for free."

"An interesting case and saving your neck aren't enough?"

"You said it yourself: You can't solve the mystery from here. You need boots on the ground, and seeing as all your other boots failed, it's not just any boots you need, but ours." My mouth was starting to ache from smiling, but the expression seemed to infuriate the woman, so I kept it in place. "What was it you said earlier? Omnia cum pretio."

"Very well. What is your price? I could return the pistole upon services rendered, removing the threat of blackmail."

"That's a start," I said. "You'll also have our Imperial friend"—I nodded toward the older woman—"file a report with Judge Cokren before we leave, naming the mage as the murderer."

Salina's eyes snapped and it no longer hurt to keep smiling. Imperial law stated that in order to overturn a murder conviction where the previously convicted was deceased, there must be physical evidence suggesting a different offender. If she gave us the pistole, she would lose her evidence and, with it, the chance to hold the crime over our heads in perpetuity. If the report I'd just asked for was filed, it wouldn't matter what judge she had on the payroll; we'd be free and clear. The treatise I'd read on that particular piece of law, between books forty-seven and forty-eight, had been dry stuff to be sure, but was proving its worth today. "Did you think we were fools?"

"No, I did not," she said, nostrils flaring slightly. "If that's what you require—"

"No, that's what you so graciously offered," I said. "And while we appreciate the sentiment, that's not going to cut it. For someone employed by the most eminent trading company in the world, you surely don't bargain well." Eld hissed a warning. "Or is this your first time?"

"I tire of this game. Name your price and be done with it," she snapped. "Or there's still the judge. . . ."

My stomach growled loudly in the silence that followed. I ignored it, ignored Salina, and paused as if considering. But I'd known what my price was as soon as I saw the catalog system. Marten's *On Religion and Power* was surely nestled somewhere in the two hundreds. One of the finest libraries in all the world, perhaps the finest, could never pass up such a seminal work. Marten was famed as a great orator, but as a writer, he was a bit dull and plodding. No one read Marten for the prose, but rather for the message.

Eighteen months ago I'd picked up that book, unprepared for the fire it would kindle within me. Marten outlined, in excruciating detail, the chaos wreaked upon the political landscape three centuries ago. That was when the New Goddess, Ciris, was discovered or awakened or whatever the fuck happened that brought her out of retirement; that's when the Sin Eaters were born. The Dead Gods—no one knows how many there are or much about them, save that they are dead and the skeleton of one of them provides the architecture of most of the capital of Normain—and their followers had had little need for manipulation and subjugation until then, but the emergence of a rival deity had ignited a secret war that left all nations dancing on hidden strings pulled by either side.

I'm not a good person, and as much as Eld jests about my lack of introspection, I'm self-aware enough to know that. I don't think good people are forged in the violence of the streets. I saw a child bashed like a rag doll against the cobblestone for dancing around a street gang while singing taunting songs and hurling made-up insults: you know, being a child. I think I was five, and lucky that all the child had already been beaten out of me, or it could have been my brains sprayed across the street. I've seen what hunger will make people do and I've done worse myself. And my sister. *Sister.*

My mind went blank.

Something flickered through my thoughts and was gone. I'm not a good person, and as much as Eld jests about my lack of introspection, I'm self-aware enough to know that . . . but if power can corrupt, it can also cleanse. If I had it my way, no child would see what I had seen reflected in the flames that danced before my eyes all those years ago, when I burnt my old life. With enough power, I can prevent another horror like myself from being created. Eighteen months ago I began to see clearly for the first time in my short years.

Achieving my goals will require a strength and hardness that would crack all but the hardest steel—and there is something in me that tends toward iron. Hard . . . but brittle. It has to be enough. It *will* be enough. Only a child could have been arrogant enough to plot a path to resew the very fabric of our society, clean the streets of their grime, and lift children out of the gutter. I am ten and seven and by the time I am ten and ten every child will be a normal child. If I was as old as Eld, I'd probably have abandoned those thoughts long ago or else drawn a blade across my wrists. Strength, hardness, but power also. The power of a nation. One not tied down by religious fanatics or insular politics. Some said the Kanados Trading Company was a nation unto itself and I intended to find out.

I pulled myself back to the moment just as Salina opened her mouth. "Our price is a writ of ownership in your Company," I said.

"Stock?"

"No, a writ of ownership," I repeated. "A stake in the Company."

"You want to be given a place among our shareholders?"

"Aye, and a seat on the Executive Board as well."

"Impossible!" I started to speak and she slammed her hand down on the table. "No, it is impossible. The shares are tightly controlled and it would take the Gods themselves in physical form to create another. And to sit on the Board?" She snorted. "Be reasonable or I'll shoot you myself."

"You'll shoot us or you won't," I growled as I found myself marching past Eld and right up to the table. The Imperial officer started to move, but my outstretched hand stopped her. I would have shown my surprise at that, but it would have ruined the effect. "You're no different in your trumped-up palazzo than the corner street tough. You've just got more expensive makeup. We're in your power, so if you'd aimed to kill us, we'd be dead. We aren't dead, so that was never your aim."

I put my other hand on the table and leaned over it so we were face-to-face. "In two weeks your Company will go belly-up and your shares will be as useless as your Board. If we solve your mystery, that can be prevented and the Company preserved and its Board with it. To my mind, that should entitle us to a seat at the table. Especial services rendered and all that."

We stared eye to eye, her nostrils twitching as if she were walking along the edge of the Tip after a feast day. "Solving the mystery won't get us the sugar we need. It will be little help if you return a week late to tell us Normain is poaching our ships after all. Solve the mystery and I'll give you the pistole." She hesitated. "Solve the mystery and fix our sugar problem and you'll be given equal share in the Company." Air hissed between her teeth. "And a seat on the Board."

"Done," I said, offering my hand.

"And done," she said, hesitating before taking it gingerly. Her palm was slick with sweat and I could feel her pulse beneath my touch. Either she was terrified of what she'd done or terrified that we wouldn't be enough. I almost told her it should be the former, but she wouldn't have believed me; they never believe a mere girl will do what's needed. Eld's the only one who's ever believed in me, and beyond a knife in the shoulder I'm not sure he's gotten much in return. But this time would pay for all.

Salina broke my grip and rang a small porcelain bell on the table. "Your writ will be on the ship, along with the information you requested."

"Just like that?" Eld asked.

She looked past me and smiled, but there was no humor in it. "Your little friend," she said, and I growled. "The signorina," she corrected, "was right. If you fail, the share is meaningless. If you succeed, I believe I can convince the Board it was a small price to pay to stave off financial ruin." She inclined her head toward the Imperial officer. "To say nothing of the Empire itself."

"Always an afterthought," the other woman murmured through tight lips.

"Like the signorina said, everything has its price. And ours are profits above all else."

"Speaking of price," I interjected before the captain could fire back whatever retort was on her lips, "we'll need money for travel expenses."

"Travel expenses?" Salina asked. "I'm providing the ship."

"We'll need supplies."

"Very well." She opened a drawer and pulled out a small purse with a pearl clasp. "You'll need to submit an itemized list of expenses upon your return or else we'll expect to be repaid for every lire missing from this purse."

"That's going to be problematic," I said. She raised her eyebrows. "Well, I've never been to the Shattered Coast, but from everything I hear, it's wild and untamed."

"It is all of that and more."

"In my experience, limited as it may seem to you, money is often needed to loosen tongues."

"Bribes?"

"Your words, not mine," I said. I also left unsaid that we'd just watched her bribe a judge. "Given how such costs can add up quickly in Servenza, I expect that there, it must be twice as bad. And you'll want us to move quickly, which means more . . ."

"Bribes, yes, I take your point." Reaching into the drawer, she pulled out another purse. "Very well, we'll forgo the itemized receipts for now."

"So long as we're speaking of difficulties," Eld said, "Imperial lire may draw the wrong kind of attention. Especially if they are newly minted."

"How did you know?" she asked.

"The sound of the bags on the table was too uniform," I said. "If there were enough clipped lire in there, and even in Servenza the average on the street is three or four clipped to every one that's not, the bags would have jingled more."

"Doubloons are a neutral currency," Eld added.

"Then make sure you visit a bank if you run out of them," she said, setting a third purse beside those already on the table.

This one jingled more. "Now, can we see about that ship?" She frowned. "Why are you smiling?"

"There's a certain sound money makes. Can't you hear it?" I picked up the purse with the doubloons and let it fall onto the table again. "Possibilities, possibilities, possibilities," I sang in time with the jingling. She smiled uncertainly and I beamed right back at her. Possibilities sure, but what I heard was of one note.

Power.

5

"A wretched girl," Salina muttered as the door swung shut with a dull boom. "I almost wish the stakes were lower; she could do with a lesson in failure. . . ."

"You think she won't fail?"

Salina stiffened, then turned slowly so the captain couldn't see her agitation. The girl had crawled under her skin far enough to make her forget she wasn't alone. The older woman stared back at her and arched an eyebrow.

"I did my research," Salina said finally. She tapped the sheets of parchment on the table before her. "She's annoying, but she has a talent for sifting through the flotsam and coming up with gold. This Buc and Eld have solved half a dozen mysteries in the past two years where all others have failed."

"Aye, but this isn't some mere mystery," the captain muttered.

"It's not," Salina agreed. "But seeing as none of the other methods have produced results, the Board decided it was time to try something new." She left unsaid that the Board still had another card up its sleeve.

"And the Empress?"

"Wouldn't have gifted me the use of you and your soldiers if she didn't approve," Salina said. *She's also the reason I can't tell you about that hidden card.* "I was more worried they wouldn't take the case and we'd have to shoot them," she admitted. "Our agents said she was hardheaded to a fault, that threats wouldn't sway her."

They also said the girl's one weakness was books. Salina studied the shelves around her and smiled. Books were a necessary evil, dull and plodding, but worth their weight in gold for the knowledge they imparted. *I'd gladly pay vast sums to distill their messages without reading them.* A chill ran down her spine and she shuddered. That was too close to what Sin Eaters did, communicating directly with one another's minds and their Goddess, Ciris.

The Board had suspicions about the Goddess . . . but Ciris's mages were the reason the Company had risen so high, so quickly. *A necessary evil. Like books.* "If she only knew that I played her like a street performer on Market Day . . ."

"Did you? I wonder if the Board will agree when they find out you've watered down their share ratio." The captain frowned and fingered the pistole on the table. "The girl gave you enough rope to hang the pair of them any number of ways. Maybe there were two performers playing today."

She held back the retort on her lips as another chill raced through her body. *The Board would understand. They had to! They were the ones who agreed to this. But.* But they hadn't agreed to give up a seat. *Well, they still might not have.* It depended on how well that girl knew the legal requirements for such documents. Still, it was a thin nail to hang her coat on.

"The Board cares about results, *Captain*. If they fail, then my offer might as well never have existed, and if they don't . . . well, the Board is going to be too busy counting their gold to worry that a slip of a girl pulled a chair up to their table."

"Perhaps," the other woman said. "At least until she opens her mouth."

She chuckled. "Well, success has a way of inflating youth's excesses. I'll grant you, she could use a dose of moderation."

"Couldn't we all," the captain said dryly.

Salina drew herself up and crossed her arms, but the officer looked unperturbed. Gods, that girl had her nerves wound tighter than a violin's strings. No, not just the girl. This whole situation was a powder keg waiting for an ember to touch it off. The Company had seen too many good years recently to lag now, not when the Dead Gods' priests were leaning on the Empress to halt their use of Sin Eaters. And Ciris . . . yes, the Board had its suspicions, but that was for another day. First to put out the ember before it caught flame.

This Buc and Eld had to succeed. It was as simple as that. Salina heard her breath whistle through her nostrils and realized she'd let the silence go on too long. Her heart pounded in her chest, but the captain couldn't hear that. Had she heard her breathing? Salina glanced at the other woman's amused expression. Damn it, she had. She coaxed a smile out of her mouth.

"I almost pity her partner," she said, changing the subject. "He had some sense to him, but he's tethered himself to her and he'll share her troubles."

"Aye, but the Gods send it's not too much. He had a nice pair of shoulders," the captain said. Salina eyed her askance and the older woman laughed. "I saw you looking, Salina. If I can appreciate the view, you can too."

"I suppose he was handsome enough," she admitted. But she wasn't thinking of the man. The Board only cared for results, but if the results weren't favorable, they wouldn't remember it was their idea to pin their hopes on a waifish girl with dark-amber skin, kan-whitened teeth, and bright green eyes that seemed to mock without trying. They would only remember who it was who said she'd handle everything. The Company might or might not fall without its sugar, but either way, Salina would. *They won't fail.*

"Dark days are coming if they do," the captain whispered.

Salina hadn't realized she'd spoken aloud, but thinking of those green eyes, she felt a little better. There was something there that spoke of a certainty she hadn't felt until just now. "They won't fail," she repeated.

6

The wind licked my face with salty wisps as the galley pulled away from port. My stomach lurched slightly with the waves, but I tried to ignore it. I'd grown up on the three islands comprising Servenza, seat of the Empire, and it was said half the Empire was ocean; what was a little more water now? My stomach tried to argue, but lost to the book in front of me. Well—half lost. The complex, gear-work diagrams on the pages were nothing like the Cannon Ship itself. It was equipped with hollow tubes from stem to stern that took on seawater at one end, piped it through the ship to power the oars, then exploded out the stern, using the ocean itself as propulsion. It sounded simple enough, but from the diagrams, it was anything but. The massive gear-work mechanism had to be wound and set loose at just the right time.

Do it too soon, before the tubes were completely filled with water, and the ship would go nowhere, potentially damaging the sophisticated gear-work mechanisms that ran through the hull; do it too late and the pressure within the tubes could cause them to rupture, turning all that gear work into expensive shrapnel that would send the ship and every soul aboard to the bottom. It required a precise understanding of the water pressure and speed to kick things off so that the water coming in was sufficient to power the gear work operating the oars, ensuring they rowed in unison, but once a cadence was established, the method was self-perpetuating.

That last bit was courtesy of magic: Ciris's magic. I wondered about that—most magic I'd read about or seen required the mage to be present, but gear work was an art that blended mechanical skill and magic in ways none could fathom. Cannon Ships were said to be twice as fast as galleys powered by slaves and if they only carried a few guns compared to larger brigs or frigates, they more than made up for that in speed. Or so it was said. It was also said they were named for the roar the water made when they were running at full speed. Right now they were quiet and with only the wind to power us—the ship's sails were unfurled—we were making slow time leaving the harbor.

"Steal that from the Company's library?"

"She said I could take what I wanted," I said as Eld joined me at the rail. He looked better in his new blue jacket with red cuffs. Of course, any clothing looks better minus blood and knife holes. Still, the clothes the Company had sent ahead of us, along with the food we'd found in our quarters, had helped. Eld's skin was its usual clammy, pale color instead of the horrid white it'd been when we'd first set foot on deck. "That's not stealing. I had the rest sent back to our place; no need to sink the ship with them."

"Ha. She didn't know what she'd agreed to." I handed him the book and he glanced at it and leaned against the rail, sighing as the wood took his weight. "It's not fair, you know." I arched an eyebrow and he smiled. "Two years of reading and you've already read more than any but the profesori at university."

"I'd have read more than them if you hadn't waited until I was fourteen to find me," I said. "And then you had to teach me."

"I'm not sure it was teaching so much as pointing you at the alphabet and getting out of the way."

I smiled at that and both of us fell silent as the shore crept away. It was the calm before the storm. I could feel it and so could he. I still wasn't sure how we'd ended up on a ship heading for a coast hundreds of leagues away. Intellectually, I knew the steps that had led us here, but I wasn't sure I believed it. There was something about those Imperial Guards being so damned conveniently close. *And that mage. Something came over him before he killed Salazar. And he just watched as Eld killed him.* It felt as if there were another staircase beside the one we trod, invisible, but intertwining with our own somehow.

"Why'd you agree to take this on?" Eld asked, breaking the silence. "Why trade for a share in the company?"

"Like we had a choice?" I snorted. "You fancied a musket ball to the brain instead? Why'd you rescue me in the first place?" Whenever anyone pokes me, friend or no, my inclination is to poke back. Hard. "Why have we been solving other people's problems ever since? That was your idea from the start."

"At the start," Eld amended. I grunted. "Solving things," he said, drawing in a breath. "Helping others, it's a way to . . ." He sighed. "Have you ever made a mistake? Even one that wasn't truly your fault, but if you had been smarter, quicker, *better,* if you had been all of that, maybe you could have prevented it? And if you could have prevented it, maybe it *was* your fault after all?"

My big sister's smiling face filled my mind's eye. That big, stupid smiling face, with a mouth that was just a little too wide, a nose a shade too bold, and eyes of different colors that drew the wrong kind of attention. She would have been gorgeous if nature had been a touch more discerning with beauty's knife. If not for her, I wouldn't have made it past the age of five . . . but without me she wouldn't have stood over that moldy sack of rice. She could have gone a few more days without food even if I couldn't. *Failure*.

"Who am I kidding?" Eld asked. "You don't make mistakes, do you, Buc?" He laughed. "You might be the only person I've met who doesn't. I think that's why I let you keep me. Solving cases, well, I keep telling myself that if I do the right thing enough times, it might make up for that mistake. I never believed it, but I had to try." He touched my arm. "But with you, Buc, I think I might start to believe."

"I did fail," I said slowly, barely hearing my voice over the dull pounding in my skull. "Once."

The sounds of the clubs had been terrible, but somehow the knife had been the worst. There's a sound sometimes, when a knife hits the chest just right, a hissing sound as if it struck the soul and all the life is leaking out. I know now it was the sound of my sister's lung collapsing, but at the time it sounded like a whisper. *Failure*. A whisper louder than the flames, if not as hot. She might have lived with half a lung . . . but the flames saw to the rest.

"Once was enough, Eld." I squeezed the railing beneath my fingers until the wood bit at them. "The world should be a better place than it is." Eld nodded. "And that's why I agreed to take on the case. It's why I bargained for a share in the Kanados Trading Company." He frowned. "The world isn't shaped by good deeds alone. There's too much weakness for that. Power is the antidote. And with enough power, aye, and some good deeds, maybe we can shape the world after all."

"You truly believe that?" he asked.

I stood up from the railing and so did he. The wind caught my curls and lifted them, exposing where I'd shaved the sides of my head and he smiled as he always did when he saw that. Something in his smile killed the seed of doubt that had been planted by that failure and while I'd never allowed the seed to take root, I'd never been able to completely destroy it either. Now, with one smile, it was gone. I don't understand emotions in others; I guess it shouldn't surprise me that I don't understand them in myself, either.

"Aye, I do." I felt my mouth twitch. "And like you said, I don't make mistakes."

Eld laughed at that and I joined him, but we were both cut short by the Cannon Ship roaring to life with enough force that I would have fallen if Eld hadn't caught me. That had been the way of it for the last two years—one of us has stumbled, faltered here and there, but the other's been there when they were needed. We hadn't made any mistakes. Even the catastrophe with Salazar had turned in our favor at the end. This was our first real chance at taking a step toward gaining the kind of power needed to change the world, so we couldn't afford to make any now. Still, with Eld's arm on my shoulder, holding me steady against the harsh tilt of the ship, it was hard to see how we could. He felt solid, unshakable.

I wish I could say the same for my stomach.

7

Eld stared out at the dark water that slid past the ship in a slick sheen, broken only by the odd wave that shone white beneath the scrap of moon that peeked out from the clouds above. Standing on the deck, railing cutting into the palms of his hands, he felt alone in a swirling blackness that was sharp with the taste of salt and not much else. The sound of the water cannons, siphoning seawater on either side of the hull and propelling them forward at an impossible speed, drowned out everything.

His thoughts swirled around the question Buc had posed to him when they'd slipped out of Servenza's harbor at dawn, almost a day ago now.

"Why'd you rescue me in the first place?" She'd shot the words at him as if from the slingshot she kept in her purse. *"Why have we been solving other people's problems ever since? That was your idea from the start."*

"I didn't rescue you," he whispered to the passing waves. Buc had gone belowdecks after dinner; something about the speed of the ship didn't seem to agree with her, and her typically flintlike tongue had sharpened to an edge that had the crew walking well wide of her. "You rescued me.

"I just never told you."

He closed his eyes, the tears burning down his cheeks echoing the fire in his shoulder, where he'd caught the knife meant for Buc. Salina had summoned a physiker to look at the wound before they left, at Buc's insistence. The woman had known her trade, but no poultice would knit his shoulder back together in a matter of hours. That would have required magic, and no one wondered that he didn't want to trust a mage so soon after killing one. Nothing left for him but to grit his teeth and bear it. If there was one thing his previous life had taught him, it was how to take pain, and if he took it so Buc didn't have to, so much the better. It was the least he could do after she'd all but given him his life back. The army had taken most of it and the price he paid in leaving had stripped the rest away.

"You're to take the company into the gap, Eldritch."

"Sirrah?" Eld's voice amplified the question. He'd been trained at the Academy, like every other noble's second and third daughter or son, and though he'd only been in a few skirmishes and one pitched battle that barely merited the name, only a fool would fail to see that the opening in the line of the Burning Lands militia was likely a trap.

True, the main thrust of the assaults and counterassaults had been to the north and east, but he'd read the scouting reports, same as Commander Seetel had: the Burnt were crawling all over the barren dunes beyond the foothills in front of them; if they had missed the small gap between the hills, it was because they'd intended to miss it.

"I know you're green, Leftenant," Seetel growled, his voice cracking as it did whenever he grew angry, "but I didn't think you yellow."

"I'm as brave as the next," Eld said. The explanation was on his lips—the gap looks too inviting; it was too easy for the scouts to find an undefended gap on the enemy's flank—but Seetel's tone kept him silent. The man was prickly about his command and liable to send Eld off, like he had the last junior officer who had pushed him too far.

Lamell had been a good leftenant, despite being barely fifteen and the youngest of them, pressed into service far too early due to the war going badly. Even her father's standing in the Servenzan nobility hadn't kept her from being reassigned to a regiment of untrained replacements. She'd done her duty in the next assault, aye, and died for it. Eld didn't even have that much protection—he wasn't Servenzan. And I don't want to die.

"If we're to exploit their weakness, shouldn't it be with the entire regiment?" He hated himself for asking, for inviting more soldiers to join him in what was likely to be a trap, but numbers had a way of covering mistakes. It was one of the few lessons Seetel had taught him.

"The regiment will be with you, but farther into the foothills, to your right, to keep any reinforcements cut off," Seetel said, his voice returning to its typical gruff, taciturn growl.

Did I really once think him an ideal officer? *The man carried himself well and his uniform was spotless, cuirass buffed to a high sheen, but there was no heart behind it and very little brains above. Seetel droned on, but all Eld could see was the crimson circle on the map, drawn around the gap in the hills. It looked like a circle of blood.*

"I should have said something," Eld said, the wind snatching his words as soon as they left his lips and taking his secret with them. "It was my command, my duty, and I failed." Buc had spoken of failure as they left Servenza, but she didn't know of his. No one living did. It'd made the memories easier to forget, but the past day's events had undone all the progress he'd made at walling that part of his life away. The last time he'd been so close to death, he'd been in the gap, fighting for his life on the shifting sands. "And I paid the price. They all paid the price."

Screams rent the air, as heated as the gunfire that cut them short. As heated as the sun that beat down upon them. It'd been dawn when they first moved into the gap, and they'd barely had a moment's rest in its shade before they'd been driven back on all sides. Seetel had ordered him to press the attack and Eld had obeyed, for all the good it'd done. Now the Company was strung out well into the far side of the gap, where hard ground gave way to soft sand. Boulders littered the sides of the hill to their left, concealing a platoon or more of Burnt soldiers who managed to keep up a steady fusillade despite their ancient matchlock muskets.

A woman stepped up beside his aide and the lad screamed when she caught the ball meant for him, brains and blond hair splattering across his cheeks. Eld's stomach tightened and a bitter taste filled his mouth before a high-pitched scream cut his reaction short: the Burnt were charging. His training took over and he began barking orders.

"Clean yourself up later, Bahrais!" he said, his words pulling the lad back to himself. "Get to First Platoon's sergeant and tell him to dig in, with swords if he has to. I'm sending reinforcements, but they must hold. Understand?" Bahrais's dark eyes were unfocused and Eld had to restrain himself from punching the youngster. He was just a year or two younger than Eld himself—but he doesn't have your training, Eld thought. A fat lot of good it's doing you, *the thought chased after, but he stepped on it. Hard.*

"Soldier! Get to the First Platoon. They are to dig in!" His shout brought the boy's eyes into focus. Bahrais saluted with a fist to his chest and took off, boots churning up sand in his wake.

"You!" Eld's voice stopped the woman rushing past him. Seetel had told him the mark of a good officer was a stout pair of lungs and an even voice and, at least, in that he hadn't lied. The soldier somehow managed a salute while continuing to reload her musket. The fire to their front, which pinned them down, slackened as Burnt held their fire, probably waiting for their comrades to flank them from the hill.

"Get back to Tensil's weapons squad and tell her I want all the grenadoes she has sent up to First on the left flank. On the double now!" His shout chased after her—unlike Bahrais, she'd taken off as soon as she

understood his intent. Marking her out for promotion if she survived the day, Eld bellowed for the platoons to hold, then rushed after his aide.

"To me, condottieri!" Eld forced a smile into his voice that felt as false as his courage. All he felt was numb, cold, but it was another's stiffness—he had a job to do. "Their muskets are as like to blow up in their faces as ours and we've got Servenzan steel to greet them with. With a kiss, aye? You've kissed your lover before today? If not, you've left it late, condottieri, left it damned late."

A few laughs greeted his words, but the First's line straightened among the boulders and scraps of sand dunes that offered what little protection there was in the Burning Lands, stiffened by their commander's words. Eld felt a flash of pride as they brought their muskets up to level as one cohesive machine. A machine of death that he meant to unleash on the veiled bastards rushing toward them. It'd been mere moments since the scream, but it'd been enough. The sergeant's voice called out the order and the line erupted in flame and smoke, obliterating the hillside. The high-pitched yell faltered but didn't stop, and Eld bit back a curse.

"Sin Eater!" The mage appeared at his side as if by magic, which perhaps it was. "Reinforcements, I need them now." The woman's dark features tightened—mages hated being ordered. "If you please," he added. "We've a regiment in front of us, if not several. Tell Commander Seetel I need the reserves brought up if I'm to hold the gap."

The woman's mouth twitched. As she began to nod, a loud rush of thunder caused them both to turn. Toward the opposite side of the line, to the right, where the hills rose higher, where the rest of the regiment was supposed to be holding the Burnt's attention. Whatever was there, it wasn't the regiment, because scores of cavalry were cascading over the ridge, pointed right toward his weakened flank. Grenadoes began to explode among the Burnt charging from the left— the countermeasures he'd ordered. The orders that now ensured their opposite flank would have no protection from the charging cavalcade.

For a breath he could do nothing. Then his mouth moved as if of its own accord. "Reinforcements, Sin Eater! Now! Tell Seetel to send every man and woman jack of them he has left in the camps." Even as he spoke, Eld realized any reinforcements would arrive far too late to do more than stop the looting of their corpses. "Belay that! Call in cannon fire on the hill."

The mage's face contorted, her cheeks hung as if she'd lost all control of herself. Her mouth moved and a voice that sounded deeper than he remembered answered him. "Not yet, Leftenant. Soon, but not yet."

"You don't give the orders," he snapped. Or tried to. Her refusal stole the breath from his lungs. He'd faced death once or twice in the past few months, but always with the knowledge that it'd be an unlucky chance that took him. Unless the Sin Eater used her magic to relay his orders, to call in literal divine intervention, the cavalry would cut through his thin ranks and roll up his line, acting the hammer to the militia's anvil. It would all be over in a few brief, bloody moments. "I do," he reminded her. It came out as a whisper.

"And I use my magic to speak with my sister who is with the artillery," the mage said in her too-deep voice. "Trust me."

Her words sent a shiver down his sweat-soaked spine. One of his profesori at the Academy had told him that in war, trust was the sound of death. Now he was staring it down. They locked eyes, her amber orbs steady and untroubled, and he almost believed her. Almost. Because to wait made no sense. He cleared his parched throat.

"Just do it," he grated. "Or we'll all die where we stand."

The Sin Eater laughed, but if she replied, Eld didn't hear her. Breaking into a run, he began bellowing for the Second and Third Platoons to form up. Second was a shell of its former self, having caught the brunt of the fighting throughout the morning, and Third was depleted from sending squads to reinforce the left flank. Despite all that, both platoons began to move into a cohesive line. Pride rose in his chest at the sight. We're doing it.

The cavalry struck.

The Burnt made for sorry infantry with their outdated weapons and ill discipline, but their cavalry was another matter. The only way to survive the harsh dunes was to travel from watering hole to watering hole and they were born to the saddle. Eld watched in horror as the thinly held line caved in, rebounded against the horse flung against them, and began to crack in places, a small hole here, a larger there. Then the heavy cavalry caught up, double-humped camels bearing two riders with matchlocks or long spear-scythes that chewed through armor and limb like a cleaver through stale bread. The cracks became gaps, became rents, and even as he shouted encouragement, Eld's Company broke, becoming individual men and women fighting for their lives. The line shattered like miscast iron against the forge.

"Now!" the Sin Eater shouted in his ear. He glanced down and saw her beaming up at him, dark braided locks framing her sunburned face. "The time is now, Leftenant." Her voice changed back to the one he remembered as she began speaking with her sister, who was almost a third of a league away at the fortifications they'd left at grey dawn. Just as the mage gave Eld a wink, her head exploded, wet hair and bone slapping him in the face. Sputtering, he swiped at his eyes with both hands. When his vision cleared, he saw bits of bone and brain and strands of dark hair covering his blood-soaked hands. The world sucked in, bending back on itself until all that existed were his hands and the low scream building in the back of his throat.

Clean yourself up later.

The words he'd shouted at Bahrais were like ice water splashed across his face. The world returned in a rush of acrid powder and bright steel and the sounds of people killing and being killed. A camel careened toward him, the rear hump empty, the front occupied by a rider who balanced a spear in one hand and the reins in the other, robes flying behind her like a banner. Eld saw his death approaching and couldn't muster up the energy to care. All around him lay blood-

drenched bodies in tattered uniforms of the Servenzan army. . . . What was one more? The rider roared and drew back her arm and Eld waited for the impact.

In the end his apathy saved him. The rider aimed for where she thought he would dodge, and he heard the whine as the spear whipped just over his head. Then the stirrup crashed into his shoulder, knocking him off his feet, and somehow, in midair, Eld grabbed the leather harness and felt himself lifted clear as the camel leapt a pile of corpses. The rider screeched as the sudden imbalance threw her off her mount. The camel really took off, running away from the smells and sounds of death, with Eld grimly hanging on.

The ground began to firm up as soon as they left the thick of the fighting, tearing at Eld's legs. He tried to let go, but his glove was caught in the harness straps. The scent of the hulking animal was pungent, like a hundred sweaty men in desperate need of a bath, a clawing, choking, retching odor. Fighting the blind panic that hadn't fully left him and was threatening to swamp him, he grasped blindly at his belt with his free hand, seeking his knife. Instead he felt the smooth handle of his pistole. Eld hesitated for a second, his lungs screaming for air, until a stunted tree tore a hole in his pant leg . . . and his skin. The pain decided for him and he drew and aimed in one motion, letting himself feel the movement of the lumbering beast.

Eld squeezed the trigger.

The animal went down in a heap, its momentum flipping it half onto its side and sending Eld free with a searing snap of harness that wrenched his arm painfully in the wrong direction. He thought he heard something break—it might have been his skull—as he careened end over end, until a small boulder brought him up short with a punch to his kidneys that drove the remaining breath from his lungs. Spots flecked his vision, dark fireflies against the bright cloud of smoke and dust that had risen around the battlefield. He could hear his breath whining in the back of his throat.

Not whining.

Shells.

Gods, no, *he thought. The Servenzan lines he'd sought to maintain had folded in on themselves, were now intertwined in with the Burnt, both sides holding their partners tightly in this dance of death. The mage had called the tune. Only that wasn't quite true, was it? He had told her to play.*

"But not this," he whispered through parched lips. His words were lost in the roar of explosions as a score of canisters burst overhead, turning the sands black with powder that was quickly replaced by blood. Solid shot fell among the swirling maelstrom, sending crimson geysers fountaining up dozens of paces into the sky, mixing human and beast and sand together until they blended into a uniform color that tore at his eyes.

The image of a mad ballroom in the desert, where swords and spears and muskets replaced corsages and drinks and light touches of the arm, with an orchestra of cannon instead of strings, filled Eld's mind. He began to wheeze, then chuckle, and finally laugh as he watched every man and woman he'd been entrusted with die before his eyes. By his orders. Orders the mage had twisted, for what purpose his broken mind couldn't begin to grasp. He laughed until he cried, tears filling his eyes so that the scene was blissfully blurred before him, sobs tearing at his raw throat.

Sometime later he became aware of a gurgling sound. It was his breathing, loud in his gunfire-deafened ears. Loud because the shelling had finally stopped. Blinking back tears, Eld pushed himself to his feet, using the boulder at his back for support. He looked around, from the sandy hills to the left of the gap to the taller foothills on the right. Nothing moved, nothing stood. Save him.

I'm the only one left.

———

Eld came back to himself, the sound of the water roaring through the Cannon Ship sending gooseflesh across his arms, echoing the artillery he'd heard that day, years before. Those cannons had broken both armies. The cannons had broken Eld as well. The weeks that followed had been a blur until he found himself discharged to Servenza, listless and searching for a purpose. At first he thought revenge would do. Seetel and the mage—one was dead . . . but one was very much alive and seemingly guilt-free.

But Eld had found revenge to be a shallow thing. He was on the brink of giving in to the inevitable and joining his fallen comrades in oblivion, until he found Buc. She'd been the gleam of light in the blackness surrounding him, promising something he'd never thought to find again: hope. He'd clung to that light ever since.

"Sirrah!" At the sound of the voice from behind, Eld turned to see a sailor running toward him in the lamplight, no easy feat on a ship cutting through the night. The short man touched a knuckle to his bandanna-covered forehead when he reached him. "Sirrah, there's something the matter with your woman."

"She's not my woman," Eld said, frowning past him toward the cabins. "I'm her man."

"Aye, well, it's just that—"

"Say! Is that smoke I smell?" Eld asked. Whatever the sailor answered, Eld didn't hear, because he was already running toward the grey plume he could see coming from belowdecks. *Buc.*

8

Port au' Sheen was a wooden pile of shit running itself down into the sea. Farther up, toward the top of the deforested hill, wood gave way to ancient stone buildings built in layers that rose to a point. Ramshackle hovels and shacks surrounded them and were piled beside one another down the hill and right up to the docks we stood on. It was hard to tell if the sea had spat out the rubble or if the rubble was slowly sliding into its depths. People strutted about, looking like fleas waiting for the ocean to wash them off their host.

I took it all in a glance, hurrying down the gangplank, not bothering to acknowledge the captain's cries of farewell. Or maybe they were curses. I'd been seasick the whole voyage, most of which had passed in a hallucinatory blur. From what I gathered, I hadn't been my usual, pleasant self. As soon as my boot heels touched the dock, I felt my stomach settle, and took in a deep, shuddering breath. *Land.* The docks shifted beneath my feet, but after days on that murder ship, going faster than the wind, I barely noticed. My head felt hollow, but the dull pounding had ceased, so there was that.

Eld dropped his pack beside me and squinted up the hill. "How you feeling?" he asked, shooting me a look.

Hard, Buc, hard. Eld pulled me off the streets and I'd tried to even the scales since, but the journey from Servenza hadn't been my finest hour. *No one gets to see me weak.* Not even Eld. I bit my tongue until it bled, and forced a smile. "I feel like ten thousand lire, fresh minted." I plucked at my new dress. It was modeled after the riding habit I usually wore, but the Company didn't know how to do things on the cheap, so the soft burgundy was cut through with thread o' gold that would shine in the sunlight. *And make me a mark for the cutpurses.* I shouldn't have been surprised—there is no fool like a rich one.

Still, they'd given me the hidden pockets I'd asked for, for my blades. A dress without pockets is like a gondola without an oar: pretty but useless. I ran my hands down my sides, feeling the stilettos I'd slipped into the usual places, plus a couple in unusual ones, and twisted my left wrist to ensure that the flat piece of double-pointed steel was where it belonged.

How they'd managed to have new clothes made for us in the few hours between our "business meeting" with Salina and our arrival at the Cannon Ship was almost magical in its own right, even if the clothes were really too rich for my taste. Eld handed me my dark leather purse and I glanced inside to make sure he'd packed it with my slingshot and a dozen lead balls plus one or two special ones of my own making. I slid the strap over my head and adjusted it so it hung by my side as I liked. Other women might have a score of items in their bags, but I didn't want to rummage through a lot of things to try to find what I needed in the moment, so slingshot and ammunition was it.

At close quarters a slingshot is nearly as powerful as a gun and infinitely faster to reload. Slingshots don't misfire, guns frequently do, and what the weapon lost in intimidation, it more than made up for in surprise. I once sent an entire street gang running after loosing half a dozen balls down a tight alleyway before they could do more than fire an old matchlock into the air. Surprise will do that for you.

"I hadn't thought to see pyramids here," Eld said.

"Pyramids?" I shifted my glance up from the purse to the stone buildings and swore. "So that's what a pyramid looks like. I've read of them of course, but I thought they'd be more . . . pointy."

"There are pyramids in the Burning Lands that are a hundred paces tall . . . and pointy," Eld said.

"What do you know of the Burning Lands?" I asked.

Eld shrugged, his face already bright in the sun or maybe burnt from the journey. "The captain said these were built to withstand the hurricanes that broke the coast up centuries ago. Relics of another age, but impressive in their own way."

"If you say so," I said. I glanced back at the ship and my stomach flipped. "About time we were getting on, don't you think?"

"Aye." Eld glanced at a man strolling past with two broad cutlasses thrust through a thick red sash that rode low beneath his broad, bare belly, which was darkened by the sun and ink from tattoos. The man caught Eld's eye and grabbed at his crotch. Eld looked away, blushing.

"Hoy, fatty!" I called. "I know he's ugly, but he's mine. Go find your own piece of meat." The man glared at me, then bellowed with laughter and kept sauntering down the docks, exchanging greetings with a few others who were as covered in tattoos as he was.

"Look at you, making friends," I said.

"Friends?" Eld sputtered. "This isn't Servenza, Buc. The only law here is that of the blade and pistole. Speak like you have been and you might find someone thinks it's worth drawing steel over."

"A good fight might be just what I need to clear my head," I said. He snorted. "I'll try to moderate my tongue, but you know how I am." I shrugged. "There wasn't much in the way of law on the streets, Eld. It's you I'm worried about."

"Me?"

"Aye, while you're trying to explain to some pirate that you were just being polite, she'll slip a knife between your ribs." I touched his arm. "These are my people, Eld. They don't see politeness as civil behavior, only as weakness."

"Is that why you always act the arsehole?" he asked, bending over to grab his pack. It was stuffed full of our clothes and a few supplies as well as Salina's coin.

"Tough to say," I murmured as we began walking down the dock. I tried to walk straight and tall despite my stomach protesting against the movement. Eld's eyes tightened and I knew I hadn't fooled him. "Was I born this way or did my environment turn me into an arsehole?" I grinned. "Maybe both?"

"Maybe," Eld said. He adjusted the straps of his pack and let his hand caress the hilt of his sword to make sure it hung where he liked it. "What's the plan?"

"Information," I said. "We'll head up yonder hill until I get a feel for where we need to drop anchor. Knowledge is the root of power, but with less than a week before our deadline, it's going to be tight. Good thing that Company bitch gave us plenty of money."

"Aye," Eld said, disapproval loud in his voice.

"It'd have been nice if she'd given us more of a lay of the land," I said by way of explanation, though it did little to improve Eld's expression. "That's all I'm saying. Some knowledge of what the world's been up to may tie into whatever we learn here."

"Well, as to that, there're some pages in this paper," he said a moment later, digging into his dark blue, nearly black jacket.

He shook the newspaper out and offered it to me. "Two days old before we sailed, but it's something."

"Bah, it was dross," I said, waving it away.

"You read it?"

"Crown Prince of some Normain province murdered in the streets!" I said, pitching my voice like one of the paper lasses standing on a street corner. A dockworker packing empty glass flagons into a crate glanced at me, shook her braids, and returned to her work. "Twenty-five times removed and piping kan into his veins. Some would-be historian who styles herself as an archae-ologist, first in her field, claims she found a shipwreck from two centuries past or more—from when explorers braved hurricanes to discover the Shattered Coast. Seeking a sponsor to finance the expedition and split the treasure. And, of course, rampant speculation about kan futures given the wet spring." I snorted. "Dross, like I said."

"When did you read it?" Eld asked.

"The first night, before I thought I was going to die. I'd try to read a whole page before running up to the deck to puke."

"So that's why you had the lantern lit in your room?"

"Of course," I said.

"But you said you didn't remember lighting it," Eld said.

"Really?" I frowned. My memory after that first night was hidden by a thick fog. "When did I say that?"

"After it caught your bed on fire and half the crew fought to keep it from taking the ship with it. It took hours before the embers were done. Meanwhile, you were raving on deck as if it were you burning and not the bed. The captain had to give you his own cabin, Buc!"

"Hmm." I shrugged. "Well, I don't remember that, but then again, severe dehydration will do that." Cold ran down my back. *Fire. Sister. I hate fire.* I suppressed a shudder and clapped him on the shoulder. "They put it out, right? No harm done." Eld sputtered, but before he could get wound up we reached the end of the docks and joined the swirling crowd milling about.

"Hush, Eld, you'll disrupt these hard workers. Have some respect." I didn't hear his response, but when I turned around, his face was dark and I don't think it was from the sun. Even so, he looked away quickly and I could tell he was embarrassed by his outburst. Manners are a terrible affliction. Thank the Gods I'm immune.

9

The air was heavy with water and together with the heat, I felt like the sweat that poured down my skin was about to ignite. I was tempted to strip to my shift, save that Eld would die of shame—and everyone would see my knives. The crowds were a singularly un-uniformed lot: tattoo-covered sailors who looked more like buccaneers that I'd heard of in taverns since I was a lass than like honest Servenzan deckhands, festooned with all manner of blades; dirt-covered beggars; merchants bedecked in suits of fine, thin silks and dresses that would have been considered scandalous in Servenza. *At least my dress won't stand out here.* If anything, I blended in perfectly, as most of the women seemed to be clothed in gilt . . . or dirt. The women were easy to pick out amongst the throng of men of every type and nature, each yelling louder than the next, striving to make themselves heard over the maelstrom.

Here and there a street urchin darted about, clad in only torn shorts regardless of sex, but they were few and far between, which made sense: Who would bring a child to this Godsforsaken corner of the world? It reminded me of Servenza on Market Day. Or any day, really.

The crowds thinned as we stepped off the cobbled plaza surrounding the docks and headed up the hill. The dirt streets were surprisingly calm; most people walked to the sides, finding refuge in the shady overhangs of the sometimes ramshackle wooden buildings that leapt up on either side of the road, all in varying degrees of falling apart. Here and there a parasol or umbrella made an appearance, but if someone had the forethought to sell any, they'd have made a killing. Farther away from the docks there was less of salt and fish in the air and more of body odor and sweat that even the sharp tang of foreign spices mixed with dust couldn't mask.

A shot rang out and I put an overweight merchant between me and the sound while Eld reached for the pistole in his sash. Another shot came a moment later, followed by laughter. None of the people around us so much as paused and Eld and I exchanged looks before resuming our climb. I made sure the fat bastard sweating through his silks was close enough to use for cover just in case. A dozen paces on we reached a crossroads and saw the source of the gunfire.

Two men faced each other across a dueling green, but as there was no grass, I suppose it was a dueling dust bowl.

"Having both missed, is Your Honor satisfied?" a thin, reedy gentleman cried.

"You'd have to have honor for it to be satisfied, whore," said the closer man. He spat into the dirt. "Mine is not."

"Mine is," the farther man said—when he spoke, I realized he was actually a woman wearing men's clothing. I ground to a halt and Eld grunted as he bumped into me, but I ignored him. As soon as I stopped seeing a man, her features became plain. She would have been pretty in a dress, but in trousers and a loose jacket there was something about her that elevated her beyond merely pretty.

"Then again," the woman said in an even voice.

"Come on," Eld spoke in my ear to be heard over the crowd. "There's no need to see this."

"She's wearing trousers," I said.

"Aye, well, who's to say she can't? Out here there are no laws, no rules, barely any guidelines. She can do as she pleases, but I'd bet a copper that if she were in a dress, she wouldn't be on that green right now."

"That's sexist of you, Eld." I clicked my tongue. "And it's not green."

"You know what I mean," Eld said. "Now come on. Either she'll kill him or he'll kill her or they'll kill each other. Only fools fight duels and this isn't getting us the information we need."

I nodded reluctantly and began moving again, now mimicking the locals, ducking into the shade of nearby buildings instead of walking up the middle of the street. The shade didn't do much, but it removed enough of the sun's harshness that my skin stopped steaming. The fat merchant had picked up a companion in an equally fine suit, his face pinpricked with scars. The fat man leaned toward him, resting his hands on a rich gilded cane carved with sugar leaves; I stepped up my pace until I was close enough to hear.

"The route's cursed, I tell you."

"It hasn't been the last seven years, man."

"Yes, but the last seven months it has been. I've started instructing my ships to eschew the sugar route and make farther north, where the kan ships sail."

"You can afford that kind of delay?" the scarred man asked.

"More than I can afford ships disappearing. I have to think of the fleet." The man's cheeks shook. "Not that you can call three ships a fleet."

"You've lost that many?"

"Don't pretend you haven't either," the fat merchant growled. "We both know—"

Another gunshot rang out and I glanced over my shoulder in time to see the man who'd called the woman a whore lying flat on his back, his plumed bicorne several paces away. The dust was growing dark around him. The woman appeared, standing over him, a smoking pistole in her hand. *Good on you, sister.* I turned back around, but the merchants were gone. I spun to look for them and spotted them ducking into a tavern, the scarred merchant arguing with the fat one.

"I guess she had honor after all," Eld said; he, too, had glanced back at the sound of the gunshot. He sighed. "You know why they call this place Port au' Sheen?"

"Assume I don't," I said.

"Because they say blood or gold, both shine in the sunlight," Eld said.

"Damn. Come on." I tapped his elbow. "I want to get a better feel for this place."

"You haven't seen enough?"

"Maybe, but I haven't heard enough. I need to understand the people, what motivates them. Beyond blood and gold, I mean," I added.

"Still think this is like your streets?" he asked.

"No." I shook my head. "It's more honest."

An hour later we were both sweating like gondoliers on the Feast of Lights despite the shade offered by the tattered awning of what served as an open-air tavern. Eld's cheeks glistened no matter how hard he fanned himself with that old newspaper and every time he took a sip of his wine punch, drops of sweat trickled into the cup. Pretty soon he'd be drinking his own salt water. I drained my mug three times—well watered, per Eld's whispered instructions to the bartender, so my mind was clear, but Gods, I still had a thirst that a hundred glasses wouldn't slake.

"I'll never complain about Servenza's heat again," I said.

"Don't go to the Burning Lands then," Eld said. "Less water in the air, but the heat is so intense, it feels like a furnace in your lungs every time you draw breath."

"Burning Lands?" I motioned for the bartender a fourth time. "You mentioned that before. When were you in the Burning Lands?"

"I did travel before we met," Eld said, but his lips were pressed together in a way that told me he didn't want to talk about it. Usually that would be my cue to pry, but my mind was boiling over with what I'd heard in the last hour and I wasn't yet well enough to hold both objectives clearly in mind. The bartender placed another clay mug on the table and took away my empty one along with Eld's doubloon, making the coin disappear so quickly into her bodice that she looked like a street performer demonstrating sleight of hand.

"We need a map."

"A map?" He took another sip. "Of what?"

"The Shattered Coast and the trade routes. Specifically, the shipping lanes."

"Turn around, then." Eld pointed behind me. "Assuming it's accurate, of course."

I glanced over my shoulder and saw, above the tavern's door, a faded map of the area drawn in dark lines that looked like charcoal. I blinked to dispel the haze in my eyes and the map grew clearer. *Gods, I am tired.* I'd put all the pieces together by my second cup, but between trying to decide if I could stand the heat and wondering where we could find a good map, I'd wasted the better part of an hour, when all along it'd been staring me in the back.

"You're still off-kilter, aren't you?" Eld asked. "You'd never miss that."

"I'm perfectly . . ." I sighed and drained my wine punch in one long swallow. "Fine, I'm not feeling great, but I can't afford weakness."

"Yes, you can . . ." Eld began.

"No, I can't." I shook my head. "You're going to give me another headache. We need to find some pirates."

Eld's mouth moved wordlessly for a few moments. "Pirates?" he asked finally.

"Aye."

"And why do we need to find pirates?"

"Because of the map."

Eld leaned forward, peering into my eyes. "Buc, are you okay? Truly?"

"Very well," I muttered, leaning forward too, more to keep anyone from hearing what I was saying than from needing the table to support my weight. Aye, maybe that, too, but start admitting your own weaknesses and pretty soon you start accepting them. And I won't do that. "I'll explain."

"That would be nice."

"Remember the two merchants we followed up here? The fat one and the scarred one?"

"Vaguely," Eld said.

"Aye. The scarred one's face was marked with old burns. The kind you get from working in a sugar refinery. The other one's cane was embossed with sugarcane leaves."

"So they own sugarcane plantations."

"Or oversee them, aye. The sugarcane plantations lie leagues to our south and the kan plantations a few leagues to the north, but the trade winds offer several potential courses. The important thing is that they said their ships were disappearing when they followed the sugar route, but if they went farther north, along the kan route, their ships made the journey unmolested."

"Okay . . ."

"And then when we first sat down here, recall the naval lieutenant at the table behind me?"

"The one talking to the physiker?"

"Aye, the ship's physiker. Both wore green sashes indicating they patrol the Southern Expanse, which means they also patrol the sugar route. The officer was complaining about the plethora of sugar, but the absolute lack of limes, pirates, or other ships."

Eld's eyes narrowed. "Now, what is that about?"

"I'd assume his ship has a problem with scurvy."

"Not the limes!"

"Oh, well, simply this: If there are no pirates and no ships in the southern shipping lanes, then what is causing the disappearances?"

"It can't be so simple as to be about sugar profits and that's why the ships are disappearing?"

"Perhaps, but I'm less interested in motivation at the moment and more in the physical cause."

"Doesn't the first lead you to the second?"

"Usually, but we don't have that kind of time," I said. "Besides, why would anyone want to draw attention to that area if they are poaching ships? That's shortsighted."

"You have to be a bit daft to take up piracy in the first place," Eld said. "Once you hoist the black flag, your life expectancy drops exponentially."

I pointed at the newspaper in his hand. "The next to last page, eight, I believe, mentions the exploits of a certain pirate, a woman with black hair filled with fire." I sniffed. "Whatever that means. Anyway, she certainly captured the reporter's imagination, but I'm less interested in her hair and more in what the reporter says her territory is: the Southern Expanse." I turned to the map behind us and nodded. "Right where the ships are disappearing, right where the navy has found nothing."

"So," Eld said, pushing himself to his feet. "Pirates?"

10

It turned out that Port au' Sheen was lousy with pirates. A few doubloons slipped to an appropriately disheveled ruffian covered in tattoos and more hair than I had known was possible pointed us toward an abandoned tannery lurking on the outskirts of the town. The man had appeared confused that we wanted to pay to find a recruiting meeting, but gold has a way of silencing questions, and his directions to the dusty side alley and the overgrown yard were easily followed. Eld and I were dressed a little too fine compared to the rest of our compatriots, but we arrived early enough to secure a spot next to one of the old tanning vats. The lingering aromas from the factory's working years still burnt our eyes, but kept everyone away from us.

"A right proper turnout!" A large woman wearing what looked like a blacksmith's thick leather apron over her dress stood up from the stump she'd been resting on. "First off, let me save any Imperial agents the trouble—we're all here as free privateers, looking to sign and sail and plunde—that is to say, *appropriate*, under proper authorities, aye?"

"Aye," twenty voices chorused.

"Not pirates."

"Not pirates!"

"Well then, now that we've established our bona fides," the woman said, "let's get down to business. There's ships what need bodies to sail them south. The northern routes are filled with peace-loving merchants of our Imperial brethren."

"Filled with man o' wars, too!" a voice cried out.

The woman laughed with the rest. "Aye, them, too. It's been too long since we sailed south and Mama Hammer"—she tapped her considerable chest—"wants to change that. If that don't sound interesting to you, then you're welcome to leave. Now. Those that stay, we can discuss the specificities of our arrangement and— What the bloody mizzen top do you want?"

A young man in a loose jerkin and even looser trousers stepped around the man in front of him. "Are you really sailing south?" His voice suggested he was used to more respect than his disheveled appearance warranted.

"That's what I just said, isn't it?" she asked, spreading her arms wide. Everyone laughed. "You think Mama Hammer is a liar?" The laughter died at that.

He shook dark hair out of his eyes and leaned forward. "I think you should sail north."

"Listen, milksop, I don't know where you left your brains today, but you'd best sit down or I'll bury you a fathom deep with one stroke." The woman pulled a blacksmith's hammer from within her apron and shook it.

A smile played across his features. There was something dark in the expression and I felt my muscles stiffen. "You still sail south?"

"I earned my name, boy. Don't tempt me."

The young man nodded slowly and his lips pursed as if he were about to say something. Mama Hammer shook her implement again and he shook his head as if in reply. He turned away and, as he moved, I saw the sun catch something bright in his hand. *A vial.* He tossed its contents back with a single swallow and a heartbeat later his body jerked as if he had a palsy.

"I told you to reconsider," he said in a voice several octaves deeper than before. "Remember." Mama Hammer started to speak and he growled. "Remember!"

"Shit, he's a mage," I spat.

"What?" Eld stood straight.

"One of the followers of the Dead Gods. Veneficus."

The word left my mouth at the same instant the lad's skin exploded outward and he fell to all fours, quivering, and then screaming in bass bellows as his bones cracked. You see mages every day, walking around in their fine robes with medallions swinging around their necks and sometimes, if you haven't had experience with them, you forget what dark powers they wield. I'd seen more than a few and had little cause to trust them. Eld hates them more than me, though I don't fully understand why. All that is to say, when a young man rips himself apart to reveal a full-on raging bull with steel horns—it's hard to ignore.

The bull bellowed and so did Mama Hammer, but her swing rebounded off the beast's horns and a moment later she followed, tossed like a piece of flotsam. The vat she hit screeched as it cracked, but her head cracked first and that was the end of Mama Hammer.

Men started screaming, fighting with one another to escape the yard, but the vats created natural funnels and where they ran, the bull ran too. Four legs are faster than two. I would have been content to watch, save Eld moved past me and leveled a pistole. It leapt in his hand and the bull howled, paws digging up giant furrows of mud as it spun around. It dropped its head at us.

"Whoops," Eld muttered.

"Gods damn it, Eld."

"Any ideas?"

"Aye. Run! And not in straight lines." I shoved him hard to get him moving, then ducked behind the nearest vat. The one we'd been leaning against tipped over with a squeal of metal on metal that was all but drowned out by the bull's roar. Or was it the mage's roar? There was a lot of roaring and none of it good. I can go on about lack of emotions all day, but sometimes they get the better of you. Turns out, all it takes is a rampaging bull up your arse and you understand fear. "Keep fucking moving!"

Eld shot past me into an opening between two vats, slid to a halt with a yelp, and backpedaled into me so that we both went down in a heap. The bull filled the opening where Eld had been a breath before. Anger flashed through me. *This is how we die?* I saw the bull's muscles bunch beneath its pink skin and readied myself for the inevitable even as Eld struggled to get to his feet. There simply wasn't enough time. The bull launched itself at us with another earsplitting roar.

Some lucky bastard in a tattered red bandanna ran around the vat behind us, tripped over my leg, and went arse over face, right into the bull's path. The creature's horns took him through both shoulders and the man slid down to their base with a feral scream. The bull shook its head back and forth, but the man was stuck, screaming into the beast's face. Eld pulled me to my feet. Fear drained away and time seemed to slow.

Left hand to slingshot. Right hand to bottom of purse. Slightly larger than the rest. The nose is the most sensitive part on large beasts. I dug in my purse, left hand closing around the handle of my slingshot, right hand burrowing farther until my fingers touched smooth lead. It took another moment to find the shot I was looking for, but Eld filled the time by drawing another pistole. The pirate's shoulders finally tore free and he flew through the air with a scream that ended in a crunch of bone and flesh. The bull lowered its head. Its eyes were pure red in its mottled pink skin. Then Eld fired and the creature disappeared in a cloud of smoke from the pistole.

I couldn't see the effect, and the beast did little more than grunt, so I wasn't exactly surprised when a mountain of flesh and horns charged at us through the smoke. I brought the slingshot up, dropped it slightly as the bull lunged forward, and released the ball at ten paces. The bull's scream turned from rage to pain and the beast slid to a halt two paces from us, nearly cartwheeling end over end as its front hooves tried to reach its nose. It shook its head, blood flecking the air. It paused, glaring at us through eyes that looked more human than they just had, and bellowed so loudly, I felt it in my chest. I didn't have time for another round and even if I did, I only had one silver ball. The creature cried again and spun around, leapt over a vat, crushed another pirate beneath its hooves, and then was gone in a whirling cloud of dust.

"Silver," I said when my breath came back. "Only thing that will turn a Veneficus."

"Aye, silly me," Eld said lightly. He stepped over the flattened pirate's bloody corpse. "Guess I wore the wrong sword."

The yard was a mess of mud and blood, twisted steel and bodies, but Eld thought there might be clues to be found and I couldn't argue with him. Mostly because he was right, but also because I was so damned tired that if I tried to talk him out of it, I'd likely lose and I never lose an argument, so he'd know something was up. I could have just told him, I suppose—three days of seasickness would kick anyone's arse—but there's a core in me that is too hard to bend. Until now it's been impossible to break, but the problem with iron is that when you start to see the cracks, it's already too late.

My musings were interrupted by a moan. Eld shoved one of the legs of a vat off two pirates. As he checked the woman for signs of life, the man beneath her moaned again. Eld turned him over carefully. His breath hissed through his teeth and when he moved aside, I saw why. The pirate was a thin, reedy fellow wearing a vest and striped trousers and nothing else. I'm not sure what color the vest had been, but now it was dark with his blood. The bull had caught him low in the stomach and his hands were the only thing keeping his intestines inside. His right forearm was twisted with recent scar tissue, but any other markings were hidden by blood.

"Hold still," Eld said gently, squatting down next to the man. "I'll do what I can to help."

"Help?" The pirate's lips were turning blue and his teeth chattered despite the heat. "Naught you can do now, maybe put a bullet through my head and end my suffering. B-bad luck. Is all," he stuttered.

"I'd say we all had some bad luck," Eld said, glancing at me.

"Own fault," the man said. Blood flecked his mouth. "I knew better than to come, but I needed the money."

"Why'd you know better than to come?" I asked. The man squinted as if trying to see me better, but damned if I was going to get down in the mud like Eld. Certainly not for someone who only had a few breaths left in him. "Did you expect this?"

"S-should have," he said. "I was on a ship in the Southern Expanse. Black flag. We were overtaken by the Widowmaker—heard she was behind the attacks to the south, but the 'hood usually leaves their own alone. Marooned for a week afore a ship came close enough to hail and get me back to port. Swore off pirating, but . . ." He grimaced and blood trickled from the corner of his mouth. "But I was broke and I got nothing else."

"What does the Widowmaker have to do with what happened today?" I asked. Eld gave me an exasperated look, but there was no time for politeness. The dying man was punching his ticket for his final gondola ride and taking any useful information with him. "Huh?"

"Rumor's been that she's in league with the Dead Gods. It's why she still sails the Southern Expanse while the rest of us disappear. I—I didn't believe it. Should have." He grunted and stared past Eld sightlessly. "That's why the Veneficus attacked. Keep us from the South."

More blood filled his mouth and Eld lifted his head to keep him from choking. "Easy, man. Easy."

"B-bad luck, is all," the other whispered.

"Bad luck aside, what do the Dead Gods have to do with the Widowmaker? What do they care about this Godsforsaken coast?" I asked.

"Luck," the man repeated.

"Aye," Eld said. He cursed and looked up at me. "I don't think he's much time left."

"No," I said. I pointed. "He's gone already, and my answers with him."

"Damn." Eld let the man down to the ground gingerly and stood up, dry washing his hands to hide their trembling from me. "That was a hard way to go. What a fucking day."

I glanced around at what was left of the yard, my mind filled with the memory of what it had looked like only minutes earlier. When I blinked, the pirates and Mama Hammer were gone, replaced by bloody strips of flesh and cloth.

"When you're right, you're right." I nudged the pirate at Eld's feet, but he was well and truly dead. "Was he lying?"

"Lying? Why would a dying man lie?"

"Why wouldn't he lie?"

Eld snorted. "I thought you said we needed to find pirates because this Widowmaker was the pirate captain of the South-ern Expanse. He as much as told you your hunch was right." He touched my arm carefully—I've been known to snap when someone touches me. Comes of being on the streets where every touch has a double meaning: money, food, power, desire. Pick a sin and it's there, on their fingers. I tensed but didn't move and he squeezed gently. "And with this much information? When have you ever been wrong?"

I heard his words, but my eyes were on the dead man. *Were you lying, you bastard?* He didn't say anything. The dead are arseholes like that. There wasn't much left to him anyway, save for the twisted scar tissue on his forearm, but next to the gaping hole in his stomach, what was that?

"Never," I said finally. *But when have I ever been this tired?* The last two years hadn't been easy, but they'd left me softer than when I'd started.

"Never," he agreed. "So lose the frown and let's go find this Widowmaker before another mage finds us."

"Aye," I grunted, and followed him to where our pack lay sur-prisingly undisturbed amid the wreckage where we'd been sit-ting, but didn't lose the frown. I was missing something. I knew it. *What do the Dead Gods care for this place? Or a pirate? Am I wrong?*

Never.

11

"Then she shot me with silver, Eldest, and I had to leave before I returned to my human form," he said. The tremors that came after Transfiguration were growing worse and the silver in his bloodstream felt like liquid fire coursing through his veins. His knees shivered violently against the rough flagstone floor, abrading his flesh, but the external pain was a fly bite beside the internal. He risked a glance up through his dark hair, saw her eyes were on him, and kept his head bowed. "She was the only one left."

"A Sin Eater?" the Eldest's voice was dry parchment, stiff and wrinkled.

"I—" He had implied as much; no ordinary human would have stood up to a Veneficus in full form . . . but lying would make him wish for the pain he felt now. He licked his lips. "I can't say, Eldest. You know their Goddess has been sending more Sin Eaters here now that our agent owns the sea."

"True," the woman muttered. "But She hasn't moved openly against us in half a century. Why now?" Breath hissed between her teeth. "Is her madness spreading?" The last barely reached his ears.

"It may be that the Sin Eater was acting on its own. Panicked?"

"A better scenario than Ciris at war with us," the Eldest said. "If it was a Sin Eater, it is well you didn't kill her, child. The Council hasn't approved direct action." Her voice didn't indicate if she was happy about that or not. But she was a Veneficus too, and they both knew the Council was run by Dead Walkers these days. A byproduct of their magic: a Veneficus could pass as human until they chose to Transfigure; a Dead Walker tended to attract the wrong kind of attention. It was hard not to when the undead followed on your heels like rotting lapdogs. So the Dead Walkers sat in the halls made from bones of their Dead Gods and the Veneficus went out into the world.

"Even accidents have consequences," she continued. "*Especially* accidents."

"Then I haven't failed?" His head shot up before he could stop himself and his heart sank at the grim expression on the Eldest's face. He knew the question was a mistake, but the pain was blinding his reason. She studied him for a long moment, her smooth, unlined midnight skin incongruous next to the ancient eyes that pierced his own. She shook her head, white braids shifting back and forth around her shoulders. "Eldest," he whispered, and in that word he felt the tension slip from his head. "My life to yours."

"You haven't failed, child, but your work isn't done." Her mouth twisted. "You're useless with silver inside you." Her hands groped in her robe and came out with a vial flecked with dark splatters and a tiny pool of liquid at the bottom. "Drink."

The vial felt warm in his hand and he searched the blood for signs of what creature she'd given him, but found nothing. His breath caught in his throat and he searched her face. *It can't be* . . . "Eldest?"

"Our Gods' blood," she confirmed. "Drink and be restored."

He tore the stopper off greedily, then stopped himself from throwing the vial back. The Gods had died—in a manner of speaking—millennia ago, having finished creating all life in the world, but they'd left their bodies behind and, with them, the Gift of their blood. Their blood was too precious to be wasted; it was only given to priests along with the hair of an animal required for Transfiguration, never pure like this. The vial shook in his grasp.

The Eldest spoke the ritual words, but he couldn't hear them over the throbbing beat of his heart in his ears. When she finished, he bit his tongue hard, until his own blood filled his mouth. Then he tipped the vial back and after what seemed an eternity, a new warm metallic tang filled his mouth.

When he swallowed, warmth flooded him, banishing the pain and tremors that had tortured him a breath before. He could feel the skin on his knees reforming, his nose straightening, and every other ache and wound mending. The brand on his right forearm itched, like it always did during Transfiguration. For a heartbeat his vision blurred, then everything snapped back into sharp focus.

"You have been blessed, child. Now listen and obey."

"I live to serve," he said, gasping.

He listened with half a mind, the rest gaping at the Transfiguration healing his body as she spoke. The Dead Gods' blood gave him and the others like him their name: Veneficus. Only this time, without having to fit into a new creature's flesh, the process was painless. It was ecstasy. But even in the throes of pleasure, her final instructions pulled him back to reality. "An arch a what?"

"Archaeologist," the Eldest repeated, enunciating the unfamiliar word slowly and clearly. "One who understands history. Think, child. The Empire's sent their servants here. That the

Empress doesn't know they dance to Ciris's siren song is small comfort, but that Archaeologist is powerful in her own way, for there is power in knowledge. She discovered descendants of the survivors from these islands before the colonizers came and this filthy port was founded. Were she to be picked up by them . . . the combination of the Empire, Ciris, and this Archaeologist would take more attention than our servant can give. You can't fail here."

"I won't, Eldest." How could he, with his Gods' blood in his veins? He was holy now. "I swear it."

"Then go, my son, and be swift."

He scrambled to his feet, his trousers stiff with dried blood. "Eldest?" The woman craned her neck to look up to him now that he stood. "What about Ciris's agent? The one who shot me?"

"She'll be dealt with shortly." He frowned and her youthful features crinkled in amusement. "You weren't the only priest in the tanning yard, child. I watched through one of your brother's eyes before he passed on." She repeated what the dead man had said and by the time she finished, they were both grinning.

"But then," he said, laughter beginning to bubble up from his lungs, "she's racing toward her doom?"

"And none will know it was our hand that dealt the blow," she agreed. Her laughter joined his and the walls echoed with it, matching the pulsing in his ears from the Gods' blood.

12

The sun was waning when we reached the main thoroughfare and the crowd was thrice its previous size we left it, houses and hovels apparently emptying now that the worst of the heat was over. Taverns were already bright with lanterns, as if to dispel the dusk, and here and there a few of the nicer places had fiddlers, one accompanied by a horn. It sounded out of tune, but the woman played enthusiastically, as if to make up for it. I looked back the way we'd come, a mere few hundred paces when you removed the warren of alleys in between. Gunfire seemed to go unremarked in Port au' Sheen, but surely the tanning yard had been close enough for people to have heard the bull's cries of rage?

"I think that mage could have transformed right in the main square and so long as it didn't disturb a drink, none would mark it," Eld said into my ear. I glanced up at him and he laughed. His grin looked out of place on his waxen features and tight eyes. "I could read it on your face."

I smiled back and from his reaction my smile was no better than his. *Gods damn it.* I was weak indeed if my face was an open book. I bit my tongue once again until the pain forced the breath from my lungs. It also forced me to concentrate and helped me fight the urge to pull a wad of kan out of my jacket and smoke it. My brain was slow enough without that. Useful thing, biting your tongue. I don't know why people waste it on keeping from saying what's patently obvious. Address the obvious and move on. Everyone seems to get uncomfortable when I do that, but it's never bothered me. By that point, I'm on to the matter at hand.

"Where are we going?" Eld asked. I dodged a particularly buxom woman with searching hands who reeked of rum and stepped over an old man who'd passed out with his mug still in his hand. I'd seen worse in Servenza, but not before the sun went down. Unless it was a feast day. Eld tripped over the old man and cursed. "Where are we going?"

"Harbormaster."

"Harbormaster?" Eld's voice was tight, whether from the mage nearly killing us or upsetting the old man, I wasn't sure. "Why?"

"You're full of questions, Eld," I told him. I left unsaid that we should have gone to her straight off to get a lay of the land from someone on the ground and my mind had been too muddled at the docks and too busy taking in all that Port au' Sheen had to offer to think of that. "We need to contact the Company bitch."

"She has a name," Eld said.

I stopped so suddenly that he bumped into me, but I'd been expecting that and was braced accordingly. The woman behind Eld wasn't so fortunate and I heard her arse hit what must have been the last cobblestone on that section of street. I turned around and arched an eyebrow. "Oh yeah? What is it?" Eld frowned as the woman found her voice and began to curse us both roundly. "Her name?"

"I—I."

"Don't remember either. She's blackmailing us, Eld. Using us, forcing us into a situation that she likely helped engineer. So I'll call her whatever I damn well please."

"You're still heated she got one over on you," he said, stepping aside and bending down to help the woman to her feet. Her red face, surrounded by brown curls, froze in surprise. Whether at Eld's gesture or his looks, I wasn't sure, but either way she stopped yelling and allowed him to help her up. "But if she hadn't, you wouldn't have the opportunity to claim a share in the Company. And that's what you claim you want. Or is this merely a feint?"

"I wouldn't risk my life over a feint," I said, shooting daggers at the woman, who had wrapped her hands around Eld's arm.

"But you'd risk mine?"

"I'd never say that," I said. Eld opened his mouth and I threw my hands up. "All right, all right, you win! I give over. We need to contact that polite but manipulative old crone so we can give her the good news."

Eld managed to disentangle himself from the woman even as she tried to snare him with her calico scarf. "She's not old. She's not much older than me. Why, she can't be more than twenty-five years!" I laughed and he cursed. "And what good news?" he growled when he reached my side again.

"That we know the Widowmaker is sinking pirates in the Southern Expanse. Given the other information we have, it's likely she's sinking merchant ships carrying sugar as well. So we'll find her mage and pass that along, and maybe if we're lucky, she'll let us go back. Case closed in a day," I said.

"I doubt we'll be that lucky, knowing her. She'll—Wait, what mage?"

"Her Harbormaster."

"Is a mage?" Eld sputtered.

"If you read the instructions left for us on the ship, you'd know that she said the Harbormaster of Port au' Sheen was a Company woman and would be able to put us in contact with her immediately."

"I read the instructions. I didn't see any mention of a mage."

"We just came across the sea on one of the fastest ships ever built, Eld. And that still took three days. So if her word is true, and in this case I'll believe her, then she must be speaking of some form of sorcery. Ergo, mage."

"We're going to put ourselves in the hands of another mage after one just tried to kill us?"

"Well, there are mages and then there are mages," I said. "Veneficus are one of the lesser known branches of the Dead Gods' order; I guess they don't want to advertise that their Gods have powers that can turn their priests into were-creatures. But they were willing to risk sending one to Port au' Sheen, which makes sense given the dead man's story that the Dead Gods are backing the Widowmaker. Who, remember, is behind the disappearances." Eld blinked and I couldn't keep the laughter from my voice. "Try to keep up, Eld. Their mage could be of the Dead Gods or they could be Sin Eaters of Ciris."

"So they could be waiting to turn into bulls or murder us like that traitorous bastard that shot Salazar and got us into this mess in the first place," Eld said. He seemed to find restating things helpful.

"Aye. So mind your manners and watch your language." I slapped his shoulder. "Or . . . you might want to try biting your tongue." I marched past him and considered smoking some kan. Needling Eld was one of my favorite pastimes and if I felt up to that, perhaps the seasickness was finally leaving and taking my weakness with it. My fingers touched the tightly wrapped leaf at the same instant the mage's face back in Salazar's warehouse flashed through my mind. Vacant eyes staring elsewhere even as his hands moved, drawing and firing the pistole, like some form of clockwork automaton. I pulled my hand out empty, and let Eld catch up to me. "We'll need our wits about us for this." I glanced at him. "What? No comment?"

"Not when you speak sense."

"If that were true, then you'd be a mute."

Eld's silence spoke volumes.

The Harbormaster was easy to find, given that the only tower in the entire port was marked with the Kanados sigil of a rolled kan leaf in a steaming cup, showing both the sedative and stimulant properties of the leaf. The courtyard confirmed it—when Eld's boot crossed the threshold, ahead of mine, a faint vibration ran through the cobblestones between us and the gilded door. The door took on a new sheen, its surface rippled, and a gemstoned handle and knocker appeared as if by magic. Which it was. Ostentatious, but then nothing about the Company had been subtle.

The serving man who greeted us didn't believe our story and seemed to take a special pleasure in denying us entry. He managed to try even Eld's famously marathon patience and another headache began building in the back of my head. Between that, his brightly gilded suit that hurt my eyes, and the preposterous feather—phoenix, if you were fool enough to believe it—in his tricorne, I was reaching for a blade when the Harbormaster herself appeared.

"Now, before you slit my assistant's throat because he has been waving a crimson flag in your face, what do you want?" the Harbormaster asked. She was almost as young as me, but fair where I was dark. Her eyes, while green like mine, looked far too old to sit in an unlined face with a button nose and dimples. She was unsettling in a way I hadn't anticipated, Sin Eater or no.

"I wasn't going to slit his throat," I said. "Just spear his windpipe like an apple on a pole."

The Harbormaster's face grew still for half a breath before she laughed. It sounded like wind chimes. Or maybe that was her medallion tapping against the silver buttons of her lavender dress. Either way she looked easily as young as I, until she opened her eyes and the wisdom of scores of years stared back at me. She wiped at her eyes with delicate fingers covered in thin silver rings that glinted in the lamplight of the courtyard. "I'm not sure he would appreciate the difference," she said.

"We're here about a . . . sweet problem the Company has been having. Sent from Servenza three days ago," Eld said before I could reply. "We need to report back and our instructions indicated you might be able to help."

"Oh—you're that lot?" She reassessed us and nodded fractionally. "Leave your pack by the door. You'd better come up."

13

The mage led us up a wide gilded staircase and into a larger study that appeared to wrap around the entire tower. A large glass window dominated the far wall, affording us a magnificent view of the harbor. As she crossed the room toward the window, it parted in half seamlessly, withdrawing into the floor and ceiling, letting in the sharp, crisp smell of the ocean and the softer sounds of the port waking up from its hot nap.

"Sit, sit," she said, gesturing to the two chairs and a small oval table to the right of the window. She threw herself into the larger, high-backed chair to the left and crossed her legs. "Our drinks will be up in a moment, but first I need to ask you—please sit." There was something in her tone that felt like . . . my arse was in the hard, wooden seat before I realized quite what I was doing. *Magic?* "Thank you, that's better," she said. *Or suggestion?* "Have either of you used the services of a Sin Eater before?"

Eld and I exchanged looks and he appeared as unsettled as I did at how quickly we'd obeyed her commands. "No," I said.

"Yes," Eld said after a pause. I kept my expression neutral, but I couldn't keep my body from tensing. *He worked with mages?* It made no sense. As long as I'd known him, he'd hated mages and magic of all kind. I hated them for their power and their waste of it, good reasons, but whatever my reasons, from what little Eld had said about them, mine were shadows in comparison to his own. "In the army," he added. *Army?*

"Ah, did you see Transference? Communication across great distances between mages?"

"N-no." He coughed to clear his throat. "Nothing so useful as that," Eld said quietly, looking away.

The woman tilted her head but didn't say anything at first. "Transference is a process whereby I will make a connection with one of my counterparts in Servenza," she said, as if the knowledge were a gift, but one she'd disposed to many listeners before. "He'll find Salina and then she will use him as a channel to speak to you."

"A channel?" My religious reading had been more focused on the way the Dead Gods pulled strings to fight their undying war with Ciris—the New Goddess, some forgotten daughter of the Dead Gods, who created all life. But when I'd stumbled across Marten's *On Religion and Power,* I'd dug deeper into his source material and found the truth in manuscripts written when the Imperial tongue was but one dialect among thousands.

The Gods didn't create our world. They aren't even of our world, not truly. An anonymous scribe, a priest of the Dead Gods, writing a secret history for their Council of Elders, told of a war in the stars and skies above, a war that had ended with Ciris's apparent defeat and the death of the Gods themselves. A truce, save that their teachings infected some of the early leaders in the time when tribes ruled a few leagues, long before the nations of today. Religion—to me, just another word for control and power—had been born. With Ciris's return, the war had resumed, with our world as the battlefield and all of us pawns. *I'm no fucking pawn.*

"How's that?" I asked. I'd read of Sin Eaters who worshiped Ciris and were given superhuman powers and others who prayed to the Dead Gods and were gifted the power to change flesh and bone or command the dead, but clearly I had more reading to do.

The Sin Eater sighed, a knowing smile playing across her lips. "Think of a horn that amplifies your voice across hundreds of paces. Now imagine that instead of amplifying your voice, the horn is focusing your voice, so that only a single person hears you across hundreds of paces." She spread her hands. "This is one of the gifts from our Goddess, the ability to find one another across great distances."

"How do you find that single person, though?" I asked.

"Well, only Sin Eaters can communicate via the signals left in the air from the Goddess's entry to our world." She shrugged. "I use the signals in the air to connect with her and she connects me with the one I want." Eld and I exchanged confused looks and she rolled her eyes. "More detail than you can comprehend. To return to the horn analogy, in this case we are the horns, but your voices are your own."

"Will you—"

"Hear or remember everything that was said through my mouth?" she asked, finishing Eld's question for him. "Everyone's always wondering about that," she said with a laugh. "After a fashion. I'll hear and remember what I hear, but I won't remember speaking the words you give to me. Another thing—ah, Albar, I hope you haven't tarried long enough that the tea's grown cold?" she asked, looking across the room. Her assistant's features were more sullen than a dog denied a bone, but he did have three steaming pewter mugs on a tray. "Which is the tea?" she asked.

"This one." He indicated the one closest to her, just across the table from us, and she took it gingerly, inhaling deeply before nodding him toward us. "And kan for you lot."

"Manners," the mage said, clicking her tongue. Albar blanched but said nothing, setting the tray on the table between us and nearly running to the stairs. "Insolent man," she muttered as his heels echoed after him. She took a sip of tea and smiled. "But he does know his brews."

"Would you be terribly offended if I had some of your tea instead?" I asked.

The mage laughed. "Did I make it look that good?"

"No." I leaned forward so my hesitation wouldn't be as noticeable. Kan is a fickle thing, beautiful when inhaled, but harmful when drunk if you've a brain like mine. "But I've had kan many times before; Servenza has a kanhouse on every corner, after all. It's been ages since I've had tea."

The mage inclined her head. "I should have asked your preference before ordering Albar. Of course you may try my tea." She smiled that strange young smile from ancient eyes. "And I suppose it won't kill me to taste some of my own brew."

I moved so we could exchange mugs, then sat back down next to Eld, who was watching me with feigned interest while his kan sat untouched on the tray. I'd thought I'd known every nook and cranny of Eld, not his history, but who he was. Now I wasn't so sure. Othotus had been an old man who had grown too fond of his own words when he wrote *The Study of Centuries,* but his final theme was clear and succinct: history repeats itself.

Eld's history included working with the types of people who had landed us in this predicament in the first place. *Mages and military.* If I had made a mistake, something I don't do, I would remedy it. But not now. I crossed my legs, adjusted my skirts, and took a sip of the mage's tea, keeping my smile light even as

I felt the foul liquid turn my tongue bitter. *I should have risked the kan.*

"Now that I have something for my throat, we can begin," the mage said. She drank some kan, frowned slightly, then tried another sip. "Sweeter than I remember, but they do put sugar in everything around here." She took another swallow, smacked her lips, and set the mug down. "I will reach out to Servenza and when I do, my voice will change." She pressed a finger to her throat. "If you'd like Salina to hear your voice, you need to provide me with a drop of your blood." She reached for the small knife in an embroidered sheath that lay on the writing desk behind her.

"Is that necessary?" Eld asked.

The mage paused. "No. You will hear Salina's voice, but she knows mine and the connection cannot be hijacked, so there's no need. Unless you want her to understand your inflections and emphases better."

"I think she'll understand our meaning just fine," I said.

"Very well." She turned back around in her seat and closed her eyes. "This will only t-take a m-moment." Her teeth chattered and her eyes snapped open sightlessly. "I have reached the central altar." A small moan escaped her mouth. "Mother." Another moan, the pleasure more pronounced than the first. "Hello, Katal."

"Good evening, sister," the mage said, speaking with a deep man's voice. "It is early here. What do you require?"

"Salina," the Harbormaster said in her own voice. "I have two with me on a mission of hers involving the sugar crisis."

"So soon?" the man's voice asked. "Very well, I shall wake her, but I hope they have good news."

"If they don't, what better way to deliver it than with a sea between them?" she asked. She chuckled in a man's voice and then blinked and her eyes focused on us. "We are still . . . connected, but I am returned for now. Some find this experience unsettling the first time."

"The first time?" I asked. "And how do you find the experience?"

"Rapturous," she breathed.

"Gods," Eld muttered.

"Precisely." Eld opened his mouth, but her face twitched; her eyes grew still and her features blank.

"Buc and Eld," the Company bitch's voice said. "Do you have any idea what time it is?"

"Time for some good news," I said, sitting up in my chair.

"You didn't give her any blood?" Salina asked. There was amusement in her voice. "I guess I'm not surprised, but I do miss your dulcet tones, Buc."

"With any luck, you'll not miss them for long." I wasn't sure how much of my tone made it through the mage's voice, but I didn't hold back on the satisfaction. "We've solved your big mystery."

"That easily? And what is the cause?"

"Pirates," Eld said.

"Pirates?"

"It's often the most likely answer that's the right one," he said.

"Pirates," Salina repeated.

"Not just any pirates, if it makes you feel better," I said. "One of the more famous ones. The Widowmaker."

"Impossible!" Spittle flecked the mage's lips. Eld and I looked at each other. I mouthed "resting bitch face" and he turned away quickly, covering his mouth with his hands. "Explain yourselves. Now."

"I don't like orders," I said. "But I like this island less, so I *will* explain." I sat back in the chair and cleared my throat. "It started with a fat-arsed sweaty merchant who'd lost a few sugar ships of his own. . . ." I laid out the evidence for her, drawing the portrait as clearly as I could, trying to fill in the places where my mind had leapt ahead so that she could keep up. It felt like I was explaining how a gondola oar worked to a child, but the mage didn't interrupt, so I must have kept the contempt from my voice. Or else Salina was willing to suffer a little to get what she wanted, the same as I was. *Now there's a thought. The two of us have something in common.* I reached for the tea to clear my throat. "And he confirmed my suspicions: the Widowmaker is in league with the Dead Gods and this island is rife with their agents."

The mage's mouth curled in a snarl at the mention of the other religion. "And how do you know he wasn't lying? Pirates lie as easy as drawing breath."

"He was dying," Eld put in. "He died as he told us, with a hole the size of a dinner plate from where the bull, the Veneficus, ran him through."

"Ah," Salina's voice lost some of its edge. "That makes sense, then."

Eld smiled triumphantly at me and I rolled my eyes. *Why wouldn't a dying man lie? He had nothing left to lose.* Sometimes I think I'm the only sane one in the world, but if that is true, then I guess I'm insane to everyone else. And . . . just because I would lie as I drew my last breath if I had reason, didn't mean everyone else would. I threw up my hands and Eld's smile grew wider.

"The Widowmaker," Salina muttered.

"Why don't you think it's her?" I asked.

"How will you find her?" Salina asked, ignoring my question.

Eld replied. "The southern shipping route is where the disappearances have all occurred. The maps indicate two routes of passage, and from the islands the naval officer mentioned, where he saw no ships at all, we know which trade winds to follow."

"We won't be finding her; you will," I added. "Or your Company will. We solved your mystery and in enough time for you to direct your ships to use the northern route."

"And why would they do that? It's weeks slower with the winds."

"Because slow is better than sunk," I said. "Done and done."

"Hmm." Salina's voice didn't sound happy to have good news. "I'm afraid we disagree on the definition of 'done.'"

"Allow me to elucidate it for you," I said.

"As entertaining as that would be, this isn't a debate. I hold the pistole; I hold your shares and your seat on the Board," Salina said. "You've done good work, but we need incontrovertible proof that the Widowmaker is responsible for sinking these ships. And even with mages helping, it will be days before we can get word to all of our plantations. The northern route is slower, so it's unlikely that more sugar will reach Servenza before our supplies run out."

"A few days' scarcity should drive prices up," I said.

"And you want a seat on the Board," Salina mocked. "We are the largest sugar supplier, but not the only one. A few weeks of no supply from Kanados will lose us more than a short shock of high prices will compensate for. The Empire will deal with Normain as easily as us. Easier in some regards."

"It's a shame their plantations lie farther north," I snapped.

"Yes, but they do, so you'll need to find a way to bridge the gap in our supply or else your shares and seat are gone," Salina said. Her voice sounded a little hoarse—or was it the mage? We hadn't been talking that long.

"I'm not going to keep dancing along to the string you're holding just out of reach," I said. "We confirm the Widowmaker is behind the disappearances and get some sugar to Servenza in the next twelve days and we're done."

"Eleven days," she growled, proving she could count.

Well, it was worth a shot.

"Take one of our warships and once you confirm it's the Widowmaker, I want her sent to the bottom of the sea." The mage rubbed her throat with one hand and reached for the cup of kan beside her.

"We're not murderers," Eld said. I shifted in my seat and he glanced at me. Eld hadn't spoken to the maid when we were solving the Frilituo murders. I had, and I still wasn't sure if condemning an innocent woman to death while the murderer walked free was right, whether the woman went along or no. But Eld didn't know that, didn't need to know that, so I made a soothing gesture and he turned back to the mage. "We're not," he repeated.

"That's not the tale the Imperial Guard gave me," Salina said. Her voice had grown truly hoarse, but I thought it sounded more like the mage's throat was giving her trouble. "You'll do this or I will turn the pistole over to them and old Judge Cokren and then you might as well turn pirate and join the Widowmaker yourselves."

A blind grope by the Harbormaster knocked her mug across the table; dark liquid puddled, then ran onto the floor. The mage's teeth grated together and I saw the veins in her neck pulsing as she clawed at her throat.

"Are you all right?" Eld jumped up. "Gods, I think she's choking."

The mage's wide eyes found mine then looked at the cup in my hand. Her body jerked and fell out of her chair, rolling onto her back. At her side in an instant, Eld fought to hold her down. A growl escaped through her clenched teeth.

"Kill her and—" Blood appeared under her nails where she'd scratched rivulets into her own skin. "Kill her!" she barked. "Kill her. Kill. Kill." The last was a harsh whisper. She abruptly went slack in Eld's arms.

He looked up at me and shook his head. "I don't understand."

I glanced at the tea in my hand and then at the spilled mug of kan. It had been meant for me. Or Eld. "I think I do," I said, pushing myself to my feet. "I'm pretty sure it was that bastard assistant."

"My lady!" Albar burst up the stairs with two others right behind him. He slid to a halt as he took in the scene and I saw his eyes bulge when they found his mistress on the floor instead of us. I'll give the bastard his due, though: he didn't hesitate. "They've killed the Harbormaster! Murder!" He stabbed a finger at us. "Kill them!"

The last was lost in the howls of his companions, who raced forward with cutlasses drawn. Eld dodged a swing, parried the back blow with his pistole, and blew the brains out of a young man in torn clothing who stood a full head taller. Had stood a full head taller. Smoke filled the air. The other one, a woman with a shock of blond hair sticking out from a dark head scarf, leapt past Eld. *Three paces left, draw stiletto with right hand. Inner jacket.*

She moved faster than my mind. I was so shocked, I just sat and watched her come on. Eld yelled and I slid back in my chair until I was brought up hard by the table behind me. Eld's untouched cup of kan jiggled and I reached for it before I had decided what to do with it. The woman started to swing and I threw the cup without thinking. I felt the sword pass over my head, its hiss muted by the woman's startled scream. The sword flew out of her hands and she clutched at her scalded face. Then I didn't need to think; instinct took over and I drew a stiletto from my jacket and buried it in her sternum. She tripped and sat down hard, clutching the hilt between her breasts, her face an angry red mess of burns.

"Bitch," I whispered.

"Bitch!" some man shouted.

Something slammed into me and I flew sideways, tripped over the mage's body, and cartwheeled over the table. The room spun until it broke my fall. My head reverberated off wood and my vision went dark, then clear, then spotty in the same instant. My mouth tasted of smoke and I spat as I sat up. I was lying on the top of the writing desk. A paperweight fell from behind me, cracked in two from my skull. I saw everything, but couldn't make sense of anything.

"Bitch!" Albar repeated, stepping over the mage's body and leveling a pistole at me. "Move and she dies!" he yelled. Across the room, Eld froze with his sword half drawn. "I'm going to enjoy this," Albar added, cocking the hammer. Something moved behind him, but he was focused on me. "You've no idea how mu—" His voice cut off with a squeal.

"Oh, I think I do," the mage whispered in his ear. She had one arm wrapped around his throat and the other wrapped around his forehead. She grabbed a fistful of hair and jerked his head up. Her mottled purple face was slowly returning to its normal color and her neck was a mass of bruises and scratches and dried blood, which gave her a feral look. Albar squealed again and her arms moved in a blur. His neck sounded like a handful of nuts in a nutcracker. His body was facing me, but his head was turned completely around, staring at his mistress. The mage let go and he fell like an abandoned rag doll. "I hate kan," she growled.

"Gods, you're alive," I said.

"No thanks to you."

"Easy now, we didn't have anything to do with that," I said. It's rare that I countenance caution, but a woman smaller than me snapping someone's neck completely in two was one of those times. "He tried to kill us, too," I reminded her.

She breathed deeply and a few of the purple blotches faded, but there were still a dozen left on her face. "You need to leave," she said hoarsely. "Now."

"We'll leave," Eld said. I noticed he'd fully drawn his sword in the few moments between Albar threatening him and dying. He motioned for me to come to him. "But Salina promised us a warship."

"A warship?" the mage asked.

"Aye, a man o' war," I said, deciding that if her memory was foggy, it was worth taking advantage of. "Biggest one you've got."

"Leave now," her voice was calm if gravelly, "or I'll tear you limb from limb."

Her tone made me blink even as it galvanized my bruised legs into motion. "Salina said—" I began.

"Fuck Salina," she spat. "It's my fucking harbor." She hunched over, grabbed her head in both hands, and growled. "Every Rebirth is like ten thousand needles in my brain. Pain only begets pain." She looked up and her eyes bulged. "You really need to leave."

I opened my mouth, but Eld sheathed his sword and swept me off my feet and over his shoulder before I could do more than protest. And by protest, I mean squeal high enough to rival Albar. The mage sank to her knees as Eld reached the stairs and the last image I had was of her weeping crimson tears. He set me down when we reached the doorway to the courtyard. I opened my mouth, but he shook his head and pushed me out the door and sent me sprawling into the yard.

"You can curse me later," he said, steadying me enough to get me moving away from the tower. "But we need to get as far away from her as possible. She's barely clinging to sanity. Even for a mage."

"How do you know?" I asked.

His face tightened. "Just trust me." He glanced over his shoulder, then pointed toward the harbor. "We need to talk our way onto a ship. Now."

"Aye, after we grab our things," I said.

"No time," he muttered.

"I'm not leaving my books. I didn't even finish the first one," I said.

"Buc!" He stopped on the edge of the road and studied me. "Did that fall knock something loose?"

"No." I felt the lump forming at the base of my head and winced. "Just hurts."

"Aye, you're not thinking clearly. That *thing*"—he pointed in the direction we'd come from—"will be back to normal in an hour or so. Maybe she decides that we didn't have anything to do with Albar's little stunt and helps us out. Or maybe she decides we have to pay for what happened to her. If she does that, the smallest thing she'll do will be to order the captains to deny us passage. That's if she doesn't snap our necks like she did Albar's.

"Besides . . . you had most of your books sent to our place in Servenza." He shook his head, then stared into my eyes. I stared back to show him I wasn't afraid and his sapphire eyes grew dark. "Gods, I've never had to explain anything to you before, Buc. What's wrong?"

I opened my mouth, but nothing came out. *He's right.* I swallowed the lump in my throat and when I opened my mouth again, everything came tumbling out. "I haven't slept for days, threw up almost all the liquid in my body, sweated the rest out while a man-bull tried to kill me, got body-slammed off a desk, broke a paperweight with my head, and nearly had my neck broken by a witch," I said in one breath.

Eld's mouth moved wordlessly. He touched my cheek with the back of his hand. "You're feverish. You need water."

"Here? This water will give me the runs," I said.

"White wine watered down then," he said.

Now that I'd admitted my weakness, I felt lighter somehow. A voice in the back of my mind began to rage, but it was barely audible over the ringing in my ears and the haze in the corners of my eyes. "We have to reach the ships. You said."

Eld cursed and caught me as I fell, hefting me in his arms. He broke into a run toward the port lights, away from the harbor. "Liquids first, Buc. You'll be fine. Just need to drink something. I promise. Lots of liquids." My vision flickered and he muttered something that slipped past me in the haze.

"You said," I whispered as the darkness took me. "You."

14

Eld sprinted down the hill, his lungs burning, his legs windmilling so quickly that he knew all it would take was a single loose stone to send him and Buc tumbling the rest of the way. *Can't stop.* Buc felt light in his arms, lighter than she should have, head lolled back so that her dark locks almost touched the ground. He murmured for her to hold on, but she didn't answer. Faintly behind him, well beyond the Harbormaster's tower, he could hear Port au' Sheen beginning to get into its cups, but down here, the street was nearly empty.

He plunged on, dodging the few dockworkers who hadn't joined in the partying. One of them asked what the matter was, another shouted at him to stop, but he ignored them all. There was a cluster of huts around the edge of the docks and he remembered seeing a few sailors drinking there when they'd disembarked that morning. Huffing and puffing, he slowed to a jog and then a walk, taking care not to jounce Buc as he reached the door of the nearest straw hovel.

"Easy, man!" the tattooed barkeep called from behind a plank overturned on two kegs that served as a bar. "No need to kill yourself—the drinks will do that for you!" A greasy-haired sailor and a bare-chested dockworker, the only other patrons in the place, barked laughter. "Say, what's going on now?"

"Wine!" Eld shouted.

The barkeep rested thick arms across the bar, hand near a rusty cleaver embedded in the wood. "Not so fast—you can't just go bringing bodies in off the street. I know we're a rough lot, but we've standards, man," he said with a smile. "Did you hurt her?" His smile disappeared and his hand caressed the hilt of the cleaver.

"Not dead! She's had too much sun and fainted." Eld winced; Buc would hate to hear him admit that. "She needs watered-down wine."

"Well, that's a different chantey altogether," the barkeep said, his shoulders relaxing as he released the cleaver.

"Now!"

"Keep your temper," the man grunted, moving around the end of the plank with a pitcher in either hand. "Well, no fears, we've got the cure for what ails yer wife."

"She's not my—Never mind," Eld said, setting Buc down gently on a stool, dropping down behind her so she fell back against him. "Water it down, man," he grunted when the barkeep reached him.

"Well, er." The other man glanced back toward the other men and dropped his voice. "It's already well watered down," he whispered. "Give her the lot and she'll barely feel a buzz. It's chilled though; that's why they"—he nodded over his shoulder—"drink it."

Eld barely heard the man. Reaching into his pocket with one hand he pulled out the newspaper he'd saved from Servenza and rolled it into a makeshift funnel. "Easy, does it, Buc. I've got you," he whispered. He tried to slip the thin end between her lips, but her head kept twisting, and it was going to require a third hand he didn't have to pour.

"Here, let me," the barkeep said, squatting down beside him, his stained apron dragging through the dust. He reached for the pitcher and Eld growled. The other man's eyebrows raised and then he nodded and took the funnel from Eld's hand.

Eld steadied Buc with one hand and used the other to carefully and slowly pour the cool liquid down the funnel. At first nothing happened, and then Buc opened her mouth slightly, and he poured faster. "There you go, Buc," he whispered. "We'll get you taken care of and then—" For a moment his mind was blank, so tightly had he focused on Buc, but now he remembered the whole debacle.

The Sin Eater wouldn't be down forever. They had to get out of Port au' Sheen before nightfall or she might decide to slit their throats and drown them for good measure. An image of burning desert flashed through his mind and for a breath he could almost taste gunpowder on his tongue.

"And then," he said as he tipped the pitcher higher, "we find ourselves a ship."

"We've all wants, man," the gnarled dockmaster said to Eld with a grin, eyeing Buc in his arms. The dockmaster seemed only mildly concerned about him showing up with an unconscious person, and once he'd explained, she seemed to find the whole situation a joke. She hooked her thumbs into her trousers and spat between a gap in her teeth. "But wants en't going to put you or yer missie on yon man o' war."

"As I told you before . . ." Eld began politely.

"Aye, aye, the Company's orders," the old woman growled, hocking something dark and wet from her throat and spitting it out over the railing into the sea. "But wot the Company don't ken is that on this dock, I make the orders."

"Madam—"

"Stow it, boyo, unless ye've got more gold than ye've flashed already."

Eld had gone through the proper channels once he'd managed to pour both pitchers of wine—and damn the barkeep, it had better have been well watered—down Buc's throat. It'd taken a fistful of doubloons and an hour to find this old crone . . . this kindly woman . . . who refused to tell him where the captain of that ridiculously oversized, well-armed ship was. Time was slipping away and in her current state, Buc was as innocent as a newborn babe. He frowned at the thought; Buc and innocent didn't go together.

"Madam . . ." he began again, and the dockmaster shook her head. The anger that'd been slowly building during the wasted minutes between leaving the Harbormaster and now swirled hotly through him. He set Buc down, carefully, against the handcart someone had decided to leave in the middle of the central dock, and stood up just as the woman began to open her mouth again. She gave a startled yelp as he slammed her back hard against the open railing. A knife appeared in his fist so quickly that even Buc would have been impressed.

"Now you stow it," he growled. "I've listened to your lot's horse piss for the last hour and I've had enough of it on my boots to last a lifetime. None of you would have a coin to rub together, save the Company employs you. None of you would dare deny their orders were their Harbormaster to come down here. And none of you would have given me half this shit if I'd spoken like this from the beginning." *Thank the Gods Buc can't see me pulling steel the moment I don't get my way or I'd never live it down.*

"You're going to listen to me or I'll put this blade twixt your ribs and twist and send you over the side for the pup sharks to chew on. And then," he added, "I'll pull what's left of you out of the drink and bring the Harbormaster down to see what she thinks about you ignoring her orders."

Neither Eld nor the dockmaster said a word: him because he'd run out of breath, her because she was obviously scared. Surprisingly, it'd been the last that had done it; mention of the Harbormaster had sent terror flitting through her eyes.

"Now, about that man o' war," he said when his breath returned.

"They'en might sail," she said after a moment longer. Eld shifted the knife in his grip and the old woman flinched. "Their physiker up and died on them a week back. The Imperial lot don't like sailing without no sawbones, but they blame the pirates, so if you've at all to do with hurting them, they might'en be persuaded."

"No physiker?" Eld hesitated. Buc wouldn't have cared, but he was supposed to be taking care of her and she needed help. "What else you have?"

"There's a frigate what just docked, will need a good hull scraping afore she's out again, but if you're willing to wait a few days . . ."

"Next," Eld said.

"Ayuh, thought so. Uhh." The old woman looked up as if reading a manifest only she could see. "There's a brig that might do. Company lot, unlike the first two, and carrying twenty-four cannon and a mortar, which en't insignificant."

"Why didn't you mention them before then?"

"Because you said you needed to send pirates to the deep and that's what Imperials do," the dockmaster spat, having regained some of her former vinegar. "Company lot just flash steel and keep moving."

"Do they have a physiker on board?"

"Why?" Her eyes flitted to Buc's still form. "You've need of a sawbones?"

"Answer. The. Question." Eld could hear his teeth grating. He hadn't been this close to rage since the final time he'd met Seetel. The encounter hadn't ended great then; he couldn't afford for this one to end similarly badly. More important, Buc couldn't either.

"Aye, they've a physiker and a good one, I'm told."

"Then that's the one," Eld said. "How do I reach them?"

"Can you even tell the difference between a man o' war and a brig?" she asked.

"Man o' war is the big one," he said, pointing at the massive ship on the far side of the harbor.

She laughed. "Ye got me there. Matter of fact, their captain sent word earlier that if 'is crew missed the last rowboat tonight, they'd be looking for a new ship in the morn. Aims to sail now," she added as if Eld were too thick to comprehend.

"Now? Damn it, woman! I need to be on that ship."

"Calm your tits and tassels," the dockmaster said. "Takes time to prepare a ship that's laid up in port half a fortnight. And there's a faster way I can send you."

"Say on."

"I should warn ye that—"

"If it's faster, then that's what I want," Eld said.

"'K then." Her eyes shifted to the blade he still held a few fingers from her chest. "If'n you put down the steel first."

Eld slipped the blade back into his pocket and scooped Buc back up. She murmured in his arms, but her eyes remained closed. *The things you have me doing, Buc.* Sighing to himself, he straightened. "After you, Madam."

———

Eld held tightly on to Buc as the little open boat they were in flew across the water, slicing through the waves so quickly that it sometimes floated on air between them. A rhythmic whumping sound filled the air, loud even above the waves. He held her partially to make sure she didn't fly out when this fiendish contraption inevitably failed, but also because of the young Sin Eater sitting hunched over in the rear. The dockmaster had tried to warn him—a fact she reminded him of when she saw his face after he realized what she intended. He then reminded her that now he wouldn't need the Harbormaster to come to the docks in person if he didn't get the ship he wanted. He'd just have the mage call her.

As bluffs went it was one of his more outrageous, but it'd ended with them in the seat of this newfangled boat. Its gilded hull was designed to cut through waves and it was shot forward by gear-driven twin propellers only the Sin Eater knew how to operate. The method would cut close to an hour's hard row down to a quarter of that time. He might have been able to appreciate the novelty of the craft, despite the fact that the dockmaster had told him it was the Company's lira that paid for such technology while the rest of the world suffered with oars . . . and some suffered as slaves chained to them, save that the mage had been strangely silent from the start.

One arm was looped around Buc. Eld's other hand, hidden by her skirts, gripped his pistole. *Every time I'm near one of these creatures, I nearly lose my head.* He feigned a smile at the other man, little more than a lad, really, and clad in a silk suit that looked out of place crouched beside the tiller. The Sin Eater affected not to notice. *And just what does that mean? Did the Harbormaster tell him to look for us?*

He kept his eyes on the mage, but his mind was on Buc. He'd grown too used to her always knowing the right thing despite her inexperience. It was hard not to, when he'd been following her lead over the past few years. Not just the genius she displayed—that had always been there, rough and uncut, but bright right from the start. No, it was watching the lost, orphaned girl he found on the streets grow into a woman with the attitude of a queen secure on her throne. He glanced down at her dark features, softened by her illness, framed by a mishmash of curls, and looking strangely subdued with the fire of her intelligent eyes hidden behind closed lids.

The truth was, he was barely two years older and she'd grown up quickly. She'd have been introduced to the Court last year if she'd been born in one of the finer Quartos. He couldn't fight the smile that touched his lips at the thought of her in a ball gown, surrounded by the stuck-up aristocracy. Buc had a way of pricking the wind from anyone's bubble and she took especial delight in doing so to anyone born with a gilded spoon in their mouth. That was one of the things he loved about her.

Love.

He felt something sharp twist in his chest and it took him several heartbeats to regain his breath. There it was. *Again.* It'd started a few months ago, a slip in the affection he felt for her from the moment they met—her dressing him down for splashing mud across her already mud-covered dress. It wasn't a slip so much as a change, a feeling that there was something more there than just the friendship they'd grown into.

The feeling hadn't been there the year before, nor certainly when they'd met. *Am I a lecher?* He'd denied it, fought it, but it was there. Buc would rake him over the coals if she knew. *She'd tell me it was just infatuation, from spending too much time away from the ladies.* It had been a while, but he didn't feel the pull of other women like he used to.

Their friendship hadn't been there right away. At first it'd been no more than partnership, but that changed as their tally of solved cases increased and she began to let her guard down. He'd seen soon enough that her mind was wise beyond its years. He chuckled quietly, the noise making the Sin Eater twitch in his seat. Well, incredible anyway, if not always wise.

Just infatuation. That's what it was. Buc didn't have anyone but him and he couldn't betray her trust and ruin everything because of a small infatuation. Something he'd laugh at in years to come. He tried to laugh again, louder, but it sounded false to his ears. If it was only a fleeting feeling, he thought, it would have left as soon as it had come, not stuck around, growing harder, more solid, more . . . real.

None of that matters.

"Ho!" the Sin Eater said, the first he'd spoken.

Eld followed the Sin Eater's arm toward the ship anchored at the edge of the harbor, rapidly growing larger as they approached. They were nearly there. "Hold on," he whispered. To Buc? To himself? He was no longer sure. *Damn it.* "Hold on," he repeated, swallowing the lump in his throat.

15

I woke up in a strange bed that swung with my weight in a way that felt soothing rather than upsetting. Cool darkness greeted my eyes and a faint breeze tickled my eyelashes. I blinked and my eyes protested, along with every other part of my body. A figure came to its feet at the sound of my moan and then they held a small clay bowl beneath my chin. I nodded and they tilted it and water with the hint of wine filled my mouth. I drained the bowl and the figure scooped some more from a bucket. I sucked that one and the next down almost without breathing. The figure returned the bowl to the bucket and I groaned.

"That's enough for now, lass." The voice sounded like two rocks sliding against each other. "You've had buckets of wine water and your body took it like a sponge, but you've got to be nearly full up."

"Who are you?" I asked.

"No one," the man—I could see enough now to make out his features—said. "A physiker," he added.

"A good one?"

He laughed silently and then moved to stand beside me. "There's a saying at sea, lass. 'Any port in a storm.'"

"We say beggars can't be choosers," I said.

He laughed his silent laugh. "That too. I'm a fair hand with tinctures and potions, but I'm no university sawbones. Luckily, you were easy. You just needed water. Lots of water, I thought you were going to wake a fish by the end of the first day."

"First day? How long have I been asleep?"

"You were feverish for two days and calm yesterday," he said. "Your friend went up for a breath of fresh air; I'll go tell him you're awake and let him explain." The man's hand was rough on my shoulder, but he squeezed gently. "Make sure you eat as much food as your stomach will hold at the mess tonight. Otherwise your body won't hold that water and you'll be in as bad a shape as you were when they brought you to me."

"Mess? Where am I?" I asked.

"The *Sea Dragon*."

"Dragons aren't real."

"Sea ones are. But not this far south," the man said.

"A ship then?" The door shut on my question and I cursed the physiker roundly until I remembered he'd given me the water. "Still a bastard," I muttered. Speaking had left a dull ache in the back of my head, so I let myself sink into the bed and it began swinging with my movement. Not a bed then. *Hammock?* I'd read of such things in books, but I'd never been on a ship that had one. Even that Cannon Ship had frame beds. The door creaked open, interrupting my thoughts, and boots scraped on the floor.

"Eld?"

"Aye, that's what the mirror tells me," he said, appearing beside me. I groaned at his attempt at humor and he smiled. "How are you feeling?"

"Like an olive put through the press and squeezed out the other side," I said.

He reached to touch my arm, hesitated, and sank down onto

the bench beside my hammock instead. "I should have taken better care of you, Buc. I—"

"You cut your hair!"

"Aye, it was getting too long," he said, absently reaching for where his sun-bleached hair ended at his shoulder instead of being gathered half down his back as I was used to.

Now that I was looking, I could see lines on his face that hadn't been there before and dark shadows under his eyes that gave him a ghostly appearance—like what everyone says Shambles look like. His cheeks were pinched and his lips thinner than before, although they were, as usual, offset by his nose. That poor thing had been broken and never set properly and it was the only distinguishing feature Eld had that wasn't perfect. All in all, he looked almost as bad as I felt.

"Sometimes I rely too much on you," he said. He stared at a point just below me. "There was a time when I made every decision, had to make every decision, and while that has its attractions, it's not the good decisions that haunt you, is it?"

"I suppose not." I pushed myself up as much as I could without falling out of the hammock.

"I put too much on you, Buc. I should have remembered that you've never been outside of Servenza and her islands, save for that brief case on the mainland."

"That was what, our second case?"

"Aye, we were chasing down leads that pointed to that bratty noble's son, when I took that knock from behind and woke to discover you'd solved the whole damned thing and it'd been the maid all along."

I flushed. "Well, those were early days. I should have trusted you more, kept you up to speed with what I'd worked out in my mind." Luckily, Eld had never asked too many questions about who had hit him.

"I never worried about that, Buc. After that, you led and I followed and I never questioned it. But I should have remembered . . ." He squeezed his hands together and looked up. "I should have remembered you're a girl of seventeen years. I'm so sorry. I—"

"You should be sorry," I snapped. He flinched and then nodded, resembling the way a convict who knows they're guilty accepts the lash. I swung my legs out so I could sit without falling out of the damned netting and pulled the strap of my slip up where it had slid down my arm. "Sorry to waste time feeling sorry for yourself because I was stupid."

"You weren't stupid; you nearly died!"

"Good, I'm glad to see there's still some fire there," I said. I brushed curls out of my face and they fell over my left shoulder. I could feel the stubble growing back in where I'd shaved the sides of my head and immediately wished for a razor, but that was just one of my obsessions speaking. It thought me weak, just like Eld, and I wanted nothing so much as to disabuse both of them. "I nearly died because I didn't take care of myself. Me. My body, my mind, my choices. Aye, you tried to get me to drink wine water and I did, but not enough. That was my fault. You think me a little girl?"

"I never said . . ." he began.

"Yes, you did." He flinched again at my tone. "You said I was a girl of seventeen years. I don't really care if someone names me girl or woman so long as they mean to scribe the lack of a penis between my legs and not a comment on my age or maturity. But that's how you meant it, Eld. Aye, you've years on me, but what of it? I grew up starving on the streets. There's no time to be a child, no parents to fawn over you or hold you back so they can keep control of you.

"You grow up or you die. And as far as years go, the more cases we have, the more I've come to realize that age has nothing to do with maturity or intelligence. Plenty of fools have scores of years, yet have learned nothing. Experience only counts if you use it the right way. So don't demean me by suggesting I'm a fragile child who needs protecting. I don't. You've been"—I paused to breathe before I fainted—"you've been a good partner, but if you think that entitles you to this selfish, possessive bullshit, you've got another think coming."

"I'm—"

"If the next word is 'sorry,' I'm going to kick you," I said.

"I'm glad you're feeling better," he said after a pause. A small, tight smile played across his features, easing some of the lines on his face. "I spoke poorly. You'd think I'd have been better prepared after three days, but you'd be wrong."

"You don't look like you've slept much."

"Who needs sleep?" He waved a hand and smiled again. "I do care about you, Buc," he said, "and I feel responsible for you, but, but"—he interrupted me—"you're right: you're more capable than many people I've met. That doesn't mean I don't get to worry about you and it doesn't mean I don't get to beat myself up when something bad happens to you. That's what friends do."

"Friends?" Something stirred in my memory. Something about being in his arms as he ran toward Port au' Sheen. It slid through my mind no matter how hard I tried to grasp it. "Is that what we are?"

"I hope so," he whispered. "I hope so," he said in a louder voice. "Friends, partners, us against them."

"Them?"

"The world?"

"Aye." I smiled. "I like that. So are we done with this self-effacing shit?"

"We're done," Eld said.

"Good, then tell me how we ended up on a bloody dragon."

"It's not a real dragon," Eld said. I arched an eyebrow and he held up his hands. "Just pointing out the flaw in your statement."

"So, you do want me to kick you."

"What's the last thing you remember?"

"You pushing me out the door of the witch's tower," I said. Again, something about being in his arms as he ran swam up from the depths of the mist, lurking in my brain. *What happened?* "After that it's a blur."

"Well, after running my legs off carrying you down to the docks, I managed to find you water. Luckily, the mage hadn't shown up yet, so I took a page out of your book."

"Who'd you stab?" I asked.

"No one." He shook his head and ran a hand through his shorter locks. "I told them Salina ordered us to take the first man o' war that was sailing and head south."

"Sweet Gods, you mean the *Sea Dragon* is a man o' war?"

"Not quite," Eld said, shrugging. "Turns out there was only one of those in port and the captain was adamant it needed its hull scraped before venturing out to sea again. She said the only thing that would make her drop sails would be the Harbormaster."

"I would have liked to have seen that," I said, laughing.

"Aye," Eld grunted, his face a shade darker than it had been a moment before. He cleared his throat. "So then I did threaten—*threaten*, mind you—to stab someone. And that led to a brig that was sailing south in the hour."

"A Company ship?"

"It didn't look like there was much else in the harbor, honestly. I thought of trying for a newly minted frigate that was putting in while I argued with the rest of the captains, but I figured it would need to take on water and that would be a delay."

"Hmm, I wouldn't have thought of that," I mused. "So where are we now?"

"A day's sail from the route where all the ships have disappeared," Eld said. His eyes narrowed. "And the crew is on edge, so tread carefully when you feel up to leaving your bed."

"You told them our mission?"

"Easy," he said, holding up a hand to ward off my expression. "No, I'm not a fool. The crew knows nothing. . . . The same can't be said for the captain, unfortunately." Eld lifted his other hand as if both would do what one did not. I tightened my glare. "Well, I had to tell him, Buc. He controls the ship."

"Fair enough," I said finally. I stifled a yawn and tried not to let the pain of the movement show. "The physiker said I was supposed to eat a lot, but I don't know if I feel up to climbing decks."

"It's only two to the top," Eld said.

"Aye, but my bones feel even older than yours. A century at least."

"Then I'll bring the food to you," Eld said. He pushed himself to his feet and half reached for my arm before stopping. "It's the least I can do, Buc." I opened my mouth and this time he touched my arm and I held my tongue. "You're no use to anyone if you make yourself weaker. You have a day to eat and drink enough to get into fighting shape."

"Aye, aye, Captain," I said, adding a thick brogue to my words.

"That's more like it," he said, and laughed. He squeezed my arm and moved past me, then paused at the door. "You know, I'm not *that* old."

"Well, how old are you?"

"I turned nineteen at the start of this summer," he said.

"Gods, that's ancient," I said with a gasp. "Nearly as old as Salina!" He sputtered and protested and I laughed, to ease him off the hook. It really wasn't that many years more than me. And I believed what I told him. Age was a meaningless number; it was what you did with the years that meant something.

"Hurry your wrinkly old arse up top then—I'm starving." He shook his head and left, muttering under his breath. When the door closed, I let the smile I'd been holding go. *Poke him and he's quick to correct.* It was useful knowledge if I was going to find out how his past involved mages and armies. He was my friend, my only friend, but I think "friend" means something different to me than it does to Eld. I've told him many times I'm not like other people; I'm the oddity, that to my eyes it's everyone else who's strange. That's the problem with being normal; it means you don't listen.

Especially to a girl of ten and seven.

16

"You did good."

Eld's eyebrows shot up. "Really?"

"Aye." I tapped the railing and looked across the deck, where a dozen hands were busy scrubbing various bits of nautical equipment. I'd come up the night before and spent the morning on deck, and it seemed like all they did was clean. If they fought half so good, then the Widowmaker was in trouble. "A man o' war might have kept the Widowmaker away, but this ship is small enough to make a tempting target."

Eld followed my gaze and swallowed. "I hadn't considered that."

"'Better a lucky happenstance than a planned folly,'" I quoted.

"Gillibrand?"

"No, she wrote better stuff than that. Ballwik's *Proverbs.* Number three." I closed my eyes and the pages appeared before me. "Simple, but a good primer for a new reader."

"You're looking in fine mettle this morning, signorina," the captain said, pausing in his inspection of the ship. I'd seen his first mate doing a round last night and this morning, but this was the first I'd seen of the captain, save for at the mess this morning, where Eld had pointed him out. He was tall and impossibly thin, with narrow shoulders that made him look like a larger man's shadow. His powder-blue jacket and slim trousers only added to the illusion. He touched the brim of his bicorn. "Very fine, indeed."

"I look like someone starved me for a fortnight before beating me within an inch of my life," I said. I'd finally seen myself this morning when I used a mirror to make sure my knives were sufficiently concealed. I can't put on weight no matter how hard I try, only in my arse, and that seems to be because it's stealing from my breasts. But even my arse had lost its usual curves, and for the first time since Eld found me I could count all of my ribs again. "But you're polite to say so, and a more than capable liar," I added when the captain flinched.

"She means the last as a compliment," Eld added, translating.

"Aye, well." The captain licked his lips and touched the tip of his pick of a nose. "Thank you kindly, signorina. Kindly," he repeated.

"While you're here, Captain, perhaps you can answer a question for me?"

"Of course."

"Sea dragons. They make their home in the north?"

"So the north men would have you believe. Massive golden beasts with wings that turn the seas into a maelstrom and scare away their slender serpent cousins," he said. His mouth twisted. "There's an old tale they tell of one that came on land and took a queen as its bride. The line of Quando claims they are descended from their offspring."

"You don't believe them?"

"Anatomically, I don't see how it's possible."

"Not the tale, the creatures in general."

"I've never seen one," he said simply.

"A wise man that trusts his eyes over others' lips," I said.

"Th-thank you," he said slowly as if unsure if I was toying with him. "Signorina," he added.

Still polite. No wonder he and Eld got on so well. "Is the pirate, the Widowmaker, real?"

"I haven't seen her," he said. He touched his nose again. "But enough others have and more than a few who were robbed by her."

"So she's real?"

"I believe so, signorina."

"Good." I patted the railing. "I aim to kill the bitch and get the fuck out of this place as soon as she turns up."

The captain laughed. When he saw I wasn't laughing, he touched his hat and resumed his circuit of the ship.

I pushed myself off the railing and cut across the deck so I'd reach the helm before the captain did.

"Where are we going?" Eld asked.

"I'm not a great hand with navigation, by which I mean I've never tried to navigate a ship before, but by the position of the sun, I'm fairly certain the captain has us a few points north of where we should be."

"Why didn't you ask him?"

"I wanted to see if he'd bring it up." I shook my head and spat as we reached the stairs that led to the wheel. One of the sailors started to curse, saw my look, and bit off the rest as she bent to wipe the deck. "I hope he's not so nervous when the Widowmaker shows up."

"Sometimes nerves are a good thing," Eld said, half jogging to keep pace with me.

"I've never found that to be true," I said.

"That's because you're unique."

"Always polite," I muttered. Eld tried to catch my hand, but I slipped his grasp and reached the helmsman a step before him. Helmswoman. She glanced over her freckled shoulder, saw me, and turned back to the wheel. Her hair was tied back in a torn piece of dark cloth, and the rest of her outfit was almost as threadbare as the other sailors'. Given her position above the main deck, with the sun behind her, there was little left to the imagination. Still, it *did* look comfortable.

"Don't even think about it," Eld whispered in my ear.

We'd had more than one argument about trousers. Dresses, even ones divided for riding, were more of a pain than they were worth. I'd take a man's eyes on what I was actually doing instead of tripping in silks any day. *Really? Dresses?* I shook myself and tried not to feel disgust.

"You!" My tone was harsher than I'd intended, but there was no taking it back, so I plowed on. "This wheel is two points too far to the north. You'll correct that, now."

The woman's freckles danced across her face. "I take orders from the officers," she sneered, "not flotsam like yourself."

"I'm sure the Company will be sorry to hear your loyalties are misplaced," I said. "It'd be a shame if someone made sure they understood those loyalties caused our mission to fail. Might be you would be misplaced as well. No?" I glanced at Eld and shrugged. "I guess she knows the Company better than us."

"She must. Salina surely gave us another impression."

"Speak plain," the woman growled.

"Adjust course or I'll pin your hands to the wheel and adjust the course for you," I said. A stiletto appeared in my fist and I spun it effortlessly, letting the sun reflect off the stainless blade. I always like to keep one stiletto bright for times like this. The spinning blade was a parlor trick, but an effective one. "And then I'll report your arse to the Company. If our mission succeeds, you'll likely be looking for another berth, but if we fail, then I don't think you'll have to worry about another berth."

"You'll be dead," Eld said.

"I think she understood that time," I said.

"I did," she said. "I've not held the helm long enough to go to another ship so soon." She sighed. "Two points south?" I nodded. "The captain will feel the motion and come running."

"Good, I want him to." The woman spun the wheel and while I didn't feel anything, I heard a startled shout and saw the lanky man appear around the corner. "That was fast."

"Ulia, who told you to change course?"

"I did," I said.

"S-signorina?" he stammered, and then turned to Eld. "I give the orders on this ship."

"Aye?" Eld looked him up and down. "Then tell her that."

"I give the orders on this ship, signorina," he said, turning back to me.

"You carry out the orders the Company gives you," I corrected him. "And you haven't done that, have you? We're hours from the route we should be on and you know it. Why?"

"I—I—"

"You do believe in the Widowmaker, don't you? And you know a few hours south is where ships disappear." He nodded. "Good—that's where we're going." I stopped the stiletto in my fist with the blade pointed at him. "I'm-a kill a bitch and be done with this song and dance." The captain's mouth opened but nothing came out. "Oh, your ship doesn't turn my stomach like those damned Cannon Ships do, but I've had enough of the Shattered Coast to last me a few years," I added.

"As you say, signorina." He touched his hat and moved on.

"I don't think he took that the right way," I said. Eld and Ulia both stared at me.

"There was a right way?"

I rolled my eyes at Eld. "Aye, my way." I gestured at the captain's back. "I hope his nerves turn out to be the right sort when the Widowmaker shows up."

17

"I've made the connection," Katal said. He arched a thick eyebrow, white against his brown skin, and Salina nodded.

"I wondered when you'd reach out," the Harbormaster's voice came from his mouth. "I suppose you want to know what happened?"

"That would be a good place to start," Salina said. She tried to mask her anger, but that left her speaking in clipped tones. "It *has* been three days. Where are they?"

"It takes time to rebuild the connections after Rebirth," the Harbormaster said.

"Rebirth?" Salina gasped. "Did the girl slit your throat?"

"Hardly," the other woman sniffed. "It was the Dead Gods. They tried to assassinate me. Well, her, I think, but my servant burst in with a Veneficus and another, so they may have been trying for the whole lot."

"Gods," Salina breathed. "I think you'd better start at the beginning." She sat down as the Harbormaster told her story through Katal's mouth. For once, Salina didn't find it strange to hear that high, melodic voice coming from his blunt features.

She'd known it was a long chalk to send that pair into the middle of a thousand leagues of Godsforsaken sea and sand, but—*But the Board wanted it and I convinced myself.*

True, they'd found clues to follow almost from the start. *That was Buc.* But they'd almost died twice. The Dead Gods and their priests played for keeps. In a way, being dead, they were worse than the Sin Eaters the Company hired. You couldn't reason with a corpse, and their priests were about as imaginative as the dead deities they worshiped.

The Empire knew religion had its uses, or else the first Emperor would have stamped out worship a millennia ago. Or maybe he had tried, but back then his writ hadn't extended past one of the three islands that made up present-day Servenza. Every ruler of every nation since had found a reason to use those religions, with each generation becoming more entangled until it became hard to discern whom was using whom. It might not matter so much if the two sides didn't hate each other with a passion that made the Empire's relationship with Normain look almost congenial in comparison.

Katal had told her once that there could never be peace until one or the other—nation or faith—had been eliminated, and that their fight, Katal's fight, was eternal. The man had seemed strangely satisfied about it all too. *I've no part in that.* The Company was supposed to be neutral, free of the restraints of statehood—but were they really free? She was speaking with a Sin Eater through another Sin Eater. If she didn't use the mages, she'd have no clue what was going on along the Shattered Coast. And no information meant disaster when it came to trade. *A fine net cast around our shoulders.*

"I found an empty vial in the dead man's trouser pocket. The girl's protector must have blown his head off before he could Transfigure or Goddess knows what creature would have attacked me. Fucking Dead Gods and their fucking disgusting undead fingers bludgeoning along where they don't fucking belong." The cursing brought Salina back to the moment. It was disorienting to hear that melodic voice speaking such dross through Katal's thick lips. But she'd never met a Sin Eater who could think rationally when it came to the Dead Gods and their priests. "We should kill every fucking one of them and burn their temples to the ground. A corpse will burn easier than you'd think."

"Enough," Salina snapped. "I don't care an olive for your war."

"You—"

"More important," Salina spoke over the other woman, "the Company doesn't pay for your war. We pay for *information*. Where did Buc and Eld go? Were they injured?"

"Not that I could tell," the Harbormaster replied stiffly. "The dockmaster said two matching their description boarded one of your ships, the *Sea Dragon,* and set sail shortly thereafter."

"*Sea Dragon?*" Salina closed her eyes and the ship leapt forward in her mind. She knew every ship they financed in the Shattered Coast, down to the smallest rigger. The *Sea Dragon* wasn't small, but the brig wasn't as formidable as a frigate, or better yet, a man o' war. "Why'd you send them away on a brig?"

"I didn't send them away," the Harbormaster protested. "I was poisoned, Salina! Katal can tell you what Rebirth is like. I wasn't myself for a day and even after that I wasn't of much use. And those two sailed within the hour. Had they stayed as I commanded them to, I would have found them something more formidable." Katal licked his lips.

"This isn't my fault. I kept them alive when that goat-fucking Veneficus would have ripped them limb from limb. Besides, do you really expect that they will come back with the Widow-maker's skull as a figurehead? When all others have failed?"

"There's failure and then there's failure," Salina said carefully.

She felt her face heat at mention of the Widowmaker. *I warned the Board about her! But no one listens to a junior partner.* "We need more information," she said when she had control of her voice. "I know the Shattered Coast is vast, but how can we not know what is happening to our ships? Our fleet—" She bit her tongue. *Can you even call it a fleet anymore?* "I don't understand."

"No, you don't," the Harbormaster agreed. "You think you do, but, Salina, you haven't been here. Vast? Is the sky vast? You can sail days without sighting land and that's after you've arrived. Then suddenly you'll find yourself surrounded by specks of islands here and there, most swarming with islanders and no way of knowing if they are peaceful or have a taste for human flesh until it's too late." Salina could hear the shudder in her voice. "The south is mostly uncharted waters, the Dead Gods are finally making the play we've been warning you of for decades, and oh, by the way, the Widowmaker is sinking every ship in her path. Is it any wonder we know nothing?"

"Buc and Eld will find it," Salina said with a conviction that she couldn't feel.

"I'm sure," the other woman snorted.

"They were smart enough to avoid being poisoned by your servant," Salina shot back.

Katal snarled, but when he spoke, the Harbormaster was calm. "Fair point. Setting that aside . . . there is something I learned during my Rebirth."

"Something you learned?"

"Aye. I think it relates to the Dead Gods and why they've shown their hand, finally. You've received our reports that they are multiplying like fleas on an old dog, here?"

"I've read your reports," Salina said.

"Then you know they're becoming an infestation that must needs be eradicated. And soon."

"And you know," Salina repeated, "that we're not interested in your petty religious war. Aren't there enough fools to convert for each of you?"

"You blasphemous bitch," the Harbormaster spat.

"Aww, so you are faithful," Salina mocked, even though she knew she was wasting time. The Company needed the Sin Eaters as surely as the Sin Eaters needed the money their services brought. Ciris had shown up out of she alone knew where only a few centuries earlier; she didn't have the resources the Dead Gods had accumulated over the millennia. But every Sin Eater knew where their loyalties lay and that thought more than any other fueled Salina's disgust with the lot of them. "And here I thought you just loved the coin we send your way. How much of that does your Goddess see these days?"

"Will you hear what I have to say or should I end this now?" the Harbormaster asked after several moments of silence. Sweat dripped down Katal's forehead, beading on his nose, and a small pool had already started to form on the table he rested his meaty forearms on.

"I'm listening," Salina muttered. *Because I have to. Because we need you today. But one day, Sin Eater, one day we'll be free of your grip.* Now, if she could only find the faith to believe that day would be in her lifetime. "Say on."

"During my Rebirth, the Goddess spoke to me," the Harbormaster said, sounding like a lover remembering a particularly passionate evening. "There is an artifact that she seeks. Something that was stolen from her and hidden away shortly after she first awoke. She has reason to believe it has now been found."

"Interesting," Salina lied. Some on the Board liked to dabble in religious politics, but she'd be damned if they heard of this from her. "I'm sure we'll be more than willing to offer the services of our ships to help your Goddess find what was stolen from her.

"After our sugar problem is resolved." *And for a price that will make your eyes pop.*

The Harbormaster laughed. "This isn't some trinket, Salina. This is an item of immense power. Power beyond your ken. Why do you think the Dead Gods are swarming here now when they've turned a blind eye to the Shattered Coast for millennia? Why do you think your ships have gone missing? Why do you think the Widowmaker's suddenly made a name for herself? A ship that went missing centuries ago started all this and now it's happening again."

"What are you saying?" Salina bit off each word and wished her stomach didn't leap with each one. She remembered that fool historian who had given herself some trumped-up title. *Archaeologist*, that was it. The woman had come from the Shattered Coast, talking of an expedition to find a lost treasure, one she couldn't recover without proper funding. Salina had sent her out the door like the dross she was. What had the Archaeologist said?

It was an ancient shipwreck.

"What are you saying?" Salina repeated as thoughts raced through her mind. "That your war is the reason for the loss of our ships?"

"Goddess's breath! No!" The Harbormaster's mirthless laugh cut off. "I am simply pointing out the confluence of events that seems to circle around an artifact of my Goddess and suggesting that since it appears our problems coincide in the same geographical location, it may be in your interests to keep an eye out for said artifact. The rewards would be . . . immeasurable."

I doubt it. And yet, the Archaeologist had been sure. *Did I miss an opportunity?* If the Board found out—*No.* Salina rubbed her arms through her thin silk sleeves and shivered. She had to focus on what was in front of her. That was enough of a shit show as it was, without dredging up might-have-beens. "Gods. Missing ships. Cannibals. Pirates. Holy artifacts. And you sent Buc and Eld into the midst of that with a paltry brig beneath their feet?"

"The *Sea Dragon* has one of our gear-work mortars," the Harbormaster said finally.

"A mortar," Salina said flatly. *True, a Sin Eater–modified one was impressive, but it wasn't enough. A mortar when they need an armada.* She didn't like any of this one jot. Worse, she knew the Board wouldn't either . . . and they didn't know about the Archaeologist. She shivered again when she realized she would have to be the one to tell them. Still, there was one good piece of news: she wasn't with Buc and Eld. *Good luck, you wretched girl, wherever you are.*

You're going to need it.

18

"Oh, there you are," Eld said. "More food? Really?"

"I had to piss again; hopefully that tapers off soon," I said. "But I bumped into that damned physiker and he shoved an orange and a piece of hardtack at me. Worried I'm going to turn into a bag of bones."

"Hardly," Eld said. I caught him looking me over and he blushed. "You do look like you've lost some weight, though."

"I have." I bit into the hardtack. "But this shit is like chewing cobblestone powder," I said, spraying crumbs everywhere. Eld looked aghast, so I bit into the orange and let the juices help clear my throat. "What'd you need?"

"I just wanted to let you know we're square in the middle of the route now. I imagine it'll take a day or two to attract the wrong kind of attention."

I moved to the railing and he joined me, both of us watching the open sea. In the distance a few small dots of land, islands where the helmswoman said unruly sailors were marooned and left for dead, broke up the monotonous blue waves. She'd told me the bit about being marooned with something like glee in her eyes, as if hoping that would be my fate. And it might have been, if the captain hadn't feared the Company more than the Widowmaker. As it was, the crew had an edge to them now—there was no more singing or laughing and while they still scrubbed the deck, most kept a blade or pistole close to hand and the first mate had ordered two more up to the crow's nest. The air felt heavier and it wasn't just my imagination. Ships had disappeared in these waters and now our ship was the only one on the horizon.

"Sail ho!"

I actually jumped at the lookout's hoarse shout and Eld laughed. "So much for a day or two," I said.

Eld shrugged. "Could be another ship foolish enough to travel this route like us."

"She's flying the black flag, Captain!"

"Gods damn it," Eld muttered.

"Where away?" The captain used a brass mouthpiece so he could be heard easily even though he stood by the helm.

"Edge of the horizon, two points starboard and moving to intercept," the man in the crow's nest hollered into a brass contraption that ran the length of the mast and magnified his voice across the deck. "She's got the angle," he added.

"Sound General Quarters. To arms." The captain's voice was surprisingly calm. Maybe he would surprise me after all. "All hands to stations and make ready the cannons. Prepare the mortar!"

"Let's go check in with the captain," I said.

"I'm not sure he'll appreciate your help," Eld said.

"Probably not, but that doesn't mean he doesn't need it."

"Spoken like a woman," he muttered half under his breath.

"What was that?"

"I said he might not like that notion."

I elbowed Eld in the ribs as I passed him and dodged sailors that ran back and forth across the decks. There was no panic in their movements, thank the Gods, but there was a hurried order that made me think the first exchange of gunfire would tell the tale for the rest of the battle. Either molding them into the force I thought they might be or shattering them like so many ships had been before them. In a few moments we reached the deck where the captain held a ridiculously long telescope to his eye. He twisted it in his hands and gears spun, lengthening and retracting it as he took in the enemy ship.

"Ask Jen for an accurate count," he said to a boy beside him. "I count three rows of six cannons and her decks show no glint of a mortar."

"Aye, aye, Captain," the boy croaked before dashing off in a flurry of tanned legs.

"Well, signorina," he said when he lowered his glass, "it looks like you'll have your battle after all."

"It's the Widowmaker?"

"There aren't many pirates haunting the Southern Expanse these days. And last I heard, her ship ran thirty-six cannon." He licked his pinched lips and glanced down at me. "She tried to run out of the sun so we'd not get a good look at her until she was closer, but the winds favor us more than her, so she had to adjust her angle. She'll catch us in another hour or so because she's got more sail and oars besides, but she's lost the element of surprise."

"How many guns do you have?" Eld asked.

"The same as when you asked me back in Port au' Sheen," he said. "Three rows of four. Luckily, we've a newly minted mortar, Sin Eater–wrought, and I don't see one on her decks."

"You plan to shell her?" I asked.

"In a manner of speaking." The captain smiled. "She'll be in range of our mortar for several minutes before we're in range of her guns. If we turn away, I can extend that time and drop a few more shells on her decks. It's a tough shot under the best of circumstances, but my mortarwoman is the best in the Shattered Coast."

"A good plan," I said.

"Aye." He nodded. "And all it takes is one shell from that angle to open a hole straight through to the sea."

"I was afraid of that," I said. The captain arched an eyebrow, but Eld paled beneath his sunburnt cheeks when he saw my expression. The captain's plan *was* good—too good. We had to confirm it was the Widowmaker before sinking her. And with the mortar, odds were even if we'd glimpse her before sending her to the bottom. I wasn't going to wager a seat on the Company over a coin toss. "Salina's orders were clear—we're to take the Widowmaker, confirm her identity, and slit her throat." Eld started to open his mouth, but I turned my glare toward him and he chewed his lip instead.

The captain either didn't see my look or didn't care. He laughed humorlessly and shook his head. "Dead is dead, girl. I'll not risk my ship and crew so you can look her in the face when she breathes her last."

"You will or risk the Company's wrath," I said. *Girl?* He'd lost the "signorina," quickly enough. *Not like Eld then.* Somehow that made the next bit easier. "Luckily for both of us, I've a plan."

"You?" He snorted. "And what do you know of naval warfare?"

"I've read Aislin," I said. "And Gatina. And Frobisher. She was number two twenty-one," I added.

The captain's eyes grew tighter at their names, but they popped back open at the last. "You read *The Silence of Black on Blue*?" he asked.

"Twice—she had a way with words," I said.

"Did you mean to attend the Academy?"

"That doesn't matter," I said. "The point is that I have more knowledge here"—I tapped my head—"than half the captains in these waters put together."

"Words," he said.

"Combined with your experience, they are a formidable weapon, Captain. Use them." He started to shake his head and I touched his hand. He jerked at my touch but didn't pull away. "I want her dead as quickly and painlessly as do you, but I also can't risk failure. The Company . . ." I glanced at the helmswoman and leaned forward. "You know the Company ties strings around all our throats and is as happy to pull them tight as cut them loose. You've a string of your own, I'm sure." I bit my lip. "None of us wants to risk their wrath."

"No one wants that," he agreed slowly.

"Then let's not," I said. I could see his pulse in his throat and knew I had him. "Hear me out."

The captain glanced back at Ulia, but she was concentrating on holding the wheel on course in the choppy waters. "Very well, what is your plan?"

"Something worthy of Frobisher," I lied. None were as masterful on the waters as she had been. "Your ship is smaller and lighter than the Widowmaker's by how many tonnes?"

"Many," he said simply.

"So while she can pile on sail, that will do her little good when she's close in."

"Anyone can see that."

"Aye, but think about it," I said. "We can easily outmaneuver her, so let the Widowmaker in close and you'll only have to brave a single volley before you can slip behind her."

"Only? She's thirty-six guns," he grunted.

"Eighteen to twelve for one broadside," I said. "There's some risk, but no more than risking hitting her with a mortar across the sea. But I suggest you hold your fire, slip behind her, and then let her have a taste of the grape up her arse."

"Grape?" The captain's mouth formed a frown, but I could see the light in his eyes.

"Aye—we're not trying to sink her, remember? So load grape instead of round shot. Her cannon won't fire themselves. And if you can take her rudder with it, she'll be unable to turn herself right. Even if you don't, you'll be able to turn and give her another round before she has you in her sights again."

"Captain! You're not actually listening to her, are you?"

Ulia's voice brought him back to reality but not before I saw through his eyes—saw the Widowmaker's decks raked with shot, sailors slipping in their life's blood that ran in waves across her decks and breaking bones while trying to reach their cannon. Just when they were righting themselves, the boarding party came over the side, loaded with pistoles and bare steel. They were lost before they'd even begun. The Company would be pleased and they rewarded those who pleased them, but more than that, he'd have a second ship to his name . . . the beginnings of a fleet. I raised my voice and painted the portrait I'd seen, covering my lack of experience with Frobisher's musings.

"I'm impressed," the captain admitted. He raised the telescope to his eye and shook his head. "We've less than a turn of the hourglass to decide."

"Do what's best for your crew," Eld said.

"At least he's not a fecking liar," Ulia spat over her shoulder.

"For the long haul, not for today," Eld added.

The woman cursed again.

"It can be done," the captain said. "It is risky, but—"

"So is the alternative," I said. "You don't sink her with your mortar and she draws level—then what?"

"Aye." He collapsed the telescope hard between his palms and nodded as he marched past me. "We'll give them a taste of the grape."

I watched him go, back stiff with steel that hadn't been there a moment ago. At my shoulder, Eld asked—loudly, to be heard over the helmswoman's vehement cursing—"Do you think it will work?"

I shrugged. "'Once the cannons are loosed, only the Sea knows,'" I quoted.

"Frobisher?"

"Frobisher."

19

"Spin those wheels before you hear my dulcet tone and I'll splatter your brains over the carriage," the first mate growled into a brass mouthpiece as he marched back and forth on the deck below us.

"Eloquent fellow," Eld commented.

"He's a good man," the captain said. "If any of them fire now, we're fucked." He glanced up from the deck and his face drew taut. "She'll be on us in another minute."

"How long before you make the turn?" Eld asked.

The captain glanced at me and I answered for him. "A heartbeat after the last moment you believe possible."

"Two heartbeats if you can hold out," he added.

The man had bought into my plan wholesale and all doubts were cleaned from him. I didn't have any doubts either, but that was because I held all the cards, even if the players didn't know it. Eld kept shooting me looks as if trying to gauge my plans—he knew me well enough to know that I wouldn't tie myself to a single plan. *A plan within a plan and another if everything goes to shit*. Not even a mouse trusts itself to one hole. And I was no fucking mouse.

"On my mark," the captain muttered to the helmswoman.

She returned his nod and if she was tired from holding the course for so long, she didn't show it. Her hands were steady on the wheel. The Widowmaker's ship was close enough now that I could see individual sailors moving on deck. From everything I'd read and heard of pirates, I expected them to be disorganized, but they moved with as much efficiency as the sailors on the *Sea Dragon*. And they had more guns. The sun glinted off their cannon as they ran them out of their ports as if to remind us of the violence they promised. Eld looked calm, but I could see the captain's shoulders tighten by degrees as the Widowmaker's ship nosed almost even with our rudder and then drew alongside. Eld's mouth moved, but no command came. And then it did.

"Clew up! Clew up! Hard to starboard!" the captain roared.

"Fire, you fuckers!" The mate's gravelly voice was swallowed by the sound of machinery as twelve wheel locks zipped in tune. The *Sea Dragon* shook and the Widowmaker's ship disappeared in a plume of smoke. Recoil made the ship swing over faster than seemed possible.

"Hard over!" the captain screamed again. It sounded distant thanks to the ringing in my ears. He saw me and clapped me on the shoulder so hard, I stumbled into Eld. "It's working, thank the Gods. It's—"

The rest was drowned out by the Widowmaker's broadside. I could actually hear the rounds screaming through the air and then wood splintered and we were enveloped in something wet and cloying that drove me to my knees. I tried to fight my way out of the canvas, but everything was dark and tangled, so I drew a stiletto and began hacking around me. You'd think canvas sheets would cut like paper, but you'd be wrong. I finally managed to

hack a hole large enough to squeeze through and emerged to find
the deck partially buried under half the mainsail, with shards of
wood littering what was visible of the rest. I could see Ulia's arms
wrapped around the base of the wheel, but the wheel itself spun
freely and there was enough blood soaking through the sheets
that it didn't seem likely she would steer anything again. The
canvas heaved as a figure stood up beneath it, then sloughed off,
revealing Eld through the large hole he'd cut with his sword. He
cursed when he saw the helmswoman, but his face lost some of
its tension when he found me standing beside him.

"What happened?"

"I don't know," I said. "I think they—" A muffled shout behind
me drew both of us over. Eld's sword made shorter work of the
canvas now that he had freedom to move. A moment later the
captain's lanky figure emerged, aided by a hand from Eld. "I think
they missed the hull and hit the mast instead."

The captain turned in a slow circle, eyes unfocused, but they
snapped back to sharpness when he saw the dead woman beneath the wheel. "They knew," he muttered.

"Knew what?"

The man glanced at Eld as if not seeing him. "They knew
we'd try to maneuver, so they loaded chain instead of ball." He
searched around and then kicked a length of chain with a small
ball still attached to the one end. "Each tried to outwit the other.
We lost." He surveyed the deck where the first mate, alive but
bleeding freely from his bald head, was trying to kick the few
sailors on their feet into some semblance of order. "We lost," he
repeated.

"We can still turn." Eld pointed at the unmanned wheel.
"We'll lose speed, but surely we'll be able to send a few salvos
over to weaken them first."

"I don't think so," I said. I'd finally spotted the Widowmaker's ship and while she was more than several hundred paces away, she was closing fast with full sail while the *Sea Dragon* limped along. We'd never be able to turn with enough speed to get the edge on her now. "They're coming up fast."

"Gods damn it," the captain spat. One eye was darkening from a bruise, but he glared at me from the good one. "If I had done as I wanted, we would have sent her to the depths."

"Likely," I agreed. "But I couldn't risk you doing so before we knew it was the Widowmaker."

"You gambled with all of our lives," he growled. "Do you think this a game?"

"Life's a game," I told him. He was on the edge of doing something foolish, but I wasn't worried. "If you lose, it's over. If you win, you get to keep playing. And you gambled right along with me. It's your ship, your toss."

"I never would have been here, if not for you." He gestured at Ulia's body. "She would still be drawing breath if not for you."

"And you as well," I told him. "Your plan would have worked too well—I needed a plan that worked just well enough." There's something in me that can't help but kick a man when he's down. Or a woman, for that matter, but generally I find men at my feet more often than women.

It's a dark piece, left over from the streets, I think, or else something broken in my moral compass. Either way, I was no more able to stop the smile from touching my lips than the waves were able to stop crashing against the ship. "And you made it happen, Captain. I'm sure the Company will keep that in mind if you make it out of this."

"You. Fucking. Bitch!" He screamed the last and reached for the pistole in his belt. "I'm going to blow your—" His face disappeared in a flash of metal and he tumbled into the wheel before falling on top of the dead woman. The wheel turned slowly from the impact, but the *Sea Dragon* barely registered it.

"He had a point, Buc." Eld wiped his hilt clean against the canvas. *And that's why I wasn't worried.* Still, too polite to stab a man in the back apparently. "Why sacrifice an entire crew for one woman? Why give her the upper hand?"

"Every choice is a gamble," I said. I almost shrugged, but I could see the anger in him and for once, I didn't feel like feeding it. I leaned against the railing and watched the Widowmaker's ship begin to align itself parallel to us. "I simply ran the odds and chose the best option. If we'd followed his plan, Salina would have hung us on uncertainty. At the very least, she wouldn't have given us a share in the Company."

"Aye? So how does this play out? If the Widowmaker is in the business of sinking every ship on this lane—and so far all the evidence says she is—then we're going to die."

"Perhaps." The Widowmaker's second volley was shot of the more solid kind, and the *Sea Dragon* shivered from the impact. The deck was surprisingly untouched, save for a piece of railing that exploded, but the ship lurched and the last of its speed disappeared. "My aim is to remake the world, Eld. I won't fail because of half measures or bad gambles." I glanced at him. "If that's your aim too, then so much the better, but if it's not, at least don't stand in my way." We stared at each other. The only sound was that of the first mate ordering the cannons run out.

"I don't have to like it," he said finally. He sighed and scrubbed at his eyes. "There should be a better way."

"Then find me one," I said. I turned back to the pirates closing fast on our port side as half our cannon exploded in flame, but as the smoke cleared, I could see they'd fired too soon. Grape won't carry like round, not at that distance. "Until then, find some rope and be quick about it."

"What?"

"Just do it," I said. Eld shook his head, but it only took him a few moments to cut a few lengths of rope from the piles of canvas strewn about. He held out a length and arched an eyebrow. "Now tie my hands. Tie them!" I glanced back over my shoulder, silently counting breaths since the Widowmaker's last volley. I felt Eld slip the rope's ends around my wrists and pull it taut. "We don't have much time. You're going to have to pull harder than that," I added.

"Any harder and you'll have marks," Eld spat.

"That's what I'm looking for. Burn me, damn it." Pain lanced through my fingers as he tightened the bonds and my hands grew darker than the rest of my skin from lack of blood flow. "Good, now cut me loose but leave the loops on my wrists."

"You make no sense," Eld muttered as he drew his sword again.

"And you never trust me," I said.

"I saw where that got the captain," he said.

"You wound me," I mocked. "Now it's your turn," I said. He set his sword against the railing and held out his wrists. I wasn't experienced in knot tying, but I'd read a few books and one not too long ago, so I didn't have to close my eyes to see the images. "You can trust me with anything, Eld." I finished the second loop and pulled as hard as I could. "So long as you don't cross me."

"Ouch!" he yelped. "Fuck sake, Buc, if I'd known you were going to try to amputate my hands, I would have pulled a lot harder. You should have gone first."

I caught up his sword and cut him free. "Aye, I was thinking the same thing." I handed back his sword and he took it, rubbing his wrists together as he did so. I pointed over my shoulder. "We need to go over the rail."

"Throw ourselves into the sea? Are you mad?"

"The Widowmaker is riding a swell and her guns are aimed low. Our ship is taking on water." I sighed. Sometimes the need to spell everything out is more exasperating than anything else. "She's aiming for the powder magazine, whether she realizes it or not. Frobisher says a crack Imperial crew can fire a broadside every hundred and fifty breaths while a typical crew is closer to twice that. I don't know how great the Widowmaker's sailors are, but I'm guessing they aren't typical and it's already been one hundred eighty breaths."

"So we jump overboard?" Eld asked. He swallowed hard and shook his head. "Isn't that the last thing you're supposed to do?"

"Only if you're the captain—which we're not," I said. Not that I would have stayed if I had captain's bars on my shoulders. Only a fool plays to lose.

"I'm not sure that's a great plan, Buc."

"One hundred ninety," I counted. "It's either that or get blown up. And her ship is in that direction anyway," I added.

"Fuck me," he muttered, but followed me down the steps.

The main deck was slick with blood and sea spray. Just what I'd promised the captain would happen to the pirates, only then I hadn't accounted for the Widowmaker. *I won't discount her again.* The pirates were close enough that I could hear someone yelling. Not yelling. Shouting commands. *Fuck.* "Dive down and swim underwater for all the breath you have!"

"I'm not an idiot, Buc," Eld growled. "But first—"

"Too late!" I screamed. I grasped his hand and heaved, spinning in a circle. I barely reach Eld's chest, but my momentum and the slick deck made up for it. He hit the railing and catapulted into the sea and I followed, letting my momentum swing me over the rail. I'd like to say I made a graceful entrance into the water, but the best that can be said is I didn't flop so much as sink like a stone. Dark blues and greens filled my vision and I wasn't sure if I was swimming away from the *Sea Dragon* or back toward it. I'd killed the captain for playing those odds, but sometimes you've a knife at your back and the only thing to do is grin and toss the dice and hope they don't come up pips.

My dress pulled me down or, more likely, my knives, and it was all I could do to move forward in the water and not sink. My lungs screamed and I could feel my eyes bulging when something swatted me from behind and twisted me down and around until my wits were well and truly scrambled. *Can't breathe.* Only the bubbles trickling from the corners of my mouth gave me an inkling of which direction to head.

I clawed upward, fighting the sea. I could feel the salt assaulting my lips, lunging for my lungs. *Can't breathe.* All I wanted to do was open my mouth, water or no. Everything in me screamed for it. *Breathe.* I couldn't resist any longer. I had to give in. I had to open my mouth. I had to.

I broke through the surface with a giant gulp and surprised myself by sucking in air instead of water. I splashed back down, sunk below a wave, and resurfaced, greedily sucking more air into my lungs. It was hot and harsh, but life-giving. And then I looked up and realized what I'd taken for the sun was the burning hulk of a ship. The deck was a writhing inferno of canvas and wood; a few dark shapes danced in the flames. It was listing so heavily to port that it looked as if it would tip at any moment and send the flames toward me, exacting revenge for the part I'd played in its demise.

"Gods," I breathed.

"Nothing good comes from the sea," Eld said, treading water beside me. His blond locks were plastered to his forehead and a small cut bled over his left eye, but otherwise he looked fine. "Let's hope the Widowmaker takes pity on us."

I couldn't keep the laugh within my chest. He laughed too, after a mulling over his words, then froze. I followed his stare and saw the pirate ship less than a stone's throw away, holding itself back from the fires of the *Sea Dragon*.

"If they see us," I said.

"Flotsam off starboard!" The lookout's voice was clear—somehow the crackling sound of the *Sea Dragon* burning and the never-ending churn of the waves was small beside the voice high in the crow's nest above us. "Two still swimming."

"It's about time our luck changed," Eld grunted.

"There's no such thing as luck," I said.

A rope landed between the two of us. "Grab hold or drown, I don't care which!" another voice shouted.

"Bullshit there isn't," Eld said.

I rolled my eyes, but there was nothing to be done but grab the rope. Eld slipped an arm through it and then we flew across the water as it was drawn back up. For a breath I thought they meant to bludgeon us off the ship's hull, but the tension eased as we neared the side. Those above shifted to a slow, steady pull that allowed us to stick our feet out, between us and the ship, so that we nearly walked up the side as we were lifted from the water. I'd been sweating a few moments before, but now that I was drenched, the winds pulling at my sodden dress sent goose-flesh across my skin.

"L-let me d-do the talking-g," I chattered.

"Your plan w-with the r-ropes?" Eld asked through blue lips.

"R-remember how we got into th-the gaolship to find Kaisa's missing heir?" I couldn't force anything else out by that point, but I saw understanding glimmer in Eld's eyes. It felt like hours but must have been heartbeats before we reached the railing and a dozen hands appeared, dragging us onto the deck. My knees were knocking from the cold, but I managed to fend everyone off and draw myself up. Never let the fuckers see you down; that was as true now as it had been on the streets. I opened my mouth to paint our tale, but a foul-looking bastard with a grizzled beard and a patch over one eye beat me to it.

"Look wot the sea barfed up." He jabbed a short-bladed cutlass at us. "Now for a little bit of sport, lads!"

20

"Sport?" a husky feminine voice called from over old ugly's shoulder. The man bristled; something dark flashed briefly across his gob. "You wouldn't be having fun without your captain, would ye?"

"Course not," the man said, scratching at his beard with his free hand. His other kept twitching the cutlass in his fist. The rest of the crew around us took a few steps back, but before he could move, a tall figure swooped in behind him, nearly knocking him over with a pat on the shoulder. "Captain," he added.

The woman kept her arm around the man's shoulder as she peered down at us. Her dark hair was held back by a red bandanna, and white sulfurous match cords were interwoven into dozens of braids. Striking as that was, her features were more so. I hadn't been expecting beauty from a pirate captain, but the Widowmaker—it had to be her—was beautiful. Olive oil skin that wasn't as naturally dark as mine had been bronzed by the sun, and the contrast with her angled midnight-green eyes and small pink lips only added to her beauty. She wore a cloak that obscured some of her figure; the dozen pistoles tied on and beneath her cloak left the rest to fantasy. I had a feeling that was no accident. Her tongue darted out as she inspected us, gaze swiftly going to the ropes around our hands, then Eld's cut, then our eyes.

"I see flotsam, not sport, Myles." She squeezed his shoulder and straightened with a smile that didn't reach her eyes. She stood a full head and shoulders over him. "I'll just have a chat with them, shall I, whilst you carry on with your duties. Gem!" she yelled over her shoulder. "You got need of Myles?"

A man nearly as wide as he was tall looked up from a group gathered around a smoking cannon. "Aye, aye, Captain."

"Well, there you go, Myles. They say a needed man is a wealthy one." She squeezed his shoulder yet again and I saw that dark look shiver up the grizzled man's features to his one remaining eye. "What say you?"

"Aye," he muttered.

"Dulcet tones to my ears," she said with that same smile that didn't rise above her mouth. She let him go and Myles gave us a hard look as he turned away. "The rest of you best get back to securing the ship and looking for any other 'flotsam.'" She looked past us and sighed. "Although I doubt there's much left but charred timbers." She drew a gear-work pistole with over-under barrels and inspected it, twisting it in her hands. "Go on now. I'll just have a chat with our new friends."

The rest of the crew moved off quickly, but not so quickly that I couldn't tell a few were worried about leaving their captain alone with two of the enemy. I filed that away, along with what I'd learned about her when she looked us over. She'd taken an account of what our clothes and bodies told her before looking at our eyes. Wise, that—the eyes can hide any number of lies.

She pointed the pistole in our general direction and motioned with it. "Now, I've just kept Myles from his sport, so hopefully you won't leave me disappointed. What's the name of the ship

I just sank and what were you two doing on it?" She cocked the hammer. "And the fewer lies you put past your lips, the better for all concerned."

"W-we were being sent to S-servenza to s-stand trial," I said through chattering teeth. I held up my wrists to show the loops of rope. "It's a long tale."

"Aye? Aren't they all?" The woman laughed, then pointed with her free hand toward the rear of the ship. "You two are going to go into shock if you don't get warmed up. I'm not letting you belowdecks until I hear your long tale. Long on detail and not on fabrications, I hope," she added. "There's a brazier that can be lit back there and I'll see about some coats. Until then, I don't want to hear or see anything pass between the two of you."

"Don't t-trust us?" I asked.

"Would you, were you me?" she asked.

"No."

"Good. Keep that honesty on your tongue and things will go a sight smoother all around. Now march that a way and I'll be along behind to help guide you."

Eld and I glanced at each other, but there was nothing to do with her pistole trained on us. He put a hand on my arm and we began stumbling down the deck. Most of the sailors seemed concerned with the one cannon that was out of commission, but a few here and there moved out of our way with a nod or touch of the forehead as they acknowledged their captain. All seemed relatively well-fed and none had signs of scurvy or malnutrition that I could see. The lines were all tied and the deck was clean given they'd just fought a battle. Taken together, it seemed like the Widowmaker was at least as efficient as the *Sea Dragon*'s captain. Then again, she'd won, so there was that.

"Now," she said when Gem appeared with two overcoats in

his arms and the brazier was glowing from the heat of burning coals, "settle in and give me your stories."

"Stories," I repeated, surprised that my teeth had stopped knocking together. "I'm not one for ventures . . ." I began, making sure my eyes never left hers. Liars often avoid eye contact—worried that their lies will show. But if you're going to lie from the beginning, it's best to let your eyes do the talking for you. "Eld isn't either, but we'd some money aside. Nothing burns a hole faster. Bought into the Gilded Flower Plantation and came across. To see the venture." I spoke in clipped tones, biting the words off and leaving no space between them so that one sentence bled into the other. "Ship was bad. Too fast. Still we made time. Time to see the venture." I could see her mate's brow furrow. "Check on our stake and then we—"

"Enough."

I paused mid-word.

"You're going on like a chattering jay that's finally caught sight of land," the Widowmaker said. "Begin again. Slower."

"You have any kan?" I asked.

"What? You want to go on twice as fast?" her mate asked.

"Not to drink. To smoke. It slows me down," I said.

"Gem," the Widowmaker said, keeping her eyes on mine.

The mate grumbled, but he dug into his vest pocket, drew out two thinly rolled cigarillos, then passed one to me and stuck the other in the corner of his mouth. "Never smoke alone," he muttered. "Tain't proper." He struck a match and lit his before offering it to me. I saw Eld's eyes flash, but the lack of propriety made me feel at home.

"Ah." I didn't have to lie about the sigh. The smoke filled my lungs, cooled the scores of messages burning brands in my brain, and let the story coalesce in my mind. "I'm not one for ventures,"

I said, letting the smoke spill out of my mouth, almost spelling my words for me.

"Neither of us are," Eld added. "But"—he shrugged—"we'd put some money by and were running a streak, so it seemed wise to do something with it."

"Aye," I spoke around the kan cigarillo in my mouth. "Otherwise we'd spend it all when the streak ran cold. So we were reading the papers and all the talk has been of the Shattered Coast. Or least it was then."

"And then our streak turned into a heater," Eld said.

"Gambling?" the Widowmaker asked.

"Dice," I said. I made one of my smaller stilettos appear in my fist and let it dance across my fingers. It was harder than it should have been—the cold hadn't leeched itself completely from my bones—but it was credible enough and I made it disappear back into my riding habit without dropping it. "I've, uh . . . nimble fingers."

"Too right you have," Gem said, spouting smoke with every word. "Gods."

"So we knew it was then or never," Eld said.

"And it didn't seem like we could lose, so we put our money on a stake on the Gilded Flower Plantation," I said.

"Grand enough name," the Widowmaker said. Her dark green eyes were inscrutable, but her pale lips kept twitching. I hadn't had enough time around her to gauge the meaning, but . . .

"So we thought," Eld said, filling the silence. "The broker, Fago, claimed he was in on half a dozen different plantations and this one was the best. Pure sugar, no kan."

"Just as well—your friend would smoke it all," she said, eyeing the nub left in my fingers.

"Name's Buc," I said. "And I might at that." I drew deeply and let the remaining ash fall to the deck. Her eyes flashed but she said nothing. "So we bought our stakes with Fago and waited."

"And waited," Eld said.

"Finally our luck began to run south and we thought a change of climate might be in order."

"You mean you were caught cheating," she supplied.

"I mean, we took a ship across to see our plantation."

"And did it live up to its name?"

"Shit, no," I said, blowing the last bit of smoke from my lungs. My mind was clear now, calm. Which, given her attention to detail, was exactly what I needed. "It didn't exist. We put into Port au' Sheen and were promptly laughed off the island."

"Fago didn't exist and neither did our plantation," Eld said.

"So gamblers and cheaters gambled and were in turn cheated," the Widowmaker said.

"I didn't know pirates put such a price on fair play," I said.

The Widowmaker's pistole filled my vision before I could blink. "In these waters you'd best be careful what words touch your lips, Buc."

"You fly a black flag and you sank our ship," I said. "Give me another word for it and I'll sing it back to you, but the only one I know is 'pirate.'"

"You've a file for a tongue," she said. "Sometimes files grind too far, too thin, until they break. Mind yours doesn't," she said, lowering the pistole.

I kept my features smooth, but I could feel heat in my cheeks; luckily, my skin wouldn't show it much. *Bitch*. She'd drawn me out and she was right. My tongue was a file—but a girl who tossed dice wouldn't last long with a mouth like that. I'd been distracted by the pistole. It'd appeared like magic, and with eyes as fast as mine that just wasn't possible. The streets had honed my vision such that any and every small movement was seen and categorized instantly. But I hadn't seen her move. Worse, her eyes hadn't changed at all; there'd been no warning. She was good, one of the best I'd sparred with. I couldn't afford to let her have any more of Sambuciña Alhurra, just Buc with the light fingers.

"Buc's always dancing past the edge of humor and falling into arseholery," Eld said. "That's how she got us nearly hung in Port au' Sheen and lost our money in the bargain." I shot Eld a hard look, but he shrugged. "No use hiding it, Buc; she'll find out eventually."

The deck trembled and behind the Widowmaker and Gem, I saw the hands crowded around the damaged cannon all jump away from it before moving cautiously back.

"Find out what?" the Widowmaker asked, ignoring the commotion. "Who'd you kill? This Fago?"

"It wasn't like that," I said, hoping Eld would tell me what it was like.

"It wasn't," Eld agreed. "We'd no money for a return passage to Servenza, so Buc convinced me to borrow a schooner."

"Borrow?"

"You're not a pirate," I said. "We're not thieves." *Gods.* The kan wasn't strong enough to keep my mind at the pace it needed to be. "We borrowed it."

"Right out into the bay," Eld added.

"Until yonder brig rounded the crescent, cleared the cliffs, and leveled her guns at us," I said.

"Ah, so that's why you wear links around your wrists," she said.

"Aye, the captain wasn't a bad sort, but the Harbormaster intended to make examples of us for absconding with one of her ships," I said. Gem growled. I glanced at him. "You've met the Harbormaster?"

"We ken the bitch," Gem said. He made as if to spit on the deck, saw the Widowmaker's expression, and swallowed instead. "You're lucky she didn't string you up there."

"Good as," I said. "She wrote our names down in the book and sent the missive back to Servenza."

"We followed after on the brig, Servenza-bound, where she intended our corpses to decorate the Grand Canal as an example of what happens to pirates," Eld said.

"You lot aren't pirates," Gem said.

"No shit, but the *Sea Dragon* had its orders and those orders named us pirates. Word of two gamblers against a Company Harbormaster?" I shook my head. "We were dead until you lot opened up on her."

"Tell me." The Widowmaker frowned. "Did they have a mortar?"

"Big tub of a cannon?" I asked. She nodded. "Aye, they were readying it, but the crew kept bitching about pay and booty and the first mate said he had a plan." I swiftly outlined what I'd recommended to the late captain, with Eld supplying some shine over the rougher edges.

"Damned close to what you proposed, Chan Sha," Gem said at the end.

"Aye." She chewed on her lip. "Could have gone badly if he'd tried chain instead of grape."

"Chan Sha?" Eld asked. Something poked at the back of my memory. *Chan Sha. Widowmaker.* Why did it make me think of spices? "We thought you were the Widowmaker," he added.

"A rough translation," Gem said. "Chan Sha means—"

"Widowmaker," I finished. *How did I know that?* The others were looking at me with confused expressions that mirrored my own. Then I remembered book number two eighty-nine. Zhe's

Cordoban Diplomacy. A bit of a misnomer, because the Cordoban Confederacy's ideas of diplomacy usually started and ended with the blade. But I'd learned a lot about the distant Southeast, beyond the Southern Expanse, and their rulers, or Shahs. "Shah" meant "ruler." Or maker. *So "Chan" means "widow"?* That didn't mesh with what I knew of the language, which was little enough. And Chan Sha didn't seem as prickly as Zhe described Cordobans. *Maybe the bastard had an ax to grind.* Never trust an author. That was something I learned early on in my reading.

"I don't care what they call me," the Widowmaker—Chan Sha—said, pulling me back to the moment. She shook her head. "What I'd like to know is—"

Voices shouted at the same time the deck trembled harder than it had before and a man screamed, "She's free!"

The faulty cannon caught the sun as it rolled across the deck and the crew scattered before it, but one figure lay back near the carriage, unmoving. Gem shouted an oath, but as fast as he was, Chan Sha was faster, gone in a whirl of dark leather and bright pistoles. She danced around the crew, conjured up a spar from seemingly nowhere, and braced it before the cannon. The hulking iron crashed into the wood beam with a crunch, rolled a quarter of the way up it, teetered, and then rolled back down. It steadied, moving only a little as the ship settled between swells.

"Jump on her, you lugs!" Gem yelled as he ran down the steps, a dozen yards behind Chan Sha. "Secure her or she'll break us all."

Eld touched my arm and leaned by my ear. "How did that go?"

"Too soon to say. Nice of you to jump on the stolen ship idea. I was going to go with Chan Sha's suggestion." I glanced at him. "You know, good old-fashioned murder?"

"Oh, well, the ship was close to what really happened and . . ." He dug at his collar.

"And you can't lie for shit," I said.

"Not everyone can be a master manipulator like you, Buc," he said.

"I'll take smoke up my arse any day of the week," I said, "but two of us on one ship is one too many."

"The Widowmaker? I mean Chan Sha?" He followed my gaze. "Aye, she's quick."

"Quick." I traced the distance between us and the cannon and it was easily sixty paces. Yet she'd crossed it, found a wood beam, and stopped the cannon before her first mate made it half the distance. Something wasn't right; the figures weren't adding up correctly. "Aye," I said. "Too quick."

21

"You've no liking for pickled eel?"

I eyed the wrinkled, limp pale worm-thing before me and could not find the likeness between that and some of the spicier Servenzan eel dishes I knew. "No, I think the fish filled me to the brim," I said.

"No eel," the woman said, and sniffed, passing it to Eld, on my left, who looked as hesitant as I had, but his manners won out and he stabbed one and dropped it onto his plate with a wet plop that released a hideous odor, like shit boiled in a vat of acid. She nodded approvingly, rolled her eyes at me, and set the plate down in front of Gem and Chan Sha.

The quartermaster was a woman who looked like she'd have eaten Gem under the table and beaten Eld at arm wrestling in her younger years, but now that grey ran rampant through her darker hair, the muscle was gone and the flesh hung from her bones, a reminder of what she'd lost. The woman was forever moving in front of me with dish after dish, obscuring my vision with her lumpy arms and nearly putting one of her folds in my soup at the start of the meal. I'd have ripped her a new arsehole then and there, but Chan Sha had been watching too intently for it to be anything but a test.

So I had to bugger off and let the old hag prod me through three courses, avoiding her oversized calico dress and the flesh within it all the while. But I put my foot down on the eel. "You know, it's a very great honor," she said, watching Eld poke tentatively at the shriveled thing on his plate. "Dining with the captain."

"Aye," I spoke around the bone I'd been nibbling on to keep my mouth shut. "So you said. Thrice before."

"And the captain had the eel as well."

For fuck's sake.

"And you know . . ." she began.

"It looks like a limp dick," I said. The quartermaster's eyes popped. "Like some poor bastard got all hot and bothered but didn't get the girl to spread her legs, so he ended up with blue balls, and then some maniac masquerading as a chef chopped his cock off and threw it in a pickling jar for good measure."

The woman sputtered, her mouth twitched angrily, and her chins began to burn in quick succession. *Here we go.* I'd tried to hold my tongue, but even I'm not immune to incessant, nagging badgery. I could see the smile in Chan Sha's eyes even if it didn't show in her lips. *Bitch.*

Gem slammed the table, nearly sending the eels flying into the quartermaster's lap. She tried to move, but she was wedged against the wall of the narrow space that served as both galley and dining room.

"That." He took a breath and laughter shook his wide shoulders. "That were the funniest." He slammed the table again, clutched at the mug in front of him, and caught it just before it fell off the edge of the table. "That were the funniest fecking thing I've heard in a while." He nudged the plate with his mug and exploded into more laughter when the eels jiggled. "They do look like shriveled-up cocks!" He wiped his eyes, tears glowing in the lamplight. "They do."

"G-Gods." Eld's windpipe bulged with eel. He cleared his throat, avoiding looking down at the half of an eel lying on his plate. His cheeks looked a little blue, or maybe green. He cleared his throat again. Gem offered Eld his mug and Eld pointed the bottom toward the ceiling and didn't break for air until foam had settled over his top lip like a strange mustache. He slammed the cup down and it echoed hollowly.

"Thank you," he whispered. He cleared his throat for the third time. "Thank you," he repeated, louder. Gem waved a hand, still giggling. "You run a tight ship," Eld said, looking across the table at Chan Sha. "I didn't expect that type of discipline among pirates."

"Discipline brings freedom," she said simply. "We all live and die together and that freedom demands a high price. We've few laws, but break them and you'll find short shrift from me."

"Or me or any of us," Gem added. "Break a law and you could doom us all and then marooning would be the worst of your troubles."

"Leave them on an island?" I asked.

"Aye," Gem said, "drop 'em off on a flyspeck of sand with naught but a pistole and one shot."

"Better make it count then," I muttered.

Gem started laughing again. "I like this one!"

"Something I said?" I asked.

"The pistole isn't for hunting or protection," Eld said. He leaned toward me. "It's to blow your brains out when you can't take it anymore." I arched an eyebrow and he shrugged. "The helmswoman on the *Sea Dragon,* Ulia, liked to talk."

"To you, anyway," I said.

"Marooning takes considerable time and effort," Chan Sha said. She rested her forearms on the table. "Oftentimes the plank is easier. Run a board out and let them walk off and the sharks will take care of the rest."

"Easier," Gem said, "but a damned hard way to go. No need for that level of savagery."

"You bite your mouth," the quartermaster hissed.

I'd hoped I'd shocked the old hag into swallowing her tongue, but there's a saying in the streets: "Shit in one hand, hope in the other, and see which fills up first." The streets are buried in shit themselves, so they know they answer, but they're honest. Sometimes.

"I'm just saying that a pistole does the trick just as easily. Dead is dead."

But sometimes there's an example to be made. I eyed Chan Sha, but her features were smooth, revealing nothing.

"Save the powder says I," the quartermaster said with a throaty chuckle. She swigged down the flagon before her and wiped foam from her upper lip, still laughing at her joke.

"I . . . see," Eld said, missing a beat.

"Well, abide by our rules and you've naught to fear of marooning or planks or sharks," Chan Sha told Eld.

"So you'll take us on?"

Chan Sha exchanged looks with her officers and shook her braids. "I didn't say that. You're guests and you'll be treated as such. Once we have the measure of you"—she paused—"the full measure—then we'll decide whether you'll be joining our crew. Savvy?" she asked.

"Savvy," Eld and I repeated.

Later, as we followed the old hag to our temporary quarters— two hammocks swung over crates at the bow of the ship—I played her words back in my mind and bit off a curse. *Naught to fear of marooning or planks or sharks.*

"But you said nothing of pistoles."

22

"Lime?" I asked. Eld eyed the barrel, which was three-quarters filled with limes and lemons and some strange fruit that looked more pink than yellow, and shook his head. "You don't want your gums to bleed and your teeth to fall out. I mean, you're old, but not *that* old. People will start to talk."

"The day you get your first grey hair, I will weep with joy," he muttered. I snorted and he smiled. "I think I got enough sustenance from that damned eel last night."

"Aye, who would have pictured you as one with a taste for shriveled cock?" Eld's face turned green again, more from the thought of the eel than my words, I'm sure. "What d'you think of our pirate captain?"

He swallowed the lump in his throat and followed my gaze to where Chan Sha strode the deck, personally supervising fitting the broken cannon from yesterday back into its newly made carriage. Today her cloak was steel grey, which matched the sky perfectly and seemed to mirror the crew's mood. Yesterday they'd all been riding a nervous high from the battle, but today everyone was melancholy. You'd have thought they'd be used to sending a few score of souls down to the deep by now, but no. A conscience is a terrible thing, I think.

"Her boots have elevated heels, so she looks taller than she really is. The cloak is thin and touches her calves, aiding the illusion, and as wild as her hair is, the matchsticks make it seem more so. More actor than pirate, then." He grinned. "There's something about her, though; she'd turn any number of heads in Servenza."

"And yours as well?" I asked lightly.

"Aye, why not?"

"Her hair looks brittle, I think," I said. "Too much salt and wind; it'd probably snap off the first time you pulled it."

"Gods, I don't mean to sleep with her," Eld said. He gave me a hard look. "You're especially prickly this morning, Buc."

"I just want to make sure your head's in the game," I said. "The right head."

"I want what you want," he said simply. He palmed a lemon from the barrel beside us and hefted it. "Though I hope you have a plan that involves exposing Chan Sha's scheme and getting us off this Godsforsaken boat before she exposes us and sends us over the side."

"Our good captain?" I asked. Chan Sha looked up from where she stood surrounded by half her crew, saw us, and began threading her way around the others, moving directly for us. "Aye, it's a cat-and-mouse game now."

"And you're no mouse," Eld said.

I smiled. "No." If you see enough cats chase mice, you'll begin to notice a sharp divide between the experienced and the less so. The younger cats will leap about, trying to muscle their way to the kill, but that fails more often than not. A mouse that's been pressed will double back on itself, slip through cracks, and escape. The wiser cat will keep pressure on the mouse, but make no move until finally the mouse has no choice but to make a move of its own. And when it does, the wiser cat is waiting.

It's hard to escape when you're dancing to another's tune and all they need do is wait for you to slip up. So I'd let Chan Sha play the mouse and dance back and forth as she tried to out us, and in the end, when she made a mistake, I'd be waiting to pounce.

"I'm no mouse," I repeated.

"You two breakfasted well?" she asked when she reached us.

"Very well," Eld said.

"I apologize I couldn't tarry, but the day after a battle is almost as busy as the day of the battle itself." She smiled that smile that never quite found her eyes. "Albeit with less danger, aye?"

"Your company was missed," Eld said, dipping his head.

I didn't bother rolling my eyes. If I did that every time he laid on the polish with a thick hand, I'd have gone cross-eyed long ago. I couldn't keep the curl from my lips though, and Chan Sha saw it.

"And you, Buc? How was your breakfast?"

"Well enough," I admitted. I was Servenzan, so fish for breakfast wasn't unusual, but everything on board tasted of smoke or pickle or dry dust. "Certainly nicer without the fat one reminding me what an honor you've bestowed upon us." Eld's eyes popped, so I added, "Not that it isn't an honor. Captain." The last sounded pulled from my mouth, which wasn't far from the truth, but if Chan Sha heard my reluctance, she didn't acknowledge it.

"I've never met a quartermaster who wasn't difficult to get along with. Ours might top the lot, but we're always in good supply, so there's that. I thought it might be better to ease you all together, though, and it seems I was right."

"Our thanks," Eld said quickly, before I could reply.

Chan Sha took it with a nod and glanced at the cannon her crew was running back into its gunport. "You say you were only a day in Port au' Sheen?"

"Closer to two by the time they'd written everything out," Eld said.

"And how came you from the Empire?"

"By ship," I said.

"I mean, what was her name?" Chan Sha said.

"Oh." I shrugged. "The biggest ship I've been on and that's about all I can tell you. Before that it was gondolas and the odd barge."

"Fat and slow," Eld said. "Or so it seemed to us, but we didn't have much choice in timing or funds."

"Cheating will deal you those cards," Chan Sha agreed. "So you're what, three weeks out from the Empire?"

"That's about right," I said. "Give or take a few days—my head's been turned upside down from it."

"Last I heard from the Empire, Normain was massing troops inland," Chan Sha said. "Was the talk of war when you left?"

Eld frowned. "The opposite; there's been no movements that I've heard of since that dustup two years back. Trade has been fair to all, if heavier in the Empire's favor. There're skirmishes from the Burning Lands, of course, and talk of the Free Cities banding together, but there's always that kind of talk."

"Well, our news is old and secondhand at best, often as not."

"Aye, I'd've thought there'd be more ships around these parts," I said. "From the papers, the sugar trade sounds like a congested behemoth of boats moving between the Shattered Coast and the mainland. Is it always like this?" I asked. I could have been asking about the weather, so easy did I make it.

"Not always, no," Chan Sha said. "But we're nearing high summer in these climes and that means hurricanes more often than not. You've got to steer a careful course then, Buc." She scratched her nose with a dark-lacquered nail and glanced down to me. "And there are some that prefer not to risk it."

So she knew I wasn't asking about the weather. I saw Eld's mouth twitch, trying to slow me down, but if she wanted to be this open, then I would take all the space she gave me. The time for hesitation was about to pass us by if it hadn't already. If we took too long to find proof, we might as well have never found any. "Hurricanes, eh?"

"Aye, not like they were a few centuries ago, when the Shattered Coast was a thing of legend and every ship that entered these waters was sunk by hurricanes the size of Cordoban and larger. But"—she sighed—"even a small hurricane dwarfs a ship, and in high summer there are no small hurricanes."

"I read a book once," I said slowly, as if the thought was just coming to me. *One forty-three.* "Volker's *Where the Gods Fear to Step,* I think it was. He claimed to have discovered religious documents detailing a conspiracy whereby fanatics triggered the Seasons of Flame and Ash. He believed that they intentionally caused the volcanoes to erupt and that these blasts let out enough heat and smoke that the world cooled. It wreaked havoc on the weather and the crops in the years that came after, in the Seasons of Famine." I shrugged. "It also ended the hurricanes."

"Religious fanatics, you say?"

"Adherents of the New Goddess, aye."

"Sin Eaters?"

"That's what Volker believed. Ciris awoke less than a hundred years before the Season, and the Dead Gods had had millennia to do whatever they pleased instead of lurking in their temples with Shambles and Veneficus to guard their secrets."

"'The Gods are like the sea,'" Eld quoted. "'Fathomless.'"

"It wouldn't be the first time mages played a tune for themselves and didn't give a fig that it set the world on fire," I said. "What better way to undermine the Dead Gods than to create hardship and heartache across the continents?"

"Fathomless," Eld repeated. He hesitated, then added, "I don't doubt their followers are just as easily misunderstood."

"Aye," Chan Sha said, seizing the bait. "They're like pirates in that regard. Little reckoned and often blamed."

I let her words hang on their own for a few moments, as if considering them. I hadn't been sure if Eld would stick to the points I'd outlined this morning, but so far he was playing along. If Chan Sha was in league with the Dead Gods, she was likely a believer and I've yet to meet a person who, when confronted with a different worldview, won't stop to take the time and correct it. Even when it needs no correcting. Maybe especially then.

"You say there are too few ships along these lanes," Chan Sha continued when I didn't challenge her. "And you're right: they are less than usual. Who gets blamed for that?" She tapped her chest. "Pirates."

"To be fair, you did sink the ship we were on," I said.

Chan Sha laughed. "Aye, true enough, but we never meant to blow her out of the water. Force her to give over, board her, and take what we needed—aye, that's the pirate's way. But sinking a ship never filled a lass's pockets nor her belly. No ships means no pirates."

"Then why sink so many?" I asked.

"And who says we have?" she shot back. She shook her head and the match locks danced in her dark braids. "Little reckoned, as I said. You say the mages are fanatics who played havoc with things better left untouched, but they did us all a favor, says I. Without cooling the air, they wouldn't have tamed the hurricanes and then there would have been no profits, no island paradise, no freedom, and no pirates." She laughed. "And no Chan Sha."

"I hadn't thought of that before," I said slowly. Which was true, I hadn't. Because who gave a fuck what happened a few centuries ago? I cared enough to know how it informed today, but thinking about what might have been otherwise wasn't in my nature. "Still, I must admit, going from plantation owner to a convict with a death sentence and now your . . ."

"Honored guest," she supplied.

"If you say so," I said. "Going from that to this feels like neither profit nor paradise."

Chan Sha studied me. "We've a saying on the seas. 'A change of breeze is but a wave away.' I could have left you floating in the sea like driftwood, but I didn't. Still, I can do more and I will." She pointed toward the door that led to her quarters. "I'll have baths prepared within the hour. Lay out your things and we'll have them cleaned and returned to you. It might not fill your sails, but I've found sloughing the dirt off helps give a new perspective."

"That sounds excellent!" Eld said, grinning.

"It does," I said, surprised to find myself agreeing with Eld. I could feel the salt caked on my skin, thick enough I'd've thought it would turn me into Eld's twin. If he were a couple years younger. And my clothes were stiff with dried dirt, sweat, and even more salt.

"Good, give my sailors the turn of the bell and find Gem. He'll handle things with our beloved quartermaster and you can join me for a light repast after." She looked into my eyes. "Perhaps you'll start to see that we're not so different, Buc, you and I. Pirates. Gamblers. Women."

"Perhaps," I said, but I spoke it to the wind because she was already moving, calling for Gem.

"I followed your lead," Eld said.

"You usually do," I muttered. I touched his elbow. "I should have developed a better approach—I practically threw my words down her throat. You provided the counterbalance necessary to lessen that weight."

"Thanks, Buc." He sounded mildly surprised, but it was hard to read his face with the reddish-blond scruff that had grown over it. "A draw, do you think?"

"She didn't give us much," I said. "If anything, she spoke in favor of Ciris, but if Chan Sha is behind the disappearances and sinkings, I don't know why she'd try to hide it." I fingered the stiff sleeve of my dress that showed below my coat cuff. It'd been white once, but was barely lighter than my skin now. "Still, hot baths and fresh clothes. I'd say point to us."

"Aye, things are finally looking up," Eld said.

23

"I have to admit, I'd forgotten how much just being clean changes things."

"I think you were dirtier than when I first met you," Eld said from the other side of the sheet that hung between us. Water splashed and he started humming again. "I'll just be glad to get this damnable itchy scruff shaved off."

I laughed and sank back into the water. The bath was really just two barrel halves put together and Eld likely had to scrunch his knees up, but even with the water growing tepid and turning dark from the dirt that had been caked on me, it felt good to be clean again. When that hag of a quartermaster came back with our clothes, it would be even nicer. Eld's razor made a rhythmic sound and I closed my eyes for a while, letting the remaining tension leech from my muscles.

"You know, I think Chan Sha is going to take us on as crew," I said. "Granted, that means we'll have to work the decks and we've little enough experience there, but it's the best alternative for now. At the very least, I don't think she intends to send us over the rail. It'd be a lot of wasted effort at this point. Don't you think?" I used a brush to scrub at a spot on the back of my arm. "Eld? You shaving your lips or something?"

It's too quiet. The sounds of his shaving had stopped at some point and I'd been too relaxed to realize.

The curtain parted, revealing Gem holding a cocked pistole pointed at Eld's face, which was red from anger or embarrassment, I wasn't sure which. Beside Gem, the leering quartermaster had something hanging from her fleshy hand. She cackled as oilskin parchment unrolled itself in the lamplight. I didn't have to squint to see what it was: The last time I'd seen such parchment had been upon leaving Servenza. It was the letter of writ, giving us a stake in the Kanados Trading Company. I'd given it to Eld to hide when I got seasick. I glanced past her toward the deck and it all made sense. I wanted to scream. It should have all made sense hours ago.

"The captain is a riddle, girl," the quartermaster said. "Mayhap she just wanted you nice and clean for the sharks. We don't like spies, do we, Gem?"

"We don't," he agreed. The burly first mate didn't quite meet my eyes, but the pistole was steady in his fist. "The two of you are going to get up nice and slow; nothing stupid, or the smart portion of Mister Eld is going to end up sliding down yonder wall. Then we'll go talk to the captain."

"You searched our things at breakfast but couldn't find anything," I said to the quartermaster. "So if we had anything, it had to be on us." I splashed the water with the brush in my hand. "Ergo the baths."

"Captain did say we'd take the full measure of you," she said. "I knew there was something off on you the moment you refused the eel. Anyone who would insult the captain at her own table." She shook her head and her cheeks moved with the motion. "Well, you weren't worthy of the honor you—"

The brush flew from my hand and took her full in the face, turning the rest of her words into a squawk. I'm good with my hands—it's why I prefer knives over swords. Swords are more about wrist and leg work, and while I'm nimble enough, my fingers are more so. That's also why I'm better with pistoles and slingshots.

I'd intended to put the brush off the side of her head and send her reeling into Gem so Eld could finish him off. A risky move, given the pistole aimed at his head, but anytime someone has you cornered with nothing but your own skin, risks are allowed. So long as I'm the one taking them.

My hands were wrinkled and pruny from the water and the brush was slick with soap, spoiling my aim. Instead of knocking the woman out and into Gem, I only smashed her nose. The brush sank into her flesh and bounced back with almost as much vigor as when I'd thrown it, and I dropped into the water to avoid catching the handle across my head. When I came back up, the quartermaster was clenching her nose with both hands, blood seeping between her fingers, and our writ lay on the floor.

"You widdle bitch," she moaned. "I'll see you—"

"I understand the toss," Gem said conversationally, "but even if she can be a lot to handle, she's our quartermaster." He spoke to a point just over my head. "You're just lucky I didn't blow your friend's brains out in the bargain. My hands sweat when I'm about to kill someone," he added.

Gods. He thought I was being a petulant little girl and didn't realize what I'd been attempting. *Lucky.* A sigh slipped from my lungs. Eld's knuckles gripped the sides of his barrel so hard that his skin almost looked translucent and every muscle was tensed, like steel coils waiting to loose. He'd known what I had been going for. A moment later his muscles relaxed and he went from looking imposing and on the edge of violence to what he was: a man caught in the bathhouse without so much as a scrap to cover himself with.

"You're lucky you didn't hurt her worse or the captain would have the pair of you shot here and now," Gem continued. "She protects her own. Now, Eld, you're going to get up first and let her—Gods, woman, it was only a brush," he growled at the quartermaster, who was still mumbling garbled threats between her hands. "She's going to tie you up. I'll keep the pistole on you so Buc here doesn't get any more ideas. I won't watch," he added.

"Watch what?" I asked.

"You getting out of the water," he said. "We've towels to wrap around you while we take you belowdecks."

"And what happens there?" Eld asked.

"Bad things," the quartermaster said. She lowered her hands, revealing a crooked nose with a bruise that looked like a dark smudge mid-beak. "Deliciously bad things."

"So you won't watch my naked body get out of the water, because that would be improper, while taking me to be tortured and murdered?" I asked.

"We're pirates, not savages," he said by way of explanation.

"Oh, we should suggest the captain maroons them on one of the islands the savages live on," the quartermaster cooed. She glared at me. "I hear they've a taste for human flesh."

My fingers ached for another brush to throw.

24

"There's got to be a better place to hide that oilskin than sewn into your sword belt," I said.

"We're back to that again?" Eld asked beside me in the darkness.

"Learning from your mistakes is rule number one," I said.

"You say that a lot, you know?"

"Then why are you surprised I'm trying to figure it out?"

"No, not that." Eld sighed. "You've a lot of rule number ones. Must be close to forty-seven of them at this point."

"You've been counting?"

"It's just a figure of speech, Buc."

"Seems rather specific, is all I'm saying." I tried to twist more toward him, but the shackles around my wrists were strung too tightly to the ceiling above and the ones on my ankles had just enough play to let the tips of my toes touch the floorboards. The thin bit of cloth they'd given us barely allowed for modesty and did nothing at all to keep the damp air from seeping into our skin. "I haven't had the time or inclination to sit down and hammer out a pecking order. All my rule number ones are important."

"Uh-huh. Well, you're the one who gave me that belt, remember? You even said the hidden pouch would come in handy. I thought it had," he added. "It's not my fault they found the writ."

Isn't it? "I suppose not," I said aloud. If I was going to claim leadership of our duo in the good times, I guess that means I get that pleasure in the bad as well. *Should have claimed modesty and hid it in his underclothes when we went into the baths.* I hadn't ever once thought to ask where he'd stowed it away. *Too seasick.* "It all goes back to that damned Cannon Ship," I muttered.

"What's that?" I heard his irons grind together as he turned toward me.

"Never mind," I said. "How long you think we've been down here?"

"Well, it wasn't too long past breakfast when they took us, so I'm guessing it's going on dinnertime. Chan Sha probably wants to enjoy her sport on a full stomach," Eld said.

"So long as one of us is comfortable."

"So what's the plan?" he asked.

"Plan?"

"Aye, you've got one, right? You always have a plan."

"I have many plans," I said before my silence became obvious. And I did, but none of them started with me hung by my wrists in the blinding dark hold of a pirate ship. "I thought that gaolship would be the last time we were strung up in a hold in chains, but at least this time we only have to worry about our own skins and not some snot-nosed noble's son in the bargain."

"He was a pain in the arse, wasn't he?"

Our laughter cut off as soon as it started. Chains and pitch darkness tend to have that effect. "I've plans, Eld, but I can't make the first move."

Eld grunted and fell silent. Even in the poorest dregs of Servenza, there was light to be found, but in the bottom of Chan

Sha's boat, it was so dark that the only color I saw was the spots dancing before my eyes. Even that didn't seem real, because I discovered if I closed my eyes, I saw the same spots as when my lids were open. Sound was magnified, so that I could feel the beat of my heart in the back of my throat and feel my thoughts pressing against my temples, fighting to break free of my skull. I half fancied I could hear Eld's heartbeat as well, but that *had* to be fancy. The sounds of the sea parting before the ship filtered through the wood, and it didn't take much imagination to realize that there were only a few planks between us and unfathomable depths. *Gods, but I hate ships.* Servenzan gondolas had lured me into believing otherwise, but they were pale imitations compared to the real thing.

"Maybe the darkness *is* the torture," I said. The sounds retreated from the echoes of my voice, but the spots remained. "Leave us down here for a few days and we'll be willing to talk, all right."

"I won't talk," Eld said. "Unless that's part of the plan, but if it is, you better speak up now."

"You'll know where to jump in," I told him. I hadn't the faintest idea of when that would be, but he was good on his feet so long as I didn't push the lies too far. "You always do."

"Your confidence in me is inspiring," he muttered. "But—"

I heard a door open, and a moment later a dim red circle appeared, hovering just below eye level. The door closed with a dull thud and the light drew closer, quivering as it moved. I could hear footsteps, several pairs, almost as if the vibrations of their movement painted a picture with my ears. I didn't even have to close my eyes to visualize them walking toward us. A little bit ago I'd been dreading the endless darkness, but now that they'd shown up I wasn't so sure the dark was that bad after all. It's hard for a color to make you bleed.

"Realized the error of your ways?" I called. My voice sounded hoarse to my ears. I cleared my throat and answered my own question. "Of course you have—I told you we paid for a share and so we did, worthless as it proved to be."

The figures, for I could just make out rough outlines of bodies in the faint glow—or maybe one outline for all of them—said nothing, but moved closer until I could see the red scarf hung over the shielded lantern. I opened my mouth to poke them again, but there was quick movement and the world exploded in harsh light that burned my eyes and stilled my tongue. Eld cried out beside me and I felt my chains dig into my flesh as my body betrayed me, fighting to cover my eyes from the unbearable brightness.

"It is funny how too much of something after it's been long withheld carries beauty and pain in equal measures, isn't it?" Chan Sha asked. "Even with your eyes closed, this must burn like a thousand suns."

"Maybe a few hundred," I growled, but I couldn't keep the tears from pouring down my face, revealing the lie. Orange blazed beyond my clenched eyelids. "Parlor tricks," I added.

"That's what most of torture is." Gem's voice sounded from my left, close to Eld.

"And we have to start somewhere," Chan Sha added.

"You've made a mistake . . ." I began.

"Several, in fact," she said, "but you've made one more than I have. You named your plantation, but that name wasn't Kanados. I hear they pinch and squeeze and might make you disappear if you bother them enough, but they don't renege on deals. Your writ isn't for a plantation, either. So why don't you tell me about that?" she asked.

"Bugger off."

Something hard and wet pounded into flesh and Eld grunted.

"Aye, keep your flinty tongue, girl," Chan Sha said. "Gem has strange notions on hurting young girls, but grown men? Not so much. So say on."

"A writ is a writ," I growled. "What if I said we couldn't read?"

Something whipped through the air again and Eld's breath left him in a gasp.

"I'd say those who can't read don't quote books to me over dinner," she said. "Like to try another lie?"

"We bought a writ off a man who said he'd bought it off the Kanados Trading Company," I said. "He claimed he needed money and he was selling cheap. It wasn't all that cheap, but it offered the chance we'd been looking for."

"You didn't verify the transaction with the Company?"

"What, and pay their fees?" I snorted. "That'd cost half again what the writ did. Two days later we had another flash a writ at us, a woman this time, tried to pay for her toss at the table with a writ that read like ours."

"Like yours?"

"Word for fucking word. It was then we started to realize something might be amiss."

"I'd wondered longer than that," Eld said, his voice tight with pain. He always knew when to make an entrance.

"So we backtracked, ended up following a trail of these writs," I said.

"Right to the docks," Eld added.

"Aye, turns out our Company man had sold a score of these things, not worth the paper they're written on. And then ran for the Shattered Coast."

"Interesting," Chan Sha breathed. "Then why not tell me this in the first place? Why the lies?"

"Because we're fools either way . . ." I began.

"But we're worse fools if you know the truth," Eld said.

"The rest was truth," I added. "We spent our last coin getting to Port au' Sheen, but couldn't find the bastard, and after a week it became clear we weren't going to make our money back tossing dice there, so we borrowed—"

"Stole," Chan Sha corrected.

"Stole that schooner," Eld said before I could go another round with her. "And it's been downhill ever since."

"Sounds like it went downhill the day you bought the writ," she said. "All you had to do was look at the seal placement and you'd have seen it wasn't there."

"What?" My eyes snapped open of their own accord. Lights popped across my vision from the lantern, but I forced myself to focus on the woman with the braids in front of me. "What seal?"

"The notarized seal—that's what you pay all the money for, not the scrap of paper it's written on. This one isn't sealed, so it's fucking useless." She glanced at the oilskin parchment in her hands and snorted. "Gods, it claims you'd be a Board member. They give those seats out over their graves."

"I said we were fools," I whispered. *That Company bitch!* She'd fucked us before we even left port—we'd been working for free this whole time and not even realized it. And now we were about to be tortured for free too. Laughter, unbidden, bubbled up to my lips.

"That's amusing?" the other woman asked.

"I was worried about looking the fool and I didn't even know what a fool looked like until now," I said, unable to keep the laughter from my voice. "You might as well shoot us both and be done with it."

"I very well might," she said, giving me a toothy smile as she rolled the writ back up into a tube.

"We told you the truth," Eld said. He was naked, save for a scrap of dirty cloth that hung around his hips and stopped well above his knees. A red bruise stood out on either side of his ribs. "What more do you want?"

"What more do I want?" she repeated. She tapped the tube against her pink lips. "Very well. I want to know why a brig carrying criminals back to the Empire for execution departed Port au' Sheen in the north, eschewed every trade route that led to Servenza, and came south instead." She leaned forward so that the lantern illuminated her face, her cheekbones obscuring her mouth in shadow. "I want you to stop lying to my face like I'm another simpleton you can throw weighted dice at. I want," she continued, her voice rising. "Gem!"

Gem stepped forward and swung a sodden knotted rope, water sluicing off it as he swung it back and forth in a figure eight until it blurred into one motion and then Eld jerked and screamed through his teeth and the rope flew back to Gem's side, blood dripping from its end. The first mate's face was hard, his eyes inscrutable, but I saw his hand clench and unclench unevenly.

"You." Eld took a shuddering breath but didn't cry out despite the livid bruises across his sides. "You didn't break them." He took another breath and stared straight into the other man's eyes. "You have to swing harder if you want to do that."

"Gem!" Chan Sha's smile was as wide as it had been a moment before, but I didn't need to see her eyes clearly to know it hadn't reached that far. "You heard the man."

"Wait!"

"I don't think so," she said.

"Hit him again, cunt, and you can save us all the trouble and blow our brains out here and now," I growled. "Or you can release us and I'll tell you everything and if we're wrong, you can beat us to death and wear our skins and change your name to some other batshit crazy moniker, or do whatever the fuck else it takes to make your smile actually mean something."

"Gods." Gem's whisper was loud in the silence that followed.

"You toss dice with that tongue?" Chan Sha asked.

"Not for very long," I said. "Usually it takes more to get me worked up." I jerked the chains. "Though, usually, I'm not strung up like a fish for gutting."

"I'm not going to release you for telling poor lies," she said. "But I'll keep Gem from Eld while you tell me better ones. Or you could tell me the truth and then maybe I will release you."

"I'll tell you the truth and you release us and give up your plans for torturing and murdering us," I said.

"You're really not in a position to bargain," Chan Sha said. "My deal is that Eld stops bleeding now, not that you won't both bleed later." She twisted one of the match cords in her hair. "Take it or be damned."

"We didn't steal a schooner," I said finally. My attempt to stare her down didn't seem to be working and the bitch was right: I didn't have anything to bargain with, save staving off the pain for a later time. Despite Eld's blind faith in me, I didn't really have a plan. But if there was no opportunity now, I'd just have to stall until one presented itself. Which meant the truth, or a version of it. I'm not sure I'd have given her the whole truth if she had lit a fire underneath me. There's something in me that would rather burn than give over. So, the truth. Ish.

"No?"

"No. We went to the Harbormaster, as she's the Company's representative in that midden heap. Explained our predicament and asked for reparations." I snorted. "That sailed as smoothly as you might expect."

"Worse, actually," Eld grunted. Pain hung on the edge of his voice. "I should have listened and stolen that schooner instead."

"Aye, well." I tried to shrug in my chains. "The Harbormaster accused us of forgery and bribery and threatened us with debtor's prison."

"That sounds about right," Chan Sha said. "She's a cold one."

"Colder than you," I agreed. "But she also offered an alternative. Seems the Company is boiling over because their sugar shipments keep disappearing and that heat was being directed at the Harbormaster, as she's in the Shattered Coast and they're back in the Empire. No one talks to the Harbormaster, though, especially pirates. So she sent us to nosing around and . . ." I told Chan Sha of the meeting at the tannery, changing some of the details and leaving out the Dead Gods entirely, but letting her know that some madman had broken it up and another madman of the dying sort had implicated her in the disappearances. "We gave the Harbormaster the information."

"And she put us on a brig and sent us south to find you," Eld said.

"I still don't understand that part," I said, letting honest confusion touch my words. Or what passed for honesty. "I'm not sure if she didn't trust the captain or she was trying to punish us further or what. But next thing, we were on a ship heading south, straight for the route where no ship has made it through in months. Straight to you."

"And you did sink the ship we were on," Eld said.

"After you overtook us. Makes me think maybe that dying pirate wasn't mad after all," I finished.

Chan Sha kept rolling the match cord between her fingers as we spoke, but there was a new tightness around her eyes. Their dark orbs shone brightly in the lamplight. "I've been keeping ships away from the sugar routes, it's true. But your ship and a few others that wouldn't take the hint aside, I've not been behind the disappearances."

"Come again?"

"Keeping word of the truth from spreading doesn't mean we're the cause," Gem said. "It's not been Chan Sha. Nor other pirates."

"If not you or your brethren, then who?" I asked.

Chan Sha dropped the match cord and shook her braids out. "A ship that flies red sails and a black flag."

"You said it wasn't pirates."

"It's not a pirate ship," Chan Sha said. "It's a ghost ship."

Her words hung in the air for several breaths.

"A ghost ship?" Eld said at last, shaking his head. "I've never heard of such a thing."

"Of course not—that's the word I've been preventing from spreading," she said. "It's crewed by the undead, so they don't want for hunger or thirst nor feel pain. And their captain is a Dead Walker. . . ." She shuddered, and for the first time I saw real emotion on her face. "He sends them against every ship that touches this route. Builds his crew with the ships he captures and sends the rest to the depths. So, a ghost ship."

"You've been putting yourself between him and the rest of the world, haven't you?" I asked. Eld cracked his neck turning to look at me, but I already knew the answer.

"If the world finds out they've something to fear more than pirates, instead of ships rolling over at the first exchange of fire, they'll start to fight." She snorted. "Contrary to your experience, I prefer not to sink ships. It's bad for business and draws the wrong kind of attention."

"The warship kind," Gem said. "That's the other half of it. If the nations know the Dead Gods are involved, half will send their ships to destroy them and half will send their ships to save them. And the companies will fight to clear their precious sugar routes. The sea will run black with powder and red with blood."

"You're not allied with the Gods?" I asked.

"Fuck no," Gem spat. "If we were, we wouldn't be running from the sight of every sail that looks too dark to be white."

His words sounded sincere and I'd observed more lookouts in the rigging than the *Sea Dragon* ran. *But.* That pirate with half his insides torn out had been sure Chan Sha was in league with the Dead Gods. The number of ships disappearing had made me expect to find a flotilla, not a single ship . . . but a ship crewed by the undead was a different story. I felt my eyes narrow, but in the light cast by the lantern, I don't think anyone noticed. Maybe Chan Sha was allied, but her crew wasn't. . . . They could be playing the game from both sides. But what was the game? Why keep everyone away from the south?

"Why does this ghost ship only sink ships along the sugar trade routes?" Eld asked.

"We don't know," Chan Sha said. "It could be they aim to keep sugar from the mainland and crash the world economy."

"Or maybe they plan to take advantage of that," I said. It made a certain kind of sense. The Dead Gods had Shambles, undead, and that would make for a large enough crew to cause some damage. Damage to the trading companies that had begun to rely heavily on Ciris's Sin Eaters. *I knew I should have picked up that book on sugar production.* I understood enough to know how sugar was farmed by the destitute or indentured and how it was processed, but not enough about the inner workings of it all. Still, I knew plenty about trade, supply and demand. "You could make a lot of coin betting against sugar if you knew it was going to fail."

"Maybe they want to set up their own Empire in the south?" Eld asked.

"Aye, or they're just fucking mad," Gem said. "We've considered all the options, but none seem any more likely than the other. In the end, it don't matter. Run afoul of the ghost ship and its captain will either claim your soul or extinguish it."

Gem was right: We'd gone around most of these scenarios back in Servenza with the Trading Company bitch and gotten nowhere. We'd spent the better part of our two weeks jumping from one disaster to the next and I'd thought we were on the right track. I didn't expect Chan Sha to spill her life's ambitions to us in the bottom of her ship, but I'd hoped to get enough confirmation that all we had to do was kill her and escape . . . after getting out of these irons. A tall enough order . . . .

Now it seemed we'd been pointed in the wrong direction the entire time. And, unlike the dead, who can have motives ranging from complex machinations to pure spite, I couldn't see an advantage in the live pirates lying to us. Not when they had us dead to rights. *I believe her, damn it.* We were no closer to ending this than before we left Servenza. The thought rankled.

"So now you know the truth," I said, bringing the conversation back around. "You'll release us?"

"I believe you," Chan Sha said, nodding. "Or most of it, anyway. But I can't just let you join my crew; things have gone too far for that."

"The chains?" I asked.

"And the beating," she said. "I don't trust that you'll let that go." *She knows me well.*

"I can be persuaded to do any number of things," I said. "You've caught me in a very amiable mood."

"Be that as it may," she said, "no. You were trying to kill me and my crew, after all, blackmailed into it or not."

"Kill you?" I shook my head. "Didn't you wonder why the *Sea Dragon* didn't use its mortar? She could have dropped bombs on your head while you were still drifting into cannon range. But the mortar stayed silent, because of me."

"You?" Gem asked.

"Both of us," I said.

"More her than me," Eld admitted. "She rode the captain hard. It was Buc's idea to try to use your size against you rather than sink you at distance."

"I saved your ship," I said, forcing Chan Sha to meet my eyes. "Isn't there a debt there?"

"There are debts and then there are debts," the woman said. She wasn't smiling, but her face didn't tell me anything more than that. "I still won't allow you to join my crew and I can't just set you ashore. 'Loose lips sink ships, but still lips none at all,'" she quoted. "I won't skin you though. Nor will I torture you further."

"Then what?" Eld asked.

Usually I'm the one with the insatiable curiosity, but for once I didn't feel the need to hear her answer. Anytime a plan hinges on honor and doing the right thing, you know you've run out of options and are tossing the dice because it's the only freedom left to you. All say they will do the right thing until the blade is at their throat. And sometimes the blade doesn't have to be there; they need only imagine it. Chan Sha seemed to have a great imagination.

"The sharks," Chan Sha said. "I'll give you the night to get your thoughts in order. Tomorrow, you swim."

Sometimes I hate being right.

25

The warm breeze blew Chan Sha's braids back as they came up on deck at dusk, carrying with it the smells of salt and pitch, steam and brine. Her mouth twitched toward a smile, against her will. The sea always did that to her. Even on a day like this, long and difficult, if unsurprising. The breeze promised a hint of chill later, but by then she'd be in bed with a blanket or three tossed over her. *Remind Gem to see the lads and lasses have an overcoat near to hand.* The nights this close to the islands were warmer than most, but after the sweat-sucking heat of the day, they felt cooler. Tonight would feel more than cool.

Her crew was good, but many couldn't think past the point of a blade and she'd yet to meet a pirate that wasn't a misery when sick. Lanterns began to flicker to life as the second day shift tidied up before heading down, giving the night watch the light needed to work as the *Widowmaker* plowed through the spray.

A happy accident that the girl didn't know Cordoban as well as she thought, or that could have given me more trouble than I need at the moment. Had she known that calling the ship *Widowmaker* would have tarred her with the same name, she might have made a different choice all those years ago. Gem cleared his throat, pulling her out of her reverie, and she glanced at the first mate, whose features were partially hidden by the fading light.

"What did you think?"

"I think they was telling the truth," he said, lighting a kan cigarillo as he spoke. "Leastways, fer the most part. Enough as it doesn't matter much at all." He glanced at her and blew a stream of smoke past his pursed lips. "Will you release them in the morn?"

Chan Sha leaned against the railing and scanned the deck. She knew what she should do . . . and yet.

"Blood of the Gods," the quartermaster snorted as she joined them from across the deck. "Release them?" She spat over the side. "I was wondering why you didn't just slit their throats and let them bleed out down below. They were trussed up like hogs— might as well have finished the thing then and there."

"Oh, aye?" Gem inhaled deeply, the cherry glow illuminating his unshaven cheeks. "That would have left one damn fine mess to clean up after, wouldn't it? Fish guts, woman," he growled, sending another stream of smoke past his mouth.

"Fish guts is right," the quartermaster shot back. "They likely wouldn't have eaten the stew for tonight anyway, not after the pair of them turned their swiney noses up at the eel."

"That's not fair," Gem said. "Eld choked down that slobby knob like nobody's business."

Chan Sha chuckled and Gem guffawed another plume of smoke from his lungs. The quartermaster eyed the pair of them askance. *She has a priest's sense of humor.* Which probably wasn't fair to the priest. But the woman was more than prickly, and there was still enough light left with the lanterns for her to see the quartermaster working herself up to another explosion. "I won't release them," she said a moment before the other woman went off. "And it's not because of the eels," she added, which snapped the quartermaster's teeth together. "You promised you'd have those reports on the bales of silk from last fortnight's haul to me yesterday. Are they ready for me to read before I turn in?"

"W-well, I . . . I." The quartermaster licked her lips. Her loose skin shook as she turned away. "I've been busy, Captain. That is to say, I've been doing your work, Chan Sha. I'll have those reports to you by—"

"The last evening bell?" Chan Sha prodded. The other woman froze; clearly she hadn't put pen to paper or, more likely, hadn't even gone to that cargo hold to begin. *Unusual for her.* "The crew won't thank us if we don't handle their interests well, Quartermaster. You know this is true."

"Too right it is," Gem muttered.

"I haven't seen a report on the rum barrels, either. Could you find the time for a sounding?"

"Gods, woman!" Gem rounded on the quartermaster. "Do you want a mutiny on our hands?"

"I told you, I've been busy!" the woman snapped. The next moment, she began apologizing so rapidly that it took Chan Sha a full minute to get a word in.

"Easy, easy," she said. "The crew trusts you. I trust you." Chan Sha's fingers found one of the match cords amongst her braids and twirled it as she studied the other woman. It was a calming routine for her, but she'd noticed early on that it made others nervous, more willing to please. The quartermaster needed it less than most, but she *was* slipping. And the stakes were too high for that. "Now, we'll leave you to your reports."

"Of course, Captain. Of course," the older woman stammered. She almost sketched a curtsy. *A curtsy!* She spun on her heel and disappeared down into the hold in a flurry of skirts.

"She hasn't even bothered to open the bales yet," Gem grunted.

"Agnes is a good crew member," Chan Sha said quickly. Gem smiled and she snorted. "I'm not saying she's not a pain in the arse. She's an unholy pain in the arse. But she's good at what she does." Her smile slipped. "But we're down a second mate, so she's been doing the work of two. You both have."

"Price we pay for keeping the seas clear of sail," Gem said, suddenly as serious as she was. He took another drag on his kan leaf and sighed. "We can't keep word of the Ghost Captain from spreading forever, Chan Sha. We need a plan. One that doesn't involve us sailing back and forth chasing sails."

"Aye, Gem, you're right." She let the match cord slip from her fingers—Gem didn't need incentives—and fought back the angry retort on her lips. *We've been over this before, old friend. Why won't you let it go?* But she knew why. . . . She wouldn't have let it go either, if she were him. Because her plan made no apparent sense. Unless you knew the larger plan. *And I can't trust you with that.*

"We need more information," she said at last. "If only there were some way to find out what that rotting bastard was actually doing, where he goes when he's not sinking ships. . . .

"You've been here the longest, Gem. Gods, you were born in these seas. Have you noticed anything on the map?" Not that she'd seen anything during the half thousand times she'd gone to the map room to stare at the little colored needles pinpricked all across the Southern Expanse. Too random for a pattern and not enough needles to find one, if one did exist. Even with her edge, she hadn't found it. Maybe Gem—

"It's like you said," the first mate responded. He studied the cigarillo, almost smoked down to a nub, and shrugged. "We need more information. Might be we need to give this plan over and go right for said rotting bastard's throat."

"Why, Gem, that's almost poetic of you," Chan Sha said. He guffawed and she smiled.

"I know you don't want to hear it," he continued, "but that girl down there has a brain on her that I haven't seen before, save once." He looked at her sharply. "And that was you. Buc reminds me of you, a little different here and there, but damned close. You consider maybe the two of you could do what one can't?"

"I'd be lying if I said I haven't," she said after a moment. She hadn't realized she'd been considering it until she heard the words, but she *had* been mulling it over. Subconsciously. The girl was smart, no question, almost preternaturally so. If Chan Sha didn't know better, she'd have guessed her a follower of one of the Gods, but that was impossible. *I'd have known. Wouldn't I?* No answer came, so she turned to Gem and shook her braids.

"Did you see her face when I called her out on not forgiving me—us—for the treatment we've given them? Even if she wanted to, I don't think the girl is capable of forgiving that. If the ship was going down, maybe I'd consider unlocking them. Eld, at least, would stand to in a fight." Gem nodded; he'd asked to bring Eld on as crew before they discovered their treachery. "But even then I'd have to think twice." She sighed, then straightened and scratched at where the railing had begun to dig into her side. "It's almost full dark—don't you want to make a round of the crew before heading belowdecks?"

Gem took a final pull of his cigarillo before flicking it over the side. He nodded and spoke in a stream of smoke, "Aye, aye, Captain. But what about the lass's story? What's it mean that someone is saying you're behind all these disappearances? It'll be a small favor if we keep the Ghost Captain's presence quiet but bring the Imperial fleet down on our heads. Who's behind this, do you think?"

"I'm not sure," she lied. "But I intend to find out. . . ." They stood together in silence. "Have you ever heard of a woman what calls herself an Archaeologist?"

"Arch-e-what?" Gem's brow furrowed. "Can't say as I have. Why?"

"No reason," she said quickly, hiding her second lie behind half a smile. "A name I came across in correspondence from that ship's captain a fortnight ago." She grinned. "I didn't know what the word meant either."

Gem shook his head. "Sometimes you can't trust words, Captain. I'll check on the crew, then."

"Oh, and Gem?" The large man paused mid-step. "Make sure the crew has something warm to hand," she said. "There's a chill in the air."

"As you say, Captain," he replied, the smile clear in his voice. "As you say."

She watched him leave. Straightening, she let her gaze roam the decks, but everything seemed up to shape, and if it wasn't, Gem would sort it out. *A good man.* Chan Sha inhaled the briny air again, let it fill her lungs. *A good crew.* A few years ago her loyalties had been easy enough because they had been singular: loyalty. But these tattooed, greasy-haired, sunburnt bastards had wormed their way into her heart. And what should she do when even the Gods were silent? Her ear twitched and she smiled. *Mostly silent.*

Her smile stiffened. She'd taken a risk, mentioning the Archaeologist, long shot that it had been. And another, telling Buc and Eld about the Ghost Captain. *I didn't tell them everything about the Ghost Captain, though.* How could she, when she hadn't told Gem or the others? And loyalties, plural, or no, she couldn't do that. Besides, why tell the pair when they would be shark bait by morning?

"Because I have to tell someone," she whispered.

Because she had to change the equation soon or the sums would keep coming up as they had been since the Ghost Captain appeared. And eventually those sums would come up with her number on them—and her crew's as well. *I can't keep lying to them. I can't keep juggling all these balls in the air.* Her breath hissed between her teeth. Balls? It was more like juggling steel blades or bare flames. Sooner or later there would be a price to pay. *But will I be the one to pay it?* In the end it kept coming back to that damned word: "loyalty." Chan Sha shivered and it had nothing to do with the chill in the air.

26

"She's really painting it on thick, don't you think?" I asked.

Eld looked up from the manacles on his wrists. He'd been fumbling with them since members of Chan Sha's crew had marched us onto the deck and then onto the thin spar they'd fastened out over the side. No leg irons, surprisingly, but given the way the spar danced in the salt-kissed wind, leg irons might have sent us over the side as soon as we stepped out. Besides, the locks on our wrists weren't simple tumbler locks, and without a locksmith's kit they weren't going to open. I told Eld that twice already, but the man seemed to think effort would overcome reason.

"You want her to tell the crew we're Company spies and send us over the side?" he asked, nodding toward where the pirates stood in a circle, listening to their captain.

"If I'm going to die"—I glanced down at the dark water below the thin board we stood on—"and all signs point that way, I'd rather do it and be done. Not listen to her assuage her feelings by spelling everything out to her crew."

"She leads more by reason and logic than she does by sheer

will," Eld said, watching Chan Sha, who was perched on an overturned barrel across the deck, delivering her closing arguments to her willing jury. "I hadn't thought to find that amongst pirates."

"Well, she only has a dozen pistoles on her and there's more than thrice that many crew members, so I don't think she can rely on force alone. Still, does she think throwing us over the side will really upset them? It won't upset the quartermaster, that's for sure."

"No," Eld said, once again bending over the irons around his wrists. "She'll smile to see the sharks take us."

"Well, they better or she'll dive in after them," I said. "Captain's honored you lot," I added, pitching my voice higher and hoarser with a bit of nasal tone added in. "Now tuck in!"

"You do the quartermaster surprisingly well," Eld said. A smile touched his lips despite the hard look in his eyes. He cursed as the bit of metal in his hand slipped and fell down into the water. He looked up. "You really don't have a plan?"

"We're shackled, standing on a pace of wood that wobbles with every rise and fall of the ship and never mind the wind, with sharks circling below us," I said. "What plan could I possibly have?"

"I don't know," he muttered. "You've always had one before. At least they gave us back our clothes."

"Yes, her conscience must really be paining her," I said.

"Gods, there are sharks down there, aren't there?" Eld asked, peering carefully over the edge of the beam. "Did you see a fin? I thought I saw a fin just now."

"Not there," I said. I pointed with my head. "That woman near the prow just dumped a pail of fish guts over the side. Look at the water there." I'd seen three different fins moving about, but as I spoke, another, larger one with a white tip swam through the bloodied water, scattering the other sharks before it.

"Fuck me," Eld whispered. My eyes widened at the curse and he actually blushed. Eld swore as often as I was polite. A wave shook the ship and we both had to bend our knees to keep from pitching off the spar. "Fuck me!" he repeated.

Chan Sha climbed down off the barrel she'd been speaking from. I could no longer pretend I didn't feel fear. We'd gone overboard before the *Sea Dragon* exploded and no sharks had taken us then, but with blood and fresh fish in the water, I didn't think we'd be as lucky this time. Chan Sha pointed at us and the crew split, letting her and Gem and that damned quartermaster through.

"She's finished," I said. The fear was in every limb now, but there was no sense in letting Eld know. "About damned time," I added.

"You're not right," he muttered. His skin was alabaster white, save for some color in his cheeks that looked blue, tending toward purple. "Fuck me, fuck me, fuck me," he whispered.

"You don't want to swim with the sharks?" I asked. "Truly?"

"No," he growled, shooting me a hard look. "And you can't swim—you proved that after the *Sea Dragon*—so you don't want to either."

"Aye." I drew myself up as Chan Sha reached us. "When you're right, you're right." I licked the salt from my lips and raised my voice. "Are you set on seeing us torn limb from limb, or do you want to put an end to this Ghost Captain once and final?" I'd like to say my words were steady and even, but there was a tremor. Put there by the uneven plank I stood upon, of course. Nothing to do with the sharks.

"Nothing's changed since we last spoke," Chan Sha said.

"The captain's done with you lot," the quartermaster added.

I almost told her that I'd go over the side willingly if she would too, but the woman might have obliged me just to please Chan Sha. Instead I gave Eld what he'd been asking for.

"I can turn the Kanados Trading Company's full might on the Ghost Captain," I said. "And I can do it without raising suspicions. So the world is still afraid of pirates and you aren't running from every red sail that crests the horizon."

The crew behind Chan Sha buzzed at that, but Gem shouted them down. Chan Sha said nothing, her hard gaze swinging back and forth between Eld and me. "And why would they do that? Because they pity pirates?" The buzz turned to laughter.

"Why would the Company want others to know the truth?" I asked. "It would hurt their trade even further. They didn't want others to know the truth when they thought it was you; why would this be different?" Chan Sha's eyebrows rose at that and even the quartermaster looked taken aback. "They just need someone to up the scale of their response and point them toward the right target. That someone is me. And Eld," I added.

"Thanks for remembering me," he muttered.

"Don't mention it," I said out of the corner of my mouth.

"Tempting," Chan Sha mused. "But—"

"But nothing. Fly another flag for now. Bring us close enough to a Company ship that I can hail them and I'll give them everything they need to know." I held up my shackled wrists. "If they don't listen to me, you can still kill us. What do you have to lose? A few days wagered on the chance to end your cat-and-mouse game?"

"The lass makes a good point," Gem said.

Chan Sha glanced at him, rolled her eyes, then threw her arms out so her dark cloak revealed the burgundy shirt she wore tucked into pants that hugged her curves. It was the first time I'd seen her real figure, and even wobbling on a thin plank over shark-infested waters, I have to admit my mouth went dry. There's something about beauty, true beauty, that catches you and holds you fast, whether you will it or no. And the bitch had beauty, I had to give her that. I saw Eld's shoulders stiffen in front of me, and the man almost went over the edge before he remembered to bend his knees again.

"Very well," she said. She brought her arms back down, silencing the crew. "Very well. Bring them in and strike their chains. We'll see what Buc's file of a tongue can do when directed at the Kanados Trading Company. We'll see if they want to save us the trouble of sending the undead to the bottom."

The crew let out a throaty, raucous cheer. Gem moved to the rail and offered us his hands.

"Go on." I nudged Eld. "Or did Chan Sha give you a hard-on?"

"It's too cold for that," Eld whispered. Still, he walked more carefully than even a man suspended over a pack of sharks would.

"Lucky for you," I said with a laugh. "I told you I had a plan," I added as Gem reached up to help me down as well. "You shouldn't have doubted."

"I didn't," Eld said. Gem unshackled him and he rubbed his wrists as he grinned at me. "I'd never doubt you, Buc. Should know that by now. Smooth sailing from here, yeah?"

"Aye," I agreed, holding up my wrists for Gem.

"Sail ho!" The lookout's piercing wail interrupted my reply. "Three points off larboard. Heading right for us. Red sails! Gods save us, red sails!"

I looked back over my shoulder as Gem loosed the manacles, and saw a faint crimson smudge on the horizon, visible only because the rising sun had caught it like a drop of blood.

"Gods save us." Gem's voice shook. That, more than his words, sent a shiver down my spine. The sharks were still there. And there was blood in the water.

27

"Mortars," Chan Sha spat the word. The telescope twisted in her hand, gear work moving the end of the piece in and out. "A pair of them, and larger than I've seen before. Not Sin Eaters' work, thank the Gods, but we'll still be in their range well before they're in ours. Damn them." She lowered the telescope and glanced at me with green eyes. "Unless you have a twin on board yonder ship? To keep the mortars silent?"

She laughed at her own joke and clapped Gem on the shoulder. "Then we fight. Give these two back their weapons and arm the others. We're going to double back on ourselves and let the wind drive us right at them; with any luck it will spoil their aim and we'll be in cannon range before they realize it."

"Aye, aye, Captain," Gem said with a fist to his chest.

"C'mon, old friend, it's time to put the crew through their paces," she said. The two of them marched off together and a moment later a crew member ran up with her arms full of knives, pistoles, my slingshot, and Eld's sword.

"Just drop them and get back to it," I said, finishing tying the laces of my dress, which Gem had returned after freeing me. The woman shot me a look, but did as I said before sprinting to where the crew was readying their cannon. Eld didn't have to deal with so many damn laces and so he had his sword sheathed and was fixing his pistoles in his belt before she was a dozen paces away. It took me considerably longer, but hiding a dozen knives on your person isn't easy when you're already dressed. After a day and a night spent in nothing but a threadbare shift, it felt good to be clothed again, dress or no, so I made do. As Chan Sha began to spin her ship around, I picked up my slingshot and nodded to Eld. "Where do you want to make our stand?"

"Not up here," he said. "If they have any muskets, they'll pick us off."

I pointed down toward the barrels of fruit that were secured against one of the smaller masts. "We'll be able to use those for cover." Eld nodded and we set off for the barrels. As we passed another pirate laden with shot and powder horns draped across his sunburned neck, I helped myself to a large pouch of lead balls, two score at least. Meant for muskets, they would do just fine in my slingshot.

"Gods, this is happening faster than I thought it would," he said when we reached our goal.

It was difficult to see the ghost ship as we were pointed right for it, but Chan Sha had begun to change course enough that we would pass within cannon range, so the prow was just barely visible. And Eld was right: it was happening fast. The *Sea Dragon*'s battle had taken several hours to develop and even after the first clash, it'd been close to half a bell before the explosion. Somehow the other ship was moving at an unworldly pace. It would be mere minutes before we closed. We might be in mortar range already.

"Here we go," I muttered. At my words a shrieking, piercing wail filled the air and Eld pulled me down beside him.

"Incoming!" A breath later the sea exploded a score of paces off the starboard bow. Another explosion rained metal and debris down upon the deck rail. Eld cursed. "They're using exploding rounds with a fuse and timer. That second one nearly hit us." He glanced at me and shook his blond hair. "They won't sink us without a direct hit, but if one of those goes off over the ship, it'll scythe through the crew like a blade through wheat."

My reply was lost in a second set of explosions, behind the *Widowmaker*. A roar went up from the crew and I felt myself grinning along with them. "She was right." Eld arched an eyebrow. "We're moving in too fast. Did you see the windage and elevation on the *Sea Dragon*'s mortar?"

"No, but I've seen a mortar before," he said.

His words wiped the smile from my face. In all that had happened I'd managed to forget his admission to the Harbormaster. That he'd spent time in the army. That he was familiar with mages and their magic. That he had a past that was hidden from me. I pushed my unease off. There would be time enough for that, but later.

"Well, assuming all mortar systems are similar," I explained, "it's much easier to adjust to aim farther out than it is to do the reverse. The captain showed me how Sin Eaters made modifications to speed up that process, but on a normal mortar, it's not so simple."

He nodded. "They can't pull their aim down fast enough to get rounds on us now."

"Chan Sha is going to have her cannon fight. And if she's as savvy as I think she is, then she might do our work for us." *Gods, we could be heading for Servenza by the morrow.* The thought was too tempting to give voice to.

"Run 'em out!" Gem's voice carried easily over the deck. He had a bullhorn up against his mouth, with Chan Sha at his shoulder, the pair flanking the helmsman. "Larboard guns, ready. Waterline and deck, you know where to send them. Hold!" Gem didn't turn to watch the approaching ship; he kept his eyes on the crew, the horn pressed to his lips. Chan Sha was focused on the ghost ship, which suddenly came into view on the port side.

Bloodred sails, twice as many as flew above our decks, and another row of cannons made it look like a monster passing in our wake. I could see crew moving around, but if they were undead, it was hard to tell.

"Fire!" Gem cried. The *Widowmaker* shook with a deafening roar and smoke obliterated my vision. "Change over!"

"Switch!" the crew hollered back, and even with the ringing in my ears I could hear the gears and springs whizzing as the cannons flipped over in their carriages, the over-under barrels meaning they could fire a second volley before reloading.

"Fire!"

The ship shook again, but a moment later flames appeared in the haze and a roar louder than either salvo beat the air with fists of lead. Something screamed in the air, clutching at us as it whipped past, and the deck lurched awkwardly. I would have fallen, save that the fruit barrel brought me up short and Eld steadied me with a hand. Another belching line of flames missed us completely and the crew began cheering and pumping their fists in the air until Gem shouted them down.

"Hard over! Hard over and prepare starboard guns. We'll put a round right up their bloody arsehole!" The ship swung around and now a pall fell over the crew as they strained to maneuver the ship, load the guns, and get a bearing on the ghost ship before it turned into firing position. Smoke hung like fog, obscuring the enemy's decks, but their crimson sails were high enough to clear the smoke and point the way.

"Round and grape. Ready. Aim. Fire!" Gem's words were lost

in another cacophony of cannon fire. "Change over! That was a good one, me hearties," he said, although how he could see anything through the smoke was beyond me. "Angle up for the distance. Ready. Fire!" Another blast shook the deck. In the silence after, Chan Sha began sending runners to various parts of the ship so their plans weren't heard by her foes.

"Damned efficient," Eld said, turning in a slow circle. The smoke was so thick now that it was as if the world had shrunk to the size and shape of the deck and everything beyond was mere fog and flame. "She might sink them yet."

"Aye," I said. I could feel the thrill in me, but my brain couldn't stop running and I dug a cigarillo stuffed with kan out of my pocket, but not before several sums occurred to me. Chan Sha was no fool: If the odds were truly in her favor, she would have sailed against the ghost ship weeks ago, or if chance was too close, gathered a coalition of like-minded pirates and attacked en masse. She hadn't done that.

Which meant she didn't think the odds were in her favor. We'd struck first, true, and while we'd taken a blast from the other ship, everything felt fine on deck, not at all like when the *Sea Dragon* was hulled. *But.* Chan Sha wasn't acting like things were anywhere near assured, even if the rest of her crew was.

Gem stood like a silent, hulking shadow beside her, his actions belying his words of encouragement. I struck a match and puffed the cigarillo into life and my thoughts slowed enough that I could begin to distill them into potential actions. I sighed, smoke burning my nostrils. Everything ended with Eld and me in the water.

"They're coming around!" The lookout's cry cut through the thick air. "Fresh cannon right at us."

Chan Sha grabbed the wheel from the helmsman and threw it hard over, swinging the ship so our rear would face their broadside, but ships take time to turn and a few breaths later flame lit the fog and the *Widowmaker* shuddered before the roar of cannon. The ship still moved, but there was a new heaviness to it, not as bad as the *Sea Dragon*'s last moment, but not good.

Eld cursed and I followed his stare to where Chan Sha stood with a wheel that spun freely in her hands. She mouthed something to Gem, then took the bullhorn from him and addressed the crew.

"We've given as good as we got, but that last broadside did something to the rudder," she said, speaking quietly so her voice didn't carry beyond the deck. "I want maintenance over the side with ropes to assess the damage. Until then, we have to assume they're going to board us; that's what they've done with all the other ships." She set the bullhorn down on a railing and pulled matches from her cloak and struck them. The match cords intertwined with her braids began to hiss and spit as they caught.

When she was finished, her dark hair writhed with smoke and flame that framed her figure like a demon from when the Gods still strode the world. "The undead want to come against us, we'll send them back where they belong! Prepare to repel boarders!"

The crew howled with her and suddenly pistoles, muskets, blunderbusses, cutlasses, rapiers, hatchets, and dozens of other implements of war shone in the sunlight that managed to pierce the veil around the ship. As they hurled invectives, Eld drew two pistoles and inspected their clockwork mechanisms. With a slight frown, he tightened the one in his left fist. His eyes were dark, the pupils huge, and I suspected mine looked much the same.

The other ship was larger than ours and if they really had no need for food or water, they could cram as many bodies into the thing as possible, saving room only for powder and ammunition. It's what I would have done if I had an army of undead. It was certainly what the Ghost Captain had done as well. Now I understood why Chan Sha hadn't attacked before. It was suicide.

"Aye," I said. Eld arched an eyebrow. "I have a plan. Several of them." *And none of them good.* "Let's see how this plays out."

"Good enough for me," he muttered, sighting down the barrel of a pistole. "You ever fought a Shambles before?"

"No. You?"

"No, but I heard some who claimed to. . . . Not many get on the wrong side of the dead and live to tell about it." His voice shook, then steadied. "You have to take them in the head. Depending on their level of decay, you can knock limbs off, but they won't stop until you sever the link between their head and body."

"Brain stem," I said.

Eld nodded and scrubbed at the stubble on his cheeks with the back of his hand. "So use your slingshot; don't rely on knives. If you run out, stay behind me."

"If I run out, then the plan has been royally fucked," I said.

"Just keep your back to mine," he replied, but I saw him mouthing my words and a smile tugged at his mouth. Give Eld half a reason and he'll smile, but there's something unique every time, like how no two sunsets are ever quite exactly alike.

"Larboard, here they come!" the lookout yelled. Grapeshot raked the decks and the barrel Eld had pulled me behind quivered. The lookout screamed for real as the mast broke with a sickening crack and fell across the deck. She kept screaming till she tumbled out of the crow's nest and disappeared into the waves.

"All hands to larboard! Maintenance with axes, cut the cloth free or the winds will trip us all up!" Chan Sha hadn't relinquished the bullhorn and her voice was surprisingly calm. "Touch off the cannon and every hand fall to. With a will, me beauties. With a motherfucking will!"

28

The Dead came over the side in a rush of cloth and bone and steel, all the more eerie, for there was no sound. Until there was.

"Fire!" Gem's voice was lost in a volley of gunfire that tore holes in the ragged line of undead. Smoke blossomed like a fist and hid the railing from view, but before it could clear, more bodies appeared. Some moved almost as smoothly as the pirates while others hobbled on yellowed bones covered here and there with some remnant of flesh or tendon or the odd scrap of clothing.

Even the slow ones bore a weapon in each hand.

"Fire!" Gem threw up his musket and fired with the rest of the crew. His blunderbuss hissed as the gears rotated another barrel into place. He fired twice more before the next line of dead came over the railing.

Chan Sha's crew moaned as a hundred more followed. A few of the dead that had tongues moaned back.

"Fire if you have aught left!" Gem strode forward and bent his blunderbuss over the skull of one of the faster Shambles, knocking its neck back at an awkward angle. He swept its legs with a boot and stomped on its neck until the head came free, spraying black ichor across the deck. Hurling away the ruined musket, Gem drew the ax at his side. "Keep 'em on the rails!"

The crew followed suit, but as fast as they were, Chan Sha was faster. One moment she was behind the crew, the next she was at the railing, smoke curling around her with pistoles bucking in each fist as she fired, dropped that pair of guns, found a new pair hanging from the tethers of her cloak, fired again, then dropped them as well. Each time she fired, a headless torso fell back into the ranks of the Shambles or else pitched into the ocean. Gem reached her as she let another brace of pistoles fall.

He took out two with a murderous swipe that matched his roar and then living met dead with only the railing between. Steel flashed and the living screamed while the dead died again.

"Elevensies," I spat, holding out my hand. Eld dropped another lead ball in my palm and I drew my slingshot back, loading and aiming in a single motion. I hesitated, waiting for the dark woman with the flame-dyed hair to finish opening up the face of the Shambles in front of her with a claw hammer. Another undead put a hand on the railing to launch itself at her and I released; its skull whipped back, a dark hole appearing just a touch to the left of where its nose used to be.

A slingshot will kill more often than it won't, at least mine will, but the rotting desiccation of the Shambles meant my lead shot penetrated and kept going—something that wasn't likely, even with a head shot, on live flesh. I'd already killed two with a single shot that way. Thank the Gods for small miracles. The Shambles dropped lifeless to the deck and the pirate buried her hammer in the face of the next corpse. *A wench after my own heart.* "Twelve," I said, holding out my hand again.

"You know," Eld said, striving to keep his voice conversational but it was too tight, too hard to be convincing. "You know, if we moved closer, I could actually do something."

"You are doing something," I said, pulling back and releasing the ball in one motion as a fat pirate went down with a cutlass buried in his face. The Shambles who'd killed him didn't have a chance to enjoy her victory before I sent her plummeting into the gap between the ships. Her green dress, surprisingly clean given her state of decay, sparkled before she disappeared. "Keeping me loaded." He snorted. "Fine, protecting me like you wanted to. Thirteen," I added.

"Aye, but I could protect you up there," he said.

"No, you could die faster up there," I corrected him. The line of living and dead was easy enough to discern—those who were alive wore clothing and those that were dead mostly wore twisted skin and bone. One was loud and the other was silent, save for the scything sounds their weapons made through the air. And one was giving ground steadily while the other was advancing. I didn't have to wait to pick targets now and within moments I had seventeen down. "If it makes you feel better, I don't know that we'll last much longer here."

A ragged volley sounded from above and behind us—the few too ill to work the deck had been given muskets, but it was only now that there was enough space between their crewmates for them to start firing. Another bad sign. A black cloak swept along the railing in a swirling, twirling maelstrom of smoke and steel and the dead fell back, a few decapitated, but most missing hands or entire limbs. Gem followed in Chan Sha's wake with his knotted rope, well soaked in seawater, wiping bodies from the railing and the far deck with every swipe, and where they passed, holes appeared in the army of corpses.

The crew rallied, screaming hoarse war cries, and the railing cleared, save for a few Shambles still moving woodenly forward, heads straight while their limbs flailed. The cries died on the crews' tongues and a breath later there was enough space for me to see why.

A cloaked figure appeared in the middle of the undead, moving too naturally to be one of them. A garish red feather hung from the corner of its tricorne and its features, pale and drawn, but definitely human, and definitely too fresh to be dead, were revealed in a pale blue glow from the book it held, open, in its hands.

The man glanced up, tilted his head so that his goatee jingled from the bells woven through it, then looked back down. The feather in his cap shook from side to side as his head moved. The Shambles all began hissing and when they moved forward again, there was a speed to their gait that hadn't been there before. Or maybe they were fresher than the corpses that had come before. It made sense to spend your furthest gone first, feeding them to fresh troops while holding your reserve in hand. The figure glanced up one more time, then disappeared behind its glowing book.

"It's the fucking Ghost Captain!"

"You don't say," Eld said with a grin. I shot him a glare but his smile had already faded. When I looked back, the railing was consumed by a horde of dead flesh and the pirates were a mere half dozen paces in front of us and giving way fast. My breath caught in my throat. A pistole appeared in Eld's hand and he dropped a Shambles bent over a fallen pirate, twin axes raised. Eld shouted something, but his shot had taken my hearing with it and so I just followed his lead, drawing a pair of stilettos. We rushed in, everyone screaming nonsense around me while I saved my breath to swing.

It's not an easy thing, severing the brain stem of a meat carcass that feels no pain, when all you have to work with is a palm or two of steel. Even when you have a blade in each fist. I can ice pick a man through the heart faster than you can blink and step back, leaving him dead on his feet before his body knows it. Women take a blink on account of their breasts, two blinks if they are especially well endowed. But ice picking wouldn't hurt the dead.

I danced around their swings; the fresher ones were fast, but more awkward for some reason. The Shambles before me had been a lad of my years, judging from the hair and skin left on its cheek. He hissed as he stepped around the lifeless body of a cabin boy younger than either of us. Blood pumped from his neck, staining the deck beneath him. *As old as my sister.* Anger raged through my veins as I launched myself at the undead. We were almost of a height, so he was probably younger than me when he died, but I didn't take it easy on him because of that. Not after he'd murdered that poor child. *Blade to right knee. Fulcrum point then—*

His cutlass nearly caught my curls and I cursed myself for not shaving every hair from my head when I last held a razor. I ducked, plunged both blades into his knee, and heaved. One nice thing about the dead, especially the truly desiccated, is they weigh considerably less than the living. The formerly living lad's knee broke and he fell, losing one of his cutlasses in the process. I trapped the arm holding the other cutlass, flesh shrunken tight against the bone under my boot, and brought both blades down where the last of the skin on his cheek met his nose. The Shambles writhed and I twisted the blades, rage flowing through the steel in my hands, before ice picking his face with a dozen thrusts. What can I say? Old habits die hard.

I stood up, hands covered in black gore, and found myself alone. The pirates had managed to push the dead back again, though not as far as the railing. The dead, both living and formerly unliving, littered the space between their lines. The Shambles were slowed by the debris, tripping and falling, some breaking legs and resorting to pulling themselves forward by their hands. Eld offered me a handkerchief, his chest heaving as he caught his breath, his slightly curved blade dripping black from hilt to tip. I tried to thank him, but Chan Sha cut me off.

"Night crew, fall back to the cabins. We'll make our stand there. Day crew, buy them some time!" She drew a pistole from what looked like her cleavage and shattered the head of a particularly decayed-looking Shambles. "Gem, you know what to do."

"Captain?" The mate's voice carried in the silence.

"Do it," she commanded.

"You lot," Gem said, his shoulders sagging, "follow me. With a will, this has only just begun."

"He means we've lost," I said. Eld arched an eyebrow. "More of these dead bastards keep pouring out of their holds," I said, pointing at the ghost ship. "There's another hundred on their decks at least. Fall back to the cabins? How are you going to escape from there?" I shook my head. It's time we were gone, Eld."

"Gone where?" He pointed over his shoulder. "There's naught but sea out there, Buc. And our whole purpose was to kill whomever is responsible for sinking these ships . . . now they stand a mere hundred paces away."

For the second time that morning, fear took hold. There's a time to cut your losses, to show the enemy your backside and return with a sharp knife when they least expect it. Everything in me screamed this was one of those times, but—but the dead cabin boy leaking his life from the hole in his neck filed my vision. *Sister.* Eld was right: the sea might not offer us much better than a deck half filled with the undead, and the bastard who could end this all and let us return to Servenza was only a ship away.

Return and take over the Kanados Trading Company. Change the world. The sharp smell of burned powder took me back to the night I watched my sister die, and the flames danced before my eyes the way they'd danced then, as they licked at my flesh and hers.

"Buc!" Eld's voice, more than his hands on my shoulders, shaking me, brought me back to reality.

"You're right," I said.

"What?"

"All right, all right." I patted him on the arm, slipping out of his grip as I did so. Tell a man he's right and you'll be months retraining him. "Stay here while I go murder the Ghost Captain."

Eld's shouts chased me as I leapt onto the barrels, thence to the stump of the broken mast, and onto the mast itself. I ran down its length, slipped over to one of the horizontal spars, and in moments I'd crossed the deck and reached one of the smaller masts still standing. I grabbed one of the yards and slashed the other end of the rope with my stiletto.

For a breath, nothing happened, then my arm was jerked almost out of its socket as the halyard ripped me upward, swinging me out just enough that my momentum kept me from colliding with the iron tackle I'd just loosed from up above. I'd wanted to try that ever since I saw a pirate do it. He'd been given a lashing for ruining perfectly good rope, but Gods, it had looked like a fun way to climb. And it was. The wind bit at my face and tears began to leak from my eyes, but then it was over and I was left dangling a span above another crossbar with a sore arm that was fast losing feeling.

I dropped onto the crossbar and ran across it. The sounds of battle reached my ears but didn't feel as immediate, as personal, as they had on the deck. I almost imagined I could wait up here until everything played out beneath me . . . wait and pick up the pieces. But I couldn't. Half the pirates had fled belowdecks and the other half wouldn't last much longer. And Eld was down there, fighting for his life. *Besides, even if the dead lose, they win. There's always more dead after a fight. This was lost the moment their sail crested the horizon.* I took another rope, this one long, and tied it to the crossbar in a tight coil while the rest of its length led up to the top of the sail, then cut the tie and let most of it drop off into space, took a deep breath, and leapt.

My battle cry rang out so violently that it almost sounded like I was screaming, but that had to be the wind in my ears. I don't scream. I plummeted toward the *Widowmaker*'s deck, then began to angle out, slowly at first but picking up speed. There was a good span or two of open air between the ships, but where the dead attacked it looked as if they had bled into each other. If ships could bleed bodies. The undead that were still not dead-dead used their fallen as a bridge and were bending back the edges of the pirates' line, forcing the living into a circle. I saw all of this in the span of a few blinks and then I was over the other ship. My gaze was pulled, almost against my will, toward the figure holding the glowing book. Surrounded by the darkness of the dead, the Ghost Captain stood out like the Point Star. They were packed so tightly that he couldn't have fallen over even if he'd wanted to. The sight of all that writhing, rotting meat sent gooseflesh down my arms. *Gods.* Dropping on him for the kill was never an option.

But I'd known that when I'd made the leap.

I felt my momentum slow and then begin to reverse. *It's now or never* . . . I was a good thirty paces over the deck and none of the dead had noticed me. The Ghost Captain was enthralled with his reading, so none knew that I was there. None saw me flip the stiletto in my hand so that it was point first. Throwing knives isn't a good idea. Even well-balanced blades can tip unexpectedly and beyond that, the power needed to deliver a killing blow often means you're better off letting your target get another step closer and stabbing them instead. Or ice picking them. But this knife was the best balanced of my blades and I'd won more than one bet with it, nailing a card to a wall at thirty paces. This was only a little more than that and even if I didn't kill the Ghost Captain, I had a growing suspicion that his book was connected to the dead. Who knows, maybe breaking up his afternoon reading would be enough to do the trick. *Slight breeze on left cheek. Cross-body throw. Adjust. Do it.*

The rope was drawing me back. My arm lashed out, wrist snapping like chained lightning, and the stiletto whipped through the air. It was a good throw. I knew it before it fully left my fingertips. I would have screamed my victory to the skies, but two things prevented that. First, a Shambles missing a leg slipped off its crutch and knocked into the Ghost Captain. Second, the rope in my hands quivered as the sound of it snapping reached my ears.

My blade buried itself to the hilt in the Shambles's neck, spraying the Ghost Captain with ichor. And then I was falling, tumbling, twisting, and when I opened my eyes the dead were watching me. Waiting for me.

With outstretched skeletal fingers.

Fuck.

29

Sharp, jagged fingers clawed at my dress, others latched on to my wrists and calves, and still others pummeled me where they couldn't grab hold. I kept screaming obscenities as I lashed out around me, but even though the dead lacked flesh and muscle and in some cases even sinew, they were stronger than I'd believed possible. I flailed uselessly as the one trying to rip my shoulder off hissed in my ear. One of its teeth bounced against my chin as its jaws snapped together, searching for my throat. I jerked away and my head rebounded hard off the deck. The taste of smoke filled my mouth and the world shrank to a few fingers in front of my face.

This is how it ends.

The thought echoed clearly through me as I felt more bony hands grasping my legs. They began pulling in different directions and my screams turned from variations of "fuck" and "fucking" to plain old screaming. The Shambles let go of my shoulder, but another grasped my wrist, bending over me so I could see the hole through the bottom of its chin, bits of flesh still clinging to a few teeth while something that felt like breath passed across its nub of a tongue. Its jaws snapped again. Closer. Again. Closer. Its teeth ground together as it fought to pull itself closer to me, impeded by the swarming host of undead around us. I could almost feel its teeth meet through my throat, severing my jugular between them.

Instead its jaw slammed shut again on air. Not there. But closer. Closer. I tried to head-butt it, but the Shambles pulled back and I missed. The Shambles hissed as it managed to elbow a few others away. It lowered itself toward me, the skull leering as its jaws spread even farther apart. A fetid, rotten stench filled my nostrils, so raw that there was almost something sweet to it. This was it.

I screamed until my throat tore and blood filled my mouth as I willed my muscles to move, but the press of bone was too much and I managed little more than a shudder. The undead thing hissed in my face, jagged mouth parting in an evil smile. Cracking, crushing, horrible sounds drowned out the sibilant hissing as a barrel bounced into my vision and out again, leaving twisted and broken bones in its wake.

Most of the hands on my arms disappeared and the few that remained no longer clutched at me, all power gone from them.

That's not right; I was supposed to die.

I reached out mechanically, caught up a humerus, and set to smashing the three or four Shambles still pulling on my legs. Turns out, bone on bone is pretty effective against the undead. I regained my feet and the world swooned in front of me. I turned in a circle, waiting to go down, and not sure why that was a bad idea. Something thought it was, but the blood rushing to my head didn't carry any answers with it. I caught myself against a headless torso in time to see a figure leap the rail a dozen paces away, pistoles blazing in each hand. Shambles fell as the figure sprinted toward me, blue jacket trailing behind. The pistole barrels glinted as they rotated, over-under, then the guns bucked again and two more Shambles fell at my feet. Eld reached me a heartbeat later. I opened my mouth as he swept me up in one arm and drew his cutlass with the other.

I kept trying to tell him something. Something that I'd forgotten until now. The last time I was in his arms. I remembered and it was very important to tell him, but he wasn't listening. We were surrounded by a crowd, but there was an open road before us and some juggernaut bouncing along in front of us. Wherever it went, bodies flew, and there was something about it that tickled me. I saw the bone in my fist and it all came together. *Funny bone.* I giggled. I tried to tell Eld about my funny bone, but the words came out all jumbled and I had the feeling he wasn't listening because he didn't stop.

If anything, he ran faster.

I saw a man holding a blazing book, staring at us as if unable to believe his eyes, and then we were past him and the thing in front of us ran right through a large, hulking Shambles and launched itself over the railing. I wanted to tell Eld the story of the broken man who couldn't be put back together again, but the thought set off another wave of laughter.

Then Eld jumped onto the railing and I found myself thrown out over something large and dark.

And wet.

I came up spluttering, bone still clutched in my hand, but for some reason it was no longer funny. A man with pale blond hair and even paler skin surfaced beside me. "Grab the barrel, Buc!" He reached for me as a wave started to separate us, but something brown floated between us and I managed to catch it with one hand. I felt one of my nails tear and pain seared through my hand, but I held on. I wasn't sure why, but hanging on seemed the right thing to do. The important thing to do. Then I swallowed a wave and it swallowed everything else.

"Hold on! Hold on!" Meaningless sounds. Something squeezed my shoulder and a slap of cold water brought sense back to me. "Hold on."

"Aye," I said, spitting seawater out of my mouth. I grabbed a lungful of air. "You don't have to shout, Eld." I tried to wrap my arms around the barrel and then I realized why Eld had been shouting as another wave smashed into us.

30

There's not much I can recommend about spending a night in the open sea. Even when you can't remember any of it, the sea leaves its mark. I woke up to a mouth that felt full of gravel. Burning gravel. I cleared my throat and nearly screamed from the pain. It took several blinks and the back of my hand to clear the grit from my eyes. When I could finally see, I considered closing them again. Vibrant blue waters stared emptily back at me from the rocky beach I was lying on. I sat up.

My dress was still damp, but drying, already so bleached with salt and sand that the emerald green had faded to a mere suggestion of color. I felt I was missing something, but couldn't think what it was, so I moved to push myself to my feet and my arm protested. Loudly.

"Gods' breath." Bruises in the shape of fingerprints decorated my shoulder as if an invisible hand still gripped me. I pulled my dress back up and used my other arm for support. After a moment of swaying where I wasn't sure if I was going up or coming back down, I managed to steady myself. My stockings squelched in my boots, the good leather already showing signs of ruin. "Gods' breath," I repeated as my brain signaled to me that something else was wrong. I'd been worrying over my clothes. Instead of. . . . *What?* Shame gave me energy and I finally began looking around, taking in my surroundings.

If the sea had little to recommend it, the island I was on had little better. Sand dunes surrounded the rocky beach where I'd woken up. Beyond them, palm fronds suggested a forest, but it was the dark clouds beyond the fronds that caught my eye. The Shattered Coast was aptly named, shattered by a millennia of hurricanes and storms that made the Empire's worst weather seem like a light rain on a warm spring afternoon.

In the last hundred years or so, the massive storms had mostly vanished as the world cooled, but there were still hurricanes. I'd never seen one before, but the tales were enough for me to say with confidence I didn't need to. *Is that what a hurricane looks like?* There was no way to say for sure, but the dark clouds stacked one atop the next so that they formed a giant glowering mass were troubling enough, though distant yet, but filled with promise. *What am I missing?*

"You're awake!" Eld's voice broke me out of my reverie and I turned so quickly, every bone in my neck cracked.

That's it. He stood on the crest of a nearby dune, missing his coat, hat, and one boot. His red vest had bled all over his shirtsleeves so that he looked like he'd bathed in blood, and my breath caught in my throat. He came down the dune, walking stiffly, but not wounded, surely not that. He'd been by my side when I nodded off on the barrel, no mean feat, that, but the sea had been rough.

I'd been awake for several minutes and hadn't realized Eld was what had been missing. *And why should I?* I'd lived most of my life alone. *Not the past two years.* True, we'd spent every moment together since and I'd come to consider Eld a friend.

My only friend. But I could go back to living alone if it came to that. Of course I could. *You missed him as soon as you woke up; you just refused to acknowledge it.* I broke that pattern of thought and focused on Eld.

Now that he was closer I could see the livid bruise that crept up the side of his cheek and disappeared into his hairline. I didn't like the way it marred his attempt at a smile. His lip was split and he walked as if someone had kicked him hard in the arse, but the bruise seemed the worst. The large stones cradled in his arms drew my attention.

"I thought I'd be back before then, but these nuts took ages to collect."

"N-nuts?" I asked. The word came out garbled, but I wasn't going to clear my throat. I could feel the raw tenderness there. "Look like stones."

"I thought so at first, but they grew from the palm trees," he said.

"I've read of them," I said slowly. "They have—"

"Water in their center," he finished my sentence. "Aye. I lost my sword, but I was able to hammer one open with my pistole. Thirsty?"

For the next while we were busy cracking open the nuts. A quick inventory revealed I had the knife belted to my wrist and my slingshot, but no ammunition, while Eld had lost all but one of his pistoles, which was wet and useless, save for cracking nuts. Still, between my blade and the butt of his gun we were able to get a drink that tasted strangely milklike. It cleared the sand from my mouth and soothed my throat, too. The white flaky meat of the nut didn't have much taste, but it was something.

"How'd we end up here?" I asked when I had enough down to start to feeling merely hungry instead of ravenous.

"Sea spat us out," Eld said. "After your suicidal rope swing,

I didn't know what to do, but I was beside the barrel and it occurred to me—"

"You picked up the barrel? The one filled with limes and fruits?"

"Aye, well, some spilled out."

"By yourself?"

"Aye. No one else was going to do it; they were too busy fighting." He frowned. "Why?"

"No reason." I glanced at Eld's sleeves. I knew he was strong in his own way. Sure, he was good in a brawl or to loom when the situation called for it—so long as he didn't speak. *He's always so Godsdamned polite.* But his sleeves were stretched tight against his biceps and I was suddenly struck by just how powerfully built the man was. He'd picked up a barrel on his own, carried it across a ship, and hurled it from one side to the other of a second vessel, but he didn't look anything like as muscle-bound as half the tavern toughs. Even roughed up, he looked like a distant storm, dangerous, but beautiful. *Damn.* "Continue."

"Well, you know the rest. We went over the side and you were fading out on me, small wonder given a horde of rotting corpses had tried to tear you apart. I managed to get a hand on your shoulder and the other on the barrel and the waves carried us away from the fight pretty damned quick." Eld breathed out loudly and scratched his chin. "It was a long night after that."

"I'll bet it was," I said. I wanted to poke him, if for no other reason than it was my nature to do so, but the man had saved my life. Twice, really. Not many would run through an army of Shambles to save another. Had our positions been reversed, I wouldn't have. I would have followed my original plan before Eld got me to thinking about taking down the Ghost Captain: hightail it over the other side and take a lifeboat with me. "So is it you I have to thank for the handprint on my shoulder?"

Eld blushed, or maybe his skin was starting to show the sun. "Sorry about that."

I waved a hand. "Anytime you've a choice between giving me a bruise and keeping me alive, choose the bruise every time. Besides, I like it rough." Eld began coughing hard, thumping his chest to clear his throat. "Chew before swallowing next time." He shook his head, still slapping his chest. "I wonder what happened to Chan Sha's crew. I don't think they were in danger of winning that fight."

"Don't know," Eld said when he managed to regain his voice. His face was still red and he avoided my eyes, staring out to sea instead. "Pretty hard to win against another crew that's already been killed."

"Aye."

"We're lucky we got off that ship at all, really," he added.

"Lucky? Luck has—"

"Nothing to do with it, I know." Eld nodded. "But you tell me. We escape the *Sea Dragon*'s explosion and are picked up by Chan Sha, who we thought was behind all the disappearances, only to discover that it's not her but some Dead Gods priest captain thingie. Then the bastard practically walks right up to us, even though there must be a hundred leagues of sea he could have been sailing in." He ticked the points off one by one on his fingers.

"Then he tried to turn us into corpses to join his ranks," I added. "Really lucky, that."

"But he didn't. Instead we escaped again and wound up on a seemingly uninhabited island that's loaded with nuts that provide food and water." Eld's teeth looked shockingly white against his red skin. "That's luck. What else could it be?"

I had just opened my mouth to let him know he'd beaten me when the universe intervened and let me keep my pride. A hissing noise made me look toward the dune Eld had come down. The head of a Shambles wearing a bandanna that had slid down over one cheek popped up over the dune. A strange wet, snuffing sound bellowed from its mouth and I felt gooseflesh break out across me. Phantom skeletal hands clutched at my skin the way they had back on the ghost ship and fear wrapped its tendrils around my throat.

The thing charged over the dune, but the head remained low to the ground, with yellowed blades jutting out from where its shoulders should be. Then it cried out again and the rest of it came into view . . . and it wasn't a Shambles at all.

The wild boar's muffled shriek of rage at the offending skull trapped between its tusks might have been amusing if, while wildly swinging its head back and forth, it didn't catch sight of us and charge, running down the hill in a haphazard fashion that kept begging for it to fall, but the pig never did. Instead the boar began throwing its tusks around with reckless abandon as if practicing for what it was about to do to us.

"Gods!" Eld jumped to his feet, leveling the pistole in his hand before he remembered it was just a lump of steel.

I stood up calmly, more calmly than I felt. *Not the undead.* Despite my fear, or maybe because of it, everything clicked into place. *Pistole. Slingshot. Skull.* "Eld. Eld!" I almost had to shout to break his concentration. "The ball," I hissed, my throat erupting in new flames. "From your pistole!"

Eld's eyes widened in understanding and he slammed the end against his palm several times. "I didn't have time to use a patch when I reloaded so it should—Yes!" He tossed me the lead ball and I caught it deftly with my right hand, my slingshot ready in the other.

The boar carrying the dead bastard's skull had gained speed going down the dune. It reached the bottom just as I drew, a mere score of paces away. I held my breath, dropped the sling-shot down a hair, and released the round, along with the breath I'd been holding in. The Shambles's skull exploded, whipping back into the boar's face. The pig screamed from the round smashing it in the nose and tripped over itself, tumbling until it came to rest on its back, all four hooves in the air. Eld crowed until the boar started moving again, sitting up on its dark hairy haunches so we could see its bristly, but well-muscled, black hide and polished tusks. The dead skull must have absorbed enough of the force of the impact to keep the lead ball from penetrating the animal's skull. Or maybe the bone was just that thick. Eld's victory shout turned to a war cry and he ran forward with me on his heels.

I swerved to the side, slid in the sand, and nearly cut myself on the remaining teeth jutting from the Shambles's broken jaw-bone. I caught up the jaw and tore after Eld. He ran up to the boar, which was nearly the size of a small pony, and drop-kicked it with his remaining boot. It spilled backward end over end on the sand with a startled squeal and Eld's momentum carried him past.

Before either could recover, I reached the pig and smacked it in the arse with the jawbone, jagged teeth facing out. The boar squealed again, its twisty tail doing circles as its hooves churned up sand in giant spurts until it caught traction and took off back up the dune, squealing with every other lumbering leap. My arm still shivered from the impact where the bone met flesh and I let the jawbone slip from my hand before sinking down beside Eld.

He opened his mouth and I stopped him with my hand. "I know, I know, luck." I shook my head and ran my hands through my salt-crusted locks. "You know what?" I looked at him. "We were lucky." A giggle escaped my chest. "Lucky there was just one of those hairy-arsed squealing bastards."

Eld laughed with me. "Aye, I don't think we could have taken two. Not with an empty pistole and a blade the size of your finger." We were both laughing so hard that we didn't hear the pig return with a pack of his friends until they were halfway down the dune. A full dozen and every one as big again as the original boar, the air reverberating with their angry grunts.

Heading right for us.

31

The lead pig was the same as before, yellowed tusks glittering in the sunlight like gilded arse fuckers in search of a hole. Its eyes rolled in its head, shifting back and forth between me and Eld. Eld adjusted the pistole in his grip, caught up the jawbone I'd dropped, and stepped forward with a growl of his own that slowed the boar down as it charged the last dozen paces. I drew the small blade strapped to my wrist and dropped into a crouch. *Here we go.*

Something whined past my ear and the boar's left tusk flew one way, its head snapping back the other. A musket's retort echoed behind me. I opened my mouth, but before I could speak, the air exploded with fresh gunfire, drowning out the waves breaking onshore. The wild pigs stopped in their tracks, hooves churning sand as they tried to run away from the veritable volley of musket fire. A few tumbled down the dunes with wet, throaty squeals, anger transformed to terror at their sudden reversal, while the rest catapulted themselves in great leaps back up the dune and disappeared, their squeals sounding their retreat as they faded into the distance. The sands were still, the dead swine lying about like dark lumps of driftwood on the light sands.

Eld and I turned around at the same moment and found ourselves blinking against the harsh light. A woman's face coalesced
out of the brilliant sunshine, her features impassive, dark braids
hanging thickly around her slender arms, twin pistoles smoking
in either hand. A tanned olive shoulder peeked out of a hole in a
threadbare shirt. She cocked her head and a matchstick slipped
from her locks and hissed as it fell.

"You!"

"Me," Chan Sha said. She brushed a few braids out of her
deep, angled eyes. "A little comedown in the world since we last
met, I'll grant you," she added. "But an unholy terror, nonetheless."

She wiggled the pistole in her fist, then swung it in an arc that
finished with it pointing at my chest, before drawing the weapon
back and resting it over her shoulder. She nodded toward the
trail of smoking muskets that lay beside her wet tracks in the
sand, which led to a lifeboat that looked as if it were made to
hold water, not ride it.

"Lucky for you I came along, else those runty pigs would
have finished you where you fell." She glanced past me and her
lip curled. "City folk think they're cute because they oink and
squeal, but farmers and islanders know: a pig will eat a human
as soon as anything else and a wild pig will defend its territory
to the death. But put down the lead boar"—she gestured toward
the original pig, which lay in a growing pool of its lifeblood—
"and the rest will think otherwise."

"You know a lot about pigs," I said with a sniff.

Eld jumped in before Chan Sha could stop blushing long
enough to reply in kind. "We thought they were Shambles," he
said, explaining what had happened with the first boar.

"Shambles?" She bent to inspect the remains of the desiccated
skull I'd destroyed with my slingshot. I leaned over it as well, but

I didn't see anything of note, save that the bandanna it'd worn had been silk. She glanced up at me. "He's got to be lurking nearby with that Godsdamned ship."

"You've the lives of a Dead Gods' priest," Eld said.

"Funny, I was going to say the same about you lot," she said, rising to her feet. "You aim to take one of them from me, Buc?"

I cocked my head at her and she rolled her eyes. "If you're going to try, you'd best find something more than that shard in your hands," she said, pointing.

I'd forgotten I'd drawn the flattened steel blade strapped to my wrist, but at the sight of Chan Sha I'd brought it up of its own accord. The streets had worked themselves into my bones and I'd reacted to the threat of her appearance without thought. Every fiber in me drew tauter as we stared at each other. *There can only be one queen.*

"Just happy to see you," I lied, forcing the tension from my limbs.

"Aye?" She shook her braids. "I've been told I can cause that reaction. Come on then, if you're not going to stab me." She marched past, letting her pistoles hang from the pair of remaining ropes hung around her neck. She drew a scimitar from her waistband without breaking stride.

"Where are we going?" I called after her.

"Can't you hear it?" She jerked her braids toward the dune the pigs had come over. "There's fighting over yonder hill." She pointed the blade at the shattered skull. "Bet you a plugged doubloon it's that undead bastard what sank my ship." Her smile was hot steel, showing every tooth. "I aim to repay the favor. Thought you lot might be inclined to feel the same."

"Friends?" Eld called.

"Allies," Chan Sha and I spoke as one.

"And temporary ones at that," I added, just for Eld's ears. His mouth twitched, so I kept talking. "The bitch tried to murder the pair of us, Eld. Do you hear anything?" He shook his head and I cursed. "There's something she's not telling us. Many somethings."

"She could say the same for us," he protested. A wet, meaty thud echoed behind me. "Gods," Eld said, glancing over my shoulder. "She just decapitated a boar with one stroke."

"Testing her blade. Better on the piggies than us," I muttered. "Allies only, aye?"

Chan Sha jogged to the top of the sand dune, while Eld and I followed more carefully, unused to moving in loose sand. As we reached the crest, the island opened itself up to us, smaller dunes running down until they met jungle. Farther out, smoke streamed lazily up from a civilization of some sort. The village looked sizable, nestled back amongst some cliffs where I could see a small waterfall and natural spring that split the settlement in two. Half their buildings were thick, squat structures built to withstand hurricanes, pyramiding up to flat roofs, the clay and stone whitewashed by the sun, while the rest were long, horizontal huts built of dried grasses and palm fronds.

There was more, but Chan Sha's cry cut my attention short. She was staring away from the village toward the beach. Thick palm trees obscured my view, but crimson sails fluttered in the wind, standing tall above the trees, and told all the tale I needed.

She was right.

The Ghost Captain followed us.

How? I cut my brain off before it could leap down that path. "How" was a question for later; the question before me was simple: Now what? Chan Sha glanced at us when we caught up to her on the downward slope, her expression inscrutable beneath her sun-darkened skin.

"Well." The word burned in my throat. "We already had one

shot at the bastard and I hate missing. I suppose we can try a second."

"That's the spirit," she spat. "C'mon, we don't want to be late to the party."

"Hold fast," I snapped. Chan Sha's eyebrows shot up. "You're running on emotion, woman. Emotion is like to get you killed, aye, and us in the bargain too. We need a plan."

"Fine," she said. "Plan is, find the undead arsehole who killed my crew and take his head off with this blade."

"Stabby. I like it." I sniffed. "But I doubt he's out there alone waiting on your pleasure. I don't suppose you have any kan?" My mind was racing and it was taking everything in me to hold it at bay.

Chan Sha surprised me by digging a small rolled-up clump of kan from her pocket and tossing it to me. "No matches to be had."

"I'll take it." I packed it into my mouth and began chewing. I'd heard of addicts doing the same, but I'd never tried it. *First time for everything.* Now that we were closer, I could hear shouts and the faint ring of metal on metal. It sounded like the islanders were putting up a fight, but I doubted the natives were prepared for an army of the undead. Chan Sha's crew hadn't been, and they'd had guns and ammunition aplenty. My mind began to slow, ever so slightly, as the kan took effect. "What we need to do is—Wait."

"Wait?" she snarled.

"No." I pointed toward the movement in the jungle I'd just seen. "Wait, I just saw something. Our luck it will be more of those fucking trotters." We were halfway down the dune and I could see almost through the jungle to the next beach over. I'd seen a flash of something in the trees. Chan Sha opened her mouth when I saw it again, moving our direction. "There." I stabbed my finger. She shook her head, then froze. "You see it?"

"Not an it. A her," Chan Sha said, squinting. "Limping. And she's from civilization."

"How do you know that?"

"She's wearing a Godsdamned dress, can't you see?"

"I can't," Eld put in.

"Oh," Chan Sha said, and her voice dropped. She took a deep breath. "Might be mistaken, but after years at sea staring for a scrap of sail, my vision is pretty good."

I tried not to stare at her. It was better than pretty good. All I had seen was a figure, definitely not a pig, but no way to discern gender or dress. Not that I'd tell Chan Sha that. Several Shambles burst through the jungle behind the woman, smashing through thick vines, not bothering to hack them away with their swords, but simply walking forward until the vines broke or their bones did. One fell down, but half a dozen kept going. Almost parallel to them, but coming from the village side, were a dozen of the native inhabitants. I wouldn't have seen them, save one had scurried up a palm tree and was now coming back down. They were pointing excitedly toward where the woman— she was close enough now for me to make out the gilt on her tawny-brown dress—had stopped, bent over, to catch her breath.

"I don't know who she is, but it seems like everyone on this island but us wants a piece of her," I said, relaying what I'd seen.

"Fuck her. It's the Ghost Captain I want," Chan Sha said.

"Aye, and he wants her," I said. With the kan helping to control my thoughts, things began to slip into place. "So we capture her and he'll come to us. 'Never let the enemy dictate the ground you fight on,'" I quoted. "If you'd learned that, maybe yesterday wouldn't have happened."

"You little bitch!" Chan Sha leveled a pistole at me.

Eld dropped into a crouch, raising the butt of his empty pistole with a growl, but I held up a hand to stop him.

"You know you didn't reload that, right?" I asked.

"I—" She glanced at the pistole in her hand as if surprised, then back at me.

I realized I'd misjudged her. Her eyes were almost dilated despite the sunlight, and there was a wildness in them that hadn't been there before. The Chan Sha of yesterday had been dangerous the way a pit viper was dangerous. Ignore her warnings or enter her lair or read as prey and she would attack, but otherwise she was content to watch and wait. That had been stripped away by the loss of her ship. Now she was like a three-fanged sea serpent during breeding season, actively looking to spread the pain.

"You want the Ghost Captain dead, aye?" I tried to force some sympathy into my voice, but the bitch had tried to kill us. After torturing Eld. If I could have done it safely, I would have thrown a candle into her ship's powder magazine myself. "Well, so do we. Need him dead, if you remember our tale. But we're not going to kill him by running straight for him. I already tried that." I shivered at the phantom sensation of the undead's fingers grasping at my skin.

"We need to catch him off guard, when he's least expecting it. And if he's sent his minions after that woman, then I'm guessing she's important to him. Important enough that he'll come looking if the Shambles don't bring her to him."

"An ambush," Eld supplied.

"Just so," I agreed.

"Ambush?" Chan Sha whispered.

"Aye, but you'd best load that pistole first," I said. "If you have any dry powder."

I stepped past her, to forestall any more arguments, and bit back a curse. From my vantage point I could see the woman, but she wasn't looking in my direction and if I tried to draw her attention, I'd likely draw the attention of the ones chasing her as well. She was staring at a point to my left and when I followed her gaze, I saw why.

A small stream cut through where the dunes met the jungle. From my perspective, I could see it was only a few paces across and shallow, but from hers? Where there was a break in the dunes, the water spilled over a number of rocks, looking wild. *She thinks it's strong enough to keep the Shambles away or carry her downstream.*

I was running before I realized it, ripping the pistole from Eld's hand and leaving the shouts of him and Chan Sha racing after me. I'd told Chan Sha we needed a plan and so we did, but I had taken it all in with the first glance. My body was weakened from being tossed about the sea like a glass bottle, but my brain was unfazed. We needed leverage over the Ghost Captain, and given the state of Chan Sha's rowboat, we were effectively marooned here.

That meant we needed to give him a reason to stay and I was betting an awful lot that this woman, whomever she was, would be enough. But only if I got to her before the gaggle of old, dead, and ugly did. I tried to will my legs faster, caught my feet in my skirt, and went tumbling down the last dune, ass over boots. When I came to a stop, I saw the woman scrambling across the stream, her sodden reddish-brown dress clinging to her, tripping her up with every step. She spotted me and froze, tears in her eyes, pale cheeks a deep red. We stared at each other.

"Who are you?" she said, panting.

"B-Buc," I said with a gasp, spitting out the wad of kan before I swallowed it trying to breathe. "Who the bloody Gods are you?"

"The Archaeologist?"

"The what?" Drawing a breath, I waved my question away. "Never mind. Doesn't matter. Why's the Ghost Captain want you?"

"You mean the Dead Walker?" she asked, nearly as out of breath as I was.

"Aye, why are his Shambles chasing you?"

"Because he wants the knowledge I have," she said, tapping her red hair. "Up here."

"You know how to kill him?" I asked, unable to keep the excitement from my voice.

"Do you have a ship? A boat?"

"Aye, but set that aside for a moment—" I began.

"Will you take me with you?"

"I was coming to get you—" I tried again.

"Oh, thank the Gods," she cried.

"Don't thank them, thank me," I muttered dryly. "You know how to kill the Ghost Captain? Kill him dead."

"He's almost dead already," she said.

"But—"

"I know how to kill him," she agreed. "And I'll tell you if you take me with you."

"Done," I spat. The Shambles came stumbling from the jungle and splashed into the middle of the stream. The woman saw something in my eyes, turned around, and screamed. "Get back!" I yelled, but she stood motionless.

"C'mon." I could feel her trembling in my grip, so I spun her and gave her a shove to start her moving. "Go! Run!" By then the Shambles were nearly on me. And all I had was an empty pistole, my slingshot, and a shard of a blade. *Damn it, Buc.*

A fine trap I'd laid for myself.

32

I sank into a crouch, swinging my arms back and forth, empty pistole held by the barrel in one hand, flat shard of steel in the other. The lead Shambles wore a sun-bleached calico dress, its bone-white fingers bright against the dark handles of the twin cleavers it wielded. I dodged the first swipe, breaking its wrist with the butt of the gun, and a notched cleaver fell to the sand between us. The Shambles moaned, blackened tongue poking between broken yellowed teeth, and I growled back. The rest of its compatriots caught up and I found myself facing a semicircle of death. *Throw the pistole. One pace to cleaver. Take out knee of one to the left. Sprint through gap. Take the rest from behind.* It wasn't much of a plan, but in my mind's eye it was the only one I saw with a chance of ending without me torn and bloody, one step from joining the Shambles' ranks.

I took a deep breath—which was driven from my lungs by an elbow that sent me sprawling into the lead Shambles. The creature's moan turned to a whine as it stumbled back, skeletal legs tangling in the shreds of its dress. It, I, and the . . . Archaeologist . . . fell to the sand. The woman was screaming, her eyes wild.

Gods damn it. My shove must have twisted her wits, because she'd run right back into the midst of the fight. I jumped to my feet, catching her arm and hauling her up though she was head and shoulders taller than me. Adrenaline will do that. So will half a dozen undead with blades all within an arm's reach of you.

"Run, you fool!" I shouted, ducking a rusty cutlass that nearly took me square in the forehead. The wind from the blade sent gooseflesh down my back.

My words must have reached her because the Archaeologist took off.

Right into the arms of one of the Shambles.

Two more stepped twixt me and the woman while the remaining three followed the one in the calico dress, lumbering back the way they'd come, with the Archaeologist flailing ineffectually between them. My howl of impotent rage was lost in her frantic screams. The two came at me, ax and sword in hand. When I dropped back a pace, my boot kicked something hard and I glanced down to see the notched cleaver dropped by the one in the calico dress. I scooped it up just in time to parry the sword of the one on my right. Shock waves reverberated along my arm and sent me down to one knee. My breath screamed in my lungs from the past few moments, and blood beat a nervous rhythm in my brain, disrupting my train of thought. The undead will do that to you. Being a breath away from joining their ranks doesn't help either.

I saw the ax coming like a hammer blow, blotting out the sun. Time stilled. The Shambles swinging the ax was tall, its pale bones thick and joined together by fresh tendon and sinew with scraps of muscle rotting between. Stronger by far than most others I'd faced. I could block their strike before it split my skull like Eld and I had split those nuts on the beach, but the force of the blow would still rip the cleaver from my hands. I didn't think the pistole in my hand would stop the other from running me through, but it was all I had. *Fall left after blocking, throw the pistole.* Only blind luck would save me now.

Time reasserted itself, the ax whistling toward my head as I desperately brought the cleaver up between us. Then a scimitar was there and the ax caromed off with a screech of steel on steel. The Shambles's desiccated skull disappeared in a flash of gunpowder and a plume of smoke and the rest of it fell into a limp pile of bone in front of me. A heartbeat later the other fell beside it, skull spinning off into the stream. A gentle hand on my shoulder pulled me to my feet.

"Gods damn it, Buc. Next time don't run off without me," Eld said, the lightness in his voice betrayed by the bright worry in his eyes. "Clue me in first."

"Aye, and me," Chan Sha said from behind me.

I'd forgotten I had Eld. We'd been partners for two years and I'd called him friend, but for my part it'd been in name only. Only recently, facing everything we had over the past week, it'd become something more. "Friend" didn't seem to do it justice, but it was the only word I had to use. I had a friend. And a Chan Sha. I feigned a smile and fought to keep the tremor from my voice as the nervous liquid fire that comes after a near-death experience flooded through my veins. "I knew you'd catch on," I said. "I didn't think it'd take you this long, but still . . . late's better than never, aye?"

Chan Sha snorted, stepping up beside us and staring at where the rest of the Shambles had run off to. "You're welcome, Buc," she said. "Now, what was all that about? I assume you let them steal the woman away?"

"Gods, no," I replied, refusing to take the bait she'd thrown out. "Fool woman got turned around and ran right back into them. You must have seen?" The pair exchanged looks over my head. "What?"

"It looked like you might have shoved her into them," Eld said, finally.

I snorted. "Why would I run pell-mell into the middle of a pile of undead just to make sure they captured the prize they sought?"

"Because they caught up to you faster than you'd anticipated and you needed a way to save your own skin?" Chan Sha asked.

"Bullshit," I growled. *I didn't do that, did I?* "I wasn't worried about my skin until she ran into me. And even then, I wouldn't sacrifice the one person who knows how to kill the Ghost Captain. Least not till after he was dead."

"She knows how to kill the Ghost Captain?" Eld asked.

"Who is she?" Chan Sha asked over him. "What was her name?"

"We didn't have time to exchange pleasantries," I lied. "And that's what she claimed. He sent Shambles after her to prevent that knowledge from spreading," I added, answering Eld. "Now you understand why I wouldn't have let her die?"

"No, you just let her be captured so she can die later," Chan Sha said.

"Fuck off," I growled.

"Ladies," Eld interjected. He held his hands up defensively when we both turned on him. "Not sure we want to fight in front of the company is all," he said. His smile looked strained as he nodded past us. We followed his gaze and saw that we were surrounded by a dozen islanders with spears and war clubs and a few arrows nocked on reed-thin bows. "Wouldn't be polite, would it?"

"No," I muttered, mind spinning with calculations and not liking the sums. "It wouldn't."

33

For a moment we all stared at one another. I elbowed Eld. "Do you speak any Shattered Coast dialects?"

"No."

"What do you think the odds are they speak Imperial?" I whispered. Eld didn't say anything, so I stepped forward. At first glance, the woman opposite me looked to be only a few years older than me, but when she brushed her dark red hair back, I could see faint lines on her cheeks. So older, but holding on to her looks well enough that she'd be the envy of many in Servenza. But we weren't in Servenza and what I'd really been hoping for was some gnarled old person who might know a few words of the Empire's tongue. Still, she was a woman, so that was something. "Do you speak Imperial?"

The woman eyed me, then whistled like a bird, opening her mouth and undulating her tongue to change the pitch. Another answered in kind behind her and she shook her head. I arched an eyebrow and she offered back a series of grunts and calls that sounded like mating pigs. I shook my head and she laughed, breaking into another series of whistles that was echoed by some of those behind her.

"I don't speak bird. Or rutting pig, either," I added. The woman's smile faded and her compatriots moved forward, tightening the circle around us.

"Hold it," Chan Sha said, pitching her voice for our ears alone. "I'm familiar with some of the islander dialects. Not quite sure I follow this one, but . . ." She thrust the scimitar through her belt and held both hands up, stepping past me. She whistled, slowly, and less surely than the woman, but her undulating tones didn't sound too dissimilar from the islander's. To my surprise, the woman answered back and Chan Sha nodded, whistling with more confidence. The pair began exchanging grunts and whistles with increasing frequency.

"Do you think they'll let me get a boot off one of the dead?" Eld asked as Chan Sha and the woman exchanged a few more calls. The rest had settled in around us, three on each side, while the others spread out a few score of paces, occupying the nearby sand dune. "I'm tired of walking with a limp."

"Unless you speak bird, I imagine they'll take that as an attempt to escape." Eld nodded glumly. "Sorry, Eld, but I've no fucking clue what they are saying." I growled in the back of my throat. *Gods, I hate ignorance.* "I wonder if the gestures are part of it?"

"Search me," he grunted. "Still, they seem to be fighting the undead so they can't be about to kill us, aye? Likely want to share some news, perhaps help us defeat the Ghost Captain, and then we'll be on our way."

"Gods, I'd give a pretty copper to know where your eternal optimism springs from," I said.

"Why, whatever do you mean?"

"Number one hundred and seven." Eld frowned. *"A Year Amongst the Inhabitants of the Uninhabitable Coast,"* I said. "Anonymous author, a poor fool marooned back when the Shattered Coast was just becoming navigable. They found some tribes are friendly, some are neutral, and some are hostile. But even the neutral ones practice ritual sacrifice and cannibalism."

"Cannibalism?"

"Aye, beyond fish and pigs, have you seen any protein on this island? Nuts have to get old after a while. Might be they are going to help us," I said, mocking Eld's accent, "to fatten us up before the feast."

"Good grief," he growled. "This is starting to get a little thick, don't you think? First Chan Sha, then this Ghost Captain and the Shambles and bloody pigs with tusks the size of cutlasses, and now cannibalistic islanders."

Chan Sha turned back around before I could answer. "Stow it," she muttered. "Like as not at least one of them kens Imperial, if not speaks it fluently. They don't give a ruddy fuck who we are—they just want to send the Ghost Captain packing before he breaks through to their village and turns them all into Shambles. And they're happy to have us along for extra muscle."

"Dulcet music to my ears," I said. "Shall we go rescue the arc—the woman"—I corrected quickly, still not sure why I was keeping her name from the others—"then, before he absconds with her?"

"Absconds?" Eld asked.

"It means—" Chan Sha began.

"That even if someone"—I nodded toward the islanders—"understands Imperial, they aren't likely to ken the word."

Eld's eyebrows rose. "So what's the plan?"

"Let them lead the way and see what the situation looks like when we get there," I said.

"I don't care what the pair of you do," Chan Sha said, "but I'm killing the undead bastard."

"Aye, so you've made clear," I said. *Let her provide a distraction.* "But unless you know how to do it, good and proper, you might want to focus on rescuing the woman first." I shrugged. "You do you."

Chan Sha muttered something under her breath, but turned back to the islanders, drawing her scimitar. She whistled a question and they all grunted back. "They're ready."

"Perfect," I said lightly, ignoring the cramp in my side. "Then let's do this, shall we?"

Chan Sha grunted something to the islanders and they tore off with high-pitched howls, heading in the direction the Shambles had taken. We followed fast on their heels. Chan Sha's feet blurred as she sprinted along the faint suggestion of a trail. We brought up the rear, me in my salt-stiffened dress and Eld with one boot on, and by the time we came out the other side, the former Widowmaker was halfway across the rocky beach, sprinting toward the Shambles. They were forming ranks in front of rowboats, the front row rapidly thinning thanks to the spears that poured from the edge of the jungle like bees from a hive. The dead let out a loud chorus of groans and ran or stumbled as their level of decay allowed. The spears stopped, and a ragged line of warriors stepped out of the grasses. *Too few.*

"The Ghost Captain!" Eld shouted. A familiar thin cloaked figure had appeared at the head of one of the boat crews. A strange light emanating from the object in his hands turned the black silk of his cloak blue while a bloodred feather pointed to the sky from the corner of his tricorne. He glanced around, standing a full head above most of the bent Shambles surrounding him before returning to his book. The Shambles swarmed toward the jungle and the islanders.

My eyes swept across the beach. "There she is!" I pointed to a group gathered beside a just-beached rowboat. "They're trying to take the Archaeologist back to the Ghost Captain's ship."

"The Ark—what?"

"I dunno, that's her name," I told Eld. "We can't let them escape with her."

"Is she really worth this?" he asked.

I nodded, the kan still sharp in my mind, modulating my thoughts, as I put everything together. Chan Sha had torn after the islanders, heading right for where the Shambles surrounded the Ghost Captain. She and her newfound friends would provide all the distraction needed. I'd a feeling the Ghost Captain used that strange book to commune with the dead and if he was too busy trying to keep Chan Sha from his throat, he wouldn't be able to stop us rescuing the Archaeologist. *To say nothing of keeping Chan Sha from our throats as well.* I told Eld that in a single breath.

"If we can't reach her in time, we'll steal a boat and follow after. We've a chance to burn that fucker's ship and maroon him with only half a hundred or so of his undead companions. Shortens the odds quite a bit."

"It would at that," Eld muttered as a roar leapt from the islanders as they met the Shambles. The ragged line swelled—dozens more fighters appeared from the jungle and I felt my mouth tug into a grin. There's nothing so sweet as an ambush—especially when you're not on the receiving end of it. The Shambles fell back even as the boatload the Ghost Captain had sent forward reached the battle line. Both sides were fully engaged, leaving no room to notice the Shambles struggling to get the Archaeologist into one of the boats. Or us stopping them. *Now I've got you, bastard. I don't make mistakes twice.* "C'mon, old man!" I shouted at Eld, and tore off across the beach.

Eld caught up to me a few paces later, awkwardly running

with one boot on so that he leapt more with one step than the next. "I'm not old!"

"You're older than me."

"Older, not old!" he shouted in the face of one of the Shambles that had stumbled toward us, turning at the last moment so Eld's shoulder sent it spinning back, heels over head. He caught the sword it'd dropped before the weapon touched the sand and as the undead thing sat up, a mass of curls pulling away from its decaying flesh, Eld put his boot through its skull. Hair and black ichor and Eld's boot flew through the air. Eld leapt forward in his sock feet, blade shining in the sun, running toward the Shambles. I dropped to a crouch, searching for smooth pebbles in the sand.

The beach was rocky, but stones aren't the same as bullets. Each bullet, even if poorly made, is roughly the same size, shape, and weight as other rounds of the same type. A few shots and I know just how it will feel in the palm of my hand, in the sling, and against my cheek before I release.

Stones are individuals and every one a stranger. But what they lack in accuracy they make up for in quantity. And quantity has a quality all of its own. I think someone said that once; if they didn't, someone should. In moments I had transformed into a machine that turned the air dark with stones that broke flesh and bone, and when I was lucky, skulls.

Eld and I were wrecking the Shambles' flank while the islanders, led now by Chan Sha, carved through their front; the Ghost Captain had no choice but to commit the rest of his force. Unlike on the ship, here he had to make do with well less than a hundred Shambles.

Unfortunately, we'd done too good a job on his flank and a score broke off from the main body to check our advance. Eld met them in a crouch, twisting this way and that, small motions and lunges doing for the first two before he leapt up with a roar and set about them with hacking strokes that parted limbs. I could scarcely see him through the inky spurts that flowed from the dying (dead?) Shambles, but his sword marked him out, always attacking while the rest were fighting to parry it. Between the pair of us, we nearly halved the Ghost Captain's boatload before they'd crossed half the distance toward us.

Fools like being the center of attention, but it's something I've always tried to avoid. In trying to rescue the Archaeologist, though, we'd inadvertently turned the Ghost Captain's flank . . . and laid a trap for ourselves. The Ghost Captain's head snapped up and he stared in our direction. He studied Eld, then I saw his tricorne flick as he glanced at me. He turned to his book and suddenly Eld's advance slowed and then stopped entirely and now he was parrying half a dozen strokes from the Shambles nearest to him. He fell back even as my stone found the dark hole where a tall undead's nose had been. The Shambles' movements were coordinated, smooth, almost as fast as living flesh. The dead may be slow, but they don't tire, while Eld's parries grew slower with each pass.

Damn.

I ran forward, leaping over scattered piles of bone and flesh, dodging a hand that still moved, and slid to a halt beside Eld.

"What are you doing here?" he grunted. The Shambles before him swung a pair of cutlasses back and forth, carving the air between them. "You're supposed to be covering my arse."

"No, I'm supposed to be finding a way to kill our ghostly captain yon."

"Aye?" The Shambles stepped in, bone showing through its tattered trousers, while a long cape obscured the rest of its body. Eld slid away from the first cut, but was forced to take the second squarely on his blade. Steel met steel and both blades stuck for a heartbeat. It was all the Shambles needed to bring its other blade around, rusty steel thrumming toward Eld's unprotected neck.

Thwack!

The Shambles's head exploded and it fell in a heap, cutlass landing harmlessly at Eld's feet. Behind it, another dropped with a dark hole in its forehead. It clawed at the sand and then went slack, tarry liquid leaking down its pale corpse-face like midnight's tears.

"You're welcome," I said, slipping another stone into the pouch of my slingshot.

"Welcome?"

"You'd really be fucked without me, you know that?" I asked.

"I would not," he said with a snort.

"Good, then I won't feel bad about leaving you," I said. Eld looked up from inspecting the faint notch in his blade. More Shambles were coming toward us, but there was an opening to the rowboats. If we both took it, they'd follow us and we'd be forced to fight, drawing the Ghost Captain's eye again. I saw understanding in his eyes and clapped him on the shoulder. "I'm off," I said without looking back.

"Seems a good way to get killed."

"Or kill," I said. I dropped to the ground to gather more projectiles.

"Or that." He took a breath. "I won't be able to follow you, but I'll do what I can."

"I know," I said. *You always do.* "Luck, Eld." I glanced up and laughed when I saw his expression. It doesn't pay to let a man get settled and Eld was first and foremost a man. So I left him with my laughter ringing in his ears and began running low across the sand, using the bones of those already killed as cover.

There were a few Shambles still on their feet, but they kept shifting position, first toward Eld, then toward the islanders, as if being driven by two indeterminate wills. Whatever the cause of their hesitation, soon I was past them. I couldn't take credit for all of the undead lying on the beach—here and there one was pinned to the sand with a spear or three—but I'd offed close to a dozen. *A few more will do the trick.*

I dropped lower as I drew closer to the Shambles holding the Archaeologist. One lay awkwardly against the boat, ichor sprayed across the hull's sun-bleached side. The rest were wrestling with the woman, who was giving a good account of herself considering four of them had her completely off the ground. *Keep it up, woman.*

One of the unencumbered Shambles looked over its shoulder and I threw myself down. The sand was hot and scratchy against my skin; the darker stones burned so that I fancied I could smell my flesh burning, but I think it was just the smell of so much ichor from the Shambles. I risked a glance up and saw the Archaeologist being tossed over the side of the boat, which was surrounded by half a dozen of the taller undead. I lowered my head but kept my eyes on the boat, slowly inching my way forward.

Dead Shambles lay thick around me and I had no choice but to crawl over bones and rotting flesh, my dress fighting me with every move as it snagged on and stuck to the gore surrounding me. The smell was sharp, rank, yet almost sweet in a way that made bile rise in my throat. I crept over one that was all bone; its rib cage, pressing against my abdomen, sent gooseflesh racing down my arms.

I risked another glance and froze—one was staring right at me. If it saw me, it gave no indication. Another half dozen joined the rest and they began to climb, awkwardly, over the side of the gunwale. *They're leaving!* With them would go my chance, but several still stood, looking around, so I bit back my impatience and kept my head down. I kept going, making every movement with frightful slowness that made me want to scream by the time I'd covered half the distance left between me and the undead circling the boat. The Archaeologist appeared once again, red hair gleaming in the sun as she clawed at the edge of the boat. For a moment it looked as if she was going to pull herself over, but dozens of skeletal hands grabbed her, yanking her out of view. The Shambles on the shore began pushing the boat back out to sea.

No longer being watched, I came to my feet, slingshot in hand, and dropped the nearest one with my first shot. Another stepped up to take its place, gnarled claws of bones grasping the side even after my second shot blew its head to shards. The boat slowed and I bit back a laugh as my third shot took out one on the far side, dropping it like, well, like a stone. The boat ground to a halt, but the Shambles didn't attack me like I'd thought they would. Instead they kept pushing, moaning as their bones began to crack from the strain. There weren't enough of them left to shift the boat, which was mired in soft sand.

Now I've got you. I bent to pick up a stone. When I straightened, my smile slipped from my face.

Another crew of Shambles had arrived, sweeping around either side of the boat like a tidal wave of death and decay. A dozen stopped to help push the boat and with their added numbers, it slid smoothly into the surf, oars locking into place and drawing it into deeper water. *No!* I'd been so close, within a stone's throw of rescuing the woman, and now just like that, she was gone. I screamed my frustration to the heavens. The Shambles heard me, answering my cry with moans of their own.

A whining noise whipped past my ear, something flickered in the air, and several Shambles fell, fought to get up, and were pinned down by flights of spears until they stopped twitching. I glanced back to see a small army of islanders racing toward me, Chan Sha and Eld in the lead. Something caught in my throat, bit me to my core, but I swallowed the emotion before it could do more. I'd pasted a bored smile on my face by the time my allies reached me, the islanders spreading out to square off against the undead.

"What are you doing here?" I asked. "I thought you were off killing the Ghost Captain."

"Nice to see you, too," Chan Sha said with a smirk.

"We were," Eld added, "until he left. Look!"

I followed his finger. The beach was littered with fallen Shambles, but those still standing were milling about the Ghost Captain's dozen or so rowboats. He himself stood on the rail of one, staring down intently at the book in his hands. The Shambles around him began moving more smoothly, and the retreat turned from a rout into a tactical withdrawal. Though many Shambles tumbled into each boat, some remained on the beach, pushing the boats out to sea. More than that, I realized, as the islanders charged past us into the ranks of the Shambles. *He needs a rear guard.*

"C'mon!" I yelled, waving the cleaver I'd taken from the Shambles in the calico dress. "I've a plan."

"Bloody wonderful," Chan Sha said.

"Shut up and follow me. No fighting, save to break through. If we hurry, we might be able to save the Archaeologist yet. Aye, and send the bastard's ship to the bottom too!" I shouted the last, sprinting after the islanders.

"Save who?" Chan Sha asked.

Eld muttered something in reply, but then my adrenaline kicked in again and all I heard was the beating of my heart, loud in my ears. A large Shambles in an overcoat faced off against three islanders with spears. I picked this one out because it was bowlegged and because its attention seemed taken up with the three blades searching for its throat. I bowled over one of the islanders and threw myself into a roll. In my mind I had thought I'd be able to break his knee with the cleaver, but when I hit the sand, it was all I could do to keep ahold on the wooden handle, slick as it was with my sweat. I bounced off the undead's undead leg instead, knocking him off balance and coming out the other side with his overcoat hot against my face. It slid away, leaving a sheen of mildew across my forehead that made me gag.

Coughing hoarsely, but clear of the line of undead, I risked a glance back to see Chan Sha and Eld take down a Shambles between them and then they were free too. Whooping, I ran on, toward the nearest boat, where half a dozen Shambles had it nearly into the water. Increasing speed, forcing my tired legs to move as fast as they could in my once-again-sodden dress, I leapt onto one of the Shambles at the rear of the boat. I used a jutting piece of its rib cage as a step to reach its shoulders, steadied myself on its shoulders, then launched myself into the boat. I landed on top of another Shambles, pinning its head and neck against the seat while at the same time falling through its chest.

The sternum and vertebrae broke with a sharp crack beneath its leather vest, spraying me with dark rancid blood. I fought to my feet just in time to dodge a knife thrust from another that was as short as me. I wiped my eyes clean with one hand and buried the cleaver in the neck of the Shambles with the other. It fell, revealing two undead rowers staring blankly ahead and . . . empty seats. *I guessed right.*

"Eld! Chan Sha! Get your arses in here!" I shouted. "Damn, I'm good," I told the rowers. I jumped up on one of the seats to get a better view and my smile died on my lips.

Eld and Chan Sha weren't climbing up over the side. They were two score of paces away, back where I'd left them, with what was left of the islanders, surrounded by Shambles. *The Ghost Captain's rear guard.*

"No," I whispered. It didn't make sense. They'd been right behind me. But blood ran down the side of Eld's face. Something had put him down after I'd glanced back. The boat shifted, then rocked, and I realized we were in the water. *Shit.* If I jumped out now, I could make it to them. Well, to the Shambles surrounding them. But this was the last boat—if I did that, then the Ghost Captain would escape with the one person who knew how to kill him. *And you'll lose everything you're here to gain. A stake in the Company. A seat on the Board. Power.*

More islanders were pouring out of the jungle now that they didn't have to worry about protecting their village. But I was closer, and as the ring of Shambles drew tighter around Eld and Chan Sha, I realized the newcomers weren't going to get there fast enough. I glanced back to sea and bit my tongue. If I didn't go back, they'd be dead. *And you'll lose Eld.*

Eld.

Mind made up, I reached for the gunwale, but a wave hit the side of the boat and I lost my footing and everything turned upside down. My head slammed off the railing and a high-pitched ringing filled my ears as my vision swam. Something bright and hard fought through the pain. *Eld.* I bit back tears, clawing my way up the side of the boat.

The shore was a far stone's throw away with dark, fathomless water between. That rogue wave had carried us past the shallows and out to sea. "No," I choked. I pulled myself up as high as I could, nearly pitching over the side, but all I could see was a maelstrom of undead around a small center of flashing steel. The center went under like a rock beneath a tidal wave and when the islanders' charge broke upon the wave, the wave shattered . . . but the rock was gone. Chan Sha was gone. Eld . . . Eld was gone.

"NO!"

I screamed myself hoarse, hot tears biting at my eyes. I'd lived my whole life alone. *Save for Sister.* Losing her had been like being stabbed in the chest with an iron poker, white-hot from the forge. I'd sworn never to love another. Then Eld had found me. Taught me how to read. Stuck with me, even when the best I could offer was a knife in the shoulder and the promise of more pain to come. *I told him not to trust me.* But he had, he always had. Just like my sister. We'd become friends, more than friends. And in the moment he'd most needed me, I'd hesitated. Because of the same greed, the same power that I claimed to be fighting to change. It'd leeched its way into my heart and I'd allowed it to betray me. My breath came in ragged gasps, spittle flecked my lips, and I couldn't keep the low, keening moan between my teeth from escaping.

"D-d-damn you, Eld. I told y-you." I swallowed the lump in my throat. "N-not to t-trust me." The world blurred behind a wet, blinding sheet of pain.

34

I was alone, save for the sounds of the sea around me. The pull of
the oar, the cracking of the undead's knuckles against the wood
between their fists, the slapping of the waves against the hull,
and the occasional gust of wind, loud in my ears. I stared at the
board my boots rested on. *Eld.* There was pain in the thought. A
shadow fell across my salt-stained boot and I looked up to see the
hulk of the Ghost Captain's ship rising before us. We'd arrived.
Only, that was wrong. It was how it was supposed to be. How I'd
planned it to be. But I'd fucked up. There was no "we." Just "I."
Singular. *I* had arrived. Alone.

A pair of ropes attached to pulleys flew down from above just
as we were within another wave of crashing against the hull and
both Shambles pulled their oars in and stood up as if on command. I suddenly remembered the cleaver in my lap and waved it
in front of them, but one turned its back on me, heading to the
rear while the other marched straight toward me, empty sockets
focused on the tackle swinging just behind me. *Must have only
one job.* I slid across the bench as the Shambles stepped past me.
It was almost completely bone beneath trousers that had been

warped by seawater so they were like casts around its femurs, and a threadbare blue-and-white-striped shirt that was missing a sleeve. Catching the rope, it looped it through a ring on the front of the boat.

The other Shambles, as skeletal as the first, if better clothed, in a faded sundress missing half its petticoats, pulled hard on the rope, using the pulley as leverage, and the rear of the boat shifted up a pace higher than the front. The one by me did the same and the boat shifted to level. Then the one in the dress pulled again, jerking the back end up until the one by me pulled to even us out. And so they went, hand over hand, and steadily we rose by degrees. I could see the rest of the boats around the edge of the ship, a few spans below the railing. They were already emptied; our boat, being the last to come in, was at the rear of the ship. *And the most likely to be overlooked.*

My mind was dark and numb, save for one throbbing thought that stood out bloodred amongst the haze: *revenge.* I'd only just realized what I had to lose: Eld. That wasn't quite the truth; I don't think I'd allowed myself to believe there was more there than a partnership, but I believed now. The Ghost Captain had killed my best friend. Check that, my only friend. Eld was . . . My mind couldn't hold the thought, so it slid away. It didn't matter. Nothing did, save that I was going to kill the motherfucker. Cut him. Watch him bleed until death shone brightly in his eyes. Failing that, I'd blow up the whole fucking ship, but one way or another I wasn't leaving without the Ghost Captain's corpse. *No resurrection for you.*

The boat jerked me out of my reverie and I realized that while I'd spaced out, the Shambles had pulled us nearly level with the rest of the boats. *That won't do.* I didn't want any of their brethren to know I was there until it was too late. I stepped gingerly across the seats, picking my way carefully so as not to alert the one in the dress, but its seaweed-infested locks didn't shift once.

I could almost wish for one of Ciris's Sin Eaters; superhuman powers couldn't hurt for what I was about to do. This was war, even if I was the only one who realized it. In the end, I'd have to take Ciris down as well, but the Ghost Captain first. After these Shambles. I waited for the other Shambles to pull the boat level again and then swung the cleaver, feeling the blade shiver as it cut through the neck of the one wearing a dress. Its bones shattered; its body fell against the side of the boat while its head went over the edge in a burst of dark spray. I spun around, waiting for her compatriot's attack, but it just stood there, desiccated fingers wrapped around the rope, waiting for the other's pull. *Would it wait for its turn forever?* I couldn't be sure, so I leapt across the seats and practiced decapitating the Ghost Captain with its bleached bones. Practice makes perfect, they say. And I needed this to be perfect. I'd get only one chance.

I've a head for heights, but usually even I wouldn't have attempted swinging myself out over open water several stories high with only a rough rope to keep me from plunging to my death. But nothing about this was usual, so I barely noticed when a gust of wind threatened to slam me off the side of the hull. Bracing myself with my legs, I used the momentum to leverage myself higher until I was level with the rest of the rowboats. My hands were beginning to tingle, my arms to burn, but I didn't allow myself to care. It was someone else's pain and I was storing it up inside like a vast keg of grain alcohol, just waiting to be dumped on someone's head and lit aflame. I was both vessel and match and I was filled to overflowing. I needed only to strike.

At last I caught ahold of the railing, taking care to wrap my fingers around the very edge of a wood post. I drew my cleaver with one hand. I was close enough to the top that all I had to do was swing my arm over and heave and the rest of me would follow. First I had to make sure I wouldn't land on top of a Shambles. The other two ships I'd been on had always had a deckhand or two toward the back of the ship. That was fine; I could deal with one or two, so long as I kept the element of surprise. *Just more practice for the Ghost Captain.* I grinned to myself when I didn't hear anything.

One.

Two.

Thre—Skeletal arms came over the side, wrapping iron fingers around my wrists, and jerked me up and onto the deck, wrenching my shoulders half out of their sockets.

I catapulted into the chest of a reedy Shambles, sending an ivory rib out the side of its leather jerkin, then landed on my arse. Dozens of Shambles surrounded me, and standing just beyond them was the Ghost Captain. This close I could see the stubble on his cheeks, dark and speckled, like the gunpowder on Eld's face when he reloads too quickly. His goatee shone from the bells interwoven in it, a bell at the bottom cleaner and shinier than the rest. *Why? Is it new? Added after he sank Chan Sha's ship? Like a notch in his belt?* The thought slid away, belonging to another person with other priorities. If I succeeded, in a few moments I wouldn't need to wonder about his demented proclivities.

"Sambuciña!" His teeth were white beneath the shadow cast by his tricorne. "You've saved me the trouble of another expedition."

My name on his tongue brought me up short. *How? Doesn't matter.* The rest of his words flew past me, as meaningless as the horde of undead surrounding me. Now that the time had come, all other might-have-beens left me. I felt that bright thought in my mind darken like blood in the sun as I shouldered aside the Shambles standing between me and the Ghost Captain and threw the cleaver toward him, overhead, with both hands.

Straight at his face. He let out a startled squawk that brought a smile to my lips. *Eat steel, bitch.*

A short Shambles leapt from nowhere and took the cleaver square in the chest. Its rib cage caved in and it fell back, limbs moving, but unable to stand.

"Damn."

I stared from the cleaver buried in the Shambles's chest to where a bone shard had just missed the Ghost Captain's throat, taking most of his goatee instead, leaving a small tuft behind. We stared at each other, my brain suddenly slack and empty.

"Another mistake, Sambuciña," he muttered. "Take her!"

Darkness flashed across my vision and clocked me full in the face. The deck rushed up to greet me, and bones gripped my flesh on every side. I screamed as one bent over me, blackened stump of a tongue spraying ichor as it hissed into my face. I'd ended up in the same fucking predicament as the first time I was on the Ghost Captain's ship, only this time there was no Eld to save me.

Eld. Rage lent me strength and my war cry actually sent the Shambles stumbling back. I fought one arm free, drew the flattened steel blade strapped to my arm, and slammed it into the empty eye socket of the one in my face. I managed to free a leg and kick myself away from the roiling mass of undead, their fetid stench so strong that I could taste it with every breath. *I'm going to kill them all.* Another inhuman roar filled my throat and then something slid over my head, taking the fury of light and sound and smell with it and turning my cry into a throaty gurgle. The masses bore me back down and my head slammed off the deck. I couldn't breathe.

I'm going to kill.

Them.

All.

The world and I parted ways.

35

The world came back to me in a bloody bruise. At least that was what it looked like as consciousness returned in fits and starts. I heard, more than felt, my heart beating in my chest at the same moment a ragged gasp whistling in my burning throat filled my lungs. I saw the sun setting, deep crimson reaching out to touch the purpled bruise marring the sky. I blinked and pain set my face on fire and my skull to throbbing. I sat up, taking another wheezing, rasping breath as I gingerly felt my face and realized I'd been looking out of one eye; the other was almost swelled shut. I moaned as I felt the edge of my cheek and sent pain waves reverberating through my face.

"So you're awake," a soft voice whispered. "Thank the Gods I'm not the only one trapped here."

"Trap-ped?" The word clung to my dried lips and I had to work moisture into my mouth to get my tongue to move properly. "Trapped?" I repeated, twisting my head around so I could see with my good eye.

"Aye," the Archaeologist said, grinning around her split lip. Her cheeks were flushed to the color of her curled hair, or maybe that was from too much sun, but her grin widened when she met my eyes. Eye. "Awaiting the pleasure of the Dead Walker."

I frowned. *Dead Walker.* "Ghost Captain," I muttered.

"That's the one," she agreed.

I fought to stand up, but my boots couldn't find purchase; they kept kicking through the air and suddenly my world spun, slowly, in a circle. Ropes creaked around me and I finally took a moment to take stock of the situation. I was sitting in a cage made of out rope with a wooden frame, almost like a hammock, but with larger holes. My boots hung in a couple of the gaps in the weave and now that I was aware of what I was seated on, I could feel the sharp indentations through my dress where my arse poked through in other places, between the woven grass ropes, which were as thick as my wrists. I looked up and realized the cage was suspended from a spar off the mainmast. Then I looked down.

I immediately regretted my decision.

A few spans below, Shambles stood waiting on the deck, crammed so close that if we were to fall, we'd land on bone instead of wood. And every dead mother's child staring up at us, a hundred empty sockets questing, searching for something unfathomable to mortals. Their eyeless gaze sent gooseflesh racing down my spine and across my arms. Memories raced with it. *The Ghost Captain. The cleaver. Eld.* I shivered, blinking back tears. My sudden movement made the cage twist in a slow circle.

"Who's Eld?"

"What?" I looked up, my thoughts broken.

"You said a name just now," the Archaeologist said. "Who's Eld? Will they come rescue us?"

"No." I shook my head and looked into the sun's dying light. "They were too stupid to save themselves, let alone us." *You should have listened to me, Eld. I had a plan!* After all, I was the one who—

I was the one who led us stumbling from one mistaken nightmare to the next. The thought poured ice water over my self-pity and rage and maybe for the first time since we left Servenza, my mind was blissfully clear. *I've fucked up everything.* Okay, perhaps "blissful" wasn't the word. But my mind was clear. I'm the leader. Me. I say so. Eld says so. Said. *And we've almost been gutted by a bull-man thing, been sunk by pirates, tortured by pirates, almost eaten by sharks, nearly drowned, almost killed by the undead—twice—and now Eld really is dead and I'm trapped on a ship at the Ghost Captain's mercy.* Sprinkled in among those highlights were a number of other mindless errors that had aided and abetted our misery. *Gods, I'm a failure.*

"Glad to see you ladies are getting along!" a thin voice called.

Below, the Ghost Captain leered up at me, hands on his hips, tricorne cocked at a jaunty angle. He leaned against an enormous water cask, which was secured to the mainmast by dozens of ropes, surrounded by Shambles. His smile grew when he saw he had my attention.

"You know," he said, "sometimes you have to fight and claw for what you want and it seems like nothing is going to break your way and then everything changes in the blink of an eye and you're handed everything you want, no questions asked."

"'Change is but a breeze away,'" I quoted by rote.

"That's it exactly," the Ghost Captain agreed. "I searched for you, Archaeologist, for months, when it became apparent I wasn't going to find that cursed island on my own. That bitch and her black-flagged brethren kept you from me." He laughed and stroked the remnants of his goatee. "I was beginning to give up hope. Then, not only do I capture you and with it the location of the island, but on the same day, the Sin Eater I need to retrieve the artifact walks right across my deck and into my hands."

"Why do you need one of Ciris's mages?" the Archaeologist asked.

"You've been to the island," the Ghost Captain replied. "So you already know the answer. The artifact didn't come from the Dead Gods. . . . It came from the New Goddess. Stands to reason, then, that the artifact won't work for me."

"But you want it anyway?" the Archaeologist asked. He nodded. "Then what will you give me for the location?"

Their words flowed through me. A small part of my mind an alyzed the conversation, sifted through it, making calculations, but the greater part of me ignored it. *Failure.* The word was all-encompassing and I couldn't seem to see past its edges. Nor, if I was being honest, did I really care to.

"If your life means so little to you, you wouldn't have fought my servitors so hard, woman. So stop trying to negotiate with me—you're in no position to bargain," the Ghost Captain said.

"I don't know the location!" The Archaeologist's voice cracked, rough with unshed tears. "I've just a general idea of where it lies . . . likely the same as you."

"That's not how that Kanados captain whose ship I took remembered it," the Ghost Captain said with a laugh. "His memory was of carrying you with all speed to Servenza to meet with the Board. And the story you told then was of a more . . . specific sort. Did he lie? Because I can call his moldering corpse up for us right now," he growled, pointing back toward the open door leading belowdecks.

"Of course I told a different story," she protested. Her knuckles were nearly translucent where she gripped the edges of the cage. "I lied! Because that's how this sort of venture works. I needed a fleet of ships to find the island and the money to pay for them. A single ship hired for a few days was never going to get more than a vague sense of where it lies.

"The trading companies wouldn't finance an expedition to no-where." She sank back against the ropes. "So I lied, and a fat lot of good it did me. I was laughed out of their office and sent back here, shipless and coinless to boot."

"Why do you want Ciris's artifact?" I asked. The question sur-prised me; it'd come from the fraction of me that still cared. The one that had been listening intently. I hated that part of me, yet allowed it to speak. "And where will you find a Sin Eater?"

"I've already found one—you!" He laughed.

I snorted. "Me? I'm no Sin Eater."

"Oh, but I've reason to believe you are, Sambuciña." He tapped the side of his nose. "The dead have a smell to them, don't they? I've come to realize the living have a smell to them as well. The dead smell sweet—too sweet sometimes, it's true, but sweet nonetheless. It's the living that smell bad, what with their sweat and odors. And Sin Eaters?" His smile hardened. "They have another smell. A hard smell. A metallic smell." He inhaled deeply, through his nose.

"Haven't you wondered how I know your name? You did well, slipping into Port au' Sheen unnoticed, but after that, you couldn't help yourself, could you?" He shook his head and winked. "Your kind never can."

"I don't know what you think I did in Port au' Sheen, but the only Sin Eater I'm aware of there is the Harbormaster. You're wel-come to the bitch for all I care, but she's there and I'm here," I said.

"Why are you prolonging the inevitable?"

I shrugged. "I'm not—why are you?"

"Your kind can't stand much in the way of pain." He licked his lips, shadows growing across his cheeks. "Not before your God-dess's taint reveals itself. Is that what you want? Because if you won't cooperate, I'll force you to. Blood and Bone, woman!" He shook his hands at me. "I haven't even asked you for anything yet."

"You're desperate," I whispered. "I can see it in you, buried just below the surface and working its way up like a corpse that just won't stay dead." My eyes flicked to the Shambles, which had begun to stir around him, perhaps feeling their master's irritation.

"I was like that once and it cost me dearly," I said. "The problem with desperation is, it plays for keeps." I took a deep breath and let it out, barely feeling my lungs move. "There's no game here, Ghost Captain. I'm not playing. I'm no Sin Eater."

"Bullshit!" He jabbed a finger at me. "There is something on that island that Ciris desperately desires, but her lust will be her undoing. I'm going to give her everything she wants and then—" He paused, panting, and forcibly took control of himself. "So." He inhaled fitfully. "Think again, won't you? If you don't do as I ask, I won't keep you safe in a cage dangling over my pets." He grinned that too-many-teeth grin.

"I'll cut you down and turn them loose on your flesh. And after I've exposed the lie in you, I'll beach my ship on yonder island and let your friends feel the bite of the dead until the waves run red with blood. When I leave, there will be nothing left but sand. No plants. No animals. No *people*." He straightened and the look in his eyes filled me with dread as he held up a glowing blue book.

"Now you understand the stakes. You have until morning to change your answer." His eyes fixed on the Archaeologist and she let out a small cry. "Both of you."

The Ghost Captain spun around, pulling his tricorne straight, and stalked away. As he did, his words swept through my mind, but the small part of me still listening caught on one. *Friends? The islanders? Or*—"Wait!" My cry pulled him up short. "What about my friends?"

He glanced over his shoulder and sneered. "Don't think that

washed-up pirate or your hulking partner will rescue you, Sambuciña. They're as good as dead, marooned on an island with cannibalistic savages. But if you care at all for them, you'll give me what I want or else they won't be dead. . . . They'll be undead." He marched off, Shambles following in his wake. Those below us began to moan softly, flexing bone and sinew menacingly.

My eyes burned, but I managed to hold the tears back. That was a hill I was ready to die on and after a few torturous breaths the dampness dissipated. *Eld . . . alive?* My breath came out more like a sob, but I let it. *Gods, I didn't kill him. There's still a chance to put this right. I didn't kill him.* The part of me that'd still been working shifted slightly and I felt my chest tighten fractionally. *I didn't kill him, but I did fail him.* I forced myself to take another breath. *Think, Buc!*

All right, I am a failure. *Why?* Why had I been making so many bad decisions? The thought hung there before the answer came. Because I'd let emotion blind me. That was one weakness I'd never thought to find in myself. Emotion comes slow to me when it comes at all, but doesn't everyone dream about a better tomorrow? The very word is a promise, a fantasy, an intangible dream that could be any number of things. Anything but the present, or worse, the present's corpse: the past. I'd dreamed of a better tomorrow for as long as I was on the streets, and the only memory I had before the streets was of a warm stone hearth and a song being sung. I can't quite catch the melody, but it's there and every bit as warm as that hearth.

My dream had changed over time, a better tomorrow not just for me, but for my sister as well. For the girl who'd kept me from starving, fended off the children who grew faster and stronger than me, and never let me slip into the gutter even though the only blood we shared came from cleaning the cuts on my face. Fire had ended that fantasy.

Now I dreamed of a better tomorrow for everyone who wasn't born with a full stomach and coin in their pocket.

That Kanados Trading Company bitch had come along and offered to give flesh to my dream. To turn it into a goal. Dreams are of the ether, but goals have more substance. They can be made real. I defy anyone who's longed for something so hard and so long that it physically hurts—twisting the stomach into knots, burning the chest, and choking the throat—to not lose their mind when that moment arrives. When all you've known is pain. And yet. And yet, the promise of it is so sweet that it's worth the agony. I'd let that sweetness overwhelm and consume me, and I'd forgotten the lessons that came with the agony. No more.

"No more."

"What?"

The Archaeologist's question pulled me back to reality. *Eld is alive. I can still save this.* Hope surged through my veins, warming me and giving my words of warning a moment before the lie. *Don't fuck this up.* I could save this, but I had to be more careful than before, more thoughtful, and I couldn't let my emotions run away with me. I hadn't even realized I'd had emotions, but now that I knew they existed, at least a few of them anyway, I could control them. Had to control them. Above all else, if I was going to change the tide, I would have to be absolutely ruthless. I felt my mouth twitch.

"You realize we're fucked? Why are you smiling?"

"Because," I whispered, "'a change of breeze is but a wave away.'"

And I'm a hurricane.

36

Eld stared past the foliage and out to sea, where the Ghost Captain's ship rode high in the water. Where Buc had gone without him. He'd tried to keep up, but something had caught him in the side of the head and brought him to his knees. His memory of the events was foggy at best. He remembered Buc shouting that they had to save the woman. *The Archaeologist.* Then Chan Sha had asked him something, but what she asked was a blank, though he recalled the surprise in her voice. The next moment he'd found himself lying in the sand and if Chan Sha hadn't appeared in front of him like a street performer, he would have been run through by the Shambles' blades.

What hit me? He reached and stopped just short of the jagged cut beneath his hairline. *Who?* He'd fought to his feet then, and carried on, working mostly on instinct as others fell around them. At the end, it'd just been him and Chan Sha, fighting back to back; then the islanders' charge overwhelmed the Shambles and sent them back to their unholy graves. But the attack had come too late and Buc had disappeared aboard the ship.

Buc. They'd been through a lot together, but this easily eclipsed everything else that had come before. Before, he'd been the one leaning on her while she quietly mocked him—well, maybe not so quietly—but in her way, she'd protected him when he overstepped. Turn and turnabout. Now their roles were reversed and the thought of her sailing alone toward the lurking ship left a bitter taste on his tongue. He took a sip of water from the broken brown nut in his hand, but it did little to wash away the taste of failure. The last time, he'd lost every man and woman who relied on him and now, alone again, he'd lost her. His throat burned and he blinked back tears. *What would you do now?*

"Are you going to stand there all day?" Chan Sha asked from behind him. "I chose this tree to take advantage of the sea breezes, but that only works if you're not blocking them."

"I'm standing watch," Eld said quietly. He turned beside the tree and caught Chan Sha smirking at him. "I shouldn't have left her out there alone."

"You've a one-note mind, don't you?" the pirate asked. She stood up from the palm frond she'd been lying on and stretched, showing peeks of olive oil–colored skin through the tears in her sun-bleached shirt. "She's not alone. She's got the Archaeologist with her and she said the woman knows how to kill the Ghost Captain. I'd bet a pretty coin your girl is plotting the best way to slit his throat as we speak. And to do that will require skullduggery. You being there with those wide shoulders would only get in the way." Her eyes hardened. "Now, are we going to talk about that parley or not? You gave your word."

"Aye, in a bit," Eld said, turning back to the sea.

"Listen, you big oaf," Chan Sha growled. "You think you're the only one what's taken losses? You didn't lose anything. Your little woman's still alive. That rotting fucking bastard sank my ship and took my crew down with it. Every woman and man on board. Dead.

"So we don't have a bit. We have right now." She rolled her shoulders and clenched her fists. "I could have taken his head off at the shoulders on the beach, right there and then. He was bent on his purpose, distracted. Then you two fools had to come charging in like some heroes out of one of those cheap novels they sell on the streets for a scrap of copper. It's a wonder the twerp didn't get *her* head taken off at the shoulders."

Anger, slow-stoked and buried deeply enough that he hadn't fully realized it was there until now, shook the soreness from Eld's body. He didn't feel tired, only ready. And angry. *Gods help me.* Bad things happened when he let his temper get the best of him. An image of another man's face, drawn taut, with blood coursing from smashed lips, flashed through his mind. Seetel's lips had been twisted in a superior sneer when the duel started. *Bad things.* His hand fell to his side, but he'd left the rusted cutlass on the beach, so he crossed his arms to keep from reaching for Chan Sha.

The movement attracted her attention. She looked at him and froze. Her breath hissed through her teeth. She looked past him and then her gaze flitted back to his face and she swallowed audibly.

"Might be I'm overwrought," she said finally.

"Might be," he said. He wanted to say more, but his throat was clenched tight.

"We both are," she said carefully.

"Agreed."

"Then let's both take us a couple of deep breaths and come sit down in the shade and work this out," Chan Sha suggested. Her eyes stared right into his as she moved away slowly, every muscle in her body taut as a wire. When she sat, she kept her feet and legs in front of her so she could move if she had to. "Neither one of us is going to help that gir—Buc—by standing around wishing things were different. We've got to play the hand we've been dealt."

Eld felt his chest expand with his breath and he took in more air until his lungs couldn't manage another scrap before he let the air out slowly, allowing the coals within him to lose some of their fierceness. Two more breaths and he could work his jaw without pain. This was Buc's territory, dealmaking, but with her gone, it fell to him. *Chan Sha matches Buc wit for wit.* He'd never thought of himself as stupid, far from it, but two years with Buc had given him an appreciation for genius. There was intelligence and then there was Buc. And Chan Sha was in the same league as Buc. He was facing veteran shock troops, and all he had were some light cuirassiers of doubtful experience. But then, that was all the Burnt had had when they'd faced him and—

We've got to play the hand we've been dealt. The pirate was right, so he buried his doubts along with the rest of his anger and sank down onto the beach beside Chan Sha.

"Okay," he said, resting his forearms on his knees. Sunlight lanced in through one of the openings in the palm fronds overhead, illuminating Chan Sha in a beam of light that made her braids shimmer in the dust mote–filled air. "Let's talk."

"You are a mule of a man," Chan Sha hissed. The sun had shifted hours ago and her features were bathed in shadow. "How many times must we go over this?"

"I told you on the beach, I'd help you get off the island," Eld said. They'd been over it a dozen times, but the repetition seemed to be getting to Chan Sha, so he kept steering the conversation back into the loop. One thing he'd picked up from Buc: needle someone and they'll slip up; needle someone in the right place at the right time and they'll dance to your tune without ever hearing the music. He wasn't sure he was capable of finding the soft spot in Chan Sha—the woman was hard as nails—but he might get her to slip up. "I'm not going to promise more until Buc is back." He nodded toward the sea. "And I'm going to get her if she's not back in the next hour," he added.

"How?" Chan Sha asked. "My boat was sinking more than floating when I washed ashore. We'll need good daylight to see what holes need to be plugged if we want to make it past the breakwaters. And that means they'll see us coming long before we reach them, assuming the dead bother to keep watch."

"That's why I wanted to float the fucking thing hours ago!"

"Aye? When you were wobbling on your feet with either eye crossed?" Chan Sha shook her head. "We were past the brink of exhaustion, Eld. Nothing to be done."

"There's something to be done now," he muttered. "But not without Buc. Until then, you'll have to deal with me."

"Deal? You mean 'parley'?" She sniffed at his expression. "Amongst pirates we call agreements, deals, or truces 'parley.' There's an entire code attached to them. Parley generally comes with terms and conditions, and all you've done is promise me vagaries. You make no sense, Eld."

"I don't have to," he said. "Buc makes enough sense for the pair of us." He fought the urge to look at the open sea. It was dark enough now that he'd be hard-pressed to see anything beyond the ship's mainsail anyway. "You've gotten about all you're going to get out of me, Chan Sha."

The pirate sat back, disgust writ large across her features. A moment later she leaned back in. "Even if she returns empty-handed, you're going after the Ghost Captain."

It wasn't a question, and in any case Eld didn't have to give it much thought. If Buc . . . *when* Buc was back, she wouldn't let the Dead Walker go. Even without the Kanados Trading Company's "offer" to consider, the Ghost Captain had bested her twice and nearly killed her the last time. That sort of thing would have inclined a normal person to think twice before running the other way—Gods, that was what Eld wanted to do. But Buc wasn't normal. No, she'd be calculating a way to slit the Dead Walker's throat—if she hadn't done so already. *But if she has killed him, why hasn't she come back?*

"Aye," he said.

"Then take me with you!" Her dark green eyes flashed. "The Ghost Captain's already bested the pair of you with just a few longboats of Shambles. How many do you think he has on his ship? You can't do this on your own."

"Buc would point out that you didn't fare much better with a crew around you," Eld said. Buc would have said that, but she would have used her words like a dagger to wound Chan Sha, while he merely stated the truth. "Why take you on? You held us in chains, tortured us, and came about as close to killing us as *he* has. By the Gods, why would we risk having you with us after that?"

"The Gods," Chan Sha repeated hesitantly. She glanced down at the sand and when she looked back up, her eyes were sharp, piercing. "You think you can kill one of the servants of the Dead Gods? We've a saying on the seas: 'Don't bring a pistole to a cannonade.'"

"Aye, 'fight fire with fire,'" Eld agreed. "What of it?"

"You said it yourself: I've come as close to killing you as the Ghost Captain has." A smile touched her features. "Haven't you wondered why?"

"Why?" Eld snorted. "Because you had the crew and we didn't."

"No, that's not it. Not it by half." Her voice lowered and drew heat from some unseen source, and when she spoke, her words sent gooseflesh down his sunburnt arms. "You have a pistole, Eld, when what you need is a cannon. Let me show you."

Cold sweat ran down the back of his spine. His heart pounded in his ears. He knew what Buc would say and he'd never doubted her. *But.* But they hadn't done much more than fall from one failure right into another since leaving Servenza. Eld licked his lips and forced himself to think, but the answers spun past him so quickly that all he could do was grasp at them in a desperate attempt to find the right one.

"Let me show you," Chan Sha whispered. "And if she's not back by morning, I'll lead the rescue effort myself."

Where are you, Buc?

37

"I wasn't sure about you," I told the Archaeologist. She arched an eyebrow. "What?" I shrugged. "First I saw you, you were running from Shambles. Then when I step in to save you, you run right back to them."

"I didn't run back to them—you pushed me!"

"I did not," I protested.

"Did!"

I studied her wide eyes in the moonlight, but if she was lying, I didn't see it. I hadn't pushed her, though. *Eld and Chan Sha thought I did.* I tried to recall the scene, but my recollection was of pulling her away, not pushing her closer. *What wouldn't I do to save myself? I nearly sacrificed Eld; what's this woman to me?* I tried to shake the thought away, but it clung with a multitentacled grip and eventually I gave over. Without kan to help me manage, my thoughts swirled around, leaving me grasping at eddies. I could control it, just, but that required enough concentration that I could feel the beginnings of a headache coming on. I didn't think I'd done what they all thought I had, but it didn't mean I wouldn't have done it if I'd thought it would save me. And it didn't mean I wouldn't do it still.

"I tried to pull you away and we got tangled up and turned around," I said finally. "I came here"—I tugged on one of the thick grass ropes—"to save you. Does that sound like the actions of one who wanted you dead?"

"N-no," she said. She hesitated. "I suppose not."

"As I was saying," I began again, shooting her a hard look, "I wasn't sure about you, but the way you stood up to big and corpse-y earlier was damned impressive." She sat up a little straighter, adjusting her skirts, although I didn't think she had much to fear from the undead seeing up her dress. "Not everyone would be able to face down a Dead Walker, especially on a ship infested with Shambles."

She cleared her throat. "Thanks, but I don't know what came over me, if I'm being honest."

"Survival," I answered for her. "Survival instinct and some steel in there that maybe you didn't even realize you had." She smiled, wincing because of her split lip. "How did you manage to lie straight to his face? I've heard the mages of the Dead Gods can read minds," I lied.

"I didn't lie," she protested. "And the Dead Gods' magic doesn't let them read minds. It transforms flesh and bone or turns the dead to life."

"I see," I said, nodding along. "Well, I may not know much of the Dead Gods, but I know when someone's lying. And you were, back then. You do know where the island is, don't you?"

"I . . ." She hesitated.

"Gods, you've *been* there, haven't you?" I bit my lip to keep from pressing further and instead let the silence drag out. Man or woman, they all like to believe they are stronger than they are. Like a dog that's never fought in the pit before, that carries its head too high and finds out the hard way that its throat is exposed. I wasn't sure how much steel the Archaeologist had in her. Some, to be sure, or she'd have never come to the Shattered Coast, let alone lie to the Ghost Captain . . . but if she had much more, she wouldn't have asked for my protection back on the beach.

She would have just kept running. That, along with the little bone I'd tossed her way, plus our general predicament, would be enough to loosen her tongue. I hoped. *If she were a man, she'd have started talking as soon as I said I was impressed.* But women weren't as foolish as men. *Unfortunately.*

"Aye, I lied," she whispered. "I have been to the island, but only long enough to confirm that a ship had been wrecked there. I'm serious," she added when I rolled my good eye. "Whatever happened, the waves must have been scores of paces higher than they are now. . . . The ship's impaled on a cliff's edge. It'd be difficult work to safely excavate it without a crew and some engineers."

"And there's the artifact to consider," I supplied.

"That too . . . He was right: it belongs to Ciris." She cleared her throat. "I wasn't trying to steal from your Goddess, Sin Eater, I promise. I had every intention of finding one of your leaders, but I had to make absolutely sure first."

"By selling it to the Kanados Trading Company?" She blanched and sank back, holding up a hand protectively. I decided it was time to let her off the hook. She'd lied to the Ghost Captain when she felt threatened and I didn't want her lying to me. "Easy, sister. I wasn't lying earlier. I'm not a Sin Eater." I laughed mirthlessly and tugged on one of the ropes. "If I were, do you really think this tawdry cage would hold me?"

"No, I guess not." She shook her head. "But he seemed so sure."

"Aye." I frowned. "I've no answer for that, but he's likely to only believe me when he's gone too far and I'm dead." I waved mention of my impending torture and demise away with a hand and settled back against the ropes. "But leave that. How'd you know for sure the artifact belonged to Ciris?"

"It's hard to explain if you haven't been there," she said, pulling gently on a lock of her auburn hair. "But there's a certain sense of power there. It ebbs and flows. I wasn't on the island long enough to know how powerful the artifact truly is, but I could sense a presence." She paused and looked at me. "Almost as if it were in my mind. Or reaching for it, at any rate."

"That doesn't make any sense." And it didn't. Sin Eaters like the Harbormaster could reach the minds of others of their kind at great distances and were near immortal. But none of them could contact regular people, or read their minds, that I knew of. *Knew of.* "Unless they've kept a portion of their powers hidden?"

She shrugged. "They definitely have telepathic powers with one another. The journal I read was written by one of their own and they didn't mention the ability to speak with nonbelievers."

"Could have been lying."

"I doubt it, since it was written in a cipher."

"Wait—this journal? That's how you knew where to find the artifact?"

The Archaeologist eyed me for a long moment, then sighed and nodded. "I was in the Cordoban Confederacy, on an expedition to explore some of their more ancient tombs."

"Grave robbing, you mean."

"*Exploring.* That's what an Archaeologist does . . . or at least that's what I do, and since it's my name, I get to decide what it means. Exploring. I came across the journal in a dusty corner of one of their oldest libraries. Most of it was boring, mundane. The author must have been a relatively new initiate, with ambitions that outpaced their talents."

"Why do you say that?" I asked.

"Because the only reason they knew about this particular expedition was that it was meant to be kept secret even from other Sin Eaters. This boy—I'm pretty sure he was barely older than that—decided the way to power was to know every little secret and controversy he could lay his hands on.

"He knew when the expedition left, and he knew its course, and when his Goddess's sudden rage confused many of his fellow Sin Eaters, he knew it was because the expedition was lost." She leaned forward. "The ship wasn't carrying just any artifact, Buc. It was carrying a shard of Ciris herself."

"Gods," I breathed. "That's why the Ghost Captain's out here— he's searching for a weapon against Ciris. Her own weapon."

"Something like that," she agreed. "Now you see why I didn't simply try to take the artifact. It's practically inviting a death sentence. But I figured something as powerful as the Kanados Trading Company could find a use for it and wouldn't be as worried about the consequences."

"Guessed wrong, eh?"

"They wouldn't even hear me out," she growled. "All I got was some prissy dressed-up bitch in blond curls who told me to be gone without ever looking down her nose to see me bowing before her."

"I think I know who you're talking about," I muttered. "She's an arsehole."

"Epic."

We laughed then, but it's hard to laugh when you're suspended in a rickety cage above undead monsters. Silence descended and with it, the last rays of the sun; darkness well and truly consumed the ship. Even with lamps lit, the Shambles were hard to see on the deck below us, save for where an odd bone stood out, dull white in the darkness. I plucked at the ropes and let my mind wander.

There was a way out of any trap, but sometimes finding the first step was the hardest. Full night and my lack of kan didn't help any. *And even if I escape, there's still the Ghost Captain and his Shambles to deal with.* "Say, you told me on the beach you knew how to kill the Dead Walker," I reminded her.

"And you said you'd get me away," she replied with a wan smile.

"And here I sit," I said, spreading my arms wide. *Properly fucked.* "But seriously, do you know how? He's not undead like the rest, is he?"

"No." She sat up. "Any mortal may die, it's true. And he is mortal, though not like you or me. But so long as his minions are under his power, if his body dies, his mind will pass into one of them. Hardly ideal, I'm sure, but it's not quite death, is it?"

"So I kill all of the Shambles."

"Sure—if you can kill several hundred before they kill you." She sniffed. "This Ghost Captain is many things, but he's no fool, and he's been recruiting from the crews he's killed."

She had a line for every one of mine, each one turning me away from the light and back to the wall. And I hate walls. "Nothing is impossible. I won't believe it. Stop trying to make it seem so."

"It's not impossible, Buc; there may be other ways," she said, her tone balancing mine. "But the one who wrote the journal only mentioned one and I think, given what they were, they would probably know." She leaned closer. "You can see it in the two warring religions. One magic cannot abide the other. Dead Walkers and all of the Dead Gods' mages use the magic of blood and bone. You want to kill the Ghost Captain? Kill him outright? That would require Ciris's magic. Mind magic."

"Sin Eaters," I whispered.

"Sin Eaters," she agreed.

"What else did your mystery author have to say?" I asked, sitting back.

"Dunno. After several hastily written entries that made references to others being jealous of his power and worry that one of them was on to him, he said he was going to lie low for a while." She showed her teeth. "That was the final entry."

"Aye," I grunted. "I'm sure he's lying low still. Buried in the ground." I shook my head. "I've no intention of waiting for the Ghost Captain to torture me, and I'm sure you don't want to see how far he'll let you carry on before he decides to torture you as well—"

"He won't torture me," she said, interrupting. Her voice quivered. "He'll just turn me into one of the undead. Didn't you hear his threat about bringing up the captain I sailed with before? He can sift through the memories of the dead."

"He can?"

She nodded. "Blood magic, remember? The dead are still of the flesh, and whatever magic the first worshippers found in the Dead Gods, it still works today. Another thing I learned from the journal. The memories will decay over time, sure, but we're only a few hours' sail from the island. My memory will be plenty fresh."

"But he doesn't know that?" I asked. She shook her head. "Then we've still some time."

"Time to do what?"

"Blow this motherfucking crypt," I growled.

38

"That wasn't part of the deal," the Archaeologist protested.

"There was no deal that accounted for all of this," I said, waving an arm around us. "The deal onshore was, I get you away, in exchange for knowledge on how to kill the Ghost Captain."

"Which you didn't do," she said.

"Aye, and you didn't either."

"Bullshit! I just told you how to kill him," she hissed.

"For which I'm very grateful," I said, smiling. "But there was no deal, then. And I don't work on gratitude." She opened her mouth angrily and I cut her off. "Listen—I didn't have to come here to save you. I could have stayed on the island and you'd be a corpse come morning."

"Aye, that's true, but I don't think you came for me," she said, glaring at me. I crossed my arms and stared back at her. The silence lengthened between us until finally she threw up her arms. "Fine, then. If I don't tell you, I'm dead anyway, so what does it matter?"

"That's the spirit," I agreed. "But, Archaeologist?" She looked up. "Like I said, I'm not like the Ghost Captain. I can hear a lie. And if I even suspect you're hedging a little bit, I'll lay down here and go to sleep out of spite alone." She nodded slowly and I could see she believed me. Which was good, because I'd been lying about sleeping, but not the rest. I would have throttled her instead. "Then go on."

"You'll need a compass," she said. "And to know how to use it."

"I know how to use a compass," I snorted. Which was true in the sense that I'd read how to use a compass. But the book hadn't made it seem that difficult and I could still see the words if I closed my eyes hard enough, so the knowledge was there, just waiting.

"Well, yon island is the starting point. Go to the southwest corner and then take a bearing when the sun's just rising over-head and . . ."

I listened intently, committing every word to memory, and when she finished, I was sure of two things: I could find the island in my sleep and the Archaeologist was either the world's best liar or I'd scared her straight. I'd seen her lie to the Ghost Captain, so I knew what she looked like when she wasn't telling the truth, and I wasn't worried about it.

"Okay," I said when she finished. I pushed myself to my feet, wobbling on the thick ropes, and caught myself. "Okay," I re-peated. "Let's take stock of our surroundings." I turned slowly, studying the ropes and the points where they intersected with the wooden planks that formed the frame of the cage at each of the corners. The Archaeologist stood up beside me, smoothing her dress. "I could wish my eye wasn't swollen shut; I'd be fin-ished in half the time," I muttered.

"You've a clot of blood beside it," she said, pointing to the cor-ner of my eye. "That's what's keeping it shut more than anything."

"Aye, well, I left my last knife in the eye of one of the undead, so nothing to be done about it."

"If it's something sharp you need," the other woman said, "would this help?" She dug into her bodice and pulled out the nib of a fountain pen, the steel tip's edge gleaming in the moonlight. "Although it might hurt."

"Pain is temporary," I assured her, holding out my hand. She arched an eyebrow and I made a noise in my throat. "I trust you, Archaeologist, but I don't trust anyone's hand but my own around my eyes." She shook her head and gave me the nib, then indicated with her own hands where the clot was. I found it and pressed gently. Pain radiated in waves as I touched the blood-filled swelling. I took a deep breath, steadied myself against the ropes, then stabbed the nib hard into my flesh and drew it down and out in a single motion that felt like drawing a line with fire. A sharp, burning sensation sprang to life in my face, flooding my cheek with warmth, which I realized was the blood running down. When it stopped, I tried to open and close my eye and found that most of my vision had been restored. "How do I look?" I asked her.

"Like murder walking," she said.

"Bloody perfect," I said, spraying flecks of blood that had run onto my lips. "Now, what else have you got hidden in your cleavage?"

It turned out the Archaeologist didn't have much more beyond a small inkwell and a compass. I took both. Turning out my own pockets, I found only my slingshot, and with no shot it was barely worth the name. I'd run out of knives between all of our misadventures, which was a damned shame given how ill made the grass ropes of the cage were. We tried the pen nib, but it was neither sharp enough nor large enough to do more than irritate a few of the fibers.

I could see the other woman's face losing hope by degrees in the flickering lamplight. It was times like these I truly missed Eld. He never doubted me. *And look where it got him.* I trod across the thought, and the one that followed on its heels: *What happened to my confidence?* It was hard to find a thing you'd never lost before, but there it was, like a small burr in the back of my mind, slowly rubbing away, leaving something raw in its place.

"This isn't much of a prison," I said. I walked in a slow circle as the Archaeologist busied herself pulling up the small water bucket, which was tied to a rope attached to the bottom of the cage. The rope was just long enough that the bucket could be swung to the massive water barrel secured to the mainmast below. The barrel was easily a dozen paces away and we had to swing the bucket just right so it would land in the barrel. Half of it spilled out on the way back up.

It was a huge barrel. Apparently the Ghost Captain wanted to make sure he'd be able to sail for weeks without stopping, even though he was the only being on board who needed to drink or cook. That was a good thing, because it'd taken the Archaeologist a score of attempts before she figured out the right momentum required to reach the damned thing at all. I expected her to take a drink, but instead she washed her face. I didn't have the heart to tell her we'd be getting a lot dirtier before all was said and done.

"Not much but grass and bark, really," I mused aloud, tugging hard on the ropes. The Shambles or Ghost Captain or whomever built it had bound it tight to the wooden frame and it barely shook. The pain from my eye had proved an unexpected boon: it kept part of my brain occupied so I could actually think. Not so nice as kan, but "beggars can't be choosers" and all that. I glanced at the water she was dumping over her face and down her chin and laughed. *I can't believe this is how we're going to escape.* "I read something once about grasses and ropes and knots, something I never fully understood, but now I think I might," I said. Her head jerked up. "Are you ready to get out of here?"

"You seriously want me to piss on the ropes?" the Archaeologist asked.

"Well, I'm going to give it a go too," I said. "I wish Eld was here, given our lack of anatomical advantage, but luckily gravity will help." She laughed. "Seriously, I want you to piss on the ropes."

"Are you going to tell me why?"

"Number two sixteen," I said, quoting the book I'd read. "It was a pamphlet on knots and their common uses. There was a small section on different types of rope and it mentioned in passing that grass ropes should never be used in wet climes because of rotting, but also because of shrinkage."

"Shrinkage is rarely good," the Archaeologist said with a smirk.

"Aye, well, I guess that's their anatomical disadvantage?" I asked her. She giggled, which was an improvement over sulking. "Well, anyway, these are fresh grass ropes, so they haven't ever been exposed to moisture. Get them wet and the knots around the frame are going to become incredibly tight." I waved away her protest. "Doesn't matter. We couldn't untie them anyway. But they are tied all along the frame of the cage, so when they tighten, they are going to pull everything tight around the frame." I touched one of the boards. "It should make getting out of here that much easier."

"Should?"

"I read a dozen pages in a pamphlet, Arch. That doesn't make me a fucking rope expert. Either we'll cut our way out or use the tension to break the boards."

"Fair enough." She held up the bucket. "So why not use the water from this?"

"We will," I said, "but we need a lot of water to cover that frame. And piss will eat through what water won't."

"Gods," she groaned. "Is this nightmare ever going to end?"

"Look at it this way," I told her. "Some speak of spitting in death's eye, but you'll be able to say you pissed in it instead. Eh?"

"That's not helping," she muttered.

"Well, I tried." I motioned for her to pass me the bucket. "Drink up if you have a need; we don't have long, Arch. It's almost full night and the Ghost Captain may come for us anytime now."

"More good news."

It turned out that urine was even better at ruining grass ropes than I'd hoped. Something I hadn't accounted for, but enough shit had happened that it was about time something good came of it instead. However, even drinking all the water we could hold and using the bucket as well, we'd barely managed to soak the four corners of the bottom part of the frame. By the time I had my dress readjusted, the whole cage smelled like the gutters the morning after a celebration day in Servenza. I couldn't see enough to know how effective it had been. At least our undead guards didn't seem to have noticed what we'd been up to.

"I can't drink anymore," the Archaeologist said. "We've been pissing for hours."

"Feels that way," I agreed. I pulled on the rope that went

through a hole in an end of one of the boards and the entire frame shook, but the rope didn't move at all. It was drawn taut, like plucking a bowstring. I gave the board a solid kick and we both had to grab hold as the cage rocked back and forth, but the board didn't show any signs of cracking. *So that's out.* "I think we've pissed away enough of our time." I drew the pen nib and knelt down in the corner. "Now to find out if I'm as smart as I think I am."

"You're going to cut through a rope the size of our wrists with a broken pen nib?" She laughed.

"The nib's not broken," I said. "The rest might be, but this has an edge to it and it's been tipped."

"Which means?"

"Gods, woman, this is your pen and you don't even know what its condition is?" She sniffed and I shook my head and turned back to the rope. Next to reading, writing was the second most important skill you could have. It being "mightier than the sword" and all that. Although in my mind, swordplay was a close third. Or, in my case, ice picking.

"Tipping means," I said as I wedged the edge between two of the twisted fiber strands and began to saw savagely back and forth, "that it's been dipped in an alloy to keep the steel from wearing away. It also means it will hold an edge longer." I grunted as sweat began to drip from my forehead and onto the back of my hand. "Unfortunately, that edge isn't incredibly sharp nor is it long enough to build up much friction. But . . ."

"But with the ropes pulled so tight, you don't need as much cutting surface," the Archaeologist said slowly.

"Correct. Or"—I felt the strand part with a silent twang and began digging out another—"as sharp an edge." I attacked the next strand with a will. "So we cut two of the ropes along the edge here to open a hole along the bottom of the frame and we'll spill out like a pair of coins from a cut purse."

"Right into the midst of a horde of the undead."

"That's the plan," I agreed. She moaned and I laughed as another strand parted. *Or at least, as much of it as you need to know.*

39

"Easy, easy!" I hissed. I stood with my boots braced wide atop either side of the rim of the water barrel, balanced precariously while the Archaeologist's stained bloomers engulfed my face. My saving grace was that the stench of the undead obliterated all other smells. Not that the woman had shit herself—just that she hadn't had a chance to wash her clothes in some time and being chased by the undead hadn't helped matters. "Hang on to the mast, woman."

"I'm trying, but my arms don't reach," she whispered. "I'm losing—"

I had grasped one of her legs and nearly had ahold of the other when her weight unexpectedly dropped fully onto me and I lost her with a muffled cry. Her cry wasn't muffled as she shot between my arms and into the barrel, the water mercifully cutting her scream short. I fought to keep my balance, arms windmilling as I wobbled, until my boot slipped and I fell half into the barrel. The Archaeologist was just coming up for air and my arse sent her right back underwater again.

"Gods damn it, if Eld could see me now," I muttered, trying

to find purchase on the wet barrel sides. After cutting us partially free, it'd taken the better part of an hour to swing with enough momentum to reach the spar our cage had been tied to. I'd had to hang half out of the damned hole to catch ahold, and it'd been a near run thing if we were going to shinny onto the spar before crashing down into the Shambles below. We'd made it, but navigating down the mast hadn't proved as easy as I'd bet on. The Archaeologist's head rammed into me from below, reminding me that she was still down there. I scrambled up and out and she surfaced with a throaty cry that made me wince.

"Shut it," I whispered. I reached over the rim and held her steady. "You're fine. I'm fine. We're all fine . . . but not if you keep carrying on loud enough to wake the dead." It was the wrong choice of words. As soon as I said it she seemed to remember where she was and her mouth opened again to scream. I sighed and shoved her head back underwater and waited for the bubbles to stop. When the surface was relatively calm again, I pulled her back up. "What part of 'shut it' don't you understand?"

"Y-you're drown-n-ing me," she said, gasping.

"Not yet, I'm not," I said. "But scream again and I might change my mind." She recoiled and I bit my lip to keep from screaming myself. "Okay, okay," I said in a gentler tone. "Give me your hands." Between my pulling and her pushing, we managed to get her out of the barrel and onto the deck. "That was the easy part," I reminded her.

The Shambles were motionless around us, spread out in a thick circle about five paces back from the barrel. As I approached one, its head twisted back and forth as if trying to work a crick out. When I stopped moving, it stopped too. I took another step and its head twisted again and I remembered what the Ghost Captain had said. About how the living smelled different from the dead. *Damn.* On a hunch I inched my hand closer, watching its head, and then snatched at its tattered shirtsleeve. The whole sleeve came away, tearing around the exposed bones, and the Shambles wobbled unsteadily for a moment, its head turning completely around to stare at me. I quickly held the shirtsleeve up between us, and the Shambles cocked its head quizzically before turning back around and resuming its former motionless stance.

"Phew," I breathed out. "I can't wait to get off this fucking ship."

"What did you do?" the Archaeologist asked, so closely in my ear that I almost jumped out of my skin.

"Damn it, woman," I whisper-growled. "Don't sneak up on me like that. Not when we're surrounded by Shambles."

"Sorry, it's just—I'm terrified."

You and me both, sister. "I'm not. Not now, anyway." I wrapped the stiff, weathered sleeve around my forearm and hand and then held it up between me and another Shambles that wore a patched and ragged overcoat. It didn't so much as twitch as I neared it, not even when I ripped one of the larger patches out of its coat, making its bones rattle.

"Here." I shoved the cloth back at her blindly. "Tie that around your arm and then you and I are going to slip out of here, back to back."

"They . . . can smell us?" she asked.

"I know," I muttered. "It's not fucking fair. They shouldn't have any olfactory senses left. But at least we have a workaround."

"I—I can't do this," she moaned.

"Oh, you're doing it," I said, turning to face her. Whatever my expression looked like, with my swollen eye it must have proved menacing, because she stepped back so quickly, she almost bumped another Shambles. "The cloth!" I hissed. She held it up, quivering in her fist, as the Shambles began to turn toward her. It paused, gloved fist in the air, and then turned away and resumed its previous hunchbacked position.

"You're doing it," I repeated, "or else I'll leave you here in the center of them."

"You promised!" she said, her voice cracking.

"Aye, but you have to hold up your end. Now get over here." I pointed toward the sky. "Dawn is about to break; it's already only dark instead of blindingly so. If we're not far out to sea by the time the Ghost Captain stirs his bones, then we might as well just slit our throats and be done with it." She squeaked and rushed to me. I had to turn her around and adjust the piece of cloth so it was affixed more firmly to her arm, but once we started moving, I was surprised to feel her back against mine as we wormed our way in lockstep through the huddled mass of bone and decay.

I'd like to say I charted a course and held to it, but the best that can be said is that I didn't let fear freeze me in place. It wanted to; every fiber in me screamed to stop moving, that I was already dead, could feel death leeching into my bones. Worse, every step sent a vibration through me that felt all too much like skeletal fingers locked onto my skin. Twice now I'd been caught by that iron embrace and I had no wish at all to risk a third. So we inched forward, feet echoing on the deck, the Archaeologist's breath loud in my ears. When we finally stepped past the final Shambles and onto clear, open deck, we sagged against each other and I couldn't tell if our dresses were sodden from the dunking we'd taken or from sweat.

"That's done," I said finally, straightening up. "Work your way toward the rear; that's where I left a boat halfway down." I scowled. "So long as the Ghost Captain didn't haul it up afterward."

"What?"

"What, what? Oh." I shook my head. "Right, nautical terminology and all that. Work your way to the stern and I'll catch up."

"Not *that*," she said. "I know where the rear is. Why aren't you coming with me?"

"I have to attend to something first," I said. "Listen," I snapped when she opened her mouth to argue, "I'll meet you there. Don't fucking touch anything until then. Go that way"—I jabbed a finger toward the rear—"and keep to the shadows. If you see any Shambles standing around, make sure you have that cloth between you and them.

"If you see any moving, treat them the way you would any living human. Hide," I added at her blank expression.

"But—"

"No buts," I said, waving aside her protests, "there's no time. Now go." And then I got her moving with a hard shove. I ran across the deck to the far side. She didn't need to know my plans; she just needed to fucking listen. As I ran, feeling the wind against my skin, no longer locked in a cage hanging over half a hundred Shambles, I felt something like iron returning to me. I'd found what I'd lost. My confidence. *And you'll never take it back now.*

"Well, that makes things easier," I said, pointing toward the shoreline. "He moved around to the far side of the island, but he didn't put out to sea like I feared."

"Aye, but if we can see that far, then it means we've overstayed our welcome," the Archaeologist said.

"When you're right, you're right." I tapped her on the shoulder. "C'mon, I'll go over the side first. It'll take both of us to lower the boat."

I went over the side before she could say anything, using the ropes tethered to the rowboat. Luckily, the Ghost Captain hadn't bothered to pull the boat up. Maybe he hadn't noticed, or maybe, without a real crew, he didn't care. Either way, it was only about two-thirds the distance down to the sea. The wind snatched at my dress, whipping me from side to side like a marionette and sending my heart into my throat more than once.

By the time I reached the boat, I was worried about the Archaeologist's ability to make the climb, but there was nothing for it. She would have to make the attempt or fall into the sea. I dropped into the boat and nearly cut my hand on a blade lying beneath the seat, amongst the bones and rags and blood left from the Shambles I'd killed earlier. I stared at the knife, not quite believing my fortune. *Must have been on that Shambles I sent over the side.*

Cooing to myself, I scooped the knife up and thrust it into the sheath on my wrist. It was too large, the blade longer than my palm, but it would do for now. The weight of it felt wonderful against my arm, like I was finally wearing clothes again.

"Psst," I called, pitching my voice low for the Archaeologist's ears. I cupped my hands over my mouth. "Your turn."

"Oh, I think I'll have a go, if you don't mind," another voice said. The Ghost Captain appeared beside the Archaeologist, wrapping an arm around her. Her skin drained of all color; she looked as pale as the Ghost Captain in the dusky light.

"You've proved yourself a worthy adversary, Sin Eater," he called to me. "And proved I was right about you, thanks to that little escape back there," he said, nodding behind him. "But even you can't survive a fusillade at this range."

He brought up his other hand, showing me his strange, glowing blue book, and suddenly the deck bristled with Shambles brandishing all sorts of firearms, from pistoles to muskets to shotguns. Several larger ones cradled what looked like swivel cannons in their arms.

"I didn't think they could use firearms!" I shouted back. "Thought the powder might ignite their bones."

"Don't be silly." He laughed. I noticed he'd tried to retie the bells into what remained of his goatee, but rather than making him intimidating, it made him sound like a penny beggar on the streets every time he moved. "They usually don't have the dexterity required to make guns worthwhile," he added, "but with a few score aiming at such a small target, I don't need them to be accurate. Anything in the general vicinity will do." His words sent ice water through my veins. "If you try to escape, I'll have them fill you and the boat with lead. And I'll kill your Archaeologist friend, too, while I'm at it."

"Fuck off!"

"No! Wait, wait!" the Archaeologist screamed. "I don't want to die."

"Blood and Bone, woman, I'm not deaf," the Ghost Captain muttered. He sneered, "Since you don't know the island's location, you're worthless to me."

Oh, you poor, stupid arse. He'd baited her and she'd swallowed it in her haste to take another breath.

"I lied. Before," she said, gasping. "I'll tell you where the island is. I can take you there, I promise. I've been there! Set foot on it."

"Have you now?" the Ghost Captain asked. His toothy smile widened. "Well, this changes things, Archaeologist." His smile hardened and he squinted at me in the predawn light. "But if your Sin Eater friend here tries to escape, I'll still have to kill you."

"I'm sorry, Buc," the Archaeologist said.

"Aye." I sighed. "Me too." I flexed my arm to gauge the weight of the blade there. *Too heavy to throw that far.* What else did I have? *Knife. Inkwell. Pen nib. Compass. Slingshot. Knife. Inkwell. Pen n—Inkwell!* I held my hands up as if to acknowledge there was nothing to be done, shifting so I could reach my slingshot. Then I moved like hail in a windstorm.

Slingshot. Inkwell on right. Adjust for the angle and the height. Move! My hands swept up, slingshot in one and inkwell in the palm of the other. I drew back in one fluid motion, trying to gauge the heft of the object as I did. When it reached my cheek, I aimed, hesitating for an instant to get a better sight picture in the bare dawn's light, and that hesitation saved my life.

The Ghost Captain cursed and pulled the Archaeologist in front of him. Half his head was still exposed. *No emotion. Have to be ruthless.* As the other woman caught herself against the edge of the railing, our eyes met and I let fly. The inkwell soared up between us, toward the Ghost Captain. The inkwell, unfamiliar in my grasp, flew hard, but as soon as I released, I realized it wasn't flying true. *Missed. Again.* I saw understanding fill her eyes; her lips parted in a silent scream and then it clipped her forehead in a geyser of ink and blood.

She fell forward and plummeted over the side. My shot hadn't killed her and she screamed as she flew, until her head slammed off the side of my boat with a meaty thunk that showered me with blood. When her body hit the water, I knew she was dead.

I looked back up to see the Ghost Captain staring down at me, tricorne gone, hair wildly flailing in the wind. He stabbed a finger at me. "You fucking bi—" I drew the blade from my wrist and he bit off his curse with another oath, grasping his glowing book with both hands.

The Shambles around him all stiffened. He threw the book down and shouted, *"No!"* but the word was lost in the explosion of a dozen muskets and two swivel cannons.

The boat shuddered as death filled the air around me with its haunting, hot, lead-filled refrain. The rope at the stern of the rowboat quivered, then frayed, then snapped with a crack. I sawed desperately at the remaining rope beside me with my knife. For a breath I hung there, motionless in the air, then the boat fell away and I followed, and chasing after us was the second volley as the rest of the Shambles fired away despite their captain's screamed protestations. The world howled around me and I was powerless to do anything.

Save fall.

40

The boat hit the dark, swirling water and exploded into a thousand pieces. Bullets tugged at my dress from above and wooden splinters from below, but somehow I managed to get my hands up to protect my face as I hit the water. The boat had broken the surface tension or I would have broken my neck, but as it was the sea punched me in the face, swung me around, and tried to pull me down to its depths.

I'd fought this battle several times already, so this time I was more prepared, if half addled. I kicked as hard as I could, cursing the sea with every jab, and when I broke the surface, I was ready. I grasped a chunk of board, hoisted myself onto it, and then fell so that I covered it completely with my body, making it look as if I floated in the water, facedown. I lay motionless, kissed the rough wood against my mouth, and drew a shallow breath. And waited. *Time to toss the dice.*

"Blood and Bone! You've not a brain between you," the Ghost Captain shrieked high above me. "I didn't tell you to fire. Why did you fire?" There was a pause, as if he expected an answer, and then he laughed grimly. "By the Dead, were you trying to protect your father? I guess I can't fault you for that, can I, my pets?" His laughter cut off. "You two—over the edge and pick up your fallen sister. I need what's rattling around inside whatever's left of her brains before it rattles itself out into the sea. Go."

Two splashes landed close enough to spray me with water and I tensed, waiting for their skeletal bite on my flesh.

"No, not the Sin Eater," he called down, bemused pride in his voice. "Honestly, you two. Her kind are useless to me, dead. The other's the one we want." The splashing near me faded as they moved farther away. "Aye, there you go. Our masters won't be pleased when they find out you've killed the only Sin Eater this side of Port au' Sheen, but finding the artifact should keep them from hurting you.

"I jest, my pets—you know I'd never let anything happen to you." He laughed. "But they are going to have to decide if they want me to keep a low profile or drag that Harbormaster bitch over here after all. A worry for another day." He sighed and kept talking.

"Just grab her, you two. I'd send a rope down, but we both know neither of you could grasp it, let alone tie it around her. Climb into the boat. Up you come, now. There you go," he said, the smile loud in his voice. "I'll have a cup of tea, shall I, and then I'll turn your sister there and we'll weigh anchor." His voice receded as he turned away. "What a morning, I tell you."

I waited several minutes, letting the waves carry me and the board where they would. My limbs grew so numb from the cold that I began to shake until I was unable to hide it. When nothing came of my movement, I risked raising my head, and when nothing else happened, I sat up. The Ghost Captain's ship rode high in the water a score of paces behind me. The waves had carried me the length of his ship and past, and when I looked ahead, I could see the island less than a few hundred paces away.

Sliding off the board, I held it out in front of me so my upper body was above the waves, and began to kick. It was slow going, like kicking through molasses in winter, even as the frost began to leave my muscles. I kicked faster and harder, my skirts getting in the way, but the waves pushed me and I began to move along at a decent clip. The shore was just beginning to take shape in the sun's first rays when I heard a high-pitched scream behind me that did more to warm me through than the swimming had done.

"D-discov-vered what I d-did to your w-wheel? Eh, b-bastar-d?" My teeth chattered, but I didn't care and I laughed as I thought of the Ghost Captain watching the wheel spin freely between his fists. I hoped it'd take him the better part of the day to fix his rudder. And by that time I'd be ready for him. I hadn't meant to kill the Archaeologist—she'd been collateral damage—but with her dead and the Ghost Captain in possession of her knowledge, it did present an opportunity. *A plan within a plan.* I kicked for the shore with renewed vigor. *I'm coming, Eld.*

41

An undercurrent looped around the island, so by the time I reached the shallows, the Ghost Captain's ship was around a bend and my sense of direction spun aimlessly in my brain, half frozen from the water and exhaustion. I kept kicking until my boot came down in soft, gritty sand, and when I stood up, I discovered the water was only knee-deep. I stumbled ashore, collapsing on the sand by the water's edge and sucking in huge gulps of air.

"You've got grit, young one," a voice said in Imperial behind me. I spun around as fast as my sodden limbs would allow and saw an islander in dark leather trousers staring at me. He wore a white fur hide around his bare tanned shoulders; the fur matched his long braided locks. He smiled when he saw my expression and lifted a hand.

"Peace," he whispered in a voice as gravelly as the beach around me. "I only came to see you reach the shore safely. You bested the Dead One on the decks of his ship," he said, stumbling over the words "deck" and "ship." "It was well done."

"Aye," I said, gasping, still catching my breath. "Well, thanks.

It was touch and go there for a bit." I glanced up at him. "But you didn't come down here to tell me that, did you?"

"You see deep for one so young," he whispered. "My name is Bar'ren," he said in a louder tone. "Sha'amen of the Arawaíno."

"Sha'amen," I said, pronouncing the word slowly. "Like a king?"

"There are no kings amongst the Arawaíno," he said. "We are a free people. But I . . . speak for the people."

"Aye, and you speak Imperial suspiciously well, for an Araw-whatever."

He laughed. "When I was a lad, a woman washed ashore after her ship was destroyed in a storm and the crew lost. She became part of our people for many years, until she longed to see her homeland and took to the seas once more." He shrugged. "She taught me your language, to read and speak and write."

"Good on her," I said. "So now what?"

"I came to see what you intend. We wish our island to return to peace." He glanced past me, to where the tops of the Ghost Captain's ship's sails were visible over the tree line, and his jaw clenched. "We've had enough of death to last a generation."

"Fair enough," I muttered. "My friend? Is he alive?"

"They both are," he said. "We aren't like some of the East Is-landers who crave their brothers' flesh." He shuddered and drew his fur tighter around his shoulders. "They're trying to fix their wide canoe as we speak." He met my gaze. "What will you do now?"

I pushed myself to my feet and staggered. He held out a hand to catch me, but I brushed it away. *Never let them see weakness. And if they do, make them second-guess themselves.*

"I'm going to find them and we'll sail away and leave your island in peace." I looked over his shoulder, to where the jungle met the sand dunes, but didn't see any hint of the other islanders who were surely watching. I remembered the sound their arrows had made, whistling overhead when we fought the Shambles, and tried not to imagine a volley launching out of the dark jungle to fill me like a pincushion. Bar'ren might not have a taste for human flesh, but that didn't mean he wouldn't fight to protect his people, and I was a foreigner. In many languages the word for "stranger" is synonymous with "enemy."

"If it helps," I added, "when I sail, I sail to put an end to the Ghost Captain. The Dead One."

Bar'ren's grey eyes studied mine and he nodded slowly. "Then you'll need a canoe."

"Aye, that's why I need to find my friend. Friends," I amended, not wishing to confuse him by trying to explain my relationship to Chan Sha.

"Their canoe is too broken," he said. "They don't see it, but they will eventually."

"Likely when they are a hundred paces out to sea," I muttered. Suddenly I realized they didn't know I was alive. Or that I had escaped.

What would I do in their situation? Wrong question. *What would Eld do?* "Try to rescue me," I whispered. *Gods, I'm surprised he hasn't tried already.* "I need to go to them. Now. Don't worry—I'll find a way to plug that leaky tub and we'll be off your shores by morning."

"Morning is come already," Bar'ren said, pointing to the rising sun. He looked at me and the ghost of a smile crept across his features. "But the Arawaíno may be able to help."

"Help?"

"If it hastens peace, if it hastens the Dead One's demise?" He shrugged beneath his white fur. "Why would we not?" He pointed down the beach toward a break in the dunes. "There is a small stream. You will find a canoe waiting for you, with food and water for three. Strike out until the current catches you and then let it guide you around the island. When it begins to die off, you'll see your friends on the beach."

"I can't repay you . . ." I began.

"No," he agreed. "I do not think you owing Bar'ren a favor will be so bad for the Arawaíno."

I laughed hoarsely. "If you see me after today, Bar'ren, then something's gone seriously fucking wrong."

He laughed with me and nodded. "Perhaps you speak true. What is your name, young one?"

"Sambuciña Alhurra," I said after drawing a breath. His smile died on his lips and I saw something flash across his eyes. "Do you know it?" *Impossible.*

"No," he said quickly. "But I think we may meet again one day, Sambuciña. In this world or the next."

"Aye?" I arched an eyebrow, not quite believing him, but I didn't ask the real question looming in my mind. "Well, if we do, I won't forget my debt. The boat's that way?" I asked, pointing. He nodded and I inclined my head. "Then I'll be off. Thank you, Bar'ren, Speaker of the Arawaíno." I ignored the itching between my shoulder blades as I walked away, my boots sinking into the wet sand. *Why'd you lie? How do you know my name?* Questions for another day. I had to find Eld before he did something stupid, or worse, courageous. Courageously stupid. It'd be just like him.

The canoe and a pair of oars lay just out of the water, at the end of a path carved through the sand, so I could push it easily into the stream and out to sea. As I drew closer, I saw, in the bottom of the boat, a number of the big tree nuts and several hides of water. There was a bundle lying on the rear seat, which turned out to be a rough slip of a dress made of reeds and a pair of thong sandals. It didn't take more than a glance at my sodden and torn dress, stained in places with blood and ichor, to decide it was time for a change of clothes.

I stripped down to nothing and sat in the water, running fingers through my hair, letting the stream wash me clean, before standing up. My eye throbbed, but the salt had helped sanitize it and it'd already begun to scab over, so I didn't mess with it. I reached into the canoe and shed my old clothes for new. The dress I thought would be scratchy, but it actually had a pleasant feel against my skin. Short, true, but I didn't think anyone this far from Imperial civilization would be shocked to see my wrists, let alone my forearms. My boots were harder to give up; it's hard to find a good pair of boots that fit as well as these had, but they were warped now, twisted by sea, sun, and sand. So I slipped the sandals on and stepped into the canoe. It rocked gently back and forth in the sand as I settled down on the seat, taking stock of my situation.

My feet kicked a small sack beneath the seat. When I opened it, a grin split my face. Lying atop a pile of small round stones was a knife. I drew it out, watching the sun play off its pig-iron blade. *I owe you one, Bar'ren.* I had to hide the knife inside the top of the dress, just below my armpit, due to the sleeves barely reaching my elbows, but it worked.

Feeling a new woman from the quick wash and change of clothes, I used the oar to inch the canoe along the sand and into the water. The stream did the rest and with a few sure, deep strokes, I was propelled out to sea. Just as I reached a depth where I could no longer touch bottom with the paddle, I felt the current take hold, sending me out and around the island.

The sun was warm on my skin and I felt as if I'd awoken from a fever dream, my illness broken. I was weak, but on the mend.

And I'll need to mend fast. It's not over yet. My smile hardened. The mysterious island, Ciris's artifact, and the Ghost Captain still awaited me.

"You won't have to wait long," I said aloud, stabbing the oar into the water. "I'm coming, you bastards."

42

I came around a sharp cut in the island and saw two figures hunched over a hulking shape in the sand at the same time I felt the current slip away. One of the figures straightened, the sun's light reflecting off their alabaster forearms, and something twisted inside me. Biting down on the lump in my throat, I thrust my oar deep into the water and began paddling toward shore. As I drew closer, I saw Eld feverishly working to jam an ill-shaped hunk of driftwood into a hole in the upturned hull. His newfound tricorne lay cast off at his feet.

Chan Sha watched idly, leaning against the hull. A long splinter danced between the fingers of her outstretched hand, scoring the hull with every stroke as she went back and forth so quickly that the sun-bleached wood was little more than a blur.

Both were engrossed in their tasks and the crashing waves hid my approach, so I was able to beach the canoe a dozen paces away and climb out without either noticing me. Then Chan Sha glanced up and her eyes widened, flicking to Eld and then back to me.

"Well, you're as alive as the last time I saw you," the pirate said, keeping the splinter moving between her fingers for another moment before pushing herself up from the boat. "You shove a blade up the Ghost Captain's arse or just go for a lovely row on the water?"

"Buc?" Eld spun around with a jolt that sent the piece of driftwood flying through the air. He was striding toward me before the wood landed in the sand; his smile lit his face up brighter than the sunlight did. "Thank the Gods! Buc, what happened?"

"I come from the Ghost Captain," I said slowly, letting my tongue stick to the roof of my mouth. Eld's smile slipped and Chan Sha muttered a curse. "May he be fucked for eternity," I said normally. "I thought about planting a blade in him, but I didn't want you to feel left out, so I decided to come back and collect you first. But I'm still alive and my tongue retains its usual razor's edge."

Chan Sha cursed again, louder this time.

"Buc." Eld's eyes flashed, but his smile returned, belying the look he gave me. "You are the biggest pain in the arse a man's ever been saddled with."

"A boil of epic proportions," I agreed.

Reaching me, he pulled me into a rough embrace. "I was worried that you'd gone to your death," he said over my head. I could smell the salt and sweat on him and beneath that, a smell that *was* Eld. Something loosened inside me even as he stepped back to inspect me again.

Chan Sha pointed at me with the wooden splinter. "I'm interested to hear how you slipped out of that bastard's rotting grasp again."

"Not as easily as I would have liked," I admitted. "The Dead Walker mistook who I was. Or at least what I was."

"Aye?" she snorted. "And what is that?"

"A Sin Eater."

I saw Eld stiffen at my words, but I could barely keep the laughter from my lips. "Aye, one of Ciris's mages. Turns out he's been searching the seas, looking for one to pair with the Archaeologist."

"Fuck me sideways."

"Archaeologist?" Eld glanced back and forth between us. "What's she saying, Buc?"

"You heard her," I said. I felt a chill in me that I kept buried deep. *She knows. Ghost Captain. Sin Eater. Archaeologist.* It was an awful lot for a mere pirate to ken, great captain or no. Show me a criminal who cares beyond their crime and gold, and I'll show you something that skinned a shark to swim in deep waters. *But what kind of shark?* "She wants to be fucked sideways." I shrugged. "You're the only one with the equipment to do that properly, Eld."

"Gods' balls."

"No, yours," I corrected him.

"You know that humor as a defense mechanism is rather obvious," Chan Sha growled, taking a step in my direction.

"What do you know about the Archaeologist and the Ghost Captain?" I asked, ignoring the jibe.

"Buc," Eld whispered, his mouth barely moving, "there's something you need to know."

"You found her on board his ship, didn't you? What did the Archaeologist tell you?" Chan Sha asked.

"You tell me yours and I'll tell you mine," I promised. *Maybe.* "What, exactly, happened to your ship? Your crew?"

She sank down onto the sand and wrapped her arms around her knees. When she spoke, her voice was bitter and guileless. "We couldn't reach the doors that led below. I tried to cut a path to the lifeboats, but the dead kept coming. I only lived because Agnes carved space with a cutlass in each hand and two others hoisted me like a paper doll above their heads and tossed me over the railing." She whispered something that sounded like "loyalty" and looked away from us. "They knew I'd go down with the ship. But they went down while I floated away, watching my ship burn."

"I'm sorry," I said. Eld's head jerked and I shot him a look. *What? I can't be sorry?* I was sorry. Sorry for the flames. Sorry she hadn't still been on the ship. But sorry was there. "You knew though, didn't you?" I asked. She looked sharply at me. "That the Ghost Captain couldn't be defeated?"

"I'm not a fool. I did the odds long ago. There's always a chance, of course; his mortars misfire or a lucky volley hulls him at the waterline. But if he closes?" She shook her braids. "The dead don't tire and they can't be killed. Bone against flesh, bone wins. Fucking Dead Gods and their dark magics." Chan Sha's breath came fast and hard. "You heard my story; now let's hear yours."

"Not much of a story—you fell off your boat and wound up here. Same story as ours." I pointed to Eld. "Besides, you didn't tell me what you know of the Archaeologist and the Ghost Captain. I'll make you a deal, though," I said, not bothering to disguise my smile. "You swim over to yonder ship and dance with the dead, and the Archaeologist will whisper all manner of things in your ear."

"This wasn't in our parley," she said to Eld.

"Buc . . ." he began.

"I make the decisions and oaths," I growled, staring at him before turning my glare on Chan Sha. "And I damn sure didn't let that filthy word pass my lips. Fuck your *parley*." Eld's elbow dug into my side and I couldn't keep the gasp between my lips. "If it's all the same to you," I added. I let my smile slip as I turned away from her and leaned toward Eld. "The fuck?" I growled into his ear. "That hurt!"

"Pain is a good teacher," he said simply. I felt my eyes pop out of my skull and was surprised not to find myself staring at the ground with them hanging down my face. "Save the drama, Buc. I know you can't do polite, but I'll settle for not being a horse's arse." I started to curse him and he gave me a look that made my teeth click together. "You're not listening, Buc. There's something I have to tell you." There was a special emphasis on "something."

"The only reason you have anyone to come back to for reinforcements is because of her," he said, jabbing a finger at Chan Sha. "That came from parley. I made the call because you couldn't. So you'll honor it as if you begged for it on both knees."

I opened my mouth, but Eld kept rolling right over me, never letting me get out more than the beginning of a word. Gods, nothing is more infuriating than some fool who thinks he knows better than you giving you the rough side of his tongue. Advice unasked for is like a bag of shit on a hot day: you can't be rid of it fast enough, and yet it lingers long after it's gone.

"You want to live, Buc? If you want to see your crazy plans ever come to fruition, you have to be alive to see them, so blunt the file on the tip of your tongue and put that beautiful brain of yours to work. We're going to need help. Allies. You tried to kill the Ghost Captain several times now and he's still drawing breath. What's your definition of insanity, Buc?"

He ran a hand through his sun-bleached hair and gave a tug of irritation I wasn't meant to see. "You might be able to put together a team that can take him down if you can get over yourself."

"Get over myself?" A stranger spoke the words, high and tight and seething with anger. Eld never talked to me like this. Never. No one did. If they did, I'd have cut their tongue out. I was the one who'd gotten us this far. I—

"Is the child going to throw a tantrum?" Chan Sha asked. "Perhaps she can have a lie down while we figure out how to get off this damned island and slit the Dead Walker's throat."

Fire filled my brain and if words could burn, I would have burned Chan Sha alive and danced around her flaming corpse. But . . . but if I did that, I'd be proving her point. Which meant I had to swallow it. All of it. Gods, but I wanted to punch Eld. I'd nearly killed myself thinking I'd led him to his death. *His death. Failure.*

I'd been letting those damn sneaky emotions creep through me again. I'd been cursed with a modicum of the portion given to others and they still managed to slip through the cracks. No wonder everyone else was so fucked up. *He nearly died for me and then he sacrificed what he had left to try to save me.* While I'd been ready to throw my life away like so much dross. Now I had a chance to change that, to take another path, and see this through. Even if, Gods forbid, it meant swallowing Chan Sha's bullshit. It still took several deep breaths to conjure up the courage.

"Fine." I touched Eld's elbow. "I'll do what's right and I'll see us through." I squeezed his arm. "Promise."

His eyebrows leapt into his hairline. Then he smiled and his sky-blue eyes warmed. "You're a good heart. You always have been."

"No, I'm darker on the inside than I am on the out," I said. "But I will see us through."

He nodded. "I trust you."

"Trust." The only word more dangerous than "promise."

43

"I'll tell you of the Archaeologist," I said, leaning against the upturned hull of the rowboat beside Chan Sha. Eld stood opposite me. I followed his gaze to her and felt an ember flare in my stomach. "Unless you'd prefer Eld to fuck you sideways first?"

"Buc!"

"I prefer women," Chan Sha sneered.

"Oh." I straightened up. "Well, this is awkward. The only woman I can stand is myself. So, uh"—I shrugged—"I don't know what was in the parley, but . . ."

"Gods, woman, you just promised!" Eld's face was as red as I'd ever seen it and I saw a horse kick him in the balls once at the behest of a particularly earnest hansom cabdriver.

"So I did, so I did." I patted his arm. "Old habits and all that.

"The Archaeologist. I caught up with her in a cage after I went a few rounds with the Ghost Captain and nearly buried a meat cleaver in his face. She told me of a Sin Eater she met a few hundred years ago what knows everything there is to know about Dead Walkers and magical artifacts and hidden islands. After she told me everything and we danced with the Shambles, I put an inkwell through her skull and let the Ghost Captain keep her bones."

Chan Sha's green eyes were wide with disbelief and Eld started to growl again, but I hurried on and after a few moments both were quiet. I told them everything. Or almost everything.

Old habits and all that . . .

"So the Ghost Captain is unkillable?" Eld asked when I finished.

"Not quite, but good as," I admitted.

"But a Sin Eater can kill him?" Chan Sha asked. She and Eld exchanged a quick look that sent alarum bells ringing through my mind. *What happened while I was aboard that ship?*

"According to the Archaeologist and whatever Sin Eater wrote that journal," I agreed.

"And this artifact the Ghost Captain's guarding on the island will do the trick?" Chan Sha asked.

"According to the Archaeologist," I lied. "That's why he wants it destroyed, but he needs a Sin Eater's blood to do that. And that's why he's built up an army of undead around him first, for protection." It sounded patently false to my ears—letting someone who could kill him get close to the artifact that could kill him—but they seemed to accept it. Start off with the truth and most will lose the trail when you venture off into fantasy.

I'd told them everything the Archaeologist had told me—up to the part about the artifact being a fragment of Ciris. After that, until I got to my escape from the Ghost Captain, I'd obfuscated or left things out entirely. I'd tell Eld more, later, but Chan Sha didn't need to know anything I didn't want her to. I hadn't considered the need for allies before, not even after the shipwrecking, but now it seemed clear. Eld said "allies," but my mind whispered *cannon fodder*. Aren't they the same thing?

We had a pirate captain without a crew when what we needed was a Sin Eater amiable to do our bidding. If we could get free of Chan Sha and play our cards right, success was still a long shot, but I'd an idea on how to keep the bone walkers occupied while Eld and I took down the Ghost Captain.

I shrugged. "Now that we're settled up"—I pointed at Eld— "we're taking my canoe to the island to have a little private conversation with the Ghost Captain."

"Our parley—"

"Eld said we'd get you free of the island," I said, cutting her off. I smiled and patted the ruined hull. "You have a boat of your own, if you will it."

"He said more than that," she insisted. Her eyes burned. "I will see my crew avenged and that undead bastard rotting along with the rest of his corpses. Eld promised me we three would be shipmates until then."

"Shipmates?" I growled. "Eld?"

"Buc, there's something you need to understand . . ." he began.

"Did you or did you not promise her we'd let her tag along?" I asked.

"I did, but—"

"But you forgot she tortured us?" *Tortured you.* Suddenly the blade I'd hidden beneath the pit of my arm was in my hand. I pointed it at Chan Sha. "She hung us up by our thumbs. She could have slit our throats and we couldn't have done anything more than drown in our blood." *How could you be so stupid?* "She was going to *kill* us, Eld, just so she could keep her big secret a secret: that she had no fucking plan to deal with this mess. You think I'm going to trust her just because she lost a ship to the bastard?" I slammed the blade into the wooden hull to keep from stabbing anyone.

"Give over the dramatics, girl," Chan Sha snapped. "Your friend made the only move he had. It's your good fortune it was the best move as well. You'd see that if you took a breath to use that brain of yours."

"This isn't between us, bitch. Now"—I swung back to Eld and my voice grated in my ears—"you're going to tell me what the fuck you were thinking." *And then I'm going to twist that to get out of this parley.* I'd promised Eld I'd do what was right, but I hadn't expected to have to do right this quickly. I could feel my limbs quivering. "You've been wanting to tell me something. So what is it?"

Eld opened his mouth, but the pirate beat him to it.

"You are a fool, Eld," Chan Sha said. "A fool to put up with her tantrums."

"I told you to stay out of this," I hissed.

"Aye, you say a lot of shit, Buc. But tell me, do you see anyone but me here?" She chuckled. "Any other friends you've got lurking about who you'd like to try? Eld is the only rational one of the pair of you right now. Tell her, Eld."

"Gods, women!" Eld threw his arms up. "I've been trying to, but I can't get a word in edgewise."

"Say another word, Chan Sha, and I'll do the job," I snarled, ripping the blade free from the hull.

"Another." Chan Sha's grin matched the strange light in her dark green eyes. "Word."

I launched myself off the hull straight at her, knife in hand.

44

Eld was quick, and I was quicker, but that tanned, braided bitch was quicker still. *Damn her.*

Though Eld's outstretched fingers brushed my legs, he couldn't stop me from piling straight into Chan Sha. The pirate's startled yelp was loud in my ears as my momentum carried us both over the end of the upturned boat and onto the ground. The world somersaulted and my head slammed off hers; black flecks danced through my vision while blood ran down her forehead and into her braids. We stared at each other, her features dark in shadow, then both looked at my blade, a mere finger's length from her chest.

Somehow she had managed to get a death grip on my wrist before we went down. I couldn't feel my fingers, could barely feel my arm, but I was still forcing the blade closer to her heart. Only the blade wasn't moving, no matter how much I willed it to.

"Are you quite done?" she hissed.

"No."

"Then you might as well know it all."

"All?"

"Buc!" Eld's voice came from behind me.

"Don't interfere, Eld." I could feel the sweat running down my cheek. My hand was turning a darker shade than the rest of my skin and I wasn't sure I could hold the blade much longer.

"I am a Sin Eater, a priestess of the Goddess Ciris," Chan Sha said. "You have threatened the life of one of Her own." Her mouth twisted in a rough smile. "And She does not take kindly to threats."

Eld cursed loudly. "That's what I've been trying to tell you," he muttered. "She's a mage."

I couldn't keep the blade where it was. She was taller, older, and stronger. Imbued with a Goddess's powers. But I moved first and I moved fast, rolling away from her. Chan Sha moved faster still, catching my other wrist in a blur and spinning me, sending the knife flying. In a blink she was on top of me, pinning me to the ground. Her dark braids framed her tanned face, but once again it was her eyes that caught me. I could see my reflection in them. Dark in a rush-woven dress.

"You did say you preferred women," I said, gasping.

Her laugh cut off in a gurgle. Eld leaned in around the choke-hold he had her in, so his lips were next to her ear. "Move a muscle before I tell you to and I'll choke the life out of you. Doesn't matter how fast you are; I'll just fall back and use your weight against you. Doesn't matter how strong you are—I can feel your heart beating against my forearm and you're sweating like a whore after the army's been paid.

"I know your kind. I know you used quite a bit of your power. Now let Buc go." Chan Sha's eyes flashed murder instead of my reflection, but she released my wrists. "Good." He shook his head. "You're losing your touch, Buc."

"How so? I knew you'd get the drop on her if I took her attention."

Doubt flickered across his features. "She told you she was a Sin Eater and you attacked her!"

"Even odds she'd have taken both of us together if I let her up. But since she wrapped me up, that left you free," I said.

"You're too smart for your own damned good," Eld muttered. Chan Sha made a loud strangling sound and he glanced down at her. "If you try anything, I'll choke you out cold," he threatened. "And too stupid," he added, looking down at me. "She told me what she was."

"She told you?"

"Too tight," Chan Sha said hoarsely, and Eld loosened his grip. She took a rattling breath and cleared her throat. "You kill me and the Ghost Captain will finally kill the pair of you like he's been trying to. Is that what you want?"

"Better that than being killed by a Sin Eater," I shot back.

"I won't kill you," she growled. Eld's face burned but he didn't shift his grip. "Parley is still on?" he asked in a higher-than-normal voice.

"It was she who attacked me," Chan Sha reminded him. "And nothing's changed. I want to see the Ghost Captain dead. I helped you while Buc was on the ship, I'm going to help you get off this island, and I'm going to help you kill that undead bastard. You just need to keep up your end and take me with you." Eld glanced at me and I shook my head. Chan Sha couldn't help but see.

"Gods! Tell him yourself, then. Tell him I'm a Sin Eater! I don't care, so long as I touch that artifact first. You said it requires my blood? Well, I'll put an end to what's left of his life!"

Her words were loud in my ears, but louder still were the Archaeologist's words, reverberating through my mind. *One magic cannot abide the other. Dead Walkers and all of the Dead Gods' mages use the magic of blood and bone. You want to kill the Ghost Captain? Kill him outright? That would require Ciris's magic. Mind magic.*

I stared up at Chan Sha and realized that the me of yesterday would have let Eld kill her here and now and piss on the Archaeologist's tale. I'd been planning something before I'd realized we had a Sin Eater close to hand. But it'd been a long shot, involving stealing the Ghost Captain's ship while he was searching for the artifact on the island, returning to Port au' Sheen, and finding the Harbormaster. *A long fucking shot.* I didn't trust Chan Sha, but I didn't have to trust her. I just had to use her. The Ghost Captain had given me something I didn't know I needed: information. He needed a Sin Eater to use the artifact—which made sense, given that Sin Eaters were the ones who had crashed on the island.

But: Why would the Dead Gods and the Ghost Captain not only let a Sin Eater near it, but seek one out? I'd read enough about war to know there are no rules; suddenly several pieces of the puzzle fell into place. Want to take down someone powerful? Let them think you weak, let them think you well in hand, disarm them with a smile . . . or a gift. Then, while they are basking in their triumph, drive the blade home. There was a certain poetic justice in letting the two religions wipe each other out. I couldn't give a copper for poets or justice, but means and ends and all that. I needed a Sin Eater. What had I been thinking of before my mind went red with rage? *Cannon fodder.*

"All right." Eld released her and stood up and Chan Sha followed him. After a moment she offered a hand to me. "Let's plan this out," I said, using her hand to pull myself to my feet. I straightened a few of the rushes that had gone askew in my dress and walked over to where my knife lay in the sand. "We're going to slip onto that island and plant this blade in the Ghost Captain's heart."

"Together?" Chan Sha asked.

Eld and I exchanged looks again.

"Together," we spoke as one.

45

We sat on the sand in the boat's shadow for some time after that, not avoiding eye contact with one another precisely, but not seeking it out, either. The silence didn't bother me, but I could tell it was driving Eld half mad, the way he kept shooting glances back and forth between Chan Sha and me. He mumbled under his breath, turning red when he held in whatever words danced on the tip of his tongue. After a while he would relax, but soon enough then the furtive looks would start again. On and on and on, each time growing redder before finally accepting the awkward silence.

"You don't trust me," the Sin Eater said finally. "And we'll never kill the Ghost Captain if we're too worried about who is going to plant a knife in the other's ribs."

When I looked at her, I saw her gaze fastened on where I'd hidden my knife in my dress. Part of me had to give it to the wench—she was trying to make this work. But the larger part of me remembered her lies and the sound of Gem's rope across Eld's ribs. She would have fed us both to the sharks. That part of me wanted to cut her. Slowly. And feed her to herself. *Now there's cannibalism for you.*

I don't like it when someone tries to kill my friend. It brings out the darkness in me. The ember the flames left behind and no amount of words would change that. Not unless she pulled something truly spectacular out of her arse.

"I have your writ," she said. She reached into her trousers and came up with the piece of oilskinned paper I'd traded our lives for what seemed like a month or more ago but couldn't have been much more than a week.

Gods, she did pull something out of her arse. I buried my laughter. "The one that's not worth the paper it was printed on?" That part still stung—bested by that Company bitch.

"I may have misled you there," Chan Sha said. Her eyes glistened in the sunlight and she came to her feet in one smooth motion, like a cat. "The writ's legal and authentic to my eyes." She let the oilskin unfold until it dangled from her fingers. "Just needs a notary stamp and it'll pass muster. Call it a peace offering. I did take it off you." She sighed. "Aye, and mistreated you, although you'd have done the same were the situations reversed."

I caught myself nodding and stopped. I would have never let us live after I started the torture. *No half measures.*

"I am a Sin Eater of the Goddess Ciris and I have powers beyond your ken. I know you've no love for mages, but you need one now to have any hope of defeating the Ghost Captain." She jiggled the writ in the air. "I'm not saying this wipes the slate clean, Buc. But it's a start."

"It is a start," Eld said. I eyed him across the sand and he shrugged. "Why'd we come out here in the first place? I'm not upset to find we still have a shot at our dream."

"We'd never have lost that shot if not for her," I reminded him.

Still, I had to hand it to the bastard; he knew just what to say. *Our dream.* "But," I continued, "you're right." I held out my hand and Chan Sha's mouth twitched. "If you're holding out for a thank-you, you're going to be waiting a Godsdamned long time."

The pirate laughed and placed the writ in my hand. I hefted it, then tossed the oilskin to Eld, who made it disappear inside his shirt. I took a breath and forced myself to go on. "I've an idea," I said. "I might have left a few things out, earlier. About the Archaeologist and Ghost Captain and the artifact."

Chan Sha snorted and Eld laughed.

"I'm . . . not surprised?" he said.

"Nor me," Chan Sha agreed.

"Fuck the pair of you," I growled, and when they laughed harder, I felt a smile pull at the corners of my lips. "Arseholes," I muttered.

"When I killed the Archaeologist to keep her knowledge from the Ghost Captain?" They nodded. Part of me, a scrap of emotion, turned over at the memory of the sound of the inkwell striking her forehead. *I never meant to kill you.* But it had turned out to be the next best option besides killing the Ghost Captain himself.

"I did it knowing the Ghost Captain would turn her into a Shambles. Then he'd have access to her memories and know the island's location." I quickly explained what the Archaeologist had told me about Dead Walkers absorbing memories of the dead.

"So the Ghost Captain knows where the island is now?" Eld asked.

"Aye. But he thinks me dead."

"So he doesn't know that we know?"

"Nope," I told him.

"Brilliant," Chan Sha whispered. "We know exactly where to find him now. And he won't see us coming."

"It gets better," I said, unable to keep my smile from spreading. "I sabotaged his rudder before I escaped, so he's lying dead in the water as we speak." *If we've any manner of luck at all, he'll stay that way.*

"Gods, so when he finally gets that repaired and sails to the island . . ." Eld began.

"We'll be waiting for him," I finished. *And none of you will see what I've got planned coming.* Eld would be upset that I hadn't told him, but I couldn't risk his streak of politeness showing up. *Not now, when the blades are out.*

It took us longer than I expected to make ready. I sat in the shade of the canoe; the past two days had finally caught up with me now that I'd stopped to catch my breath. I was bone-tired. The only good thing about this was that my thoughts no longer needed kan to slow them down. It took everything in me to keep my plans from falling apart in my head. *Can't afford that. Not now. We're so close.*

"You two about done?" I called, forcing an enthusiasm I didn't feel, that sounded flat even to my ears. "We're wasting time and I don't know how long it's going to take us, rowing."

"Aye," Eld said, straightening with a saber in his fist. He knuckled the small of his back and winced. "We've been talking about that, Chan Sha and me." He nodded to the pirate, who had pulled out a pair of boarding axes and was hefting their weight. "We're not sure you're up to it, Buc."

"What?"

"To rowing and then taking on a crew of the undead and the Ghost Captain? It's a lot, Buc. Not questioning your commitment," he said quickly, holding up his free hand.

"Just your physical fitness," Chan Sha added. She thrust the axes through the sash around her waist and sauntered over to where I sat in the shade. "You're weak, Buc."

"You're lying," I growled.

"You know I'm not. Yours is the hardest core I've ever seen and I've known some hard motherfuckers in my time," Chan Sha said. She shook her head. "The mind is always stronger than the body and yours more than most. But it's not enough."

"I'm not staying behind," I said, reaching for the blade in my dress.

"We'd never ask you to," Eld said, stepping up beside Chan Sha.

"Then what?"

"She can . . . heal you," he said, not quite meeting my eyes.

"You mean magic?" I laughed mirthlessly. "I hate magic. You *despise* it, Eld. And now you want me to let her use it on me?"

"Desperate times and all that," Chan Sha said lightly. She smirked. "If it's any consolation, I'm not exactly thrilled about sharing my blood with you."

"Your blood?"

"Only way to heal nonbelievers. Prick your finger and give me your blade."

"That's it?"

"Just do it."

I looked back and forth between the two of them, hating their smarmy, all-knowing faces. Hating them more because they were right. It was all I could do to keep myself upright, even seated. I'd never make it several hours on the open seas, to say nothing of what would come after. But I'd come too far to fail now. She was right. I was desperate. So I ran the tip of my thumb across the edge of the pig-iron blade and hissed when it drew blood. I let it well up, then smeared it along the blade and handed the knife to Chan Sha.

She took it wordlessly, then licked it clean and grimaced.

"I'm no Dead Gods' whore," she said when she saw my expression. "I've little love for this part, but—" She gave a short moan, swayed on her feet, then steadied herself. Just as I'd done, she cut her finger on the blade and smeared its length with her blood. "Here"—she shoved it at me—"lick it clean." I took it from her, hesitant, and she snorted. "If I wanted you dead, I'd snap your neck, Buc."

"This won't turn me into one of your kind?"

Eld shifted beside her and Chan Sha shook her braids back and forth. "No, no. It doesn't work like that. Do it before my blood dries or we'll have to start again," she added.

Still, looking at her blood, dark against the iron blade, I wasn't sure. I glanced up and saw Eld watching me, a hint of a smile on his face. *He's expecting me to do the impossible. And I can't. Not like this.*

"Fine," I said, and ran my tongue along the knife, tasting the metallic tang of her blood. "Tastes sweet," I lied. "Who would have thought?" I started laughing and then my tongue burned and every drop of Chan Sha's blood sent fire vibrating through my body and I fell back, gasping. I heard Eld shout from a great distance, but a crackling fire filled my ears.

Images flashed before me. Telling the Kanados Trading Company woman to go fuck herself. Wheedling the Sea Dragon's *Captain into sacrificing his ship. Gleefully confessing my ultimate plan to Eld. Overriding his protestations.*

Then I was a girl again, in a warehouse. A warehouse I had no business being in. My sister tried to pull me away, but I reached for the door that led deeper in. I'd told her I was going in and I wasn't going to break now. I didn't break then. I don't now. I never do.

"What is worth breaking for, Buc?" a voice whispered in my mind. "Don't break and you fail, and likely the world with you."

"I'll do what needs doing," I said, not believing the words even as they left my lips. I never do, I thought.

"Don't break and your sister's death was for nothing. What if you have to break more than once?" the voice whispered sibilantly. "Can you? Can you break twice, three times?" The voice rose. "Or will you tear yourself into a hundred pieces if you try?"

"I'll do what needs doing!"

"How? How, when you're already broken and won't admit it?"

"I'm not broken."

"No?" More images danced in the ether: me throwing the cleaver at the Ghost Captain, the blade catching the thin Shambles in the chest; a shroud over my head, the weight of untold numbers sending me to the ground. Pain blossomed in my face and suddenly my mind went blank.

"You can't be honest with yourself, Buc. When the time comes, where will the lies get you?" The voice raged through my mind. "Remember, daughter of the flames."

The flames were between me and my sister's broken body as the men ran out the warehouse's far door. I saw her hand move and I went toward her, but the fire pushed me back. I pressed on, felt my flesh begin to blister. . . . I couldn't do it.

"Remember where the lies led you, Sambuciña! Remember your sister!"

The voice filled me like the sea fills a glass and I broke and everything in me bled out.

46

I woke up with the sun bright in my face. I felt swung around, as if I were lying in the world's largest hammock. The wind was loud in my ears as I sat up and Eld's broad back was in front of me as he dipped his oar into the sea. His sea-faded vest lay folded on the seat beside him, and his shirtsleeves clung to him in spots where he'd sweated through. He took a few strokes on the right side—the starboard side—then switched to the port. He glanced back and smiled.

"You're awake?"

"Aye." I pushed myself up onto the bench and rubbed the sleep from my eyes. "How long have I been out?"

"Few hours," he said.

"Gods, then where are we rowing to?" I asked. "I didn't tell you the coordinates."

"But you did, Buc. Don't you remember?" he asked.

"She doesn't and she won't," Chan Sha said from behind me. I cricked my neck turning to look at her and she grinned, teeth bright against her tanned skin. "I told you, healing does more than just heal the body. It heals the mind as well. And most wouldn't want to remember that, even if they could."

I arched an eyebrow. *Fuck.* "So, uh"—I kept my tone neutral, slightly curious—"what did I say? Because all I remember is my life flashing before my eyes as I passed out." *And that voice.* I shivered, and not from the wind.

"Gave us the navigation to the island," Eld said from one side.

"And the compass," Chan Sha added, hefting it in one hand. She tossed something at me with her other hand and I caught it without thinking. It was a curved, slightly squishy yellow fruit. "It's called a banana. Peel the skin off first. It's good. Eat that— and as much food as you can pack in. My magic healed you, but some of its power came from you, and if you don't eat, you'll feel as weak as a day-old kitten come tonight."

I nodded as I peeled the banana. My vision was clear, my eye no longer ached, and all the bruises and bone-deep soreness I'd felt before were gone. I felt like a new band on my slingshot, one that hadn't been stretched or tested yet. But I could sense a gnawing hunger lurking within, so I wolfed the banana down in three bites and reached for another.

"Where are we?" I asked around a mouthful of fruit.

Eld laughed and leaned to the side, pointing forward. "Look and see."

Over his shoulder I saw a lump of land in the not too far dis- tance. A wave carried us until we were level with the island for a moment, then swooped us back down before leveling out. The canoe wobbled a bit but kept upright. Apparently the thing was seaworthy, if small. The Archaeologist had said it would take a few hours to reach the island, but that was using sail. Behind the oar of a canoe, it looked more like the better part of a day. Then Chan Sha started rowing again and I realized we'd be there in an hour or less. Her supernatural speed sent us flying across the waves. Eld helped with a dip or two of his paddle when he could.

I offered to help, but the pair of them insisted I keep eating so I'd be ready when we reached the shore. Truth be told, once I started eating, I didn't want to stop. I had a moment of worry about the motion of the waves and my stomach, but whether Chan Sha's magic was still in my veins or I was just too hungry to care, I didn't get sick.

An hour later we put in on a rough gravel beach on the south side of a wide bay that was divided by a rocky outcropping. The outcropping rose to a pinnacle in the center, blocking our view of the rest of the island. Chan Sha and Eld had both wanted to circle the island in search of safer portage, but now that we were here, I felt time racing against us. Who knew how long we'd have to prepare before the Ghost Captain arrived?

As we drew closer, I saw reefs all around that would tear a hole in the bottom of the canoe long before we neared land. Even the bay we opted for was dangerous; the dugout canoe left bits and pieces of itself in the flotsam washing against the rocks before we landed. When we were close, Chan Sha thrust her axes into her belt and jumped out, ignoring Eld's protestations. The sea molded the dark leather of her pants around her legs so her muscles stood out. She pulled us up onto land with one mighty heave.

Eld followed and he and Chan Sha scouted up and down the beach while I sorted out my knife and slingshot and the small pouch of stones Bar'ren had given me, keeping my eyes on Chan Sha as much as possible. I'd seen her in action before, but back then I'd thought her human. Incredibly skilled, but human. I could defeat human; I'd done it before and I'd do it again. Flesh is a known quantity to me.

But this? This was something more, something unknown. As the Ghost Captain was an unknown. They were warriors, combatants in a war that had gone on since before their Gods fell from the stars and took up the fight again, turning our world into their battleground. She'd fought a horde of Shambles single-handedly, rowed herself ashore, fought a second battle, healed me, rowed all of us across leagues of open sea—and at the end, still had the strength to pull a fully loaded canoe out of the water as if it were nothing.

Unknown didn't begin to describe mages and their magic. But we needed an edge, Eld and I. Otherwise we would be little better than mosquitoes caught between the servants of rival Gods. Sometimes mosquitoes are ignored . . . but sometimes they are slapped flat without a second thought. And I couldn't take that chance. *Ruthless.* For once my mind was blessedly clear, even without the kan. *Because of her healing?* It didn't matter; I knew what had to be done.

"C'mon, Buc," Chan Sha said, dark calves flashing in the sun as she trotted back to the canoe. "Time we were gone, yea?"

Ruthless.

"Aye," I said. I'd been rolling one of the round stones between my fingers; now I slipped it into the pouch of my slingshot, pulled in a lungful of air, and steeled myself for what came next. I leveled my weapon, pulling it back, well past my ear, until the wooden frame cried out. Chan Sha echoed the frame a moment later, collapsing to the sand. She made to rise and screamed again.

"What'd you do?" Eld rushed up beside her.

"I didn't break parley," I said, gasping.

"You killed her, damn it!"

"No. Kneecapped her." I jumped out of the canoe and strode across the sand. Chan Sha glared up at me through the pain writ large over her face. "We're going to need her for the Ghost Captain."

"You can't do this."

"You keep saying that," I said. "But look." I pointed through the jungle toward the cliff's edge, just visible through the canopy ahead. "We've almost reached the top." Chan Sha limped along, leaning heavily on an oar that Eld had converted into a crutch. She'd spent the first hour cursing me roundly, but I'd found a loaded slingshot aimed at her face did wonders for her cooperation. Even weakened, her God-given supernatural strength let her keep pace with us and I was sure she was healing even as we walked. "So, given the facts, I think we can do this. Right, Eld?"

"Aye." He wasn't smiling, but his neutral expression was better than the frowns and accusations he'd hurled at me when we'd left the shore for the jungle, his sense of honor having been trampled all over by my actions. Since then, I'd had time enough to explain why I'd done what I had. I'd kept to the parley, too, damn it. Maybe not the spirit, but the word. Eld was like most men—he'd rear his head and bridle when faced with something he didn't like, but give him some time to work the bit in his mouth and he'd come around. Eventually. When the seas froze over. *Men.* I sniffed, and turned back to Chan Sha.

"You're both a pretty pair of fools," she spat.

"Call us what you will, so long as you keep pace," I said.

"This is larger than you realize," she said, digging her crutch into the dirt. "You think I operated out here for so long without the Kanados Trading Company's knowledge?"

"What are you saying?" Eld asked from behind her.

"I'm saying that no pirate captain worth their salt survives a year on the seas if they take as many prizes as I have, let alone three. I took more ships than any two captains combined, yet I never had to flee Company ships. Or the Empire's, for that matter."

"And you hid all of this from your crew?" I asked.

"Both of you shooting questions at me is making my head spin."

"Sorry," I lied. But then, I was pretty sure she was lying too. A pretty pair we made.

"Uh-huh. Aye, they never knew," she said. She grunted when her bad leg came down on a tree root. "None needed to know, and so long as I took prizes from the Free Cities or Normain, the Empire turned a blind eye."

"Must be nice," Eld muttered, "having the world's largest navy off your back."

"I'm a pirate," she said.

"And a priest of the Goddess," I added.

"That, too. Which is why I stayed in these seas when all others fled."

"Ciris told you to?"

"My Goddess wants the artifact," she said. "She knew it was lost somewhere in the Shattered Coast, but the region covers hundreds of leagues of open seas. She sent me to find it." Chan Sha's eyes clouded. "Imagine, missing a piece of yourself. An arm, a leg, part of your mind. What would you do to have that returned to you?"

"Does the Kanados Trading Company know you're a Sin Eater?"

"No." She shrugged at the twist of my mouth. "My Goddess wasn't sure who caused the disappearances. Not at first. And then . . . we didn't know if the trading company was behind it all or not."

"You mean, in bed with the others?"

"The Dead Gods, aye," she said.

"I don't think you have to worry about that," I said. "Unless they are playing the deepest game ever imagined. We know the Ghost Captain is a Dead Walker, a priest of the Dead Gods. We know he's behind the disappearances. We know the Kanados Trading Company wants him gone," I said, ticking off the points one by one.

"So we kill him and our deal is finished. Our deal," I repeated. We needed to use Chan Sha, but it still made sense to make sure she was weak enough to need us just as much. If I'd had more than a moment alone with Eld, I would have clued him in. Then maybe he wouldn't have spent half the hike sulking.

"You're not thinking clearly," Chan Sha said. "If I work for the Company same as you and they want Ciris to succeed—if you prevent that, do you really think they'll just look past it?"

"You're the one not thinking," I said.

"Aye," Eld growled. Poke the man and he blinked. Poke me, and if he wasn't the one doing the poking, he turned into a bear. I've never tired of wondering how men can be such fools, but in his case I was grateful. "If the Company knew about your Goddess, then perhaps you'd be right . . ." he began.

"But you just told us they don't know," I finished. "How long has Ciris been using them? You think they'll look past that?" I suddenly remembered the mage with Salazar. He'd been an official priest of Ciris and he'd acted strangely before murdering Salazar, almost as if he were listening to someone who was there, but not. *What if he was told to kill Salazar, to set this all in motion?* As soon as the thought entered my mind, I knew it was true. Or close to the truth. "What does your Goddess want?" I spun around, letting my slingshot hover within a breath of her face. "It's more than just an artifact."

"I don't know." The slingshot squeaked as I drew it taut. "I don't," Chan Sha repeated. "She doesn't explain herself to her priests."

"Never?"

"Rarely."

"If you were a Goddess, would you?" Eld asked over her shoulder. "You barely do now."

"Fair point." I squinted. "You want the artifact out of the Ghost Captain's hands?"

"I do," she said.

"And you want him dead?"

"I do."

"And you understand why I broke your knee?"

"Because you're a fucking idiot," she snapped.

"No, because you're too damned powerful. If whatever inside you that makes you crazy strong is preoccupied with trying to knit all those fragile bones and tendons back together, it levels the playing field somewhat." *Because I need you off balance, so you're not thinking clearly. And because you let your man torture Eld.* I leaned in. "Am I lying?"

She glared at me and then leveraged her crutch to take a halting step beside me. "No. Damn you. You're not lying."

"All right." I relaxed the slingshot. "Then we keep to the parley."

47

I knew where the wreckage lay, in theory at least, so I led the way to the top of the hill, with Chan Sha hobbling along beside Eld behind me. There were a few trails worn through the underbrush by animals of one kind or another, but they were faint amongst the twisted grasses and thornbushes that littered the hillside. The odd palm tree rose up here and there, but otherwise there wasn't much beyond hard rock and undergrowth, which made for slow going.

The sun greeted us full in the face when we finally reached the top of the hill. I leaned against a tree, blinking in the sun and letting my eyes take in the sprawling scene before us. Across the way, where the bay met the shore, was the cliff the Archaeologist had told me of. Squinting, I suddenly saw the wrecked ship wrapped around the crest of the cliff, more weathered and battered than I'd imagined. The bleached planks were of a similar color to the cliffs as if both had bled into each other, and had I not known where to look, I might have missed it. Below the cliffs, driftwood lay scattered around the sand as if scores of trees had been split into kindling.

"Look!" Eld grunted.

I followed his finger out into the bay and had to grasp the tree to keep upright. There, in the center of the bay, on the opposite side of the pinnacle of rock that jutted up like a large broken fist, the Ghost Captain's ship rode high in the water. "He beat us here! How?"

"Not hard to imagine," Chan Sha spat, leaning heavily against her crutch. "Bastard has oars, aye? And plenty of hands to row them?" She gestured toward the ship. "We didn't account for that. He could have used them to steer readily enough while he had some of the Shambles over the side to repair whatever you did to the rudder. Slowed him down, sure, but not enough." She shook her braids. "Damn it, not enough."

"Still, it looks like they've just arrived," Eld said as a boat began moving away from the ship and toward the shoreline, where a dozen more boats were already beached.

"Ever the optimist, Eld," I muttered.

"By Her name!" Chan Sha's breath left her in a sibilant hiss. "So many. We never stood a chance."

I abruptly realized that all the dark marks I'd taken for flotsam were Shambles, many standing motionless. A hundred dark marks, blighting the sand. Some were erecting a tent on the shore. I squinted. More moved in the higher grasses and a few had ventured into the thick undergrowth farther up the hills and cliffs. Maybe several hundred. Half their number would have been too many.

"That's a lot of bodies," Eld said.

"A few crew loads," Chan Sha said.

"And more on the ship."

"Likely," she agreed with him.

"You're both focusing on the wrong details," I said. Eld arched an eyebrow while Chan Sha's expression made me want to punch her. I pressed my palms firmly against my hips to resist the urge. "They are undead and most aren't moving, so no one is commanding them right now."

"How do you know that?" Chan Sha asked.

"Because the Ghost Captain controls them through some strange book," I said. I pointed down the hill at the tent that had been erected in the middle of the masses. "None have reached the shipwreck, so I'm guessing either he's waiting in yonder tent or he never left the ship. Either way, so long as he's unaware of us, so are the Shambles."

"You're sure?" Eld asked in a careful tone that spoke volumes.

"Of course," I lied. *Sure?* Only another Dead Walker would know for sure, but I'd seen the man on his ship, studying that strange glowing book, and I'd seen him use it.

"You seem to know a lot," Chan Sha said. "But do you know that the Shambles do more than kill? They infect." A shadow crossed her face. "A bite from one is a death sentence, and since Walkers command the dead, a bite will make you his slave for eternity. Or until your bones fall apart and you turn into a pile of ichor.

"I'm protected by my Goddess's magic, but you two are not." She glanced between us. "One bite and you are his." She shuddered. "There are hundreds upon hundreds down there, with teeth waiting to taste your flesh. Now do you understand why we can't just go charging in?"

"You've convinced me," I said. Chan Sha's eyes brightened. "But there's no way we can reach the artifact without going through the Shambles. So we have to become Shambles."

They began arguing, until I cut them off with an icy glare. "I learned things on that ship. Shambles can smell the living. Don't ask me how; magic makes no sense—that's why it's magic. But somehow they can." Swiftly, I told them how we'd used pieces of clothing from other Shambles to slip past.

"We'll have to do one better now," I added. "We'll have to be disguised well enough that the Ghost Captain won't notice us either."

"I'm not sure how we make our bones show through and still live," Chan Sha muttered.

"And I'm not sure how you captained a crew for so many years with that piss-poor attitude," I shot back. Her eyes glowed murder and I held up a hand. "Too soon, I know. But you don't make it easy, woman." I shook my head. "I'm not suggesting we get up close and personal with him, at least not until you're ready to slit his throat. We just need to pass the sniff test at a distance."

"They can really smell us?" Eld asked.

"They can really smell us." He cursed. "I'm sure you smell fair, Eld. That's the problem." He muttered under his breath. I turned back to the bay below us and squatted on my heels. "So the plan is we deaden three of the undead. Put on their rags or what have you, then work our way to the cliff and set up a trap for the Ghost Captain when he comes for the artifact."

"Simple as that?"

"Simple as that," I said, turning to Chan Sha. "Remember, he thinks me dead and the pair of you marooned—he's not expecting us. So we kill him and then you figure out how you want to scale those cliffs and get your Godsdamned artifact."

"It's too easy," she protested. "I thought I convinced you of that!"

"You did; that's why we're not charging in." I grinned. "And you might not think it's so easy when you're trying to climb over rock with a busted knee," I said.

"That you gave me."

"And I'm about to give you everything you said you wanted as well," I said. I studied the woman before me, tall, unbent, but dancing to the strings of another. *And I thought you my equal?*

For a brief moment I'd even considered that she might have the edge on me, but in the end, she served her Goddess, whether she agreed with her or not. I felt my lips curl at the thought. "Unless you keep arguing until he begins moving?"

"Just get me down the hill."

I almost obliged her. One boot in the arse and she would have cartwheeled end over end into the very center of the camp. But that might have killed her. Worse, it would have alerted the Ghost Captain. The Archaeologist had given me the clues I needed to put this all together, but we needed to get closer and I couldn't afford for him to know we were here . . . yet.

"Let's do it, then," Eld said, as if sensing my mood. I met his eyes and looked away. He knew me too well. "We'll not get a better chance."

If the climb up the hill was difficult and tedious, the climb down was pure torture. Have you ever tried to move silently? Not quietly, but completely silently? And then you take a step and your weight makes a stone roll or a stick snap or your very bones betray you, cracking loud enough to wake the dead. Now imagine that, but knowing that any noise at all actually *could* wake the dead.

It seemed as if our boots echoed off the rocks where vines didn't trip us and threaten to spill us down the slope. Chan Sha had the worst of it; perhaps I'd made a mistake by breaking her knee after all. Even with Eld holding her by the collar of her jacket she slipped with every step, and every jolt and jounce made her whimper. Each time, I reached for the knife hidden in my dress, ready to open her throat if she betrayed us to the Shambles.

A bird squawked loudly, annoyed by our passage, and its cry was taken up by a dozen others. Still, the dead stood motionless. With each sound my nerves grew tighter and soon I stopped sliding the knife back into my dress and simply held it concealed in the palm of my hand.

Nearer the bottom, we came face-to-face with our first corpse. It moved through the brush a pace off the path, seemingly oblivious to the path itself. Its shoulders and head sagged onto its desiccated chest, breasts more bone than flesh and dark holes in place of eyes. The three of us froze, staring at the Shambles, but it kept moving in a direction that would pass us by a dozen paces. *Scouting?*

"What are you waiting for?" Chan Sha hissed.

I shot her a look and pulled my slingshot level. I wasn't sure what would happen when I killed it—would the Ghost Captain sense that? With hundreds down there and dozens active, would he notice if three went missing? There were too many unknowns, each a knife held against our necks. One misstep and we'd slit our own throats with our ignorance. But I didn't have any better ideas, so I let the stone go and braced myself as it took the Shambles between the eyes, spraying dark rotten blood into the bushes behind it.

A heartbeat later, I fetched up beside it and stripped the loose, flowing shirt off its bones. The fabric had been dark once and had faded to an ash grey, but it fit well enough around my shoulders, though the woman must have been buxom in life. I reached for the Shambles's trousers, but they broke off in clumps when I tried to work them free, so I settled for wrapping the remnants of a sash around my forehead. The stench bit deep into the back of my throat, making me wretch, but there was nothing for it.

We picked off two others that had scouted out farther than the rest of their undead brethren—sometimes ambition is a bitch—and soon Chan Sha had a tattered robe draped across her shoulders and Eld had exchanged his tricorne for one more battered and bloody and added a greatcoat that hung loosely, even over his frame. None of us really looked like a Shambles, but packed in amongst the rest, we shouldn't draw the Ghost Captain's attention. I was betting the rotten clothing would be enough to keep the Shambles at bay too. The weight of it all was beginning to settle in around me like a cloak three sizes too small.

I bit down on my doubts and led the way through the undergrowth. A few paces farther and the rocks gave way to sand and the undead began popping up like some sort of putrefied fruit that sprang up from the ground like grapes. Only instead of wine, their harvest was death. Each step took us closer to the tent and farther into the army of undead. The cloyingly sweet stench of decay tickled my nostrils and turned my stomach.

A Shambles walked in front of me. It was almost of my height, its eyes level with mine—save one socket was empty and the other had a bulging, sightless eyeball that had popped out and hung just over the socket. As we passed, its neck cricked slightly and I felt a shiver run through me, but it kept walking and I saw the back of the head was caved in. Eld gagged, but the undead gave no sign of caring. Another stood head and shoulders above me, its massive neck still covered in wrinkled flesh. One arm was flayed to the bone and hanging limply while the other was half raised, as if in defiance of its end. Dark ink crisscrossed its skin and I paused to study it out of habit more than curiosity—the marks looked like some language I'd never seen before.

I leaned forward, but the squiggles wouldn't give up their meaning and I shook my head. *Did he see me? Smell me?* His eyes were dull, rotting, and sightless in their sockets, but a breath before, I would have sworn they were bright with intelligence. I clenched the knife in my hand, holding my breath, but the dead eyes remained dark.

"Keep moving," Chan Sha whispered.

I really wanted to stab the bitch, but moved on instead. The oppressive sense emanating from the dead burrowed its way inside me. *Resist it.* I glanced over my shoulder and saw Eld struggling with the same emotions. "Almost there," I whispered.

"I think one of the Shambles just looked at me," he croaked through clenched teeth. He nodded toward a woman in a tattered shirt that hung to the knees of flayed pants that revealed more bone than flesh. She seemed to be walking with more purpose than she had been a few steps before. If the Ghost Captain hadn't really been controlling the ones farther out, he was definitely controlling these.

"You're being paranoid," I lied. We were probably close enough now, but I'd take every step I could get. It wouldn't do to bring Chan Sha this far only to have her killed by the undead before the Ghost Captain realized what she was. I glanced over my shoulder to confirm the big dead one wasn't following us. Its body wasn't, but the head had turned around so far that it made me wince, and its bright eyes stared at me. No, *past* me.

I turned back around and saw the Ghost Captain striding through the undead, holding his book in one hand and the waxy grey hand of the Archaeologist in the other. She stumbled along at his side, her red-brown dress bleached in several places from salt and sea and sun. Her face was a ruined mess of black and blue and grey, and half her hair was torn out on the side where she'd hit the edge of the rowboat. Sharp white skull shone through in patches, and her glassy eyes stared sightlessly ahead.

All three of us froze, but when the undead around us began to shuffle forward, we were forced to follow or else stand out by our lack of movement. We were being carried straight into the path of the Ghost Captain. *Shit.* I managed to put myself just behind another Shambles who was of a height with me, and but with the lurching, hunchback step I affected, I was effectively hidden. I glanced back and saw that Chan Sha wasn't so lucky. Her gait looked as unnatural as that of those around her, but the crutch stood out as wrong and there was a small, open space between her and the nearest Shambles. *Double shit.* Eld actually blended in the best of us: with his greatcoat covering him from head to toe and that decrepit hat on his head, even I missed him at first glance. But Chan Sha was going to fuck us if she didn't find a way to hide. She seemed to realize it at the same time I did and I saw her features flicker with fear. *Damn it, not now, woman!*

Chan Sha hesitated, then she switched the crutch over to her good side, pressed it against the length of her body, and straightened her good leg while bending her bad one back so it didn't touch the ground. I could see sweat pop out across her brow, but she didn't cry out, and when she moved, she stayed almost parallel to the Ghost Captain, so her crutch was completely hidden. Her gait was painful to watch, but it actually aided in her disguise and after a few tense steps I realized she blended in better than she had before. I let out the breath I'd been holding.

The Ghost Captain marched right past the Shambles in front of me, with the Archaeologist on his arm, and I nearly choked as I dropped my gaze to my feet. His boots were loud in the rocky sand and I waited for them to stop, but they didn't. I risked a glance and saw him looking over his left shoulder toward the part of the mob where Chan Sha and Eld were, but then he turned back to the Archaeologist and leaned down, whispering in her ear and then laughing loudly—had he told her a joke? *Gods.* I hated having to keep up one side of a conversation, let alone two.

The Archaeologist glanced back toward the tent and the sea beyond, her neck moving more smoothly than most of the other Shambles. *Likely because she's still fresh.* She started turning back to the Ghost Captain and our eyes met across the sand. Her pupils were light and watery and deep and I felt something grip me low in my stomach and pull hard. *I did that.* For a moment nothing happened and then her lips moved. Feral moans joined her like a dark chorus, falling upon us with the sun's waning rays.

"I'm glad you came!" The Ghost Captain's voice pulled me back. He was facing me, standing beside the Archaeologist, book open in his hands. The glow illuminated his face in shades of blue. "I was really wrought up over the thought of you dying after that mishap. Sometimes my pets get overprotective despite my instructions," he said. "The dead don't bleed, by the way," he added, pointing at Chan Sha. At her bandaged knee and the blood that had begun leaking down the side of her leg. The knee I'd shot.

Damn.

"I'm not sure that I need the spares, Buc, but you'll be useful at any rate."

He was hard to hear over the hisses and moans of his minions. But even if he had been clear as a signal cannon over still waters, I wouldn't have listened. He didn't understand and he had to or this was all for naught.

Stone. Slingshot. Back over shoulder. Four paces. Repeat. I dropped my hand to the pouch at my side, plucked a stone, drew my slingshot, and blew off the top half of the Archaeologist's skull. It was the least I could do for her, given the circumstances. Chan Sha echoed my scream and slammed her axes into a Shambles's throat. The blades wedged in the vertebrae, so the pirate ripped off one of the Shambles's femurs and began bludgeoning another with it while Eld decapitated a third with one swing of his sword.

I grabbed a stone and put another down, tearing away its worn bandanna along with half its face. The dead closed around us and a single Shambles filled my vision. Letting my slingshot dangle from my wrist, I slashed her across the face with my knife. The Shambles hissed at me, spraying black ichor, but otherwise seemed unimpressed by the blow. I flipped the knife and stabbed it in the throat; the Arawaíno's pig-iron blade caught on the upper spine and I sawed viciously back and forth, rocking the Shambles' face side to side, her remaining bleached hair turning dark with gore. And then the blade caught and when I pulled, her head fell backward, hanging by a piece of gristle while the rest of her fell limply to the sands.

In just a few heartbeats we'd put down half a dozen Shambles, but my breath burned in my throat and my blade was too short. When I looked over my shoulder, I saw that Eld was barely doing better with a cutlass against four blades at once and Chan Sha was doing worse than either of us. We weren't going to hold out another moment, let alone another minute. Chan Sha tripped and fell with a scream of pain and the dead man in front of her fell on top of her, clawing at her braids.

"Enough!"

Everything stopped.

"Enough," I repeated. I hadn't expected everyone to come to a grinding halt. I could feel my pulse in my head and hear Eld breathing behind me. Chan Sha's breathing was quieter, with the Shambles atop her, but still there. "There's been a serious misunderstanding," I said.

The Ghost Captain stepped over the Archaeologist's body with a look of regret and took a cup from one of the undead beside him. He sipped, holding his glowing book in the other hand.

"Oh really? Do tell."

"Eld and I were sent by merchants to find out why their ships are disappearing," I said. It was a struggle to keep my voice calm, my face smooth. The dead's ichor stained my dress and every breath made my stomach clench. Beyond the stench I could feel their eyeless stares boring into me from every side. But panic would put the matchstick to powder and I had no wish to test the Dead Walker's control over the Shambles. I'd seen how well that worked when they'd nearly blown me to smithereens.

"We were to investigate only," I added. I had to spend my words like a miser: too much and I'd give him enough information to see the lies I was painting . . . too little and he'd kill us all before he grasped the importance of what I was saying. I hadn't kneecapped Chan Sha and tiptoed through the undead to bring us directly under his thumb only to be squashed now like an ant.

"Say I believe you," he said, handing the cup back to a Shambles and letting another straighten his black jacket. "You attacked my brethren in port and tried to kill me thrice now. Why, if you're not Ciris's agents?"

"You're looking at the same information, just drawing the wrong conclusions."

"You expect me to believe that?"

"I don't." I shook my head. "That's why I brought along proof. You think Ciris is here. And you're right. Eld," I said, keeping my eyes on the man in front of the tent. Chan Sha screamed when she fell in front of me. "And this is my proof."

"A washed-out cripple?" His lips curled.

"No, Chan Sha, the famed pirate. And a Sin Eater—priestess of Ciris. She's the one who's been after you and the artifact."

"Chan Sha?" He mouthed her name again and nodded, weighing the information. "Perhaps. Yes, I think so. Ingenious." He smiled, mouth spread wide across his face. "I might actually let you leave alive, if that's true." He glanced at my feet. "Do you desire the artifact, Sin Eater?"

Chan Sha glared up at me, anger warring with the pain on her face. "I do," she growled.

"Then we agree on something."

Her head snapped back around. "What lies are these, Dead Walker?"

"Your kind always spits that as an epithet, but few are chosen to command the dead, Sin Eater. It is an honor."

"It is an abomination."

"Ah, but having a lifeless God in your head is not?" His laugh was dry and crackling. "We can spar all morning, but if that dead voice wants the artifact, then I suggest you come forward." The dead moved around us, every moan and hiss disappearing into an eerie silence as they formed a corridor between us and the Ghost Captain.

"Now," he commanded, all humor gone.

I stepped around Chan Sha, keeping the ichor-stained knife in my hand. Eld stopped to help her up and she cursed him even as she leaned on his shoulder and followed after. They were better actors than I'd given them credit for, but then again, I don't think she was acting. I kept my eyes on the Ghost Captain as I walked down the aisle. I'm not sure it's possible to look commanding in a torn dress made of dried rushes. Not with my bones showing through from the last two weeks and my hair knotted on one side and fuzzy from lack of shaving on the other. And then there was my age to consider.

But.

When I was younger—young enough that I still depended on my sister to survive—I saw a woman hanged. I don't know what crime she was convicted of, but I remember thinking it wasn't her first and wouldn't have been her last, if not for the noose. She had one eye blacked beneath the soot on her face and a split lip, but she'd taken the stairs as stately as any queen mounting her throne. When she put her head through the loop of rope, it seemed like she was allowing the executioner the honor of crowning her.

She swung in the end. Aye, and kicked, too, like the rest. But she died like a queen and the streets were loud with her death for weeks after. I'd taken the lesson to heart. If she didn't give up at the end, I wasn't going to let a little grime and hard days bend my knee either.

The Dead Walker's eyes widened when I reached him. It was just a brief motion and then his self-serving smile slid back in place, but I'd seen it first and it was easier to meet his smile with my own. He wagged a finger at me. "You should have told me the other night, Buc. On the ship. I would have taken her then."

"I would have if I thought it that simple," I said. I heard Eld and Chan Sha catch up to me. "You could have just told the Goddess where the artifact was and been done with this farce months ago," I added.

"I would have," he said. His smile crept into a grin. "If I thought it that simple." He shifted his attention behind me and fingered the tuft left over from where I'd sliced his goatee away. "I don't think you'll be able to make the journey unassisted, Sin Eater," he said.

"Journey? It's a few hundred paces." Chan Sha's voice was hoarse, but even. "I can manage that at least."

"It's a little more than that," he said. "Head up the hill"—he gestured—"there is a rope ladder hanging off the larboard side." He tapped his head. "Luckily, our dear Archaeologist's memories are still with me. Once there, you'll need to scale the ship and head across the fissure between the bow and aft. It's the only way to reach the captain's chamber."

I looked up the hillside. It was rocky and steep where it wasn't covered in thick undergrowth. I couldn't see the rope ladder, but I could see numerous fissures running through the wreckage. "You think you can manage that with a busted leg?" I asked.

"You broke a bone or two—that doesn't heal in a few hours, girl. But I'll have to manage, won't I?" she asked. Her green eyes burned in the morning sun. I won't lie; it was a relief when she turned her gaze on the Ghost Captain. There was a fire in them that hadn't been there before. *From her, or from her Goddess?* "What then?"

"I've not been in the room, but one of the Archaeologist's servants was. In the corner across from the bunk, in an alcove built into the ship's planking, there's an altar made of black obsidian." He gestured with his book. "According to her, it will come to life when it senses your presence. Then you must place your palm on the altar."

"I put my palm to the altar and that's it?" Chan Sha asked.

"I think so. Gods' bones, I don't know; the Archaeologist wasn't fool enough to try it. Ask your Goddess." The Ghost Captain's youthful features twisted and I could see he hated not knowing. A feeling I could appreciate. "Complete the ritual and the artifact will be yours. But you must take care, as the ship is well and truly rotted and the rear of the cabin is open to the elements. One misstep and you could fall through every deck and end up in who knows how many fathoms of water. Or dashed on the rocks."

"You're right," I said. Everyone turned to look at me. "She's not going to be able to do it on her own. Not with that leg broken at the knee."

"What?" Chan Sha sneered as she stood straight, wincing without Eld's support. This hadn't been part of the plan—at least not the one I'd told her about. "Are you offering to go with me?"

"Hardly." I didn't try to hide my smile. "I'm simply suggesting you won't make it on your own. Our friendly Captain"—I nodded to the Dead Walker—"has countless willing servants. Perhaps they can help?"

"I'll be damned if—"

"Will you do it, Sin Eater?" the Ghost Captain cut Chan Sha off. "Will you take the artifact?"

I kept my face still as my shoulder blades tightened. Would she accept it? Ever since I'd broken her knee, I'd been doing my level best to keep her off-kilter, to nudge her toward the path I needed her to walk. Still, I wasn't sure she could make it on her own, but if she could, I didn't want her up there alone with a piece of her God that might make her magnitudes more powerful than before. A few undead might not do much, but they might give her pause. And a pause was all I needed.

"Why?" she asked. "The girl was right. . . . You could have told us at any time and we would have come. You knew we were searching for it and yet only now do you want me to reclaim the artifact. Why?"

"Because this war has gone on for far too long. Our Gods weren't able to make peace when they came here, but perhaps their servants can. Take the artifact back to your Goddess and give her our peace offering."

"Peace?" Chan Sha's laughter drowned out the crashing surf. "When has there ever been hope of that, mage?"

The Dead Walker shook his head. "Would you believe anything I told you?" Something flitted across her features and he snorted. "I thought not. We've fought for millennia, Sin Eater. Trust died long ago. But perhaps this offering can change that. Otherwise, what is our future but mutual destruction? So, trust or no, will you do it?"

"Aye. Yes."

Some of the knots loosened in my back, quickly replaced by others. *Was that her talking, or her Goddess? Did that matter?* Too many questions and not enough answers, but the first part of my plan was right on the money. I hadn't been sure how much control the Ghost Captain had over his undead, but I figured if we got close enough for him to recognize us, he'd hold them off. If only to gloat, but give me a sliver of an opening and I'll drive a wedge into it. And Chan Sha made one hell of a wedge. She was a fool to believe him . . . if she really did believe him. I was more inclined to believe that whatever was up in that rotting ship, her Goddess wanted it badly enough to risk her life.

"Then it matters not how you get there." His fingers danced across the book, and two of the nearest Shambles, head and shoulders taller than Eld, stepped forward with grating, crunching sounds of bone on bone and grasped Chan Sha by either arm and began walking away. "They will see you there safely."

"Like damn they will," Chan Sha growled. Her good leg kicked uselessly, a hand above the ground while her bad did little more than wobble. The Shambles on her right, a mass of muscle piled on muscle under a thin jacket that was peeling in parts, revealing decaying flesh, glanced down but didn't stop. The other, hidden by a cloak that nonetheless couldn't hide an equally large frame, didn't even glance down. "Dead Walker!"

"I won't gamble my hopes on your whims, Sin Eater. I'll not see them dashed to pieces on the rocks with what's left of your brains. So kick if you must, but make sure you don't kick too hard." Her oath made him laugh. As the two monsters bore her away, she managed to fix him with a glare and the laughter died in his throat. She nodded and turned to face forward, somehow conveying the feeling that the Shambles were escorting, rather than carrying, her.

"The bitch has got style, I'll say that for her," I said.

"Aye, she does that," Eld agreed.

48

The Ghost Captain tucked his book into a pocket in his black oil-skin jacket and clapped his hands together. "Well, that's started." He glanced back and forth between us. "You know you don't have to wear those scraps anymore, right? My pets can't smell you, but I can see you, so it matters little. Unless you like the smell of rotting death?"

Eld and I shed our borrowed garments as fast as we could; Eld scratched at his scalp after chucking the moldy hat.

"Okay," I said, fighting the impulse to scratch my arms where the Shambles's shirt had touched my flesh, "how about you let us in on whatever the catch is, now that she's gone?"

"Buc, Buc." He shook his head. "There's no catch. I meant every word I said."

"I'll just bet you did," I muttered.

"What else did you mean, that you left unsaid?" Eld asked. "You're nervous." He took a step forward, brushing his hair back out of his eyes, and shook his head. "No, you're scared. Holding it at bay, I'll give you that. But scared. Why?"

Gods, save me from honest men. If I was a scalpel, then Eld was a bone saw. If all diplomats were as blunt as him, then wars, alliances, and treaties would be the work of hours, not days or weeks. Then again, there'd likely be far fewer of the latter if all spoke their truths as baldly as Eld did, instead of hiding their meaning in the shades of ink drying on the page. I opened my mouth to smooth things over, but the Ghost Captain answered before I could begin. *Men.*

"You don't understand," he said slowly. "My Gods are dead." I snorted and his eyes flashed. "Dead, but their teachings are no less prescient. They guide us from beyond the grave. Even a casual pupil will soon realize that they came to us out of dire need: the War. A war that had lasted for a millennia between them and Ciris. When there were a thousand upon a thousand of Ciris. It only ended when both Gods, old and new, left the heavens and embraced mortality."

"Ended?" Eld asked.

"So we thought," he said. He struck his thigh with a fist. "Then Ciris awoke, no longer strong in numbers, but alive just the same, where our Gods are not. She was fragmented, but as her followers have begun to draw those fragments back together, a new strategy has emerged. It's clear she believes the War can still be won and none of our envoys have been able to reason with her. Not since she was parted with the only piece of her that holds any hope of peace. The artifact," he finished with a nod.

"Aye, but what is the artifact?"

"A . . . piece of her." He threw his hands up in the air. "I don't have the words. I'm not old enough to be trusted with a free hand in the Archives." My ears pricked up at that. Archives sounded like books. *Forbidden* books. "But the Eldest has said that it is Ciris's . . . conscience. Stolen away by one of her own—a high priest who thought by removing it he was ensuring her victory, because without it, she will never surrender."

"So you decided to pull the rest of the world into your religious war?" Eld asked, heat in his voice. "Because your antics have done just that."

"It's the way of religions," I said. My jaw clenched. "To ensnare and destroy that which they can't have."

"Fools," he hissed. "You still don't understand. Why do you think we're here? To save the world!" He pointed up the hill, where the two Shambles carrying Chan Sha had almost reached the top. "You think the Gods came to our world by choice? Who would choose death over immortality? They came because their war destroyed their own worlds." He swept his arms out. "Imagine all of this . . . gone. It is enough to make me want to put out my own eyes."

His chest heaved and the fear he'd kept hidden marched across his features. "That is why I came here and why I am helping a Sin Eater. If Ciris remains incomplete, then it is only a matter of time before she destroys this world trying to win a dead war. Even if she wins, we're damned."

"Then why fight her? If there's no fighting, there's nothing to destroy," Eld said.

My eyebrows twitched. "He has a point."

"Try not to sound surprised," Eld muttered. I laughed and he made a sound in his chest that made me laugh louder.

"You're asking for genocide," the Ghost Captain growled. "Scores upon scores of our priests would die and their thousands of followers. Entire nations worship the Dead Gods. They wouldn't go quietly into the night and even if they did, it wouldn't matter; the records are clear on that. Ciris would find another enemy, another reason. She is the last remnant of an entire world and her grief will blot out all reason. Unless she is whole. And even then . . ." He took a breath and his voice broke.

"It may not be enough, but we must try. If she stops fighting, so will we. We weren't born into this war and we've none of our Gods' hatred. Or hers. There's room enough for more than one religion in the world, if it's peaceful. Chan Sha's fight . . . our fight . . . is for our world."

"So you are giving her back a piece of herself both as an attempt at a truce and with the hope that this artifact may make her amiable to peace?" I snorted. "Even a faceless man would smell bullshit."

"I'll not deny that there were attempts to . . . use the artifact against her," the Ghost Captain said finally.

"Weaponize it, you mean."

"Aye, early on that was a potential strategy," he admitted. "But when it became clear that it wouldn't work, we realized this might be the opportunity we've been waiting for, but never thought to try. Chan Sha doesn't believe us, you don't believe us, but what if it's so audacious that it actually works?"

"Say we believe you," I said. And I did believe him . . . just not the lies he was telling us. "Then what?"

"Then join us," he whispered. "Help us win or this war will continue for another millennium."

The Ghost Captain's offer caught me off guard. I'd spent more than a year planning for this—oh, not this exact situation, but when I read about the Gods and their religions and realized it was all bullshit? That they weren't our Gods, but foreigners come from the skies to use us for their own purposes, the way the master drives the slaves? When I spent hours studying their motivations and their machinations that plucked the strings of the world, searching for a perfect melody that would bring them what they really desired: Power?

When I read that, I knew I'd have to confront them, Gods or no. But I hadn't bargained for them to ask for my help. The Ghost Captain's explanation had a lot of holes in it, sure, but what the Archaeologist had found in that journal filled in some of those holes all too neatly. I closed my eyes and for a moment I saw the land and seas rent with fire and thunder that tore the world apart. *The War*. Prehistory was necessarily fragmented and contradictory and given to all kinds of flights of fantasy, but all agreed on one point. The Gods' War had nearly destroyed our world at the dawn of time and now they were awakening again.

The Dead Walker might believe his Gods dead, but if their war continued, it didn't matter if they met his definition of alive or not. The same with Ciris. I wasn't sure which was worse: Gods that were dead or one that was alive and insane. To have both together was something I could never have planned for. *And yet, here it is. Do I change my plan or hold course?* I glanced at Eld, but there was no way to signal him, and besides, I'd whispered to him that we were committed.

"You think this artifact will end the power struggles between your religions?" I asked.

"Aye. It has to," the Dead Walker said.

Why? It would have been easy to let the location slip to Sin Eaters. But he didn't. And I had gambled everything on why he hadn't. Now it was down to what Chan Sha came back with. A large gamble, but if the two sides hadn't found peace in thousands of years, what hope was there that today would be any different? *None at all.*

"How do you know your Eldest didn't lie to you?" I asked. "You said you haven't seen these Archives, whatever they are, yourself. So how can you know?"

The Ghost Captain's brow furrowed and he scratched his chin absently. The bells he'd tied in his scrap of goatee rang against his fingers. "Lie? But why would they lie to one of their order?"

"True," I said. *Fool.* Why wouldn't they lie was the better question. Here was another, so enmeshed in the power structure that he couldn't take a step back to look at the situation objectively. Even if they were telling the truth, would the world go back to the way it had been before? Put out the fires they created and devolve to a utopia? *No.* That door had been opened and ending the struggle wouldn't close it now. Destroying one side completely before the other would only make it that much harder in the end. I eyed the Ghost Captain and nodded, but I was agreeing with myself and not him. I couldn't trust a fool.

But I can use one.

49

"You make a good point," I heard myself say.

"She's there!" The Ghost Captain pushed past Eld and me, pointing toward the wreck on the hill. I followed his arm and saw Chan Sha limping across the deck. She slipped and tumbled forward, arms clawing, and kept sliding until a rock poking up through the deck arrested her fall. Her scream carried down to us. The Ghost Captain cursed and dug into his jacket, pulled his book back out, and began sliding his fingers across it. The pair of large Shambles appeared over the railing at his command and climbed onto the deck.

"I told them to stay with her!" He glanced back at us and shook his head. "They have their uses, but sometimes, I swear they don't think."

Eld and I exchanged glances and Eld spun his finger in a circle by his head. I nodded. The man sounded like a father speaking of his children. Exasperated, but loving all the same. Spending all your time with the dead didn't seem to be good for your mental stability. Who knew?

The larger Shambles in the ripped jacket pulled Chan Sha

to her feet, tossed her over his shoulder, and leapt across the open fissure in a single motion that sent another scream echoing down to us. I didn't fault Chan Sha that one: having a corpse do that to you had to be unnerving. I turned to Eld and saw he had a similar opinion: his mouth hung open and his head was tilted in an odd way. I elbowed him and he straightened with a start.

"Blast that," he muttered.

"Aye."

The Shambles landed awkwardly, going to a knee, then set Chan Sha down on the deck hard enough that I thought I heard her knee snap. If it did, she didn't show it, walking no more awkwardly than she had before. We watched her hobble the length of the deck and seemingly disappear into the cliff where it had swallowed the ship. She reappeared farther toward the edge, pausing before drawing herself up to her full height and entering a door that opened reluctantly, fighting her.

"She made it!" The Ghost Captain glanced at us and his mouth twisted in a tight smile. "That's the cabin."

Color leapt from the cabin. Strange patterns of warm blue spread across the deck, visible even in the sunlight. It looked as if someone had painted the grey sand-swept deck in the blink of an eye.

"Blood and Bone, she did it!" The tension leeched from his shoulders and he sighed. "She did it."

A scream rent the air. The warm blues shimmered, faded, and resolved into a darker red that bathed the whole ship in the color of blood. The door slammed open and Chan Sha reeled out, clutching her head and running, even with her broken leg, running. And screaming. A short scream, a long breath, and then a never-ending scream that tore at the world like a God plucking at a scab. And if it tore away, what would pour out?

"No, no, no!" The Ghost Captain shook the book in his hands. "Save her."

The Shambles that had jumped across with Chan Sha lumbered toward her. She ran right into him, knocking the corpse back a pace. She twisted to run away from him, but her legs buckled, sending her to the deck. The air twisted around her. The second Shambles leapt the fissure and the pair advanced on the writhing Chan Sha.

"Gods, she's . . ." Eld began, just as the two Shambles pulled Chan Sha upright and burst into sooty flames. "On fire," Eld finished.

Chan Sha flailed wildly, slipping from the grasp of one Shambles. As the other whipped around due to the living woman's momentum, their legs twisted together and Chan Sha flew across the deck with the Shambles beneath her. They slammed into the railing and the weathered wood exploded in splinters and bodies and they soared out and fell like stones on the shore side of the cliff. Chan Sha screamed the whole way down, until they hit the rocks at the bottom hard enough that dark ichor exploded like a geyser. For a moment there was silence.

The Shambles on the ship ignited into a fireball. The Ghost Captain cursed and bent over his book and the undead ran across the deck and threw himself over the side even as flames tore at his remaining flesh. The second ball of fire went out with a hiss when it hit the water not far from where Chan Sha had vanished. Oily smoke sinuously slid up from the rocks and then a wave came in and there was nothing.

"Fuck me," Eld said, gasping.

There was nothing but the sounds of our breathing. Then Chan Sha leapt from behind the rocks with a crackling roar and tore into the ranks of the Shambles that stood motionless on the beach. She disappeared from view for a moment and when she came back up, a blade glittered in each fist she'd ripped free from the Shambles and the dead fell away from her in their haste to escape. She was halfway across the sand in an instant with only a few undead between us and her.

"Do something!" I yelled at the Ghost Captain. My plan was working too well—Eld and I were closer to Chan Sha than the Ghost Captain was and Chan Sha had lost all sense. He shook his head, transfixed, but his fingers leapt over the pages of his book. Too late. The last undead was already down in a shower of ichor. I reached to grab him. "You useless pile of—"

Eld leapt past me at the last instant, his own curved blade in his hand, and stepped between me and Chan Sha. The pirate paused, studying him, but if she recognized him, it didn't show in the way she twirled her blades and sank down into a waiting crouch. Her face was dark with soot and one eye was milky white. Her clothes hung in tatters and where flesh showed, it was burnt and bloody. But she met Eld's attack as if she were fresh from a good night's sleep. They danced on the sands with only the Ghost Captain, me, and the undead as witnesses.

50

I've underestimated Eld. Vastly.

His sword flashed like chained lightning, the blade appearing in a dozen places at once as he fought the pair of swords in Chan Sha's hands. I say fought, but it was more than that. I've seen enough sword fights to know that they often don't last longer than it takes to take a breath and release it. Oh, the buildup can take time, true, but when there's steel involved, it's often a matter of slipping past a parry or catching your opponent out and then steel touches flesh, and flesh gives over. A man can take a dozen cuts or even thrusts and still have time to give his lifeblood for revenge. But the actual fighting part? That is over and done with long before the end.

This wasn't like that.

Eld flowed around Chan Sha, who had settled from her initial rush into a waiting guard. Eld circled and she followed and their swords met between them like a trio of lovers caught in the throes of passion. Sweat poured from Eld's face and bits of his shirt showed through where steel had cut his jacket. Still he kept up his frenetic attack, though I knew, *knew,* that he would eventually falter. Flesh can only push so far. I knew that, but I guess Eld didn't. Because he kept pressing, seeking, and fighting, to the point that I began to wonder if perhaps he wasn't a Sin Eater himself. Until he proved himself human.

Eld fell with a grunt, half his sleeve torn away and blood turning his shirt and shoulder crimson. Chan Sha glanced past him and her melted lips parted in an ashen smile. So maybe the bitch did remember. She fell with a hoarse scream as Eld hacked at the leg I'd broken earlier, rolled away from him, and came up into a crouch a dozen paces away. Blood soaked one shoulder and the other was twisted strangely, but the blades were steady in her hands. She opened her mouth to speak.

The dead washed over her like high tide and she disappeared in a maelstrom of blood and bone.

"About Godsdamned time," I told the Ghost Captain.

"Would you want him caught up in that?" he asked. We both watched the dead writhing and tearing in a mass on the sand. A rogue wave washed across them and when it left, the dead were gone and Chan Sha with them. "I thought not," he said, answering his own question.

"What now?" Eld asked, rejoining us. He was battling with a scrap of his shirtsleeve, so I moved beside him, tearing it and wrapping it around the wound on his shoulder. It wasn't deep, but it was long and the scrap turned bright red before I finished tying it, so I reached for another.

"Well, she didn't kill him for us," I whispered.

"My fault," he muttered through clenched teeth.

"No. She might have killed him just now, but she would have killed us getting to him. Hard to steal his book and use it on her if we're already dead." I took a breath and forced myself to tell the truth. "You were . . . Eld, you were magnificent," I said.

"Magnificent." He smiled through the pain. "I like the sound of that. It has a ring to it."

"It can't be one of my order," the Ghost Captain said, interrupting us. "Our magic is anathema to Ciris." He glanced down at his book and some of the undead stopped combing the beach looking for Chan Sha's corpse and moved back toward us. "We thought it had to be a Sin Eater, but it seems obvious now that they can't do it either. They're already bonded to Ciris. Gods' bones, I wasted months here, when the answer was staring me right in the face." He flicked the bells in his goatee.

"It really is a pity the dead can't perform this particular service." He smiled at us. "It has to be one who hasn't touched magic. It seems that one who is pure and unmarked can touch the artifact, the same as any initiate can receive the Dead Gods or Ciris. It has to be one of you." His smile broadened. "The only question left is, who will it be?"

I stopped tying a third bandage around Eld's arm and looked over my shoulder. "You're joking. After what we just saw?" He shook his head, smiling that inane smile. "Fuck off."

He shook his head again, touched the book in his hands, and one of the dead dove for me. Eld shoved me out of the way and caught a wrist and the woman's bones snapped, but her dead eyes showed no pain. He reached for her other hand and she let him grab it. They were caught like that for a moment and Eld glanced over his shoulder at where I lay sprawled in the sand, started to say something. To apologize.

She lunged forward and sank her rotting teeth into Eld's good shoulder.

Eld screamed and shoved her back and she let him, absently wiping at the ichor that leaked from her gums, and moved calmly away, joining the rest of her undead brethren. I leapt up and caught Eld as he fell, but his weight bore us both to the ground. Blood ran from the cuff of his shirtsleeve and I could see a blackened tooth caught in the fabric. I started to assure him it was all right, that the wound wasn't deep, even as Chan Sha's warning echoed through my mind. *The dead are infectious.* But then the Ghost Captain took that chance away from me.

"I'm rather fine with you dying," he said. "The dead carry their disease in the tissues of their body; the ichor that commands them will soon command you. And when you're dead, then you'll do whatever I ask of you."

"You're dead," I spat. I climbed to my feet. My knife was in my hands and I could already visualize the steps between me and the Dead Walker. I wouldn't stop till I sawed his head completely off. "You're fucking dead."

"Kill me and I'll take possession of one of my servants," he said. He shrugged at the thought. "Unpleasant, but not unprecedented. Or you could go and retrieve the artifact and I'll remove the taint from Eld." His mouth twitched. "And all will be well."

"You fool." Eld's laughter turned us both around. He had managed to prop himself up on one arm, but I could see his veins through his skin. They were turning dark beneath his paleness. "You finally made a mistake." He smiled even as his body shuddered. "You should have had the Shambles bite Buc. I lo—" He coughed. "I am . . . weak. Too weak to refuse." He glanced at me and something filled his eyes. What that something was, I couldn't read.

"I *am* weak, Buc; I would have gone up." His gaze hardened on the Ghost Captain. "She is strong where I am not; she sees logic where I see emotion. And there is no logic in giving in to you.

"Not even to save me."

His words twisted something inside me. Something I felt when my sister was still alive—the last time I really felt anything until I thought I'd murdered Eld. Emotion is strange to me, a language I can't understand, much less speak. There is one emotion, though, one that everyone recognizes. Even a hollow husk like me. I remembered now. The words I'd tried to speak to Eld when he carried me in his arms from the Harbormaster in Port au' Sheen. The words I'd thought as I sank beneath the waves. The words I hadn't been able to contemplate when I thought I'd lost him forever. *Love.* I'd thought it dead and burned away with my sister, but I'd been wrong.

Wrong like Eld. *I love you.*

"I'll do it," I said.

"Buc, don't!" Eld gasped and glanced at his shoulder. "I—"

"You think I have no feelings," I said. "No regard for others. That I care only for power and my goals. You're not wrong," I admitted. *But that's not the full measure of truth either.* I took a breath and that feeling suffused me so that every fiber of my being was soaked through with it. My breath caught in my throat, held in place by the lump there, and tears burnt my eyes. "I'd do anything for you, Eld." I swallowed the lump and glared at the Ghost Captain. "I get the artifact and you cure him?"

"That's the deal."

"And you can cure him?"

"Aye." He held up a finger. "If you do it before he dies. The process doesn't take that long, but if you do it before then, I can remove the taint." He waved me away. "So you'd best be quick about it."

I sank down beside Eld but couldn't quite meet his eyes. I could already feel my cheeks burning from what I'd said. *Godsdamned emotion.* "You'd better not die," I said, my voice husky with unshed tears. "Or I'll kill you."

"Buc." His laughter cut off as his weight shifted on his arm. "Buc, I—"

"Don't say anything, you poor fool. Just don't die on me. Promise?"

"Promise," he whispered.

I stood up and squared my shoulders and the dead made a path to the cliff. "Then I'm off to meet a God."

51

The climb up the hill set my lungs to burning so that by the time I reached the shipwreck, I gasped and wheezed. Even so, I immediately took ahold of the rope ladder that hung from the bone-white bow and began climbing. Chan Sha's magic seemed to have worn off and while I wasn't as weak as I'd been back on the other island, I wasn't at full strength. My limbs felt leaden. I gritted my teeth and kept climbing. I was halfway up when I smelled smoke and remembered the Shambles engulfed in flames as it went over the side. The planks were dryer than dry—of course they would catch fire from even a brief exposure.

Acrid and cloying, the stench filled my nostrils, waking memories I'd buried long ago. Buried and sowed the ground with salt for good measure, but it hadn't been enough. I froze, halting so quickly that the ladder swayed back and forth, first closer so that I got a proper mouthful of smoke, then farther, so I had barely enough time to force my lungs to work and suck in good air. Back and forth. Death and life. Back and forth. And in the space between . . .

The day my sister died.

The warehouse was falling apart around itself, like the rest of this section of the Quarto that had forgotten better times. Mold, mildew, and urine clung to the air; every breath stung. Plaster hung like rent flesh from the walls, sometimes revealing air and sometimes the wooden bones of the warehouse, and every now and again pieces fell from the ceiling, exposing the floor above. Sister jumped whenever part of the building died and when she jumped, I felt every nerve in my body glow.

I wanted to tell her to give it a rest, but I could barely breathe and walk at the same time. This morning when I woke up and tried to walk to the gutter to take a piss, I'd almost passed out, finally confessing to her that spots had filled my vision for two days now. We both knew starvation well, well enough to recognize the signs of the final stages.

One of the other children had bragged that the Krakens were going to ambush the Blackened Blades at the Tip. Street gangs fought all the time, but now there were whispers that Blood in the Water herself was leading the Krakens and that meant more than a canal war. That meant extinction for one of the gangs. And opportunity for us.

"Do you remember where they had their supplies?" Sister asked.

"I—" I stopped walking, waited a breath for the black flecks to clear from my vision, and nodded. I knew, but it was slow in coming to me, my brain rendered moribund from lack of nutrition. At length I remembered.

"Last message I carried for the Blades, they made me wait yonder," I said, lifting a bony finger to indicate the dozen chairs arranged in a semicircle around a broken window. Half were lacking backs, and more than one was off-kilter for want of a leg. "They were behind me, but I could hear the stairs creaking as they walked, and when they came back down, they gave me bread and cheese and a bit of fish." After I spoke, I remembered I had eaten the fish then and there and hadn't told Sister of it. But she wouldn't mind, not now that we were both starving to death, me faster than her. "It has to be upstairs then."

"Upstairs?" Her brow furrowed in a way that would have been cute, save that her front teeth were overlarge for her mouth and gave all of her expressions a hint of idiocy. She wasn't dumb, but her teeth would never let anyone think her clever. She was clever enough to find you and latch on, though, wasn't she? Maybe that was Sister's best talent: finding those who had skills she lacked and making friends of them. Friend-making was something I was incapable of, but with Sister it didn't matter. She made friends enough for the both of us. Until the inland wars had finally touched Servenza, starting a few months back, and food became scarce. The friendships disappeared with the food.

"Buc?"

"What?" I asked. I looked around and saw her halfway across the warehouse, standing by the stairs.

"I asked if you were coming. Didn't you hear anything I said?"

"I was listening for them," I lied. Sister's bony shoulders shook beneath the threadbare calico dress. She didn't need to ask who "them" were. If either gang found us here after the battle, we'd be lucky if they just killed us. "I'm coming," I said, hobbling across the bare, dust-covered floor.

My hunger left a low, constant buzzing in my head, and with the plaster falling down all around us, it was difficult to discern real from imaginary. Sister grabbed my hand when I reached her and practically dragged me up the stairs, sometimes taking the wooden planks two at a time, ignoring my squeaks of pain when my shins hit a step. Or maybe my cries were only inside my head; it was hard to feel if my lips moved or not.

The upper floor was similar to the lower, save that it was dark. Any windows were boarded over, and the ceiling was intact, fresh boards tacked up here and there where it had caved in, so that the only light came from cracks around the boarded windows. Unlike below, there were dozens more crates and less dust. Clearly the Blades trusted *that any who wandered into the seemingly abandoned warehouse wouldn't bother searching past the decay below. And on any day but today, even if someone did bother, they wouldn't have made it this far without meeting a dozen or more toughs with cudgels, knotted ropes, and maybe a dagger or two. Today the place was as empty as a corpse, and in a few hours, if not already, most who had been here would be corpses themselves. I'd told Sister that when I convinced her to come and she'd actually managed a tear for the poor bastards, but she'd still come. Servenza might not kill softness, but it did weakness.*

"There. Those sacks," she said, and gasped. "That's the mark for rice." She pulled me into a lurching run that made my knees scream. But as loud as they screamed, my stomach was louder, and soon she didn't have to pull to keep me even with her. We reached the sacks together and Sister giggled. "Rice we have to boil first, but here's a heel of cheese," she said, handing me a small piece of white cheese with a rind that was only just beginning to mold. "And dried salted fish," she added, holding up a thin tin with the picture of whitefish engraved on it. "They must have robbed a noble's store for some of this."

"Mmphh—who cares?" I asked around a mouthful of cheese. I swallowed it only half chewed and began gnawing on the rind. When it landed in the pit of my stomach, pain radiated through me in nauseating waves that narrowed my vision to a haze of undulating black. But even so, I swallowed the rest of the rind and took the crust of bread Sister offered me. This time there was plenty of mold, but I couldn't bring myself to care. When I laughed, Sister laughed too, spraying crumbs everywhere.

"Looks like La Signora was right!" a husky voice boomed through the warehouse. Both of us whipped around and Sister squeaked in fright. A boy old enough to call himself a man, easily head and shoulders taller than Sister, with meaty arms that hung out of a loose, sleeveless shirt, stepped onto the upper floor. Half a dozen others filed up as well, flanking him on either side as they studied us. Two carried

lanterns that illuminated the lot of them and the smallest was twice as large as Sister. "The rats will come when they sense blood."

"We just came for our payment, sirrah," Sister lied. My neck cricked when I looked at her and she reached out and squeezed my hand. She was never a good liar, but I had to admit I was impressed she found the lie so soon. "From the missives we carried. The Blades told us to come back today for the rest. If you speak to—"

"Whoever you name is already dead, girl." The boy's thick lips twisted in a sneer. Or maybe he meant it for a smile. "La Signora only deals in one justice: the steel kind."

"La Signora, sirrah?"

"He means Blood in the Water," I whispered.

"Blood in the Water," he said, speaking on top of me. He scratched at a scar that pulled at the corner of his left eye.

I kept ahold of Sister's hand, popped the rest of the crust of bread into my mouth, and reached for the knife I kept hidden in my dress. It was barely longer than my little finger, but it was steel. If we hadn't found food today, Sister would have sold it for a few bites tomorrow. Now there might not be a tomorrow.

"She sent us here to secure their secret"—he said the word with another sneer—"warehouse. She said that when word reached the streets of the battle, street rats would flood this place in search of food. Vermin always do."

"We're not street rats, sirrah. We came for the food they owed, but none were here, so we helped ourselves." She dropped a tin of fish and let it settle on the floor with a wobbling metallic ring. She didn't reach for the others she'd stuffed into the pockets of her dress. "We'll leave without taking more. It's yours."

"It's the Krakens'," he growled. "None of us were happy about missing the fight, were we, lads?" The others muttered, but none looked too upset. Not like him. "Looks like we might still have some fun ourselves. La Signora means to show the gutter trash what's what today, *and I'd bet a copper you won't be the last rats what come searching for crumbs. We'll take the food, of course, but better if they see what happens to rats that come poking around where they're not wanted."*

"Sirrah?" Sister's voice had gone several octaves higher, her tone the kind that always made me roll my eyes.

"Sirrah?" he mimicked her. "I'll give you fecking sirrah." He whipped a blade from his belt and pointed it at us. "Bring them to me!"

One of the lantern bearers stayed beside him; the other five advanced toward us and all, save the one holding the second lantern, pulled out cudgels and maces. One of the taller ones, thin, but fast like lightning, leapt forward when they reached us. Sister stepped in front of me. She screamed something, but her words were lost in the others' laughter. The boy dropped his wooden cudgel and grabbed her, twisting her thin pale wrists back behind her, and Sister's scream changed from protest to pain. She half fell and the boy fell forward with her, catching himself at the last instant and heaving her back up. She sagged and he went right back down with her.

That time I was waiting.

My blade bit into his throat. Once. Twice. Half a dozen times in quick succession, each time leaving a bloody tear in his flesh so that before he could escape my reach, his throat leaked like a crimson faucet. He made an effort to stand, but Sister grabbed his wrists and now it was her turn to twist. He tried to speak, but his words were lost in blood and he collapsed against Sister, pushing her to the floor.

For a moment nothing happened. The world slowed to a crawl around me. I'd stabbed someone before, several someones, but only to send them on their way. I'd never killed before, but I knew the blood pooling around my feet was too much for him to have lived. The rest of the toughs who'd lagged behind came up laughing, unable to see in the dim light.

"Leave us have a go, Tem!" one called. "Tem?" The boy with the

lantern stepped past the rest and held the light up high, but the light didn't quite reach us.

"You playing us on?" he asked in a higher voice. He took another step and the light touched the blood pooling around Tem and Sister. The boy's face went slack; then his lips quivered and his chest heaved as he drew in breath to scream.

Once again, I was waiting. I leapt up, but he was shorter than I gave him credit for and my knife missed his throat, piercing him just below the jaw, so his scream came out garbled and short. My blade pulled free when I landed and he screamed louder, dropping the lantern to clutch at his mouth.

"She's kerred Tem!"

"And you too," I muttered, kicking the lantern. It hit him in the knees, rebounded, and broke open atop of one of the fallen sacks of rice. Oil spread across the sack and went up in bright blue flames. Shouts filled the room, but I was transfixed by the inferno I'd unleashed.

Then Sister's screams joined the others.

The large boy was illuminated by the remaining lantern bearer. Sister was in one hand, hanging like a rag doll, while his other hand held a blade. He watched my expression and a smile spread across his face, incongruous with the lancing scar beneath his left eye that almost looked like a teardrop. "You've a pair on you, lass or no. But you know how this ends, don't you?"

"With my blade in his throat!" I yelled, diving at the same time for the nearest tough. But hunger had drained me and I was too slow and the lad, smaller though he was, was still twice my size. He sidestepped easily. I slid forward, ending up in an uncomfortable crouch. "Or yours, if you don't let her go," I said, trying to hide my mistake.

"La Signora said to send a message." He glanced at the growing fire that licked hungrily at the food stores and nodded. "Burning this place to the ground is a message."

"*The fire crews will be here in minutes*," *the lantern bearer said in a diffident tone.*

"*Maybe, but I doubt they'll try to save this heap.*" *The leader shrugged.* "*And if they do, they'll still find a message. You want to save her?*" *he asked.*

I nodded.

The blade moved in his hand and I screamed, throwing myself forward, but the others grabbed me before I moved more than a step. My little knife fell forgotten from my hands and while I could hear something loud roaring in my ears, all was silent within me as I watched that blade. It hesitated, then plunged into Sister's chest.

When it came out, I heard her life come with it. Heard it above the sound of my screams. The dirt on her dress turned red with blood and he tossed her aside like so much refuse.

Into the flames.

She hit the rice sacks, then rolled off them and out the other side, dress singed, but not on fire.

"*Save her then, but you'll have to burn.*"

52

I blinked and found myself staring at the side of a rotted, weathered ship, swaying slowly from side to side. Swaying because I was on a rope ladder. In a rush, it all came back to me. *Gods, how many minutes wasted?* I shrugged it off and began climbing again. Eld was dying, alone with that madman, who was waiting to turn him into one of his creatures. It was the same as at the warehouse all those years before. I'd tried to get through the flames, but they leapt higher every moment. The heat had actually started to blister my skin.

No matter how much I loved Sister, I couldn't convince my weak flesh to brave the fire. Instead I'd stood and watched, so that she didn't pass alone. It was only when my dress caught, from floating embers, that I came to myself and managed to escape as the building collapsed around me. Later, much later, I'd told myself I didn't try to save her because she never moved—she was already dead. But that was a lie.

It would be different this time. *It had to be.* I was here to save Eld, not watch him die. I reached the railing and pulled myself over before my brain could focus on what my senses were telling me: that the flames were nearby once again. My legs wobbled when I landed on the deck, more from the steep angle than anything else. The ship followed the contour of the cliff and the deck sloped away from me, disappearing for several paces and then reappearing on the other side of the rent. It was there the flames gathered, but they were surprisingly thin. Oh, they'd caught on the deck, but the Shambles hadn't really turned into fireballs until after it plunged over the side. I've read that excess air will do that to a fire. Up here the flames hadn't gone out, but they hadn't started from much so they hadn't grown. Yet.

"They will if you keep standing here," I said. I've lived my whole life around fire: fireplaces, candles, lamps, lanterns . . . in a lot of ways, fire is life. But open flames make me nervous. And these flames kept pulling me in, whispering to me as if they were kin to the kind that kept me from Sister. Kept me from her until naught was left but ash. I felt something I hadn't felt since then.

Powerless.

"Eld." I don't know why I spoke his name, but when I did, the tightness inside loosened. Breath was still hard to come by, but I *could* breathe. And I could move. I walked forward, my rush-plaited sandals sliding across the smooth, warped deck. "Now jump." My legs were immobile. I took a deep breath, pulling in smoke and ash and terror in equal measure.

I watched the fire, focused on the flames. It wasn't a hot fire. That would come if it managed to eat more of the deck, but now it wasn't hot. It wasn't a physical threat, only a mental one. *Only a mental one.* I closed my eyes, willed myself to not be that little girl. But it wasn't enough. It wasn't enough five years ago and it wasn't enough now.

Then I knew why I'd said Eld's name. It wasn't about me; it was about him. And I had to do this thing to save him. The way he'd saved me so many times before. From the gaolship when

I confessed I didn't know how to swim. Dueling that Montay brother when I'd overstepped, even though he knew it meant a fight to the death and no way of knowing whose: both Montays were known for their skills with a blade. Catching me when I fainted from dehydration. Sprinting across the decks of two ships, clearing Shambles and pirates alike from his path so he could reach me and spirit me over the side. Meeting Chan Sha blade for blade.

When I needed him, Eld was there. When he'd needed me, on the shore below, I hadn't been there. I'd failed. Now he needed me again. *I won't fail this time.* The thought drove something through me and my legs moved.

I jumped.

I'd thought the flames young yet, but when I landed on the other side, my feet burned in my sandals and if I hadn't thrown myself into a roll, I think the dried grasses of my dress might have caught fire. As it was, I rolled past the fire and came up hard against the far railing with a resounding crack that fractured the rotted wood. I froze. All I could do was watch the flames, but while they were growing, they weren't moving my way. Instead they followed the slope down to the edge where Chan Sha and the Shambles had gone over. Cutting off my escape route.

Later. Time enough to think about that after you have the artifact. I pushed myself to my feet and eyed the open door at the end of the ship. The cabin inside was dark, but I thought I could see a faint, pulsing light. Even in the sunlight with more than a score of paces between the door and myself, I could tell there was something there. The thing that had killed Chan Sha.

It should have scared me, rooted me to the ground again, but after the trial of fire, I wasn't that fazed by it. *Kill me or don't.* I headed toward the door and fingered the blade hidden in my dress.

53

Up close the cabin didn't look any more ominous, although I could see a steady, pulsing glow coming from one of the walls within. I'd wasted enough time conquering the flames, so I didn't give myself time to think—no easy feat, that—and slipped inside the shadowed room. The air smelled crisp, like after a lightning storm when the rain suddenly lifts as if by command and there is that pause full of promise: Is it over or is the bolt coming for you? No bolt came for me, and my sandals were loud in the silence as I walked toward the artifact.

I could see it now: an altar of strange, dark, sleek metal molded into the wood. In the center of its black, impossibly smooth, impossibly polished surface, was a flickering blue light. I was peripherally aware of the cabin, of the bunk with its desiccated mattress sunk beneath rusted springs and the open drawers yawning emptily from the writing desk. All was as foggy as a dream; only the artifact, the altar, were real. I won't say it called to me, but something did, not unlike what the Archaeologist described.

To me, it felt the way a new book feels in your lap when you're about to open it for the first time. *If the Ghost Captain had shown me this, he'd never have had to twist my arm. Eld could have told him.* I never leave a book unopened or a page unturned.

My hand hovered over the obsidian surface before I realized I was there. I forced myself to take a breath, but knew I wasn't going to turn back now. I couldn't have even if I'd wanted to, and I didn't want to. My face was reflected in the cold, slick darkness, cheekbones sharper than normal, lips pressed together in a firm line. I nodded at myself.

I pressed my hand against the altar, only then remembering Chan Sha's screams as she fell. I tried to jerk my hand back and the altar exploded in bright light.

My hand wouldn't move.

I jerked my body backward, but my hand was stuck to the obsidian altar. But it wasn't obsidian. It didn't quite feel like polished rock for one thing, and I could barely feel my hand for another. Even as the thought crossed my mind, the sensation of a thousand needles sent stabbing pains across my palm and I yelped as a numb yet tingling sensation burned my skin and sank deeper, scouring my bones. A light from the altar bisected my eyes. Something reached out through the blindness and bit me on the neck, just below and behind my ear. I drew breath to scream, but the numb sensation returned tenfold, flooding me, and all thought was carried away on its waves. My eyes, nose, mouth, shoulders, breasts, legs, everything buzzed and tingled and warmth made cold sweat run down my body in rivulets. My breath came in gasps. I watched it all through clenched eyes, still half blind from the sudden burst of light.

"An initiate?"

I jumped, but my hand held me fast even as I searched for the source of the voice.

"It has been a long time. Too long," the voice said evenly.

"Blood calls to blood. The truth of blood. The power of blood. The magic of blood. We'll have much to discuss, you and I. If the ritual doesn't kill you," it added.

The voice was crisp, cool, and definitely male. With gnawing certainty, I realized it was coming from inside my mind. "What fuckery is this?" My question echoed off the walls, unanswered.

"It begins," it whispered. I started sputtering, but the voice began speaking as if it couldn't hear me. "The dust has settled. Three breaths, initiate." I inhaled. "The truth of blood. Three breaths and I'll cleanse you," it whispered.

I fought to keep my lungs still, but something in them betrayed me and I sucked in another gulp of air.

"The power of blood. Three breaths and you'll give me life," it hissed.

Now I strained, every muscle in my chest screaming, but a ragged gasp tore through my lips.

"The magic of blood. Three breaths and our bonding will be . . . complete!"

"Answer me, damn you," I snarled mentally, lungs screaming as if I'd just run a league.

"Hello, Sambuciña," he said, his voice filling my mind.

"Who the fuck are you?"

"I'm your SIN."

"Sin?"

"No, SIN," the voice said. "With a *C*."

"What sin?"

"Nothing like immorality." He sighed. "A common misunderstanding of your kind, but if we can set aside the lies the Dead Gods and their priests have spread for a moment, I'll explain in terms your mind can grasp. I'm a ritual left over from times before your kind attained enough evolutionary hierarchy to form complete thoughts. If you are made of stardust, then I'm made of the star itself. I'm your SIN and if you'll accept me, we can move beyond to the next ritual," he added. "The Rite of Possession."

My mind reeled. I'd only understood one word in three, but the little I got was that the artifact was in me. *Inside me, Gods!*

"Yes, you can imagine how thrilled I am," he said. Amusement touched his voice. "I'm sure you have many questions, I know you do, and I can hear them all. But if you'll allow me to take Possession, we can get going. Eld doesn't have much time left."

"So you represent my Sin—Wait a minute, Eld? How do you know about him?"

"With a *C*—your kind are frustrating with your limited— Very well. Sin it is. Now, Eld . . . everything you know, I know," he said as if explaining that one and one were two. "And you don't have to shout. You only have to think your words and I'll hear them."

"That's weird," I said mentally. "Everything I know, you know?"

"Yes. Blood calls to blood," he repeated. "Those words are a truth, Sambuciña. A truth you will come to see more clearly over time."

"So you know—" I began out loud.

"What? That you intend to destroy all religion and magic and bring the world into some utopian order?" He laughed. "Yes, I know, Sambuciña. All Sin Eaters bring a level of ambition with them, but yours may be larger than we are accustomed to. I think I can manage, if you can."

"So you don't mind that I intend to destroy Ciris?"

"Mind? Sambuciña, I *am* Ciris."

I choked on my reply and fought to breathe while both mind and mouth moved silently. "Call me Buc," I said when I found my words.

"Very well, Buc. Will you allow me to Possess you?"

"You're coming on a little hot and heavy. A woman likes some foreplay before she's fucked," I muttered. "You're Ciris, you're the Goddess?"

"I'm a piece of Ciris in the same way she's a piece of me. Once you allow me in, by performing what is called the Rite of Possession, we'll be bonded. She'll begin to sense me and I, her. After we make the proper sacrificial offerings, we'll sense each other always. Blood calls to blood, but the mind knows all. She is the knowledge and we are her limbs, you and I."

"A voice started speaking in my head a few minutes ago," I said. "I'm going to want to think about this before committing to everything."

"By which you mean you have no intention of completing the Rite or letting Ciris near us," he said. "And it hasn't been a few minutes, less than half of one, actually."

"How?"

"The magic of dilation."

"Come again," I said.

"Time dilation, it's—Ugh," he grunted. "I'm trying to dumb this down for you."

"Fuck you."

"You kiss Eld with that mouth?" he asked. I could practically feel him smirking. "No, but you'd like to, wouldn't you?" He cleared his throat. In my *mind*. "Your brain is like the night sky, where every star is a thought and the space between stars pathways for those thoughts. Communicating that way is orders of magnitude faster than speaking aloud as your kind does. If you didn't insist on speaking aloud to me, even less time would have passed."

"Gods," I breathed.

"Yes, imagine the possibilities," he whispered. "You saw some of what Chan Sha could do and you saw the Harbormaster. Limbs that never tire, a brain that can finally handle your thoughts without the needs of some whoring drug to slow it down, and healing abilities that turn us practically immortal."

"Whoring?" I asked mentally.

"As our ritual bonding becomes more firm, we'll begin to pick up each other's . . . mannerisms. Soon I'll have as foul a mouth as you. Now, there's a depressing thought," he added.

"Well, you've some sense of humor at least," I said. "And while that sounds tempting and all, I've no wish for a God inside my head. Its voice is bad enough." I frowned. "You keep asking for permission to Possess me. So you can't do it if I don't agree to it?"

"N-no," he said hesitantly.

"And how will you know?"

"I know your every thought, every hint of a thought. If you wish it, I will know."

"I don't wish it."

"I know," he said, and now some of his coolness evaporated.

"And you have to obey me?"

"Sort of, not quite."

"That's not a very good answer," I said.

"It wasn't a very good question," he shot back.

"Fair enough. You can't control me and I have some control over you." I nodded and straightened my shoulders. "All right, I'm ready to go, release me." Sin grumbled, but when my mind didn't waver, the altar—only Sin thought of it as some word that I'd never heard of and wasn't even sure it was part of a real language—went dark.

Suddenly I could feel my hand again. I inspected it, but aside from being a little red, it was no worse for wear. My neck still stung from whatever had bitten me during the ritual, but when I felt the spot, my hands came away clean, no blood.

"Healing," he whispered.

"Hush you," I said. I turned and walked out of the cabin to see that the flames had spread across the deck from side to side. A trickle of fear touched me, but with Sin filling my mind, it didn't have the same hold on me as before. *Perspective.* My thought or Sin's? I wasn't sure, but it didn't matter. What mattered was getting across to the other side.

"How are you at jumping?" I asked.

54

"You did it! I knew you would," the Ghost Captain lied when I reached the main group of Shambles. I could hear it in his voice—he hadn't thought I'd survive, not really. Which made what he did to Eld as good as murder. The dead all stood as they had when I left, in two lines between me and where the Ghost Captain stood beneath the awning outside his tent. When he grinned, his features softened so that only his goatee prevented him from looking as young as me. "Well-done!"

"Aye, well fucking done and now it's your turn." I couldn't let my gaze stay on Eld, or the anger I could feel building would burst out. Now wasn't the time for violence. *Not yet.*

A single glance showed me all I needed to see. His veins had turned black beneath translucent skin and his clothes clung to him from sweat; his cheeks were tinged in shades of blue and green. When he smiled, it was like a dagger to my chest.

"Heal Eld."

"In a moment, in a moment," the Ghost Captain said. "I need to know that you let the Sin into your soul before I help Eld."

"He doesn't have a moment," I protested, and took a step forward.

"Hold there." The dead shifted around me. "You've come up in the world, Buc. I feel safer with you out there and me in here." He glanced down at Eld and shook his head. "No, he doesn't have many moments." His smile disappeared. "All the more reason to be quick about it then. I need surety that you are a fully-fledged Sin Eater . . . one that will be compelled to return to Ciris after today's events and take our offering of peace with you."

"I've done it. I did it back on the ship before . . ." I swallowed an imaginary lump in my throat. "Before I knew what I was doing. It promised to save Eld first."

"Aye? Then where is Ciris to be found?"

I frowned. *Sin?*

"Accept Possession as the Dead Walker asks and I'll give you the answer," Sin said.

"It doesn't work that way," I said mentally. "You told me so yourself. You have to obey me."

"There are certain restrictions on that," he said dryly. "More restrictions now than after we're Possessed. If you'd just—"

"No," I repeated. "She's on the mainland," I said aloud.

"No shit, she's on the mainland," the Ghost Captain said. He shook his head. "I knew you wouldn't surrender to her that easily."

"You honestly think Sin Eaters would tell one of the Dead Walkers where their Goddess is?" I asked.

"If you knew where she was, you'd know that we've known, almost since she awoke, that Ciris was out of our grasp." The Ghost Captain sighed and flicked the remaining bells in his goatee.

"Eld has a few breaths left in him—he's still living, so I can't say how many for sure—but a few. Why don't you take one or two of his last breaths to decide what the fuck this has all been for?" He spread his arms wide. "You know I'm not doing this for some nefarious scheme. The world rides on this, Buc. I've spent over a year out here on a Godsdamned suicide mission, with only the dead for company." He slammed a fist into his chest. "I've sent hundreds of innocents to the bottom of the sea in search of one who can unlock Ciris's conscience. And I'll murder Eld if that's what it takes.

"So . . ." He took a breath. "Think it over and decide if you're going to let all that wash away like flotsam because you can't find it in yourself to sacrifice something for the greater good."

Surrender. Sacrifice.

The voice that had whispered to me when Chan Sha healed me, washed over me. *"Don't break and your sister's death was for nothing. What if you have to break more than once? Can you? Can you break twice, three times? Or will you tear yourself into a hundred pieces if you try?"* Call it what you want, dress it up in noble platitudes, but surrender or sacrifice is nothing more than breaking.

There's something in me that won't bend, no matter how much force is exerted. I'll break first—that's what I've always told myself, but the truth is, I don't think I'm much better at breaking than I am at bending. I'll die first. Just ask the captain of the *Sea Dragon*, whose ship I sent to the bottom with my lies. Or the score of others lying wasted in my wake. Or Chan Sha. I'd thought I'd broken already by forgiving her enough to let her join us, but . . .

What if you have to break more than once?

The words pulled the veil away and I saw, truly saw, what they meant. I'd already broken. I broke with Chan Sha. I broke when I said I would go to the ship for Eld. I sacrificed myself for Eld once. I could do it again, couldn't I? Or was the Ghost Captain right? Was it more than just Eld? While I'd watched my sister burn, I'd pledged to change the world. Was it the world that needed my sacrifice?

And if I do bend the knee and surrender, what then? Sin will force me to go to Ciris and she'll control me the same way she controlled Chan Sha. If I do this, I'll give myself up so completely, there will be nothing left. A moment ago I hadn't been sure I could trust my own mind, not with Sin lurking there, but I already knew the answer, because I knew the truth. I'd been betting on others this whole time, but now, now, it was time to bet on myself. And that thought was pure Sambuciña Alhurra.

"I'll do what needs doing," I said, finally.

"You'll become a Sin Eater?" the Ghost Captain asked. He frowned as he said it, his bright eyes focused on mine. "If you—"

"You misunderstand me," I cut him off. "I'll do what needs doing. I'll send you to your grave and heal Eld myself." I didn't try to hide my smile. "And you won't be rising."

55

"Take her!" the Ghost Captain howled. Spittle flecked his lips. "Alive if possible, but stop the Sin Eater!"

The Shambles closed ranks around me, their moaning and groaning drowning out the pounding of my heart. Their reaching, clawing hands were mere paces from me and all I had was what I wore: grass sandals and dress and a shoddy iron knife. I'd let the Ghost Captain get to me, not his fault, but mine. Gods, but I hated ultimatums and that, along with what he'd done to Eld, had sent me over the edge. But it was too soon. *Real smart, Buc.*

"Something you said, maybe?" Sin asked.

"Ha, ha," I whispered mentally.

"You're the soul of diplomacy, Buc."

"I'm many things, but not that."

"There's a way out of this," he said. "Take my power and carve your way through the dead. They'll fall like saplings in a storm."

"I'm not—"

"Not going to allow me to Possess you," he finished. "Yes," he added, speaking insultingly slowly, "I understand your prejudices there. I'm not asking you to do that. Later, perhaps, but first we need to get out of this alive and that won't happen unless you let me help you."

"I'm not giving you control!"

"Then we'll die!" Sin's façade of calm vanished. "Is that what all of this was for? Use me, woman. Let me show you what we're capable of."

"Never!"

"Don't be a fool," he hissed. "Think! I can save Eld, Buc. I promise you, I can. But first you have to kill the Ghost Captain and you'll never manage to kill him on your own, let alone cut through a hundred Shambles just to reach him. Listen," he pleaded.

I started to shake my head and then Eld began screaming. It sounded as if his soul were being ripped from his flesh and it was even more horrifying given his sickly figure—no one that weak should be able to scream that loud. The Shambles had barely moved—more of Sin's magical time dilation. But that made Eld's scream last forever and the sound tore open my heart. For the first time I knew that there was breaking and then there was *breaking*.

"I don't give you permission to Possess me," I said mentally. "But I'll let you help. If you can save Eld."

"I can't," Sin said, "but *we* can." Tingling, burning sensations rippled through my body and Sin whooped. "Time to dance, motherfuckers!"

"Well," I muttered, "Eld always said I was a corrupting influence."

Time unfroze and the dead howled around me. *Two steps right, duck then jump, right elbow to forehead. Left instep to the knee. Catch the ax before it falls.* I was moving before the thought finished. I ducked beneath the ax a large Shambles swung at my head. Wind whipped around me, scattering sand, and then I rose with a leap that brought my elbow into his forehead and the remnants of his tricorne exploded along with the front of his skull. My elbow tingled, but I felt no pain as I landed on the Shambles's knee with my left foot, then pushed off so hard that he stumbled backward.

Catching the haft of his ax, I ripped it from his hands. It felt light in mine even though the haft was thrice the length of most boarding axes. I swung it in a tight circle to get the feel and Sin nodded approvingly.

The maelstrom of dead swirled around me and I gave myself over to the dance. My partner was the ax and where we twirled, the dead fell in droves, black ichor staining the sands. Sin and I were one, our thoughts blending and his strength numbing my limbs so that I felt nothing but tingling and a faint shiver through the haft when blade met bone.

Two Shambles came at me from either side and I swept in a circle, low to high, cutting the legs from one and the head from the other, ending with my blade buried in the chest of the first. Ichor painted the air when I drew it out of him and my laughter filled my ears. I wove my way across the sandy dance floor and bodies marked my progress. I was surrounded by death and I'd never felt more alive.

I'm not one to stand and fight. Not fairly, at least. That's why I use a slingshot and carry a dozen knives when I can. Why I prefer ice picking a bastard before he can draw his sword. I'm small and I'm fast and I've an understanding of leverages, and if I can catch you by surprise, I'll kill you. I'm good at surprises. But in a knockdown, drag-out brawl, I'm just a girl, and brawls tend to be more about weight and endurance than speed. But with Sin feeding me supernatural strength and speed my size was actually an advantage, giving me angles and room to maneuver that a man wouldn't have had.

"*Buc!*" Sin's voice filled my mind.

"No need to shout."

"I've been shouting for the past second," he growled. "Which is a long time in your mind."

"Sorry?"

"We need to get to the Ghost Captain; I can't keep this up much longer."

"What do you mean?" I decapitated a woman in a tattered ball gown whose single skeletal arm held a cudgel that fell from her now dead-for-real fingers. "You said you could make me immortal."

"No, I said we were close to immortal. There's a cost, Buc. This isn't magic."

"Bullshit, it's not."

"It's beyond your ken," he snapped. "Magic isn't limitless—there are boundaries. Hard ones. The tingling you feel is happening because impossibly tiny bits of myself are overriding what your body can do on its own—but the spell only lasts for so long. And then you're going to need a fuck ton of rest."

"So you're giving me extra strength and speed now, but later I'm going to be weaker than weak?"

"In a manner of speaking. But the point is, we can't kill every Shambles before going for the Ghost Captain. We have to go now."

"How much time do we have?"

"We have to go now," he repeated.

"Then do it on my mark."

Sin started to protest but I cut him off, slid between the legs of a tall Shambles, thankful that he was all bone and sinew below the waist or I would have had a mouthful of his balls, and came out the other side in a crouch. *Dodge left, then right, drive that big one with the black bandanna back, and run like mad.*

"Black bandanna or blue?" Sin asked.

I squinted. "Blue," I corrected.

"When?"

"Now!" I screamed in the face of the Shambles before me and she hissed back through broken teeth. I elbowed her out of the way, sprinted left, then cut hard right, spinning around another Shambles, using their body as a slingshot, and slamming the head of my ax into the chest of the big Shambles with the blue bandanna. Bones cracked and his boots lost purchase on the loose sand. Another shove and he cleared a path through the Shambles behind him and I was off. Sand spurted beneath my sandals as I leapt over the last pair of Shambles and rolled into the awning, coming up in front of the Ghost Captain.

"Buc, don't be a fool . . ." he began.

The rest was cut off by the blade of my ax, which I sank deep into the side of his neck. Bright blood squirted out in time with his fading heartbeat. His words gurgled in his throat and his surprised eyes stared at me even as life left them. The sag of his body pulled the ax out of my hands as he crumpled to the crimson-stained sand. I stared at him until a rasping chuckle pulled my attention away.

"Fool," the nearest Shambles hissed. Its short green coat was covered in dark stains—probably its lifeblood—but the eyes that stared through a mask of knife cuts that marred its face were bright with intelligence.

"Stop calling me that," I said.

"I told you, kill me and I'll take another," it said. "Aye, you've done well so far, but you're tiring, Sin Eater. You can't keep this up much longer and I've another hundred Shambles in the brush and beaches of this island. Will you kill us all?"

I shook my head. "No." I turned back to the Ghost Captain's corpse and pulled the ax from his neck. Blood dripped down the haft as I raised it over my head and the Shambles rasped another laugh. I feinted toward him, then swung around and brought the ax head down onto the glowing blue book that had fallen from the Dead Walker's pocket when he died.

"No!" The Shambles's howl echoed the sound of the book and blade breaking together. A soundless, sightless explosion pushed against my chest, almost a mental scream that clawed at me as it rushed past, and then pieces rained across the sands. The army of undead stopped where they stood. Some, carried by their momentum, fell over and lay unmoving on the sand. "Nooo!"

"Like that?" I asked Sin.

"Exactly like that," he said.

"You don't know what you've done," the Ghost Captain's voice came from the Shambles's mouth. "You fool!"

"I told you—" He jumped me, or tried to. I felt my arms burn as I caught him and twisted, sending him to the ground; our legs intertwined and I fell with him. We rolled over until the Ghost Captain's body brought us up short. With me on top. And the knife I'd hidden in my dress in my hand.

"I. Told. You. To. Stop. Calling. Me. A. Fool." I sawed at the Shambles's throat with each word. The pig-iron blade had gone dull and it took several strokes to cut past the petrified flesh and gristle into the windpipe and spine. The Dead Walker's head whipped back and forth with the sawing of my blade.

"You don't know what you're doing, Buc!" he screeched. "This is our only hope to end a war that has lasted a millennium." Ichor stained my hands and flecked my dress and arms, and cold blood sprayed my face as I sawed away at his neck. He tried to fight me off, but then my blade caught vertebrae and he gave up. "It only paused when they left heaven for our world and nearly wiped us out. Do you want that again?"

"I don't trust any Gods, old or new, to do what's right," I said, gasping. "Number twenty-three!" The Ghost Captain stared back, uncomprehending. "Marten had it right, all those years ago. Magic, no matter the flavor, corrupts!"

"Kill me," he rasped as my blade cut deeper. I couldn't see my hands or his lips for the ichor flooding out from the wound I'd hacked into his throat. "I don't care, but take the artifact to Ciris. It's the only way." He gasped. "W-w-way to restore her sanity and prevent the War."

"He's lying," Sin whispered.

What?

Images flashed in my mind, courtesy of Sin. The Ghost Captain's arrival. Even sooner than we'd guessed. A small piece of something that glinted in the fading light, that he quickly slipped into the altar, but not before I saw the strange designs carved into its surface. When he pulled it out the designs were gone, its surface smooth. He had left something behind. Something small and insignificant . . . save that it would have killed Ciris when the artifact was returned to her. Killed her the same way a plague kills its host. Invisibly, and from the inside.

"The Dead Walker made a mistake, sending Chan Sha first. Her Sin recognized the corruption and took it, leaving me whole. She scoured herself clean with fire so the Dead Gods' weapon would never touch Ciris."

"You're lying," I spat at the Dead Walker, and told him what Sin had shown me. "And now you're going to die knowing you failed."

"You don't trust me, but you trust another God?" the corpse asked. "Even if it's not lying, why wouldn't you try to take it back to Ciris? Kill her and all of this ends." He blinked. "Don't you care about the world?"

The question brought me up short. Actually made me pause. Then I remembered what Eld had said when the Ghost Captain chose him instead of me. Eld understood, and now the Ghost Captain would too.

"No," I said. "I don't." He opened his mouth and I ripped the blade hard across his throat. His head fell off and rolled away from his body, nothing but bones. "Not the way you do," I finished.

Silence felt oddly out of place after all the shouting and screaming and killing. I eyed the Ghost Captain's body. Both of them. *And the dying.* I could hear the waves lapping at the shoreline as they had done for a millennium and would do so for another millennium if I had anything to say about it. The wind was beginning to whip across the waves and onto the beach, and up on the cliff, flames danced high above the railing, consuming what was left of the long-wrecked ship. I was of a mind to let it burn; with luck, it would spread and cleanse the whole island of corruption. Sin nodded within me as I settled back on my haunches and drew a shuddering breath.

"You planned this all along," Sin said.

"What do you mean?" I asked.

"What I said. You planned this as soon as you spoke with that trumped-up historian. The Archaeologist. The Ghost Captain gave you the missing piece to your puzzle. You always meant to let Chan Sha be the sacrifice and use her to kill the Ghost Captain."

"Well, I didn't know she'd die before I killed him," I said. "Or that the artifact was actually an insidious mind fucker."

"Hey, I take that as an insult."

"Don't," I said, "it's a compliment. I knew I would have to gamble, aye, and I never meant to let either one of them leave the island alive, but had I known the odds?"

"You still would have gone through with it," he said.

"You do know me," I said, laughing. "Aye, I would have, but I wouldn't have been so brash about it."

"Do you know any other way?"

"Careful," I warned.

"Buc?" Eld's voice pulled me out of my head. It was barely more than a whisper, but in the silence it could have been a shout. I leapt off the skeleton and half fell in my haste to reach him. He looked wasted beneath his sodden clothes and his face was darker, almost the color of my own, but where my skin looked alive and vibrant, his looked decayed. His mouth tried to form a smile when he saw me, but couldn't quite make it. He coughed and blood flecked his lips. "He's dead?"

"Aye, they all are," I said.

"Not. All." He shuddered and I wrapped my arm around his head, supporting him. "Th-thanks. I thought if you killed him, the poison would recede, but . . ." He coughed again and more blood came up. "I guess I'll be the last Shambles on the island." The blueness of his eyes bit into me, still sharp even surrounded by his dying body. "Will you make it quick?"

"Eld."

"Will you make it quick?" he repeated.

Sin. HELP. PLEASE. HELP.

"Kiss him," Sin said after a long pause.

I hesitated, then bent over him. Eld's eyes clouded with confusion before snapping wide when my lips touched his. Warmth met cold and we both gasped in surprise.

"Divining," Sin said. "There's a parasite. I've a spell for this form of healing. Just give me a fraction."

There's nothing so romantic as a dead voice sifting through information.

"Get fucked," Sin said, but there was a smile in his words. "Now, kiss him again. With your tongue, this time."

"Sin!"

"Do it, if you want him to live. The spell's in your saliva."

"Buc?" Eld asked.

"Hush," I said, and this time when my mouth met his, I let my lips linger, let my warmth heat his cold flesh. When I touched the tip of my tongue to his, he didn't fight me; he welcomed it. All the while, we stared into each other's eyes and I felt a shiver run through me that made Sin's numbness and tingling feel like mere pinpricks in comparison. When we broke apart, I felt all the strength leak from my bones; I half fell against Eld so the pair of us lay intertwined on the beach.

"I should have made completing the transition the price of Eld's healing," Sin whispered. "I could have Possessed you."

"Never would have worked," I said.

He didn't call me out on the lie.

The three of us lay there for a long time, listening to the waves crashing onshore. I felt drained, as if all the life within me had evaporated with our kiss. Now I understood what Sin had meant by cost. It was like waking after Chan Sha healed me, but worse. In time I felt Eld's skin begin to warm beneath mine and the bit of his arm I could see began to return to normal, the veins disappearing beneath his usual paleness. He murmured something that sounded like it might have had the word "love" in it, but I was too afraid to ask him to speak louder. Too afraid to ruin the moment, if indeed I hadn't ruined everything already by kissing him. Things wouldn't be the same between us, couldn't be. Men aren't content to let things like this lie; that much I knew. *Gods, won't that be a fun conversation?*

"What will we do with the artifact?" Eld asked.

"I won't let this—What?" I bit off what I was going to say.

"The artifact. What does it look like?"

"Oh." *Thank Gods he doesn't mean to start the conversation now.* "It's not much to look at, really," I said. Sin growled in my mind. "If you didn't know what you were looking for, you'd never know it was there," I added. Eld had apparently been too far gone to understand what had happened onshore. The question was, would I tell him the truth?

"Do we keep it or give it away?" he asked.

I didn't say anything. "Do you want magic around us?" I asked, finally.

"You know I hate magic," he said. "Even if it's saved us a few times now. Hey, are you okay?" I nodded against his chest. "It's just that you froze up against me for a moment."

"I'm fine, just weak." The admission didn't even hurt. It was infinitesimal compared to what we'd just endured.

"Magic is dangerous, Buc. When you've seen what I have . . ." He trailed off and then his breath whistled through his teeth. "What will we do with it?"

I kept my face pressed against his chest, hoping he couldn't feel my tears through his shirt. "I guess we'll have to give it away," I whispered. Even as I said it, I felt Sin's words in my mind, confirming my fears. There was no giving it away, no going back.

The magic was in me.

56

"You stretched the bounds of our deal," Salina said. Her wine sat untouched on the rough-hewn bar table. She plucked at the thread o' gold in her grey dress—a color that made her look sickly—and shook the pile of gilded curls back over her shoulder. I opened my mouth and she forestalled me with a wave of her hand. "The Company is satisfied that you met the terms. And you have Servenza's thanks. The Empire's, too, though none know it."

"As good citizens, you've no idea how much that means to us," I said dryly.

"Yes?" She leaned forward. "But did you really have to steal a Normain Cannon Ship?"

"We did, if you wanted the sugar within the fortnight," I said. I hid a yawn behind my wineglass.

"I appreciate that," she said in a tone that indicated she didn't at all, "but maybe you don't appreciate how perilously close to war this could bring us."

"Surely you can cover that up?" I asked. *And that will distract you from trying to cover us up along with it.*

"Perhaps." Her lips thinned. "That would have been easier, had you not released the crew before sending word you'd made port."

Eld cleared his throat and both of us glanced at him. *That part hadn't been in the plan.* He blushed a darker shade, but didn't say anything.

"I don't suppose you'll tell me how the two of you managed to force the surrender of an entire crew and then sailed almost single-handedly through one of the deadliest hurricanes the Shattered Coast has seen in a decade? No?"

"Come now," I said with a false smile, "surely you understand: a lady can't be expected to share all her secrets."

"And surely you understand, you're no lady."

"Easy," Eld growled.

"Now he speaks," Salina said.

"You said we've satisfied our end of the deal," I said, setting down my wineglass and leaning across the table. "Our stake-holder's writ was lost when Chan Sha's ship went down. We want another one."

"I've brought that." She snapped her fingers and held a hand out that was half obscured by the length of her sleeve. One of the men who had entered the tavern with her stepped forward, placed a piece of rolled parchment in her hand, then stepped back to the wall. "You'll need it to be stamped," she said as she handed it over.

"Nice of you to mention that," I muttered, thinking of Chan Sha mocking us for being fools to not notice the lack of notarization. *She's not mocking anyone now.* "I don't suppose?"

"That I brought a notary?" Salina asked. "As a matter of fact, I have. But before I send for him . . ." She glanced over her shoulder, but her guards hadn't moved. She leaned forward and her voice dropped to little more than a whisper. "There was mention that this Ghost Captain had a partner named the Archaeologist. What do you know of her? Did you meet? What did she tell you?"

"How much did you know and not tell us when this all began?" Eld asked. Salina's thin lips curved in a smile, but she said nothing. "Gods damn it, woman. We almost died."

"There was a woman named the Archaeologist," I said. Eld stiffened, but Salina's eyes were already on me, so she missed his slip. I shrugged. "Listen, a woman tells me she knows where an item of immense power is located, I don't send her away empty-handed." I bit my lip to keep from laughing at the blushing red that crept across Salina's face.

"Unfortunately, I never got to find out if she was full of shit or not. Chan Sha murdered her to keep the Ghost Captain from her," I lied. "He seemed quite put out by it."

"I'm sure," she murmured. "And you let Chan Sha near her? Convenient."

"If you'd told us that she was working for you but that you didn't trust her, maybe we wouldn't have," I said. "Trust is a weapon that cuts both ways."

"Speaking of that," Eld added, "I hope you brought the pistole with you."

"Sorry?"

"You know, the one that started this whole thing," I said.

"Oh, of course," Salina said. She didn't bother hiding the falseness in her words. She snapped her fingers and the same guard stepped forward, reached behind his back, and held out a thick-barreled pistole. "I nearly forgot how we got here in the first place," she added with an equally false laugh.

"I'm sure," Eld said.

Sin? My eyes burned with magic from the spell, and the pistole leapt in my vision so that it was as if I held it up right in front of my face. The maker's mark was wrong. "We're all friends here, so I hope you won't take this the wrong way, Salina," I said, "but do I need to take the real pistole off your corpse?"

Her guard and Eld stiffened at the same time, but Salina just shook her head and opened her hand. The guard removed the pistole and replaced it with another. She slid it across the table and stood up, all humor gone from her eyes. "You really are the most perfect arsehole."

"Aye." I grinned at her. "So I remember you saying when first we met."

"And nothing has changed."

"Oh, a lot has changed, Salina," I said. She stiffened at my use of her name. "We'll see you at the next Board meeting."

"One of you, anyway," she said, straightening her skirts and not meeting my eyes. "If you're smart, you'll send Eld. At least he's not a complete fool," she said, turning toward the door.

"Don't forget the notary," I called after her. She paused in the doorway and cursed, before disappearing with her men.

"I'm surprised a noblewoman knows that word," Eld said after she left. I smiled but said nothing.

A few moments later a beefy man walked in, sauntering as he cut around the tables between the door and us. His cloak hung to his heels, not quite hiding the pronounced paunch visible below his jerkin, and not masking the width of his shoulders, paunch or no. His hair was cropped short and a faint scar traced a path down from his left eye. There was something in his gait that tugged at my memory, but I couldn't pull the thread out.

He reached us and his thick lips twisted in a sneer even as he set a small black leather bag on the table and began pulling inkwells, stamps, waxes, and seals out until his half of the table was covered in accoutrements. He paused then, as if waiting for us to ask the obvious question, and his sneer deepened when we didn't before he sat down and motioned for the writ in my hands.

"You'll be wanting that notarized then?" he asked.

And you'll be playing the part of Captain Obvious?

I smiled at Sin's comment but said nothing, just passed the writ across the table. There was something about the man that suggested familiarity, but I was damned if I knew what. He swept his cloak back and laid the writ out, reading it as he set a stand over a candle and set wax in the pan at the top. His eyes grew wider as he read and by the time he reached the end and had uncorked a dark inkwell and prepared a pair of stamps, he was muttering under his breath.

"Looks like someone's come up in the world, eh?" He sneer-grinned at us. "Not a talkative lot, eh? Which will it be then? Stakeholder or no—it's just one name. So you'll be an island alone."

"It's for Eld."

The notary grunted. "Aye, well better a larger island than a small one. Name?"

I glanced at Eld. "You know, I'm not sure you've ever said your full name."

"Haven't I?" he asked.

"No."

"Eldritch Nelson Rawlings," he said. I whistled and he smiled. "And now you know why you haven't heard it before."

"Rawlings? En't there a house of Rawlings? In the Foreign Quarto?"

"There might be," Eld said with a shrug. It was a passable lie for him, but I stored it away for future use. *His Lordship Eldritch Nelson Rawlings, formerly of the Servenzan army. Or was it the Imperial army?* Eld flushed under my gaze, so he knew that I knew. "I've never heard of it before."

The notary grunted and turned back to the writ. I leaned forward and watched as he bent to his work. First came Eld's full name in a spiraled script I would have thought beyond the notary's fat thumbs. Then a blob of melted wax became the Servenzan seal on one side while ink was used to stamp the mark of the Kanados Trading Company on the other. He sifted a thimbleful of sand across the parchment and blew carefully before sitting back with a sigh. Sweat sprinkled across his brow as if the effort had cost him much. He glanced up and frowned when he saw my interest.

"There's your island," he said, shoving more than sliding the writ back across the table.

"You're not very pleasant," Eld said.

"Not paid to be pleasant," the notary said. He pushed his chair back and stood up and began collecting his things. "I don't know what blackmail the pair of you have over the Company," he said sourly, glaring across the table, the light playing off his scar, "but I hope you burn for it."

I knew who he was now, and everything drained from me.

"You who?" Eld asked me.

"Aye, who?" the notary asked.

I hadn't realized I'd spoken aloud. I was a lifetime away, back in a burning warehouse where a big, beefy lad, nearly full grown, held a blade to Sister's chest. *"Save her then, but you'll have to burn."* His words reverberated through my body. "You worked for La Signora, before." *Before I killed her.* I hadn't been able to find him—no one remembered just another thug in a street gang—but I'd made that old bitch pay before she died.

"Blood of the Gods, how do you know that?" he asked.

"Buc?" Eld's voice was tight. He knew some of my past, not everything, but enough.

"Remember a warehouse you burnt down?" I asked. "When Blood in the Water wanted the Krakens to eliminate the Blackened Blades?"

"We did eliminate them," he muttered. Then his eyes leapt

to mine and he shook his head. "You're the lass from the ware-house?"

"Aye. And you're the bastard who murdered my sister," I growled.

"What of it?" He drew himself up but was plainly shaken. "What are you going to do about it? If I killed a bitch who—"

The rest was lost in the explosion of a pistole.

When the smoke cleared, the man was lying on his back, arms outstretched, a dark hole just below the scar under his eye, and the back of his head gone. For a moment there was nothing but the high-pitched ringing from the gunshot. Eld waved his hand, dispelling the remaining wisps of smoke, then set the still-smoking pistole on the table and reached out to touch my arm. I jumped at the contact, my eyes still on the bastard growing cold on the floor. I looked at Eld, who shrugged.

"Accident," he said. "That hair trigger keeps getting me in trouble."

"Eld," I whispered. He pulled me into a rough hug and held me as I cried. I hadn't shed tears in years and now, in a fortnight, I'd turned into a blubbering child. But with the tears went some of my pain and with both Eld and Sin telling me it was okay, I was powerless to argue.

Sometime later I pulled back and Eld didn't try to hold on. Then again, he wouldn't—he knew I was tainted. We hadn't talked about it, not really, just skirted the periphery of what I'd become, but it was there. And it would come out eventually. I hated magic. Eld hated magic. And now I was consumed by it.

"We'll have to leave some extra coin for the tavern keeper's trouble," Eld said. I nodded and Eld let his smile go. He looked better when it wasn't forced. "Why'd you have him sign my name, Buc?"

"Because he was right," I said slowly. "An island won't do

much." I dug into my fresh silk dress—silk!—and pulled out a heavily wrinkled piece of parchment. "But islands, plural, are another story. The Empire started from a handful of islands." I unrolled the parchment, revealing the original writ Salina had given us, the one Chan Sha had returned in exchange for our help. *Some help.*

"You and I, Eld, Board members together." I began setting the notary's tools back up. "Who would have thought?"

"I wouldn't have it any other way," Eld said, and this time his smile was genuine.

So was mine, Gods damn me for it. So was mine.

The world is a fucked-up mess, a place where girls starve in the streets and are left to burn when they reach for something more. A place where companies and nations play with the lives of people like pieces on a game board, while over it all, the Gods lurk and smile as their endless War continues. Even if one side wins, we all lose. Now Eld and I had taken the first step toward changing that. Oh, it was a small step in the grand scheme of things; we still had to figure out a way to take over the Kanados Trading Company, win over nations, and kill Gods in the bargain. But it was a step I'd thought I was ready for. Before.

Before, when I thought I really was just an island on my own, needing no one. Now I know the truth. And if I know, that means Sin knows too, and if I make a slip, his Goddess will know as well. The truth is I need Eld. Me, Sambuciña Alhurra, the girl who has never needed anyone before. Leave Sister out of this. I've. Never. Needed. Anyone. But Gods, I need Eld. And Need? Need is a noose we slip round our necks and wait for the world to pull it tight.

Fuck me.

Epilogue

———※———

Her eyes opened on a wine-dark world that rose and fell with a soothing regularity that felt utterly incongruous with the bone-deep pain that filled her completely from head to toe. She blinked and the sea came into sharper focus. Half of it. Her left eye was useless no matter how hard she willed it not to be. The driftwood beneath her was uncomfortable—she couldn't quite get her arms around it, but at the same time, it was not large enough to properly support her weight. Instead she clung precariously to it like an insect and prayed her grip wouldn't slip. There were fathoms upon fathoms of sea waiting to welcome her if she let go. *Pray.* She snarled at the thought and tried not to let it turn into a whimpering scream.

Where are you?

Chan Sha felt her body begin to tremble and she fought it off with everything left to her. Which was depressingly little. *It's gone.* Her Goddess, her Sin, her magic, all gone . . . wiped clean by the artifact, leaving her a hollow husk. Leaving her to be filled only with pain. She closed her eyes, although she really only needed to close one, and memory coursed through her. *I'm sorry,* her Sin had whispered in his gravelly voice. Then he'd fled, and where he ran, fire ran with him, scouring the magic from her veins.

It's not his fault. That thought came to her later, after she was able to stop the shuddering sobs that racked her torn body. And it wasn't. Her Sin had a reason for what he did. Something to do with the artifact. The artifact that Buc and Eld had forced her to take. The Goddess had said nothing of her taking it. The last time Chan Sha had felt Her presence, Her orders had been clear: find the Archaeologist and keep her from the Dead Walker. Kill him or, failing that, keep his presence secret. Buc and Eld had offered a way to do all of that and then the bitch-girl had knee-capped her and shifted the balance of power between them. And that, more than anything else, had forced her to accept the hideous girl's offer. *Or did you want the power that would come with the artifact?* She bit down hard on the thought.

"Not my fault," she whispered hoarsely. Flames crept up in her throat from want of water. She opened her good eye and glanced around her and tried not to cry at the irony. A world of water and not a drop to drink. "Not my fault," she repeated. "Them. The pair. D-dead." She'd make them pay if she could, but without her Sin, she had no way to heal herself.

It was a small miracle she was still alive at all. Her eye was the most permanent damage done, but she had numerous wounds and injuries. Salt water had cleansed them and many were already beginning to heal, but a few were still little better than open sores. If any of them bled, the sharks would be on her in minutes.

Would have been better to let the dead finish me off. Instead a wave had swept them, and whatever connection they'd had to the Ghost Captain, away, and her with them. The dead had floated, keeping her alive, but there had been a moment, several really, where she could have slid off of their bones and let the depths take her. *And why didn't I? All I've done is postpone my opportunity to give the sharks something to dine on.* Even if she didn't bleed, one of them would get curious eventually. As worn as she was, she wouldn't warrant more than a few mouthfuls. Not a proper dinner then, but something.

If.

Gods. *If.* If she could find an island, she could recover. If she could recover, she could build herself back to fighting strength. If she did that, she could wait for a passing ship. If she found passage, she could find her Goddess and restore her power. And if she did *that*—they'd all pay. Eld first and the girl last. *If.* It was the only magic left to her, yet there was so much power in that word. *All the power of a dream.* She knew it as surely as she knew the shadow she'd just seen pass below her wasn't a shadow. It wasn't the first time she'd seen such a shadow, but it was the first time she'd seen one linger. *I'm going to die.*

Chan Sha took a breath, tasted the bittersweet, salty life on her tongue, and then cast about for one more view of the world before the end came. She knew what color that end would be. *Red.*

To the right, a never-ending wall of blue, the light cast of the cloudless sky and the darker blues of the sea, broken here and there by the white-tipped crest of a roller. Then to the left, twisting to see what her blind eye couldn't. More sky, more sea in the same shade of blue, broken again by waves and by—Chan Sha's breath caught in her throat.

The profile of a ship, its bow pointing right for her. If it came on as it was, it could reach her in an hour. Perhaps less. She glanced down at the shadow looming lazily below her.

If . . .

It was the only magic left to her.

The Selected and Annotated Library of Sambuciña Alhurra

Numbered and listed in order read, with notes by the reader. At the time of the events detailed in this volume, by her own count, Buc had read three hundred and sixty-seven books and an uncounted number of pamphlets.

3
Félicis Ballwik
Proverbs

Ballwik's simple advice is dispatched in humble lines that make fine practice for an early reader, if one doesn't mind the tone of an aged auntie dispensing wisdom from the rocker.

Buc's notes: *Slow going at first, but I think I shocked Eld by finishing it in three days. I hope reading holds more mysteries than "a copper saved is a copper earned." That's not how economics works.*

11
Geniver Gillibrand
A Twist of the Tongue

Gillibrand may have poached her better lines from writers and poets and philosophers from throughout history, but she's not above a few originals of her own and even the weakest among them rival Ballwik's best.

Buc's notes: *She has much faith in what passes for truth as I have. Wonder what gutter she was swaddled in?*

23

Jens Marten
On Religion and Power

If his contemporaries are to be believed, Marten was better at speaking than writing. Still, this is a detailed—too detailed, some might say—accounting of the rise of Ciris and the new world wrought by rival Gods, told in a straightforward, if somewhat boring, manner.

Buc's notes: *Why does no one speak of this? This accounts for everything I've seen on the streets. I always thought it was the hoary old Empress's fault, aye, and she deserves a full measure of the blame, but in part only. These fucking Gods set everything in motion that led to the streets. They're why Sister died and I'll—*(rest of page torn away).

24

Yanton Verner
Disciple of the Body—Anatomy

Verner's magnum opus caused issues with the bookbinders upon its release, but if one wishes to understand the anatomy of the body in all its glorious complexity, one must study this work.

Buc's notes: *Nearly passed this one over for want of a cover. There's a feel a book has though, cover or not, that beckons and I'm glad I heeded the call. Else I might be emptying my guts over the side like Eld. Easy crossing my arse.*

37
Félcher
Discourse on Planetary Bodies

As far as any can determine, Felcher had only one name. The woman takes no prisoners here in reaching out to the stars themselves and deciphering their ways for the reader. Many have questioned her proofs—found in the companion volume, *Planetary Functions and Problems*—but none seem to be able to disprove them. Approach with caution and tea for the headache her knowledge brings.

Buc's notes: *I may have finally bitten off more than I can chew with this one. I've read it thrice and every time I begin to ken what she's saying, my mind breaks. Are we really just living on a speck of dirt amidst an endless ocean of inky black?*

52
Elain Ducasse
Look to the Stars

Ducasse's introduction to the night sky delves deeper than its thin pages suggest; she asks more questions than she answers.

Buc's notes: *Blast, this would have been useful to have read before Felcher. I guess I've a fourth reading of that in the offing. I'll need a lungful of kan first. Two, perhaps.*

62
Othotus
The Study of Centuries

One necessarily expects a historical work looking back a millennium to be a weighty tome, but Othotus's love of three sentences where one will suffice turns weight into labor.

Buc's notes: *I've never not finished a book, but Gods, Othotus tested me with this one. I'm not sure I quite agree that history is a cycle that repeats itself. I read somewhere else, written in a far keener hand, that history rhymes. There's some truth there, I'm sure, but I need to understand the meter if I'm to do anything about it.*

88
Kasina Alyce
On Sculpting

Kasina Alyce, maestra to some of Servenza's most famous artists, including Alina and her younger sister Malina, was said to be a talented artist in her own right, though one would be hard pressed to name a sculpture attributed to her today. She committed her life's work to parchment while exiled to Normain, where the bones of the Dead Gods form the basis of all their architecture, providing little in the way of artistic demand.

Buc's notes: *Why do the rich care so much about useless blocks of marble? The casting bit may come in useful one day, but marble?*

107
Unknown
A Year Amongst the Inhabitants of the Uninhabitable Coast

Of questionable origin—one doesn't find many common sailors of this era who knew how to write—it nonetheless provides an all too accurate accounting of the disparate native tribes along the Shattered Coast. The intrepid traveler would wish for more on ways to parse friendly tribes from those with a taste for human flesh.

Buc's notes: *Is that blood on the parchment? Or jam? Wet finger says not jam . . .*

143
Eint Volker
Where the Gods Fear to Step

Eint Volker, one of the few northmen who cared more for spilling ink than spilling blood, married an elder daughter of a Cordoban lady and soon thereafter stumbled upon the origin of the family's fortunes: as agents of Sin Eaters. Even in his simple hand, the tale pulls the reader in . . . agents of Ciris risking all on rickety vessels to brave the hurricanes of the Shattered Coast and ignite chains of volcanoes in worship to their Goddess. Is it fact as Volker claimed, or mere fiction, as Ciris's followers would have one believe? The reader must judge.

Buc's notes: *Half the world starved if everything else I've read about that time is true. The sun blotted out behind an unending cloud of ash. Funny how when it cleared, the Empire grew and the Kanados Trading Company with it. And the Sin Eaters with them both. Hmm . . . what did the Sin Eaters want in the Shattered Coast that the hurricanes hid?*

189
Royale Aislin
Black Flag's Shadow

Privateer turned savior of Southeast Island, Aislin died a century ago, but not before she wrote out the unbelievable story of her life—which ended in an Imperial jail, both legs replaced with pegs. She was fond of joking that she didn't need her legs to swing, and swing she did, but not before completing the

autobiography that every would-be leftenant reads before joining the Academy.

Buc's notes: *A hard woman and now I understand the stories
about her insanity. But it's only insanity if you don't win and she
won every fight, save the last.*

201
Errol Gatina
A Captain's Mast

Gatina became Maestro of the Servenzan Naval Academy,
reckoned just below the Imperial Naval Academy, after two
decades before the mast. An average sailor, he proved a better
teacher, confirming that those who can't do, teach.

Buc's notes: *If I wanted a field manual on how to run a ship, I'd
have bought one. Aislin led me to believe all salts were salty, but now
I wonder. Frobisher's coming up in the pile, but is she another slog?*

216
Anonymous
On Knots and Ropes

Written in a cramped hand, in language that suggests the author is Southeast Islander in origin, it's lacking diagrams but
includes directions for more knots than a sailor ten years before
the mast would need to know.

Buc's notes: *Useful, if only to know how to tie Eld up when he gets
too polite and balks at my next stratagem.*

221
Joann Frobisher
The Silence of Black on Blue

Frobisher rose from lowly cabin girl to High Admiral of the Imperial Navy. A lifetime insomniac, she worked the deck by day and wrote her memoirs by candlelight, thrice seeking healing from the Dead Gods for her ruined sight. Amongst her numerous victories were the Battle of the Channel, where she single-handedly rewrote the rules of engagement for ships of the line, and the Fortnight War, where she shattered the Free Cities' navy for decades after.

Buc's notes: *I don't trust writers—everyone lies and writers doubly so—but I think I may trust Frobisher. I wonder how it feels to throw the ship over and deliver a broadside such that it propels the entire floating monstrosity back around for a broadside from the other cannons? Talk about a one-two punch . . .*

289
Zhe
Cordoban Diplomacy

Zhe's history of diplomacy in the Cordoban Confederacy reads more like an eyewitness's breathless account of one unceasing duel.

Buc's notes: *Diplomacy is about blades, eh? If only, Zhe, if only.*

Acknowledgments

Stephen King said writing a novel is like crossing the Atlantic Ocean in a bathtub and I've never known the man to lie. If you're fortunate, you find some mates to help you row, and I've been incredibly lucky to find a whole crew along the way.

Rachel, my wife, to whom this book is dedicated, was there for every pull of the oar and kept my sails full over many years of battling writing headwinds.

My family: Mom and Dad, who taught me a love of reading from an early age and always encouraged me. Adam, my brother, who shared my love of reading and all things fantasy. Aunt Deanna, who bought me a bunch of Brian Jacques books when I was ten years old and fed the flames that C. S. Lewis and Susan Cooper had ignited.

Dan Knorr, my best friend and the only person alive who has read every book I've ever written (for which I apologize). Always my first beta reader, he's never steered me wrong.

Arnaud Koebel, a fellow writer in the trenches and another longtime reader, whose advice is invaluable when it comes to making a good book great. A kinder human you will never meet.

DongWon Song, my agent and coconspirator. Not only is the man an amazing editor in his own right, he's a wonderful champion and master strategist and without him this book and my career would be all the poorer.

Melissa Ann Singer, my editor and Tor Champion, who understood Buc from page one and asked for more. She's improved everything in this book from the line-by-line sentence structure to the entire series arc.

The No Excuses Writing Circle, who are a talented bunch in their own right and whose feedback and encouragement helped me in the drowning waters of querying through publication.

"Writing Excuses" has been my constant companion since Season 2 and infinitely improved my writing. Special shout-out to Dan Wells and Brandon Sanderson, who saw the diamond in the rough that was the earlier version of Buc's journey. Their advice and support were invaluable.

Team DongWon and Drowwzoo were my aunties and uncles, graciously giving me their sage advice on everything from writing to career advice. Especial thanks to one auntie and uncle in particular: Elizabeth Bear and Max Gladstone, who went above and beyond on more than one occasion. You are the authors I aspire to be.

And to you, Dear Reader, thank you for taking a chance on an unknown. Buc and I wrote this book for you. Her story is yours, if you'll have it. I hope we get to meet some day, but if we don't we'll always have the pages between.

If it takes a crew to row, it takes a city to build a seaworthy vessel and launch her into that brave new world: the bookshelf. I've tried to include as many as I could, but know that there were more; there always are. No one goes into publishing for the riches, they go for the love of the next page in the story, and they all give more than they take. Tor Books, one of the finest shipwrights in fantasy, is no exception.

A very big thank-you to . . .

Amanda Schoonmaker, senior contracts manager, who drew up the contracts. Ariana Carpentieri, assistant to Lucille Rettino, who got the ABMs made. Nathan Weaver, managing editor, from whom all production floweth. Jim Kapp, production manager, who interacts with the printers, among other things. Megan Kiddoo, production editor, who handles the different stages of production. Kaitlin Severini, who was the copyeditor (any mistakes, I made her STET). Laura Dragonette, who proofread first pass, and Ruoxi Chen, who proofread second. In audio, Tom Mis was our producer and Sarah Pannenberg ran the marketing. Greg Collins, designer, worked on the interior design of *The Sin in the Steel*. Peter Lutjen, art director, has a fine eye; he commissioned the art and designed the cover. David Palumbo, cover artist, took the few pages of ideas we sent him and truly brought Buc and Eld and this world to life. Julia Bergen, associate marketing manager, was the point person for all our marketing efforts on the book. Caro Perny and Giselle Gonzalez, publicists, brought the world to Buc and showed them the ride they were in for. Lucille Rettino, vice president, associate publisher, director of marketing and publicity, was, as I understand it, the boss of many who came before and a force of nature.

Devi Pillai, vice president and publisher of Tor Books, is a feared name within the genre. Editor to the stars, she is known for taking no prisoners. The first time we met, in an elevator at a convention, I had no idea who she was, and when she bought me a drink later I nearly spilled it when I realized who I'd been making small talk with. She treated me as if I were a best-selling author when I hadn't sold a thing, let me pitch to her editors, and put the full weight of Tor behind this book. I'm forever grateful (and still slightly terrified). Thank you.